The Lunar Chronicles

★ "It's another Marissa Meyer roller-coaster ride, part science fiction/fantasy, part political machination with a hint of ROMANCE....
With at least one more Lunar Chronicle to come, the SUSPENSE continues."
—*Booklist*, starred review

★ "Returning fans of Meyer's *Cinder* will gladly SINK THEIR TEETH into this ambitious, wholly satisfying SEQUEL."
—*Publishers Weekly*, starred review

"In an interesting mash-up of FAIRY TALES and SCIENCE FICTION, the book is a cross between *Cinderella*, *The Terminator*, and *Star Wars*."
—*Entertainment Weekly* on *Cinder*

"TERRIFIC." —*Los Angeles Times* on *Cinder*

"Prince Charming among the CYBORGS."
—*The Wall Street Journal* on *Cinder*

Scarlet

Scarlet's story continues . . .

The Lunar Chronicles

Cinder

Scarlet

Cress

Winter

Fairest

Stars Above

Book Two

Scarlet

The Lunar Chronicles

WRITTEN BY

Marissa Meyer

SQUARE
FISH

Feiwel and Friends
NEW YORK

For Mom and Dad,
my best cheerleaders.

SQUARE
FISH

An Imprint of Macmillan
175 Fifth Avenue
New York, NY 10010
macteenbooks.com

Square Fish and the Square Fish logo are trademarks of Macmillan and
are used by Feiwel and Friends under license from Macmillan.

Square Fish books may be purchased for business or promotional use.
For information on bulk purchases, please contact the Macmillan Corporate
and Premium Sales Department at (800) 221-7945 x 5442 or by e-mail at
specialmarkets@macmillan.com.

Library of Congress Cataloging-in-Publication Data
Meyer, Marissa.
Scarlet / Marissa Meyer
p. cm. — (Lunar chronicles ; 2)
Summary: Scarlet Benoit and Wolf, a street fighter who may have
information about her missing grandmother, join forces with Cinder
as they try to stay one step ahead of the vicious Lunar Queen Levana
in this story inspired by Little Red Riding Hood.
ISBN 978-1-250-00721-6 (paperback) / ISBN 978-1-250-03763-3 (e-book)
[1. Science fiction. 2. Cyborgs—Fiction. 3. Missing persons—Fiction.
4. Extraterrestrial beings—Fiction.] I. Title.
PZ7.M571737Sc 2013   [Fic]—dc23   2012034060

Originally published in the United States by Feiwel and Friends
First Square Fish Edition: 2014
Book designed by Barbara Grzeslo
Square Fish logo designed by Filomena Tuosto

20   19   18   17   16   15   14   13   12

AR: 5.8 / LEXILE: 810L

BOOK
One

She did not know that the wolf

was a wicked sort of animal,

and she was not afraid of him.

One

SCARLET WAS DESCENDING TOWARD THE ALLEY BEHIND THE
Rieux Tavern when her portscreen chimed from the passenger
seat, followed by an automated voice: *"Comm received for Mademoiselle Scarlet Benoit from the Toulouse Law Enforcement Department of Missing Persons."*

Heart jumping, she swerved just in time to keep the ship's
starboard side from skidding against the stone wall, and threw
down the brakes before reaching a complete stop. Scarlet killed
the engine, already grabbing for the discarded portscreen. Its
pale blue light glinted off the cockpit's controls.

They'd found something.

The Toulouse police must have found something.

"Accept!" she yelled, practically choking the port in her
fingers.

She expected a vidlink from the detective assigned to her
grandmother's case, but all she got was a stream of unembel-
lished text.

28 Aug 126 t.e.

Re: Case ID #AIG00155819, filed on 11 Aug
126 t.e.

This communication is to inform SCARLET
BENOIT of Rieux, France, EF, that as of 15:42
on 28 Aug 126 the case of missing person(s)
MICHELLE BENOIT of Rieux, France, EF, has
been dismissed due to lack of sufficient
evidence of violence or nonspecific foul
play. Conjecture: Person(s) left of own
free will and/or suicide.
CASE CLOSED.
We thank you for your patronage of our
detective services.

The comm was followed by a video ad from the police, reminding all delivery ship pilots to be safe and wear their har-
nesses while engines were running.

Scarlet stared at the small screen until the words turned
into a screaming blur of white and black and the ground seemed
to drop out from beneath the ship. The plastic panel on the back
of the screen crunched in her tightening grip.

"Idiots," she hissed to the empty ship.

The words CASE CLOSED laughed back up at her.

She released a guttural scream and slammed the port down
on the ship's control panel, hoping to shatter it into pieces of
plastic and metal and wire. After three solid whaps, the screen
only flickered in mild irritation. "You idiots!" She threw the port

at the floorboards in front of the passenger seat and slumped back, stringing her curly hair through her fingers.

Her harness cut into her chest, suddenly strangling, and she released the buckle and kicked open her door at the same time, half falling into the alley's shadows. The grease and whiskey scent from the tavern nearly choked her as she swallowed her breaths, trying to rationalize her way out of the anger.

She would go to the police station. It was too late to go now—tomorrow, then. First thing in the morning. She would be calm and logical and she would explain to them why their assumptions were wrong. She would make them reopen the case.

Scarlet swiped her wrist over the scanner beside the ship's hatch and yanked it up harder than the hydraulics wanted to let it go.

She would tell the detective that he had to keep searching. She would make him listen. She would make him understand that her grandma hadn't left of her own free will, and that she most certainly had *not* killed herself.

Half a dozen plastic crates filled with garden vegetables were crammed into the back of the ship, but Scarlet hardly saw them. She was miles away, in Toulouse, planning the conversation in her head. Calling on every last persuasion, every ounce of reasoning power she had.

Something had happened to her grandmother. Something was wrong and if the police didn't keep looking, Scarlet was going to take it to court and see that every one of their turnip-head detectives was disbarred and would never work again and—

She snatched a gleaming red tomato in each fist, spun on her heels, and pummeled the stone wall with them. The tomatoes splattered, juice and seeds spraying across the piles of garbage that were waiting to go into the compactor.

It felt good. Scarlet grabbed another, imagining the detective's doubt when she'd tried to explain to him that up and disappearing was *not* normal behavior for her grandma. She pictured the tomatoes bursting all over his smug little—

A door swung open just as a fourth tomato was obliterated. Scarlet froze, already reaching for another, as the tavern's owner draped himself against the door frame. Gilles's narrow face was glistening as he took in the slushy orange mess Scarlet had made on the side of his building.

"Those better not be *my* tomatoes."

She withdrew her hand from the bin and wiped it down on her dirt-stained jeans. She could feel heat emanating from her face, the erratic thumping of her pulse.

Gilles wiped the sweat off his almost-bald head and glared, his default expression. "Well?"

"They weren't yours," she muttered. Which was true—they were technically hers until he paid her for them.

He grunted. "Then I'll only dock three univs for having to clean off the mess. Now, if you're done with target practice, maybe you could deign to bring some of that in here. I've been serving wilted lettuce for two days."

He popped back into the restaurant, leaving the door open. The noise of dishes and laughter spilled out into the alley, bizarre in its normality.

Scarlet's world was crashing down around her and nobody noticed. Her grandmother was missing and nobody cared.

She turned back to the hatch and gripped the edges of the tomato crate, waiting for her heart to stop hammering behind her sternum. The words from the comm still bombarded her thoughts, but they were beginning to clear. The first wave of aggression was left to rot with the smashed tomatoes.

When she could take in a breath without her lungs convulsing, she stacked the crate on top of the russet potatoes and heaved them out of the ship.

The line cooks ignored Scarlet as she dodged their spitting skillets, making her way to the cool storage room. She shoved the bins onto the shelves that had been labeled in marker, scratched out, and labeled again a dozen times over the years.

"*Bonjour*, Scarling!"

Scarlet turned around, pulling her hair off her clammy neck.

Émilie was beaming in the doorway, eyes sparkling with a secret, but she pulled back when she saw Scarlet's expression. "What—"

"I don't want to talk about it." Slipping past the waitress, she headed back through the kitchen, but Émilie made a dismissive noise in the back of her throat and trotted after her.

"Then don't talk. I'm just glad you're here," she said, latching on to Scarlet's elbow as they ducked back into the alleyway. "Because he's back." Despite the angelic blond curls that surrounded Émilie's face, her grin suggested very devilish thoughts.

Scarlet pulled away and grabbed a bin of parsnips and radishes, passing them to the waitress. She didn't respond, incapable of caring who *he* was and why it mattered that he was back. "That's great," she said, loading a basket with papery red onions.

"You don't remember, do you? Come now, Scar, the street fighter I was telling you about the other ... oh, maybe that was Sophia."

"The *street* fighter?" Scarlet squeezed her eyes shut as a headache started to throb against her forehead. "*Really,* Ém?"

"Don't be like that. He's sweet! And he's been here almost every day this week and he keeps sitting in my section, which definitely means something, don't you think?" When Scarlet said nothing, the waitress set the bin down and fished a pack of gum from her apron pocket. "He's always really quiet, not like Roland and his crowd. I think he's shy ... and lonely." She popped a stick into her mouth and offered another to Scarlet.

"A street fighter who seems shy?" Scarlet waved the gum away. "Are you listening to yourself?"

"You have to see him to understand. He has these eyes that just ..." Émilie fanned her fingers against her brow, feigning heatstroke.

"Émilie!" Gilles appeared at the door again. "Stop flapping those lips and get in here. Table four wants you." He cast a glare at Scarlet, a silent warning that he'd be docking more univs from her fee if she didn't stop distracting his employees, then pulled back inside without waiting for a response. Émilie stuck her tongue out after him.

Settling the basket of onions against her hip, Scarlet shut the hatch and brushed past the waitress. "Is table four *him*?"

"No, he's at nine," Émilie grumbled, scooping up the load of root vegetables. As they passed back through the steamy kitchen, Émilie gasped. "Oh, I'm so daft! I've been meaning to comm and ask about your grand-mère all week. Have you heard anything new?"

Scarlet clenched her jaw, the words of the comm buzzing like hornets in her head. *Case closed.*

"Nothing new," she said, then let their conversation get lost in the chaos of the cooks screaming at each other across the line.

Émilie followed her as far as the storeroom and dropped off her load. Scarlet busied herself rearranging the baskets before the waitress could say something optimistic. Émilie attempted the requisite "Try not to worry, Scar. She'll be back" before backing away into the tavern.

Scarlet's jaw was starting to ache from gnashing her teeth. Everyone talked about her grandma's disappearance as if she were a stray cat who would meander back home when she got hungry. *Don't worry. She'll be back.*

But she'd been gone for over two weeks. Just disappeared without sending a comm, without a good-bye, without any warning. She'd even missed Scarlet's eighteenth birthday, though she'd bought the ingredients for Scarlet's favorite lemon cake the week before.

None of the farmhands had seen her go. None of the worker androids had recorded anything suspicious. Her portscreen had been left behind, though it offered no clues in its stored comms, calendar, or net history. Her leaving without it was suspicious enough. No one went anywhere without their ports.

But that wasn't the worst of it. Not the abandoned portscreen or the unmade cake.

Scarlet had also found her grandmother's ID chip.

Her *ID chip*. Wrapped in cheesecloth spotted red from her blood and left like a tiny package on the kitchen counter.

The detective said that's what people did when they ran away and didn't want to be found—they cut out their ID chips. He'd said it like he'd just solved the mystery, but Scarlet figured most kidnappers probably knew that trick too.

Two

SCARLET SPOTTED GILLES BEHIND THE HOT TOP, LADLING
béchamel sauce on top of a ham sandwich. She walked around
to the other side, yelling to get his attention, and was met with
annoyance.

"I'm done," she said, returning the scowl. "Come sign off on
the delivery."

Gilles shoveled a stack of *frites* beside the sandwich and slid
the plate across the steel counter to her. "Run that out to the first
booth and I'll have it ready when you get back."

Scarlet bristled. "I don't work for you, Gilles."

"Just be grateful I'm not sending you out to the alley with a
scrub brush." He turned his back on her, his white shirt yellowed
from years of sweat.

Scarlet's fingers twitched with the fantasy of chucking the
sandwich at the back of his head and seeing how it compared to
the tomatoes, but her grandma's stern face just as quickly infiltrated the dream. How disappointed she would be to come back

home only to find that Scarlet had lost one of their most loyal clients in a fit of temper.

Grabbing the plate, Scarlet stormed out of the kitchen and was nearly bowled over by a waiter as soon as the kitchen door swung shut behind her. The Rieux Tavern was not a nice place—the floors were sticky, the furniture was a mismatch of cheap tables and chairs, and the air was saturated with grease. But in a town where drinking and gossiping were the favorite pastimes, it was always busy, especially on Sundays when the local farmhands ignored their crops for a full twenty-four hours.

While she waited for a path to clear through the crowd, Scarlet's attention landed on the netscreens behind the bar. All three were broadcasting the same news footage that had filled up the net since the night before. Everyone was talking about the Eastern Commonwealth's annual ball, where the Lunar queen was a guest of honor and where a cyborg girl had infiltrated the party, blown up some chandeliers, and tried to assassinate the visiting queen...or maybe she'd been trying to assassinate the newly coronated emperor. Everyone seemed to have a different theory. The freeze-frame on the screens showed a close-up of the girl with dirt smudges on her face and strands of damp hair pulled from a messy ponytail. It was a mystery how she'd ever been admitted into a royal ball in the first place.

"They should have put her out of her misery when she fell on those stairs," said Roland, a tavern regular, who looked like he'd been bellied to the bar since noon. He extended a finger toward the screen and mimed shooting a gun. "I'd have put a bullet right through her head. And good riddance."

When a rustle of agreement passed through the nearest patrons, Scarlet rolled her eyes in disgust and shoved toward the first booth.

She recognized Émilie's handsome street fighter immediately, partly due to an array of scars and bruises on his olive skin, but more because he was the only stranger in the tavern. He was more disheveled than she'd expected from Émilie's swooning, with hair that stuck out every direction in messy clumps and a fresh bruise swelling around one eye. Beneath the table, both of his legs were jogging like a windup toy.

Three plates were already set out before him, empty but for splatters of grease, bits of egg salad, and untouched slices of tomato and lettuce.

She didn't realize she'd been staring at him until his gaze shifted and collided with hers. His eyes were unnaturally green, like sour grapes still on the vine. Scarlet's grip tightened on the plate and she suddenly understood Émilie's swooning. *He has these eyes . . .*

Pushing through the crowd, she deposited the sandwich on the table. "You had le croque monsieur?"

"Thank you." His voice startled her, not by being loud or gruff as she'd expected, but rather low and hesitant.

Maybe Émilie was right. Maybe he really was shy.

"Are you sure you don't want us to just bring you the whole pig?" she said, stacking the three empty plates. "It would save the servers the trouble of running back and forth from the kitchen."

His eyes widened and for a moment Scarlet expected him to

ask if that was an option, but then his attention dipped down to the sandwich. "You have good food here."

She withheld a scoff. "Good food" and "Rieux Tavern" were two phrases she didn't normally associate with each other. "Fighting must work up quite an appetite."

He didn't respond. His fingers fidgeted with the straw in his drink and Scarlet could see the table beginning to shake from his bouncing legs.

"Well. Enjoy," she said, picking up the dishes. But then she paused and tipped the plates toward him. "Are you sure you don't want the tomatoes? They're the best part, and they were grown in my own garden. The lettuce too, actually, but it wasn't wilted like this when I harvested it. Never mind, you don't want the lettuce. But the tomatoes?"

Some of the intensity drained from the fighter's face. "I've never tried them."

Scarlet arched an eyebrow. "*Never?*"

After a hesitant moment, he released his drinking glass and picked up the two slabs of tomato and shoved them into his mouth.

His expression froze mid-chew. He seemed to ponder for a moment, eyes unfixed, before swallowing. "Not what I expected," he said, looking up at her again. "But not horrible. I'll order some more of those, if I could?"

Scarlet adjusted the dishes in her grip, keeping a butter knife from slipping off. "You know, I don't actually work—"

"Here it comes!" said someone near the bar, spurring an

excited murmur that rippled through the tavern. Scarlet glanced up at the netscreens. They showed a lush garden, flourishing with bamboo and lilies and sparkling from a recent downpour. The red warmth of the ball spilled down a grand staircase. The security camera was above the door, angled toward the long shadows that stretched out into the path. It was beautiful. Tranquil.

"I have ten univs that say some girl's about to lose her foot on those stairs!" someone shouted, followed by a round of laughter from the bar. "Anyone want to bet me? Come on, what are the odds, really?"

A moment later, the cyborg girl appeared on the screen. She bolted from the doorway and down the stairs, shattering the garden's serenity with her billowing silver gown. Scarlet held her breath, knowing what happened next, but she still flinched when the girl stumbled and fell. She crashed down the steps and landed awkwardly at their base, sprawled across the rocky path. Though there was no sound, Scarlet imagined the girl panting as she rolled onto her back and gawked up at the doorway. Shadows cut across the stairs and a series of unrecognizable figures appeared above her.

Having heard the story a dozen times, Scarlet sought out the missing foot still on the stairs, the light from the ballroom glinting off the metal. The girl's cyborg foot.

"They say the one on the left is the queen," said Émilie. Scarlet jumped, not having heard the waitress approach.

The prince—no, the emperor now—crept down the steps and stooped to pick up the foot. The girl reached for the hem of her skirt, tugging it down over her calves, but she couldn't hide the dead tentacle wires dangling from their metal stump.

Scarlet knew what the rumors were saying. Not only had the girl been confirmed as a Lunar—an illegal fugitive and a danger to Earthen society—but she'd even managed to brainwash Emperor Kai. Some thought she'd been after power, others riches. Some believed she'd been trying to start the war that had so long been threatened. But no matter what the girl's intentions were, Scarlet couldn't help a twinge of pity. After all, she was only a teenager, younger than Scarlet even, and she looked wholly pathetic lying at the base of those stairs.

"What was that about putting her out of her misery?" said one of the guys at the bar.

Roland jutted his finger toward the screen. "Exactly. I've never seen anything so disgusting in my life."

Someone near the end leaned forward so he could look around the other patrons at Roland. "I'm not sure I agree. I think she's kind of cute, pretending to be all helpless and innocent like that. Maybe instead of sending her back to the moon, they should let her come stay with me?"

He was met with robust laughter. Roland thumped his palm on the bar, rattling a mustard dish. "No doubt that metal leg of hers would make for a real cozy bedmate!"

"Swine," Scarlet muttered, but her comment was lost in the guffaws.

"I wouldn't mind the chance to warm her up!" someone new added, and the tables rattled with cheers and amusement.

Anger clawed its way back up Scarlet's throat and she half slammed, half dropped the stack of plates back onto the booth's table. She ignored the startled expressions around her and shoved through the crowd, circling to the back of the bar.

The bewildered bartender watched on as Scarlet pushed some liquor bottles out of the way and climbed up onto the counter that stretched the length of the wall. Reaching up, she opened a wall panel beneath a shelf of cognac glasses and plucked out the netlink cable. All three screens went black, the palace garden and cyborg girl vanishing.

A roar of protest bellowed up around her.

Scarlet spun to face them, accidentally kicking a bottle of wine off the bar. The glass shattered on the floor, but Scarlet barely heard it as she waved the cable at the incensed crowd. "You all should have some respect! That girl's going to be executed!"

"That girl's a Lunar!" a woman yelled. "She *should* be executed!"

The sentiment was enforced with nods and someone lobbing a crust of bread at Scarlet's shoulder. She planted both hands on her hips. "She's only sixteen."

A brash of arguments roared up, men and women alike clambering to their feet and screaming about Lunars and evil and *that girl tried to kill a Union leader*!

"Hey, hey, everyone calm down! Give Scarlet a break!" Roland yelled, his confidence bolstered by the whiskey on his breath. He held his hands out toward the jostling crowd. "We all know crazy runs in her family. First that old goose runs off, and now Scar's defending Lunar rights!"

A parade of laughter and jeers marched past Scarlet's ears, but were muddled by the sound of her own rushing blood. Without knowing how she'd gotten off the counter, she was suddenly halfway over the bar, bottles and glasses scattering, her fist connecting with Roland's ear.

He yelped and spun back to face her. "What—"

"My grandma's not crazy!" She grabbed the front of his shirt. "Is that what you told the detective? When he questioned you? Did you tell him she was crazy?"

"Of course I told him she was crazy!" he yelled back, the stench of alcohol flooding over her. She squeezed the fabric until her fists ached. "And I bet I wasn't the only one. With the way she keeps herself holed up in that old house, talks to animals and androids like they're people, chases folk away with a rifle—"

"*One* time, and he was an escort salesman!"

"I'm not one tinge surprised that Granny Benoit split her last rocket. Seems to me it's been coming a long while."

Scarlet shoved Roland hard with both hands. He stumbled back into Émilie, who'd been trying to get in between them. Émilie screamed and fell back onto a table in her effort to keep Roland from crushing her.

Roland regained his balance, looking like he couldn't decide if he wanted to smirk or snarl. "Better be careful, Scar, or you're going to end up just like the old—"

Table legs screeched against tile and then the fighter had

one hand wrapped around Roland's neck, lifting him clear off the floor.

The tavern fell silent. The fighter, unconcerned, held Roland aloft like he was nothing more than a doll, ignoring Roland's gagging.

Scarlet gaped, the edge of the bar digging into her stomach.

"I believe you owe her an apology," the fighter said in his quiet, even tone.

A gurgle slipped out of Roland's mouth. His feet flailed in search of the ground.

"Hey, let him go!" a man yelled, leaping off his stool. "You're going to kill him!" He grasped the fighter's wrist, but he might have grabbed an iron bar for as much as the limb budged. Flushing, the man let go and pulled back for a punch, but as soon as he swung, the fighter's free hand came up and blocked it.

Scarlet staggered back from the bar, dully noting a tattoo of nonsensical letters and numbers stamped across the fighter's forearm. LSOP962.

The fighter still seemed angry, but now there was also the tiniest bit of amusement in his expression, like he'd just remembered the rules to a game. He eased Roland's feet back to the ground, simultaneously releasing him and the other man's fist.

Roland caught his balance on a stool. "What's wrong with you?" he choked out, rubbing his neck. "Are you some lunatic city transplant or something?"

"You were being disrespectful."

"*Disrespectful?*" barked Roland. "You just tried to kill me!"

Gilles erupted from the kitchen, shoving through the swinging doors. "What's going on out here?"

"This guy's trying to start a fight," someone said from the crowd.

"And Scarlet broke the screens!"

"I didn't break them, you idiot!" Scarlet yelled, though she wasn't sure who had said it.

Gilles surveyed the dead screens, Roland still rubbing his neck, the broken bottles and glasses littering the wet floor. He glowered at the street fighter. "You," he said, pointing. "Get out of my tavern."

Scarlet's gut tightened. "He didn't do any—"

"Don't you start, Scarlet. How much destruction were you planning on causing today? Are you *trying* to get me to close my account?"

She bristled, her face still burning. "Maybe I'll just take back the delivery and we'll see how your customers like eating spoiled vegetables from now on."

Rounding the bar, Gilles snatched the cable out of Scarlet's hand. "Do you really think you're the only working farm in France? Honestly, Scar, I only order from you because your grandmother would give me hell if I didn't!"

Scarlet pursed her lips, holding back the frustrated reminder that her grandmother wasn't here anymore so maybe he *should* just order from someone else if that's what he wanted.

Gilles turned his attention back to the fighter. "I said get out!"

Ignoring him, the fighter held his hand out to Émilie, who

was still half curled against a table. Her face was flushed and her skirt was soaked through with beer, but her gaze glowed with infatuation as she let herself be pulled to her feet.

"Thank you," she said, her whisper carrying in the uncanny silence.

Finally, the fighter met Gilles's scowl. "I will go, but I haven't paid for my meal." He hesitated. "I can pay for the broken glasses as well."

Scarlet blinked. "What?"

"I don't want your money!" Gilles screamed, sounding insulted, which came as an even further shock to Scarlet, who had only ever heard Gilles complain about money and how his vendors were bleeding him dry. "I want you out of my tavern."

The fighter's pale eyes darted to Scarlet, and for a moment she sensed a connection between them.

Here they were, both outcasts. Unwanted. *Crazy.*

Pulse thrumming, she buried the thought. This man was trouble. He *fought* people for a living—or perhaps even for fun. She wasn't sure which was worse.

Turning away, the fighter dipped his head in what almost looked like an apology and shuffled toward the exit. Scarlet couldn't help thinking as he passed that despite all signs of brutality, he looked no more menacing now than a scolded dog.

Three

SCARLET PULLED THE BIN OF POTATOES OUT FROM THE lowest shelf, dropping it with a thud on the floor before lugging the crate of tomatoes on top. The onions and turnips went beside it. She'd have to make two trips out to the ship again and that made her angrier than anything. So much for a dignified exit.

She grabbed the handles of the lower bin and hoisted them up.

"*Now* what are you doing?" Gilles said from the doorway, a towel draped over one shoulder.

"Taking these back."

Heaving a sigh, Gilles braced himself against the wall. "Scar—I didn't mean all that out there."

"I find that unlikely."

"Look, I like your grandmother, and I like you. Yes, she overcharges and you can be a huge sting in my side and you're both a little crazy sometimes—" He held up both hands defensively when he saw Scarlet's hackles rising. "Hey, *you're* the one who climbed up on the bar and started making speeches, so don't try to say it's not true."

She wrinkled her nose at him.

"But when it comes right down to it, your grand-mère runs a good farm, and you still grow the best tomatoes in France year after year. I don't want to cancel my account."

Scarlet tilted the bin so that the shiny red globes rolled and thumped against one another.

"Put them back, Scar. I've already signed off on the delivery payment."

He walked away before Scarlet could lose her temper again.

Blowing a red curl out of her face, Scarlet set the crates down and kicked the potatoes back to their spot beneath the shelves. She could hear the cooks chortling over the dining room drama. The story had already taken on a legendary air from the waitstaff's telling of it. According to the cooks, the street fighter had broken a bottle over Roland's head, knocking him unconscious and crushing a chair in the process. He would have taken out Gilles too, if Émilie hadn't calmed him down with one of her pretty smiles.

With no interest in correcting the story, Scarlet dusted her hands on her jeans and paced back into the kitchen. A coldness hung in the air between her and the tavern staff as she made her way to the scanner beside the back door—Gilles was nowhere to be seen and Émilie's giggles could be heard out in the dining room. Scarlet hoped she was only imagining the dropped glances. She wondered how fast the rumors would spread through town.

Scarlet Benoit was defending the cyborg! The Lunar! She's clearly split her rocket, just like her . . . just like . . .

She swiped her wrist beneath the ancient scanner. Out of habit, she inspected the delivery order that appeared on the screen, making sure Gilles hadn't shorted her like he often tried and noting that he had, in fact, deducted three univs for the smashed tomatoes. 687U DEPOSITED TO VENDOR ACCOUNT: BENOIT FARMS AND GARDENS.

She left through the back door without saying good-bye to anyone.

Though still warm from the sunny afternoon, the shadows of the alley were refreshing compared with the sweltering kitchen and Scarlet let it cool her down while she reorganized the crates in the back of the ship. She was behind schedule. It would be late evening before she got home. She would have to get up extra early to go to the Toulouse police station, otherwise she would lose a whole day in which no one was doing anything to recover her grandmother.

Two weeks. *Two whole weeks* of her grandmother being out there, alone. Helpless. Forgotten. Maybe . . . maybe even dead. Maybe kidnapped and killed and left in a dark, wet ditch somewhere and why? *Whywhywhy?*

Frustrated tears steamed her eyes, but she blinked them back. Slamming the hatch, she rounded to the front of the ship, and froze.

The fighter was there, his back against the stone building. Watching her.

In her surprise, a hot tear leaked out. She swiped at it before it could crawl halfway down her cheek. She returned his stare, calculating if his stance was threatening or not. He stood a dozen steps from the nose of her ship and his expression seemed more hesitant than dangerous, but then, it hadn't seemed dangerous when he'd nearly strangled Roland either.

"I wanted to make sure you were all right," he said, his voice almost lost in the jumbled noise from the tavern.

She splayed her fingers on the back of the ship, annoyed at how her nerves were humming, like they couldn't decide if she should be afraid of him or flattered.

"I'm better off than Roland," she said. "His neck was already starting to bruise when I left."

His eyes flashed toward the kitchen door. "He deserved worse."

She would have smiled, but she didn't have the energy after biting back all the anger and frustration of the afternoon. "I wish you hadn't gotten involved at all. I had the situation under control."

"Clearly." He squinted at her like he was trying to figure out a puzzle. "But I was worried you might draw that gun on him, and such a scene may not have helped your case. As far as not being crazy, that is."

Hair prickled behind her neck. Scarlet's hand instinctively went to her lower back, where a small pistol was warm against her skin. Her grandma had given it to her on her eleventh birthday with the paranoid warning: *You just never know when a stranger will want to take you somewhere you don't mean to go.* She'd taught Scarlet to use it and Scarlet hadn't left home without it since, no matter how ridiculous and unnecessary it seemed.

Seven years later and she was quite sure not a single person had ever noticed the gun concealed under her usual red hoodie. Until now.

"How did you know?"

He shrugged, or what would have been a shrug if the movement hadn't been so tense and jerky. "I saw the handle when you climbed up on the counter."

Scarlet lifted the back of her sweatshirt just enough to loosen the pistol from her waistband. She tried to take in a calming breath, but the air was filled with the onion and garbage stink of the alley.

"Thanks for your concern, but I'm just fine. I have to go—behind on the deliveries . . . behind on *everything.*" She stepped toward the pilot's door.

"Do you have any more tomatoes?"

She paused.

The fighter shrank back further into the shadows, looking sheepish. "I'm still a little hungry," he muttered.

Scarlet imagined she could smell the tomato flesh on the wall behind her.

"I can pay," he quickly added.

She shook her head. "No, that's all right. We have plenty." She shuffled backward, keeping her eyes on him, and reopened the hatch. She grabbed a tomato and a bundle of crooked carrots. "Here, these are good raw too," she said, tossing them to him.

He caught them with ease, the tomato disappearing in his large fist and his other hand gripping the carrots by their lacy, leafy stems. He surveyed them from every angle. "What are they?"

A surprised laugh tumbled out of her. "They're carrots. Are you serious?"

Again, he seemed embarrassingly aware of having said something unusual. His shoulders hunched in a vain attempt to make himself seem smaller. "Thank you."

"Your mom never made you eat your vegetables, did she?"

Their gazes clashed and the awkwardness was immediate. Something shattered inside the tavern, making Scarlet jump. It was followed by the roar of laughter.

"Never mind. They're good, you'll like them." She shut the hatch and rounded to the door again, whisking her ID across the ship's scanner. The door opened, forming a wall between them, and the floodlights blinked on. They accentuated the bruise around the fighter's eye, making it seem darker than before. He flinched back like a criminal in a spotlight.

"I was wondering if you could use a farmhand?" he said, the words slurred in his rush to get them out.

Scarlet paused, suddenly understanding why he'd waited for her, why he'd stalled so long. She scanned his broad shoulders, bulky arms. He was built for manual labor. "You're looking for work?"

He started to smile, a look that was dangerously mischievous. "The money's good at the fights, but it doesn't make for much of a career. I thought maybe you could pay me in food."

She laughed. "After seeing the evidence of your appetite in there, I think I'd lose my shirt with a deal like that." She flushed the second she'd said it—no doubt he was now imagining her with her shirt off. Yet, to her shock, his face remained serenely neutral, and she hurried to fill the space before his reactions caught up. "What's your name, anyway?"

That awkward shrug again. "They call me Wolf at the fights."

"*Wolf?* How . . . predatory."

He nodded, entirely serious.

Scarlet swallowed a grin. "You might want to leave the street fighter bit off your resume."

He scratched at his elbow, where the strange tattoo could barely be seen in the dark, and she thought maybe she'd embarrassed him. Perhaps Wolf was a beloved nickname.

"Well, they call me Scarlet. Yes, like the hair, what a clever observation."

His expression softened. "What hair?"

Scarlet settled her arm on top of the door, resting her chin. "Good one."

For a moment he seemed almost pleased with himself and Scarlet found herself warming to this stranger, this anomaly. This soft-spoken street fighter.

A warning tingled in the back of her head—she was wasting time. Her grandmother was out there. Alone. Frightened. Dead in a ditch.

Scarlet tightened her grip on the door frame. "I'm really sorry, but we have a full staff already. I don't need any more farmhands."

The glint faded from his eyes and in an instant he was looking uncomfortable again. Flustered. "I understand. Thank you for the food." He kicked at the stem of a dead firework on the pavement—a remnant from last night's peace celebrations.

"You should head to Toulouse, or even Paris. There are more jobs in the cities, and people around here don't take too kindly to strangers, as you may have noticed."

He tilted his head so that his emerald eyes glowed even brighter in the wash of the ship's floodlights, looking almost amused. "Thanks for the tip."

Turning, Scarlet sank into the pilot's seat.

Wolf shifted toward the wall as she started the engine. "If you change your mind about needing a hand, I can be found at the abandoned Morel house most nights. I may not be great with people, but I think I'd do well on a farm." Amusement touched the corners of his lips. "Animals love me."

"Oh, I'm sure they do," Scarlet said, beaming with fake encouragement. She shut the door before muttering, "What farm animals don't love a wolf?"

Four

THE CAPTIVITY OF CARSWELL THORNE HAD GOTTEN OFF TO a rocky start, what with the catastrophic soap rebellion and all. But since being transferred to solitary, he'd become the personification of a well-mannered gentleman, and after six months of such commendable behavior, he'd persuaded the only female guard on rotation to lend him a portscreen.

He was quite sure this would not have succeeded if the guard wasn't convinced he was an idiot, incapable of doing anything other than counting the days and searching for naughty pictures of ladies he'd known and imagined.

And she was right, of course. Thorne was mystified by technology and couldn't have done anything useful with the tablet even if he had had a step-by-step instruction manual on "How to Escape from Jail Using a Portscreen." He'd been unsuccessful in accessing his comms, connecting to newsfeeds, or scouting out any information on New Beijing Prison and the surrounding city.

But he sure did appreciate the suggestively naughty, if heavily filtered, pictures.

He was scrolling through his portfolio on the 228th day of his captivity, wondering if Señora Santiago was still married to that onion-smelling man, when an awful screeching disrupted the cell's peacefulness.

He peered upward, squinting at the smooth, glossy white ceiling.

The sound ceased and was followed by shuffling. A couple thuds. More grinding.

Thorne folded his legs atop his cot and waited while the noise grew louder and closer, hiccupped and continued. It took him some time to place this new strange noise, but after much listening and pondering he was convinced it was the sound of a motorized drill.

Maybe one of the other prisoners was remodeling.

The sound stopped, though the memory of it lingered, vibrating off the walls. Thorne glanced around. His cell was a perfect cube with smooth, shiny white wall panels on all six sides. It contained his all-white cot, a urinal that slid in and out of the wall with the press of a button, and him in his white uniform.

If someone was remodeling, he hoped his cell would be next.

The sound started again, more grating this time, and then a long screw punctured through the ceiling and clattered to the center of the cell's floor. Three more dropped after it.

Thorne craned his head as one of the screws rolled beneath his cot.

A moment later, a square tile fell from the ceiling with a bang, followed by two dangling legs and a startled cry. The legs wore a white cotton jumpsuit that matched Thorne's, but unlike his own plain white shoes, the feet attached to those legs were bare.

One wore skin.

The other a plating of reflective metal.

With a grunt, the girl released her hold on the ceiling and fell into a crouch in the middle of the cell.

Resting his elbows on his knees, Thorne tilted forward, trying to get a better look at her without moving from his safe position against the wall. She had a slight build and tanned skin and straight brown hair. Like her left foot, her left hand was made of metal.

Stabilizing herself, the girl stood and brushed off her jumpsuit.

"I'm sorry," Thorne said.

She spun toward him, eyes wild.

"It seems that you've stumbled into the wrong jail cell. Do you need directions to get back to yours?"

She blinked.

Thorne smiled.

The girl frowned.

Her irritation made her prettier, and Thorne cupped his chin, studying her. He'd never met a cyborg before, much less flirted with one, but there was a first time for everything.

"These cells aren't supposed to be occupied," she said.

"Special circumstances."

She surveyed him for a long moment, her brows knitting together. "Murder?"

His grin grew. "Thank you, but no. I started a riot on the yard." He adjusted his collar, before adding, "We were protesting the soap."

Her confusion grew, and Thorne noticed that she was still in her defensive stance.

"The soap," he said again, wondering if she'd heard him. "It's too drying."

She said nothing.

"I have sensitive skin."

Her mouth opened and he expected sympathy, but all that came out was a disinterested "Huh."

Drawing herself up, she kicked the fallen ceiling tile out from beneath her feet, then proceeded to turn in a full circle, surveying the cell. Her lip curled in annoyance. "Stupid," she muttered, nearing the wall to Thorne's left and placing a palm against it. "One room off."

Her eyelashes suddenly fluttered as if dust were stuck in them. Growling, she smacked her palm against her temple a few times.

"You're escaping."

"Not at this very moment," she said through her teeth, roughly shaking her head. "But, yes, that is the general idea." Her face lit up when she spotted the port in his lap. "What model portscreen is that?"

"I haven't the faintest idea." He held it up for her. "I'm putting together a portfolio of the women I've loved."

Pushing herself from the wall, she snatched the portscreen away and flipped it over. A tip of her cyborg finger opened, revealing a small screwdriver. It wasn't long before she'd undone the plate on the underside of the port.

"What are you doing?"

"Taking your vid-cable."

"What for?"

"Mine's on the fritz."

She pulled a yellow wire from the screen and dropped it back into Thorne's lap, then sank cross-legged to the floor. Thorne watched, mystified, as she tossed her hair to one side and unlatched a panel at the base of her skull. A moment later her fingers emerged with a wire similar to the one she'd just stolen from him, but with one blackened end. The girl's face contorted in concentration while she installed the new cable.

With a pleased sigh, she shut the panel and tossed the old cable next to Thorne. "Thanks."

He grimaced, shrinking away from the wire. "You have a portscreen in your *head*?"

"Something like that." The girl stood and ran a hand over the wall again. "Ah, that's much better. Now how do I . . ." Trailing off, she pushed the button in the corner. A glossy white panel slid up into the wall, ejecting the urinal with smooth precision. Her fingers fished into the gap left between the fixture and the wall, searching.

Inching away from the neglected cable on his cot, Thorne cleared his mind of the image of her opening a plate in her skull, once again calling up the personification of a gentleman, and attempted to make small talk while she worked. He asked what she was in for and complimented the fine workmanship of her metal extremities, but she ignored him, making him briefly question if he'd been separated from the female population for so long that he could be losing his charm.

But that seemed unlikely.

A few minutes later, the girl seemed to find what she was looking for, and Thorne heard the motorized-drill sound again.

"When they locked you up," Thorne said, "didn't they consider that this prison might have some security weaknesses?"

"It didn't at the time. This hand is kind of a new addition." She paused and stared hard at one corner of the alcove, as if trying to see through the wall.

Maybe she had X-ray vision. Now *that* he could find some good uses for.

"Let me guess," Thorne said. "Breaking and entering?"

After a long silence of examining the retracting mechanism, the girl wrinkled her nose. "Two counts of treason, if you must know. And resisting arrest, and unlawful use of bioelectricity. Oh, and illegal immigration, but honestly, I think that's a little excessive."

He squinted at the back of her head, a twitch developing in his left eye. "How old are you?"

"Sixteen."

The screwdriver in her finger began to spin again. Thorne waited until there was a lull in the grinding. "What's your name?"

"Cinder," she said, followed by another swell of noise.

When it died down: "I'm Captain Carswell Thorne. But usually people just call me—"

More grinding.

"Thorne. Or Captain. Or Captain Thorne."

Without responding, she wriggled her hand back into the alcove. It seemed like she was trying to twist something, but it must not have budged, as a second later she sat back and huffed with frustration.

"I can see that you're in need of an accomplice," Thorne said, straightening his jumpsuit. "And lucky for you, I happen to be a criminal mastermind."

She glowered at him. "Go away."

"That's a difficult request in this situation."

She sighed and dusted the flecks of white plastic from her screwdriver.

"What are you going to do when you get out?" he asked.

She turned back to the wall. The grinding persisted for a while before she paused to roll her neck, working out a crick. "The most direct route out of the city is north."

"Oh, my naive little convict. Don't you think that's what they'll be expecting you to do?"

She jabbed the screwdriver into the alcove. "Would you please stop distracting me?"

"I'm just saying we might be able to help each other."

"Leave me alone."

"I have a ship."

Her gaze darted to him for only a beat—a look of warning.

"A spaceship."

"A spaceship," she drawled.

"She could have us halfway to the stars in less than two minutes, and she's just outside the city limits. Easy to get to. What do you say?"

"I say if you don't stop talking and let me work, we won't be getting halfway to anywhere."

"Point taken," Thorne said, holding up his hands in surrender. "You just think it over in that pretty head of yours."

She tensed, but kept working.

"Now that I'm thinking of it, there used to be an excellent dim sum bar just a block away too. They had mini pork buns that were to die for. Rich and succulent." He pinched his fingers together, salivating over the memory.

Face scrunching up, Cinder started to massage the back of her neck.

"Maybe if we have time we could stop in and pick up a snack for the road. I could use a treat after suffering through the tasteless junk they call food in this place." He licked his lips, but when he refocused on the girl, the pain on her features had tightened. Sweat was beading on her brow.

"Are you all right?" he asked, reaching for her. "Do you need a back rub?"

She swatted him away. "*Please*," she said, hands braced between them. She struggled to draw in a shuddering breath.

As Thorne stared, her image wavered, like heat rising off

maglev tracks. He stumbled back. His heartbeat quickened. A tingle filled his brain and raced down his nerves.

She was . . . beautiful.

No, divine.

No, *perfect.*

His pulse thumped, thoughts of worship and devotion swimming through his head. Thoughts of surrender. Thoughts of compliance.

"Please," she said again, hiding behind her metal hand. Her tone was desperate as she slumped against the wall. "Just stop talking. Just . . . leave me alone."

"All right." Confusion reigned—cyborg, prison mate, *goddess.* "Of course. Anything you like." Eyes watering, he stumbled backward and sank blindly down to his cot.

Five

SCARLET'S THOUGHTS SEETHED AS SHE HAULED THE EMPTY crates out of the back of her ship and through the hangar's yawning doors. She'd found her portscreen on the floor of the ship and it was now in her pocket, the message from the law enforcement office burning against her thigh as she mindlessly traipsed through her evening routine.

She was perhaps most angry with herself now, for being distracted, even for a minute, by nothing more than a handsome face and a veneer of danger, so soon after she'd learned that her grandma's case had been closed. Her curiosity about the street fighter made her feel like a traitor to everything important.

And then there was Roland and Gilles and every other backstabber in Rieux. They all believed her grandma was crazy, and that's what they'd told the police. Not that she was the most hardworking farmer in the province. Not that she made the best éclairs this side of the Garonne River. Not that she'd served her country as a military spaceship pilot for twenty-eight years, and still wore a medal for honorable service on her favorite checkered kitchen apron.

No. They'd told the police she was crazy.

And now they'd stopped looking for her.

Not for long though. Her grandma was out there somewhere and Scarlet was going to find her if she had to dig up dirt and blackmail every last detective in Europe.

The sun was sinking fast, sending Scarlet's elongated shadow down the drive. Beyond the gravel, the whispering crops of cornstalks and leafy sugar beets stretched out in every direction, meeting up with the first spray of stars. A cobblestone house disrupted the view to the west, with two windows glowing orange. Their only neighbor for miles.

For more than half her life, this farm had been Scarlet's paradise. Over the years, she'd fallen in love with it more deeply than she'd known a person could fall in love with land and sky—and she knew her grandma felt the same. Though she didn't like to think of it, she was aware that someday she would inherit the farm, and she sometimes fantasized about growing old here. Happy and content, with perpetual dirt beneath her fingernails and an old house that was in constant need of repair.

Happy and content—like her grandmother.

She wouldn't have just left. Scarlet knew it.

She lugged the crates into the barn, stacking them in the corner so the androids could fill them again tomorrow, then grabbed the pail of chicken feed. Scarlet walked while she fed, tossing big handfuls of kitchen scraps in her path as the chickens scurried around her ankles.

Rounding the corner of the hangar, she halted.

A light was on in the house, on the second floor.

In her grandmother's bedroom.

The pail slipped from her fingers. The chickens squawked and darted away, before clustering back around the spilled feed.

She stepped over them and ran, the gravel skidding beneath her shoes. Her heart was swelling, bursting, the sprint already making her lungs burn as she yanked open the back door. She took the stairs two at a time, the old wood groaning beneath her.

The door to her grandma's bedroom was open and she froze in the doorway, panting, grasping the jamb.

A hurricane had come through the room. Every drawer was pulled out from the dresser, clothes and toiletries had been dumped onto the floor. The quilts from the bed were piled haphazardly at its foot, the mattress at an angle, the digital picture frames beside the window all pulled from their brackets, leaving dark spots on the wall where the sunlight hadn't managed to fade the painted plaster.

A man was on his knees beside the bed, tearing through a box of her grandmother's old military uniforms. He jumped up when he saw Scarlet, nearly hitting his head on the low oak beam that spanned the ceiling.

The world spun. Scarlet almost didn't recognize him—it had been years since she'd seen him, but it could have been decades for how much he had aged. A beard was taking over his normally clean-shaven jawline. His hair was matted on one side, sticking up straight on the other. He was pale and gaunt, like he hadn't had a proper meal in weeks.

"Dad?"

He clutched a blue flight jacket to his chest.

"What are you doing here?" She surveyed the chaos again, heart still pounding. "What are you *doing?*"

"There's something here," he said, his voice rough and unused. "She's hidden something." He peered down at the jacket, then tossed it onto the bed. Kneeling, he started digging through the box again. "I need to find it."

"Find what? What are you talking about?"

"She's gone," he whispered. "She's not coming back. She won't ever know and I . . . I have to find it. I have to know why."

The smell of cognac swirled through the air and Scarlet's heart hardened. She didn't know how he'd found out about his mother's disappearance, but for him to just assume all hope was lost, so easily, so quickly, and to think he would be entitled to a single thing that belonged to her, after he'd abandoned them both. To go so many years without a single comm, only to show up drunk and start tearing through her grandmother's things—

Scarlet had the sudden urge to call the police, except she was mad at *them* too.

"Get out! Get out of our house!"

Unfazed, he started to pile the mishmash of clothes back into the box.

Face burning, Scarlet rounded the bed and grabbed his arm, trying to yank him to his feet. "Stop it!"

He hissed and fell back onto the old wooden floorboards. He scurried away from her as he would from a rabid dog, clutching his arm. His gaze was stark madness.

Scarlet drew back, surprised, before planting clenched fists on her hips. "What's wrong with your arm?"

He didn't answer, just kept nursing the arm against his chest.

Setting her jaw, Scarlet stomped toward him and grabbed his wrist. He yelped and tried to pull away, but she held firm, shoving his sleeve up to his elbow. Scarlet gasped and let go, but the arm continued to hang in midair, like he'd forgotten to retract it.

The skin was covered in burn marks. Each one a perfect circle and placed in a neat, perfect row. Row upon row upon row, circling his forearm from wrist to elbow, some shining with wrinkled scar tissue, others blackened and blistering. And on his wrist, a scab where his ID chip had once been implanted.

Her stomach turned.

Back against the wall, her father buried his face in the mattress, away from Scarlet, away from the burns.

"Who did this to you?"

His arm fell, curling against his stomach. He said nothing.

Scarlet pushed herself off the wall and ran to the bathroom in the hallway. She returned a moment later with a tube of ointment and a roll of bandages. Her father hadn't moved.

"They made me," he whispered, his hysteria fading.

Scarlet eased his arm away from his stomach and began to dress the wound, as tenderly as she could despite her shaking hands. "Who made you do what?"

"I couldn't get away," he continued as if he hadn't heard her. "They asked so many questions and I didn't know. I didn't know what they wanted. I tried to answer them, but I didn't know . . ."

Scarlet glanced up from her work as her father tilted his head toward her and stared blankly across the tousled blankets. Tears had pooled in his eyes. Her father—crying. It was almost more shocking than the burns. Her chest clamped and she froze, the bandage wrapped halfway up his forearm. She realized that she did not know this sad, broken man. This was only a shell of her father, her charismatic and selfish and worthless father.

Where anger and hatred had flared before, there was now an aching sense of pity.

What possibly could have caused this?

"They gave me the poker," he continued, his eyes wide and distant.

"They *gave* you—? Why—?"

"And they brought me to her. And I realized, she was the one with the answers. She was the one with the information. They wanted something from *her*. But she just watched . . . she just watched me do it, and she cried . . . but they asked her the same questions, and she still wouldn't answer them. She wouldn't answer them." His voice hiccupped, his face flushing with sudden anger. "She let them do this to me."

Struggling to gulp, Scarlet finished off the wrapping and

leaned against the mattress, her legs beginning to tremble. "Grand-mère? You saw her?"

His attention flashed back to her, crazed again. "They had me for a week and then they just let me go. They could tell she didn't care about me. She wouldn't give in for *me*."

Without warning, he pushed forward and clambered toward Scarlet on his knees, grasping her arms. She tried to shrink away but he held her firm, his fingernails digging into her skin. "What is it, Scar? What's so important? More important than her own son?"

"Dad, you have to calm down. You have to tell me where she is." Her thoughts stammered. "Where is she? Who has her? *Why?*"

Her father's eyes searched her, panicked and shimmering. Slowly, he shook his head and dropped his attention to the floor. "She's hiding something," he mumbled. "I want to know what it is. What is she hiding, Scar? Where is it?"

He turned to rustle through a drawer of old cotton shirts that had clearly already been riffled through. He was sweating now, his hair damp around his ears.

Scarlet used the bed frame to hoist herself onto the mattress. "Dad, please." She tried to sound soothing, though her heart was thumping so hard it hurt. "Where *is* she?"

"Don't know." He dug his fingernails into the space between the molding and the wall. "I was at a bar in Paris. They must have drugged my drink, because next I woke up in a dark room. It smelled damp, musty." He sniffed. "They drugged me when they let me go too. One minute I was in that dark room, then I was here. I woke up in the cornfield."

With a shudder, Scarlet pulled her hands through her hair until the curls knotted up around them. They'd brought him *here*, to the same place they'd kidnapped her grandmother. Why? Did these people know that Scarlet was his only family—did they think she would be the best person to take care of him?

That didn't make any sense. Clearly they weren't worried about her dad's well-being. So what else? Was leaving him here a message to her? A threat?

"You must remember something," she said, her voice taking on a tinge of desperation. "Something about the room, or something someone said? Did you get a good look at them? Could you describe one of them to a profiler? *Anything?*"

"Was drugged," he said, quickly, but then his brow drew together as he struggled to think. He made to touch his burn marks, but then let his hand fall into his lap. "Wouldn't let me see them."

Scarlet barely resisted the urge to shake him and scream that he had to think harder. "Did they blindfold you?"

"No." He squinted. "I was afraid to look."

Frustrated tears were beginning to sting her eyes and Scarlet tilted her head back, gulping down patient breaths. Her worst fears, those sneaking, horrible suspicions, were true.

Her grandmother had been kidnapped. Not just kidnapped, but kidnapped by cruel, brutal people. Were they harming her as they'd harmed her son? What would they do to her? What did they want?

Ransom?

But why hadn't they asked Scarlet for anything yet? And why

had they taken her father too, but then let him go? It didn't make sense.

Terror clouded her thoughts as all the possible horrors streamed through her imagination. Torture and burning and dark rooms . . .

"What did you mean, when you said they made you? What did they make you do?"

"Burn myself," he whispered. "Handed me the poker."

"But how—"

"So many questions. I don't know. I never knew my father. She doesn't talk about him. I don't know what she does here in her big ancient house. What happened on the moon. Don't know what she's hiding—she's hiding *something*." He pulled weakly at the blankets on the bed, glancing halfheartedly beneath the sheets.

"You're talking nonsense," Scarlet said, her voice breaking. "You have to think harder. You have to remember *something*."

A long, long silence. Outside, the chickens were clucking again, their scaly feet scratching across the gravel.

"Tattoo."

She frowned. "What?"

He placed a finger over one of the burns, on the inside flesh of his arm, just below his elbow. "The one who handed me the poker had a tattoo. Here. Letters and numbers."

Her vision prickled with bright lights and Scarlet gripped the rumpled quilt, for a moment feeling like she could faint.

Letters and numbers.

"Are you sure?"

"L...S..." He shook his head. "I can't remember. There was more."

Her mouth ran dry, hatred overtaking the dizziness. She knew that tattoo.

He'd pretended to be kind. Pretended he only needed honest work.

When—days? hours?—before, he'd tortured her father. Kept her grandmother prisoner.

And she'd almost trusted him. The tomato, the carrots... she'd thought she was helping him. Stars above, she'd *flirted* with him, and all the while, he knew. She recalled those moments of peculiar amusement, the glint in his eyes, and her stomach twisted. He'd been laughing at her.

Ears ringing, she peered down at her dad, who was turning out the pockets of a pair of pants that probably hadn't fit her grandmother in twenty years.

She stood. The blood rushed to her head, but she ignored it. Marching to the corner of the room, she grabbed her grandma's portscreen from where her father had tossed it onto the floorboards.

"Here," she said, throwing the port onto the bed. "I'm going to the Morel farm. If I'm not home in three hours, comm the police."

Dazed, her father reached out and grasped the port. "I thought the Morels were dead."

"Are you listening to me? I want you to lock all the doors, and don't leave. Three hours and then comm the police. Do you understand?"

Again he succumbed to that frightened, child-like expression. "Don't go out there, Scar. Don't you get it? They used me as bait for her and you'll be next. They'll come for you too."

Clenching her jaw, Scarlet zipped up her hoodie to her chin. "I intend to find them first."

Six

GREEN TEXT TREKKED ACROSS CINDER'S VISION, documenting the crimes of one Carswell Thorne, who had already led a very productive life of lawbreaking despite having just turned twenty a few months ago: one count military desertion, two counts international theft, one count attempted theft, six counts handling of stolen goods, and one count theft of government property.

That last conviction hardly seemed to do the crime justice. He'd stolen a spaceship from the American Republic's military.

Hence, the spaceship that he was so proud of.

Though he was currently serving a six-year sentence in the Eastern Commonwealth for attempted theft of a second-era jade necklace, he was also wanted in Australia and, of course, his own America, and would be standing trial and no doubt serving time in both countries for the harm he'd done there as well.

Cinder slumped against a breaker panel, wishing she hadn't checked. Escaping from prison herself was bad enough, but assisting the escape of this criminal—a *real* criminal—and doing it in a stolen spaceship?

Swallowing hard, she peered back through the opening she'd made between the mechanical room and the prisoner's cell. Carswell Thorne still sat on his cot with his elbows propped on his knees, thumbs twiddling.

She wiped her damp palm on her bleached-white jumper. This was not about Carswell Thorne. This was about Queen Levana and Emperor Kai and *Princess Selene*. The innocent child Levana had tried to murder thirteen years ago, but who had been rescued and smuggled down to Earth. Who remained the most-wanted person in the world. Who just happened to be Cinder herself.

She'd known for less than twenty-four hours. Dr. Erland, who had known for *weeks*, decided to inform her that he'd run DNA tests proving her bloodline only after Queen Levana had recognized her at the annual ball and threatened to attack Earth if Cinder wasn't thrown into jail for being an illegal Lunar emigrant.

So Dr. Erland had sneaked into her prison cell and given her a new foot (hers had fallen off on the palace steps), a state-of-the-art cyborg hand with fancy gadgets that she was still getting used to, and the biggest shock of her life. He'd then told her to escape and come meet him in Africa, like that would be no more difficult than installing a new processor on a Gard3.9.

This order, simultaneously so simple and so impossible, had given her something to focus on other than her newfound identity. Good thing too because when she dwelled on that, her entire body had a tendency to seize up, leaving her useless, and this was a bad time to be suffering from indecision. Regardless of what she would do when she got out, she was sure of one thing: *not* escaping meant certain death when Queen Levana came to claim her.

She peered back at the inmate again. If she had a close destination in mind, and a working spaceship at that, it could be the key to her escape.

He was still twiddling his thumbs, still obeying her command—*just leave me alone.* The words had been fire in her mouth when she'd said them, while her blood had boiled and her skin had burned. The sensation of overheating was a side effect of her new Lunar gift—powers that Dr. Erland had managed to un-lock after a device implanted on her spine had kept her from using them for so many years. Although it still seemed like magic to her, it was really a genetic trait Lunars were born with that al-lowed them to control and manipulate the bioelectricity of other living creatures. They could trick people into seeing things that weren't real or experiencing made-up emotions. They could brainwash people into doing things they wouldn't otherwise do. Without argument. Without resistance.

Cinder was still learning how to use this "gift" and she wasn't entirely sure how she'd managed to control Carswell Thorne, just as she wasn't sure how she'd managed to persuade one of the jail guards to move her to a more convenient cell. All she knew was that she'd wanted to strangle this inmate when he wouldn't stop talking, and her Lunar gift had surged at the base of her neck, spurred on by stress and nerves. She'd lost control of it for a moment and in that breath Thorne had done precisely what she'd wanted him to do.

He'd stopped talking and left her alone.

Her guilt had been instantaneous. She didn't know what kind of effect it had on a person, all that brain manipulation. And, more than that, she didn't want to be one of those Lunars who took advantage of her powers just because she could. She didn't want to be Lunar at all.

She huffed, blowing a strand of hair away from her face, and ducked through the hole that had been created when she'd pried the urinal out of the wall.

He looked up as she came to a halt before him, arms akimbo. He was still dazed, and though she hated to admit it, he was actually rather attractive. If a girl happened to like that square-jaw, bright-blue-eyes, devilish-dimples kind of thing. Although he was in desperate need of a haircut and a good shave.

She took in a stabilizing breath. "I forced you to do what I wanted you to do, and I shouldn't have. It was an abuse of power and I'm sorry."

He blinked down at her metal hand and the screwdriver sticking out from one finger joint. "Are you the same girl who was just here?" he asked, his voice surprisingly clear, even with his heavy American accent. For some reason, she'd expected him to slur his words after the brain manipulation.

"Of course I am."

"Oh." His brow furrowed. "You seemed a lot prettier before."

Bristling, Cinder considered retracting her apology, but instead crossed her arms over her chest. "Cadet Thorne, was it?"

"Captain Thorne."

"Your records say you were a cadet when you deserted."

He frowned, still puzzled, before he brightened and cocked a finger toward her. "Portscreen in the head?"

She bit the inside of her cheek.

"Well, if you wanted to be *technical* about it," he said. "But I'm a captain now. I prefer the sound of it. Girls are much more impressed."

Cinder, unimpressed, gestured toward the mechanical room on the other side of the wall. "I've decided you can come with me if we can make it to your ship. Just . . . try not to talk too much."

He was off his cot before she finished speaking. "It was my irresistible charm that convinced you, wasn't it?"

Sighing, she retreated through the hole, careful to step over the disconnected plumbing. "So this ship of yours. It *is* the stolen one, right? From the American military?"

"I don't like to think of it as 'stolen.' They have no proof that I didn't plan on giving it back."

"You're kidding, right?"

He shrugged. "You have no proof either."

She squinted back at him. "*Were* you planning on giving it back?"

"Maybe."

An orange light blinked on in the corner of Cinder's vision— her cyborg programming picking up on the lie.

"That's what I thought," she muttered. "Is the ship traceable?"

"Of course not. Removed all the tracking equipment ages ago."

"Good. Which reminds me." Holding up her hand, she retracted the screwdriver and, after two attempts, released the stiletto knife. "We need to remove your ID chip."

He drew half a step back.

"Don't tell me you're squeamish."

"Of course not," he said with an uncomfortable laugh, cuffing his left sleeve. "It's just . . . is that thing sterilized?"

Cinder glowered.

"I mean—I'm sure you're very hygienic and all, it's just . . ." He trailed off, hesitated, and then held his hand out toward her. "Never mind. Just try not to hit anything important."

Bending over his arm, Cinder angled the blade to his wrist as carefully and gently as she could. There was a faint scar there already, presumably from when he'd cut out another ID chip when he'd first been on the run from law enforcement.

His fingers twitched at the invasion, but otherwise he was

still as stone. She extracted the bloodied ID chip and tossed it into a bundle of cords on the floor, before cutting a strip of cloth from his sleeve and letting him wrap it around the wound.

"Is it just me, or is this a big moment in our relationship?"

Cinder scoffed. Turning away, she pointed at a grate near the ceiling. It was surrounded by tethered wires that snaked out from the breaker panel and disappeared into dozens of holes along the walls. "Can you boost me up there?"

"What is it?" Thorne asked, already lacing his fingers together.

"Air duct." Cinder stepped onto his palms and ignored his grunt as he lifted her. She'd expected it, knowing that her metal leg made her a lot heavier than she looked.

With the added leverage, she had the grate removed in seconds. She set it quietly atop some overhead plumbing pipes, then pulled herself into the opening without hesitation.

She called up the blueprint of the jail's interior structure to check the direction while she waited for Thorne to clamber up behind her. Switching on her built-in flashlight, Cinder started to crawl.

It was hot and clumsy work, with her left leg scraping against the aluminum every few inches. Twice she stopped to listen, thinking she heard footsteps somewhere below. Would there be an alarm when their escape was discovered? She was surprised there hadn't been one yet. Thirty-two minutes. She'd left her cell thirty-two minutes ago.

The sweat dripping off her nose and the rapidness of her heartbeat made the time stretch on and on, as if the clock in her head had gotten stuck. Thorne's presence was already filling her with doubts. This was going to be hard enough with just her— how was she going to sneak both of them out?

The thought passed through her skull, startling and clear.

She could brainwash him.

She could convince him that he wanted to tell her where the ship was and how to get to it, and then she could make him decide that he didn't want to come with her after all. She could send him back. He would have no choice but to listen to her.

"Everything all right?"

Cinder released the air that had stuck in her throat.

No. She wouldn't take advantage of him, or anyone. She'd gotten on just fine without any Lunar gift before, she would get on just fine now.

"Sorry," she muttered. "Just checking the blueprint. We're almost there."

"Blueprint?"

She ignored him. Minutes later she rounded a corner and saw a square of checkered light on the duct's ceiling. A tinge of relief, of hope, fluttered inside her as she inched her head out over the grate and peered down.

She saw an expanse of concrete with a small puddle of standing water beneath her and, not six steps from that, another grate, this one larger and round.

A storm drain. Right where the blueprint said it would be.

The drop was a full story, but if they could make it without breaking any legs, this was almost going to be easy.

"Where are we?" Thorne whispered.

"Underground loading dock—where they bring in food and supplies." As gracefully as she could, she climbed over the grate and maneuvered back around so that she and Thorne could both peer through the grid.

"We need to get down there, to that storm drain."

Thorne frowned and pointed. "Isn't that the exit ramp over there?"

She nodded without looking.

"Why aren't we trying to get *there*?"

She peered up at him, the grate casting peculiar shadows across his face. "And just walk to your spaceship? In bright white prison uniforms?"

He frowned, but any response was silenced by the sound of voices. They ducked back.

"I didn't see him dancing with her, my sister did," said a woman. Her words were coupled with footsteps, then a rolling door being hoisted up on clunky rails. "Her dress was soaking wet and wrinkled as a garbage bag."

"But why would the emperor dance with a cyborg?" said a man. "And then for her to go off and attack the Lunar queen like that . . . no way. Your sister was seeing things. I bet the girl was just some crazy person who wandered in off the streets. She was probably bitter over some cyborg injustice."

The conversation was cut short by the rumbling of a delivery ship.

Cinder dared to peer through the grate again and saw a ship

wheeling its way beneath them, backing up toward a recessed loading bay and stopping directly between Cinder and Thorne and the storm drain.

"Morning, Ryu-jūn," said the man as the pilot descended from the ship. The rest of their greetings were drowned out by the hydraulics hissing on an adjustable platform.

Taking advantage of the noise, Cinder used her screwdriver to remove the grate. When she gave Thorne a nod, he carefully eased it up.

Sweat trickled down Cinder's neck and her heart was palpitating so hard she thought it might bruise the inside of her rib cage. Lowering her head, she peered around the dock, checking for any other signs of life and spotted, not arm's distance away on the concrete ceiling, a rotating camera.

She jerked back inside, pulse hissing in her ears. Luckily the camera had been facing the other direction, but still, there was no way they would both make it down undetected. Then there were the three workers unloading the delivery to deal with, and every moment gone was one more moment toward some guard discovering their empty cells.

She shut her eyes, imagining where the camera was, before snaking her arm out. Her hand floundered, flat against the ceiling—the camera was farther than it had seemed in that momentary glance—but then her fingers found it. She grasped the lens and squeezed. The plastic was crushed as easy as a plum in her titanium fist, making a satisfying crunching sound that seemed deafeningly loud.

She listened, relieved as the same sounds of shuffling and chatting continued below.

Their time was up. It wouldn't be more than a minute now before someone realized a camera had been disabled.

Raising her head, she nodded at Thorne and pulled herself forward over the opening.

She dropped onto the roof of the delivery ship and it clanged and shuddered beneath her. Thorne followed, landing with a muffled grunt.

The talking silenced.

Cinder spun around as three figures emerged from the loading bay, their faces contorted in confusion.

They spotted her and Thorne standing atop the ship and froze. Cinder could see them taking in the white uniforms. Her cyborg hand.

One of the men reached for the portscreen on his belt.

Clenching her jaw, Cinder held her hand out to him, thinking only of how he could not get to his port, could not send out an alarm. Thinking of his hand petrified in space just centimeters from his belt.

At her will, his hand stalled and hung motionless.

His eyes filled with terror.

"Don't move," said Cinder, her voice hoarse, guilt already clawing at her throat. She knew she was every bit as panicked as the three people standing before her, and yet the fear on their faces was unmistakable.

The burning sensation returned, starting at the top of her

neck and spreading down through her spine, her shoulders and hips, stinging where it met her prostheses. It wasn't painful or sudden like it had been when Dr. Erland had first unlocked her Lunar gift. Rather, it was almost comforting—almost pleasant.

She could sense the three people standing on the platform, the bioelectricity rolling off them in waves, crackling in the air, ready to be controlled.

Turn around.

In unison, the three workers turned around, their bodies stiff and awkward.

Close your eyes. Cover your ears. She hesitated before adding, *Hum.*

Instantly, the buzz of three people humming filled what had become a silent delivery dock. She hoped it would be enough to keep them from hearing the grate open in the concrete floor. Her only hope was that they would assume she and Thorne had left through the dock exit or smuggled themselves aboard a delivery ship.

Thorne was staring, slack jawed, when Cinder turned back to him. "What are they doing?"

"Obeying," she said heavily, hating herself for making the command. Hating the hums that filled her ears. Hating this gift that was too unnatural, too powerful, too unfair.

But the thought to release her control over them never crossed her mind.

"Come on," she said, half jumping, half sliding off the ship. She crawled beneath it and found the grate between the landing wheels. Though her hands were shaking, she managed to twist the grate a quarter turn and pull it up.

A shallow pool of standing water glistened up at her in the darkness.

The fall wasn't far, but her bare feet landing in the oily water made her queasy. Thorne was beside her in a second, replacing the grate over the hole.

There was a round concrete tunnel set into the wall, barely reaching Cinder's stomach and filled with the stench of garbage and mildew. Wrinkling her nose, Cinder crouched and crawled into it.

Seven

THE CLUSTER OF ICONS ON EMPEROR KAI'S NETSCREEN WAS
growing denser by the hour, not only because there were so
many things for the new emperor to read and sign, but because
he wasn't putting much effort into reading or signing any of
them. With fingers buried in his hair, he gazed blankly at the
inset netscreen panel currently elevated out of his desk and
watched the icons multiply with a growing sense of dread.

He should have been sleeping, but after countless hours of
staring at the shadows above his bed, he'd finally given up and
decided to come here instead and attempt to do something productive. He was dying for a distraction. Any distraction.

Anything to chase away the thoughts that kept rotating
around in his brain.

So much for those good intentions.

Taking in a measured breath, Kai glanced up at the empty
office. It was supposed to be his father's office, but the room
struck Kai as far too extravagant to be a place for work. Three
ornate tasseled lanterns were lined up on a red-and-gold ceiling,

hand-painted with elegant dragons. A holographic fireplace was set into the wall to his left. A sitting area with carved cypress furniture surrounded a miniature bar in the far corner. Silent videos of Kai's mother shimmered from picture frames by the door, sometimes paired with flashes of Kai growing up, and sometimes all three of them together.

Nothing had changed since his father's death, except the room's owner.

And perhaps the smell. Kai seemed to recall the aroma of his father's aftershave, but now there was the distinct stench of bleach and chemicals—remnants of the cleaning crew scrubbing the room raw after his father first had contracted letumosis, the plague that had killed hundreds of thousands of people all over Earth in the past decade.

Kai's attention fell from the pictures and snagged on the small metal foot that sat on the corner of his desk, its joints caked with grease. Like a revolving wheel, his thoughts came full circle yet again.

Linh Cinder.

Stomach tightening, he set down the stylus that he'd been gripping and reached for the foot, but his fingers stalled before they could get to it.

It belonged to her, the pretty young mechanic at the market. The girl who was so easy to talk to. The girl who was so authentic, who didn't pretend to be something she wasn't.

Or so he'd thought.

His fingers tightened into a fist and he drew back, wishing he had someone he could talk to.

But his father was gone. And now Dr. Erland was gone too, having resigned from his position, and left without even saying good-bye.

There was Konn Torin, his father's, and now his, adviser. But Torin, with his ever-present diplomacy and logic, would never understand. Kai wasn't sure *he* even understood what it was he felt when he thought of Cinder. Linh Cinder, who had lied to him about everything.

She was cyborg.

He couldn't dismiss the memory of her lying at the base of the garden steps, a foot disconnected from her leg, a white-hot metal hand having melted away the remnants of a silk glove—gloves that had been his gift to her.

He should have been repulsed by her. Reliving the memory again and again, he *tried* to be repulsed by the sparking wires and her grime-packed knuckles and the knowledge that she had fake neural receptors taking messages to and from her brain. She was not natural. She was probably a charity case, and he couldn't help but wonder if her family had paid for the operation or if it had been government funded. He wondered who had taken such pity on her that they'd determined to give her a second life when her human body had been so damaged. He wondered what had caused her body to be that damaged in the first place, or if perhaps she was born disfigured.

He wondered and wondered and knew he should have been more disturbed by each unanswered question.

But he wasn't. It was not her being cyborg that had curdled his stomach.

Rather, his repugnance had started the moment his vision of her flickered as if she were a broken netscreen. He'd blinked, and she was no longer a helpless, rain-soaked cyborg, but the most intensely beautiful girl he'd ever laid eyes on. She was blindingly, breathtakingly stunning, with flawless tanned skin and shining eyes and an expression so ravishing it threatened to buckle his knees.

Her Lunar glamour had been even more striking than Queen Levana's, and *her* beauty was painful.

Kai knew that's what it had been: Cinder's glamour, fading in and out even as he stood above her, trying to make sense of what he was seeing.

What he didn't know was how many times she'd glamoured him before that. How many times she'd tricked him. How many times she'd made him out to be a complete fool.

Or had the girl at the market, muddied and disheveled, been the real girl after all? The girl who had risked her life to come to the ball to give Kai a warning, unsteady cyborg foot and all ...

"It doesn't matter," he said to his empty office, the disconnected foot.

Whoever Linh Cinder was, she was no longer his concern. Soon Queen Levana would be returning to Luna, and she would take Cinder back as her prisoner. It was the arrangement Kai had agreed to.

At the ball, he had been forced to make a choice, and had refused Levana's offer of a marriage alliance once and for all. He was determined to never subject his people to life beneath such a heartless empress, and by that point Cinder had been his last bargaining chip. Peace, in exchange for the cyborg. His people's freedom, in exchange for the Lunar girl who had dared to defy her queen.

It was impossible to know how long such an arrangement would last. Levana still refused to sign the peace treaty that would ally Luna with the Earthen Union. Her desire to be either empress or conqueror would not be sated long by the sacrifice of a mere girl.

And next time, Kai didn't think he would have anything else to offer.

Crumpling his hair, Kai pulled his attention back to the amendment on the netscreen and read the first sentence three times, waiting for the words to register. He had to think of something else, anything else, before the never-ending questions drove him insane.

A monotone voice interrupted him, making him jump. "Entrance requested for Royal Adviser Konn Torin and Chairman of National Security Huy Deshal."

Kai glanced at the time. 06:22.

"Entrance granted."

The office door breezed open. Both men were dressed for the day, though Kai had never seen either of them so disheveled. It was clear they'd gotten up in a hurry, although he suspected from the dark circles beneath Torin's eyes that he hadn't gotten much more sleep than Kai had.

Kai stood to greet them, tapping the corner of the netscreen that sent it sinking back into the desktop. "You're both getting an early start."

"Your Imperial Majesty," said Chairman Huy with a deep bow. "I'm glad to find you awake. I'm sorry to inform you of a breach of security that requires your immediate attention."

Kai froze, his thoughts racing ahead to terrorist attacks, out-of-control protestors . . . Queen Levana declaring war. "What? What happened?"

"There's been a jailbreak from New Beijing Prison," said Huy. "Approximately forty-eight minutes ago."

Nerves knotting up his shoulders, Kai glanced at Torin. "A jailbreak?"

"Two inmates have escaped."

Kai pushed his fingertips into the desk. "Don't we have some sort of protocol in place for this?"

"Generally speaking, yes. However, this is an extraordinary circumstance."

"How so?"

The lines deepened around Huy's mouth. "One of the escapees is Linh Cinder, Your Majesty. The Lunar fugitive."

The world turned over. Kai's gaze dropped to the cyborg foot, but he snapped it back up. "How?"

"We have a team analyzing the security footage in order to determine her exact method. We understand she was able to glamour a guard and persuade him to move her to a separate wing of the prison. From there, she was able to breach the air duct system." Suddenly embarrassed, Huy held up two clear bags. One contained a cyborg hand, the other a small, blood-crusted chip. "These were found in her cell."

Kai's jaw worked, but he was dumbfounded by the sight. He was simultaneously intrigued and unnerved by the dismembered limb. "Is that her *hand*? Why would she do that?"

"We're still working on the details. We do know, however, that she made her way into the prison's loading dock. We are working to secure all possible escape routes from there."

Kai paced toward the floor-to-ceiling windows that overlooked the palace's west-facing gardens. The whispering grasses still glittered with morning dew.

"Your Majesty," said Torin, the first he'd spoken, "I would advise you to deploy military reinforcements to track down and recover the fugitives."

Kai massaged his brow. "Military?"

Torin spoke slowly. "It is in your best interest to do everything in your power to recover her."

Kai found it difficult to swallow. He knew that Torin was right. Any hesitation would be seen as a sign of weakness, and possibly even suggest that he'd assisted with the escape. Queen Levana would not take kindly to it.

"Who's the other fugitive?" he asked, stalling for time while he struggled to grasp the implications. Cinder—a Lunar, a cyborg, a fugitive, who he'd all but sentenced to death.

Escaped.

"Carswell Thorne," said Huy, "an ex-cadet for the American Republic air force. He deserted his post fourteen months ago after stealing a military cargo ship. At this time we don't consider him dangerous."

Kai neared his desk again, seeing that the fugitive's profile had been transferred to the screen. His frown deepened. Perhaps not dangerous, but young and inarguably good-looking. His prison photo showed him flippantly winking at the camera. Kai hated him immediately.

"Your Majesty, we need you to make a decision," said Torin. "Do you grant permission to send in military reinforcements to secure the fugitives?"

Kai stiffened. "Yes, of course, if that's what you think the situation requires."

Huy clicked his heels and marched back toward the door.

Kai wanted to call him back immediately as a thousand questions filled his brain. He wanted the world to slow down and give him time to process this, but the two men had both gone before the hesitant "wait" fell from his mouth.

The door shut, leaving him alone. He stole a single glance at Cinder's abandoned foot before collapsing over his desk and pressing his forehead onto the cool netscreen.

He couldn't help but imagine his father sitting at this desk, faced with this situation, and knew he would have been sending comms already, doing everything he could to find the girl and apprehend her, because that's what would be best for the Commonwealth.

But Kai wasn't his father. He wasn't that selfless.

Knowing it was wrong, he couldn't help but wish that wherever Cinder had gone, they would never find her.

Eight

THE MORELS *WERE* ALL DEAD. THEIR FARM HAD BEEN deserted for seven years, since both parents and a troop of six children had all been carted to the Toulouse plague quarantines during a single October, leaving behind a collection of rotting structures—the farmhouse, the barn, a chicken coop—along with a hundred acres of crops left to fend for themselves. An arched storage building that had once housed tractors and hay bales remained intact, standing solitary in the midst of an overgrown grain field.

An old, dusty pillowcase, dyed black, still flapped off the house's front porch, warning neighbors to stay away from the diseased house. For many years, it had done its job, until the ruffians who ran the fights had sought it out and claimed it for their own.

The fights were already underway when Scarlet arrived. She sent a hasty comm to the Toulouse police department from her ship, figuring she had at least twenty or thirty minutes before they responded, useless as they were. Just enough time to get the information she needed before Wolf and the rest of society's outcasts were taken into custody.

Downing a few breaths of chilled night air that did nothing to settle her rapid-fire heartbeat, she marched into the abandoned storage building.

A writhing crowd shouted up at a hastily constructed stage, where one man was beating his opponent in the face, fist flying over and over with sickening steadfastness. Blood started to leak from his opponent's nose. The crowd roared, egging on the dominating fighter.

Scarlet skirted around the audience, hanging close to the sloping walls. Every surface within reach was covered in vivid graffiti. Straw littered the ground, trampled nearly to dust. Rows of cheap lightbulbs were strung on bright orange cords, and more than a handful of them were flickering and threatening to burn out. The hot air reeked of sweat and bodies and a sweetness from the fields that didn't belong.

Scarlet hadn't expected there to be so many people. There were well over two hundred onlookers, and she didn't recognize any of them. This crowd wasn't from small-town Rieux—likely many of them had come in from Toulouse. She spotted a number of piercings and tattoos and surgical manipulations. She passed a girl with hair dyed like a zebra's and a man on a leash being dragged around by a curvy escort-droid. There were even cyborgs in the crowd, the rarity made stranger by the fact that none of them were hiding their cyborgness. They flaunted everything from polished metal arms to black, reflective eyeballs that protruded eerily from their sockets. Scarlet did a double take when she passed a man showing off a small netscreen implanted into his flexed bicep, laughing at the stiff news anchor inside it.

The crowd roared suddenly—guttural and joyful. A man with the tattoo of a spine and rib cage tracking down his back was left standing on the stage. Scarlet couldn't see his opponent beyond the dense crowd.

She tucked her hands into the pockets of her hooded sweatshirt and continued her search of the unfamiliar faces, the strange fashions. She was drawing attention in her plain jeans with the ripped knees and ratty red sweatshirt that her grandma had given her years ago. Usually the hoodie was like camouflage in a town of equally careless dressers, but now she was dressed like a chameleon in a room full of Komodo dragons. Everywhere she turned, curious gazes followed her. With ruthless defiance, she glared back at them all, and kept searching.

She reached the back wall of the building, still stacked high with plastic and metal crates, without spotting Wolf. She backed herself into a corner for a better viewpoint and tugged the hood forward over her face. Her handgun dug into her hip.

"You came."

She jumped. Wolf had materialized out of the graffiti and was suddenly beside her, green eyes catching the dusty flickers of the lightbulbs.

"I'm sorry," he said, shuffling back half a step. "I didn't mean to startle you."

Scarlet ignored the apology. In the shadows she could just make out the edge of the tattoo on his arm, which had seemed so unimportant hours before but was now burned into her memory.

The one who handed me the poker had a tattoo....

Heat rushed to her face, the rage she'd buried in return for calm practicality rising to the surface. She closed the distance between them and thumped her locked fist into his sternum, ignoring how he towered a full head above her. Her hatred made her feel like she could crush his skull with her bare hands.

"Where is she?"

Wolf's expression was blank, his hands limp at his sides. "Who?"

"My grandmother! What have you done with her?"

He blinked, his expression at once confused and speculative, like she was speaking in another language that he was slow to translate. "Your grandmother?"

Gritting her teeth, she slammed her fist harder into his chest. He flinched, but it seemed to be more from surprise than pain. "I know it was you. I know you took her and you're keeping her somewhere. I know it was you who tortured my dad! I don't know what you're trying to prove, but I want her back and I want her back *now.*"

He shot a furtive glance over her head. "I'm sorry ... they're calling me to the stage."

Pulse pounding against her temples, Scarlet simultaneously grabbed his left wrist and yanked out her gun. She pressed the barrel against his tattoo.

"My dad saw your tattoo, despite your attempts to keep him drugged up. I find it unlikely that there are two identical tattoos like this, and that you happen to show up in my life the same day my dad's kidnappers let him go after a week of *torturing* him."

His eyes momentarily cleared, but the look was followed by a deep frown, accentuating a pale scar on the side of his mouth. "Someone kidnapped your father . . . and your grandmother," he said, slowly. "Someone with a tattoo like mine. But they let your father go today?"

"Do you think I'm an idiot?" she yelled. "Are you really going to try and convince me you had nothing to do with it?"

Wolf peered up toward the stage again and she tightened her grip on his wrist, but he made no move to walk away. "I've been at the Rieux Tavern every day for weeks. Any of the wait-staff can vouch for that. And I've been *here* every night. Anyone will tell you so."

Scarlet scowled. "Sorry if the people around here don't exactly seem like the trustworthy types."

"They're not," he said. "But they do know me. Watch. You'll see."

He tried to slip around her but Scarlet turned with him, her hood slipping back. She dug her nails into his skin. "You're not leaving until you—" She paused, looking past Wolf at the crowd by the platform.

Everyone was watching them, appreciative looks darting up and down Scarlet's body.

A man on the platform was leaning against the ropes, smirking. He raised his eyebrows when he saw he'd caught Wolf's and

Scarlet's attention. "Looks like the wolf has found himself a tender morsel tonight," he said, his voice magnified by speakers somewhere overhead.

A second man stood on the stage behind him, leering at Scarlet. He was twice the size and a foot taller than the one who had spoken and entirely bald. His hair had been replaced with two rows of bear's teeth implanted like gaping jaws into his scalp.

"Think I'll be taking that one home after I've destroyed dog-boy's pretty face!"

The audience laughed at the taunts, making cat calls and whistling to one another. Someone nearby asked Wolf if he was afraid to test his luck.

Unruffled, Wolf turned back to Scarlet. "He's undefeated," he said in an explanatory tone. "But so am I."

Annoyed that he could think for a second she cared, Scarlet sucked in a furious breath. "I already commed the police and they'll be here any minute. If you just tell me where my grandmother is, you can leave, you can even warn your friends if you want. I won't shoot you and I won't tell the police about you. Just—just tell me where she is. *Please.*"

He peered down at her, calm despite the growing rowdiness of the crowd. They'd started chanting something, the words muffled by the blood flowing through Scarlet's ears. She thought for a second he was crumbling. He was going to tell her, and she would keep her word long enough to find her grandma and get her away from these monsters who had taken her.

Then she would have his head. Once her grandma was safe

at home, she would track him down, and whoever else had helped him, and make them pay for what they'd done.

Perhaps he noticed the darkening bitterness on her face, because he reached for her hand and gently pried up her fingers. On gut instinct she dug the gun into his ribs, though she knew she wasn't going to shoot. Not without answers.

He didn't seem worried. Maybe he knew it too.

"I believe your father did see a tattoo *like* mine." His head dipped toward her. "But it wasn't me."

He pulled away. Scarlet dropped her arm, letting the gun hang limp at her side, and watched the chanting crowd part for him. The onlookers were intimidated, but also amused. Most were smiling and jostling one another. Some were moving through the crowds, scanning wrists, collecting bids.

He may have been undefeated, but it seemed clear that most bets had been placed on his opponent.

She squeezed the gun until the textured metal of the handle left an imprint on her palm.

A tattoo like *mine* . . .

What had he meant by that?

He'd only been trying to confuse her, she determined as Wolf launched himself over the stage's ropes, agile as an acrobat. The coincidence was too much.

No matter. She'd given him a chance, but the police would be here soon and take him into custody. She would get her answers, one way or the other.

Shaking with frustration, she tucked the gun back into her

waistband. The thrumming in her temples was beginning to mellow and she could make out the crowd's chanting now.

Hunter. Hunter. Hunter.

Dizzy from the heat and rush of adrenaline, she glanced toward the building's enormous opening, where she could see overgrown weeds and wheat stalks lit by the moon. She noticed a woman with close-cropped hair glaring at her like a jealous girlfriend. Scarlet returned the look before shifting her attention to the stage. Lingering at the back of the crowd, she pulled up her hood again, drawing her face beneath its shadows.

The crowd surged forward, carrying Scarlet closer to the fight.

Hunter had ripped off his shirt, displaying a mass of raw muscle as he rattled the crowd. The row of teeth embedded on his head glinted as he bowled from one side of the stage to the other.

Wolf was tall, but he looked like a child next to Hunter. Nevertheless, he was all composure in his corner of the platform, radiating arrogance with one foot up on the ropes, practically lounging.

Hunter ignored him, pacing back and forth like a caged animal. Growling. Cursing. Working the crowd into a frenzy.

The one who handed me the poker . . .

Scarlet's gut twisted. She needed Wolf. She needed answers. But in that moment, she wouldn't have minded seeing him ripped to shreds on that stage.

As if sensing her onslaught of rage, Wolf's gaze flickered toward her. The smug amusement dropped away.

Scarlet hoped it showed on her face just who she was root-
ing for.

A holograph flickered to life, hanging over the announcer's
head. The words slowly rotated and flickered.

HUNTER [34] VS. WOLF [11]

"Tonight, our reigning, undefeated champion—*Hunter!*" cried
the announcer. The crowd bellowed. "—takes on undefeated
newcomer, *Wolf!*" Mixed boos and cheers. Evidently not everyone had bet against him.

Scarlet was hardly listening, straining hard at the holograph.
Wolf [11]. Eleven wins, she suspected. Eleven fights.

Eleven nights?

Her grandmother had been missing for seventeen days and
counting. But her father—hadn't he said they'd only kept him
for a week? She frowned, frustrated from the calculations.

Hunter yelled, "We're having wolf for dinner tonight!"

Hundreds of hands slapped against the edge of the platform
like a roll of thunder.

Wolf's concentration darkened into something thirsty but
patient.

The holograph flashed bright red, then evaporated with the
sound of a bellowing horn.

The mediator dropped down into the crowd, and the fight
began.

Hunter threw the first punch. Scarlet gasped, the movement

almost too quick to follow, but Wolf ducked easily and skirted out from Hunter's shadow.

Hunter was impressively fast for his bulk, but Wolf was faster. A series of blows were deflected, until Hunter's fist finally connected with a sickening crunch. Scarlet recoiled.

The crowd erupted, pushing and screaming against her. The frenzy was palpable, the crowd salivating for blood.

Moving as if it were all choreographed, Wolf aimed a solid kick to Hunter's chest. A loud thud shook the ground as Hunter was knocked onto his back. He was only down for a moment, before jumping to his feet. Wolf inched away, waiting. Blood was dribbling from his lips, but he didn't seem bothered by it. His eyes glowed.

Hunter attacked with renewed vigor. Wolf took a punch in the stomach and crumpled over with a grunt. It was followed by a blow that sent him careening to the edge of the stage. He stumbled to one knee, but was up on his feet before Hunter could come closer.

He shook his head in an oddly doglike manner, wild hair flying, and then crouched with his big hands poised at his sides, staring at Hunter with that peculiar grin.

Scarlet wrapped her fingers around her sweatshirt's zipper, wondering if that tic was how Wolf had gotten his nickname.

When Hunter came barreling across the stage again, Wolf lunged to his side and aimed a kick square in Hunter's back. Hunter collapsed to both knees. The crowd booed. A roundhouse kick, this one at Hunter's ear, sent him sprawling on his side.

Hunter made to get up, but Wolf aimed for his ribs, sending him back onto the stage. The crowd was in a fervor, screeching and calling foul.

Wolf stepped back, allowing Hunter time to pull himself up by the ropes and settle back into his fighting stance. There was a new glint in Wolf's eye, like he was enjoying this, and when his tongue darted out to lick the blood from his mouth, Scarlet grimaced.

A raging bull, Hunter charged again. Wolf blocked one punch with his forearm but took another in his side. Then his elbow shot out, catching Hunter in the jaw, and Scarlet knew he'd taken the hit intentionally. Hunter stumbled backward. A heel in the chest nearly knocked him off his feet again. Wolf landed a punch to his nose, and a spurt of blood oozed down Hunter's chin. A knee in Hunter's side had him crouching over, groaning.

Scarlet flinched with each blow, her stomach roiling. How people could stand to watch this, to *enjoy* this, baffled her.

Hunter fell to his knees and Wolf was behind him in a breath, his face violently contorted, his hands on each side of Hunter's head.

... handed me the poker ...

And this man—this monster—had her grandmother.

Scarlet clamped both hands over her mouth, smothering the cry, as her ears waited for the snap of Hunter's neck.

Wolf froze and blinked at her. His eyes flickered, empty and mad one moment, then almost dazed. Surprised to see her there. His pupils widened.

Revulsion burned through Scarlet's nerves. She wanted to look away, wanted to run, but she was anchored to the ground.

Then Wolf leaped back, letting Hunter slump to the stage under his own weight.

The horn blared again. The crowd was a mixture of cheers and boos, delight and anger. Outright glee at seeing the great Hunter defeated. None of them minded the blind cruelty, or the fact that they'd almost witnessed a murder.

As the mediator climbed up onto the ropes to announce Wolf as the winner, Wolf peeled his focus away from Scarlet, shoved past the man, and hauled himself over the ropes. The crowd surged away from him, shoving Scarlet backward. She barely kept her balance as she was nearly crushed from the shuffling crowd.

Wolf sprang up, using his hands and feet to propel him forward. Sprinting full speed, he disappeared through the yawning exit and dashed off into the silvery weeds.

Red and blue flashed in the distance.

The crowd swarmed, buzzing with confusion and curiosity. The muttered consensus seemed to be that Wolf was a new hero, but a savage one.

It wasn't long before someone else noticed the lights and panic swept through them, people at first spouting defiant words against the police, before rushing for the door and scattering across the abandoned farm.

Scarlet was shaking as she pulled her hood up and fled with them. Not everyone was running—someone behind her was trying to call order. There was a gunshot and mad laughter. Up ahead, the girl with the zebra hair was standing on a storage crate, pointing and laughing at the cowards who would flee from the police.

Scarlet escaped into the midnight air and the noise faded without the warehouse's echo around her. She could hear the sirens now, mixing with the thrum of crickets. On the dirt road outside the building, she spun in a full circle as the crowd jostled around her.

There was no sign of Wolf.

She thought she'd seen him turn right. Her ship was parked to the left. Her pulse was racing, making it hard to breathe.

She couldn't leave. She hadn't gotten what she'd come for.

She told herself that she would be able to find him again. When she'd had time to gather her wits. After she talked to the detectives and persuaded them to track Wolf down and arrest him and find out where he'd taken her grandmother.

Tucking her hands into her pockets, she hurried around the building, toward her ship.

A sickening howl stopped her, sucking the air out of her lungs. The night's chatter silenced, even the loitering city rats pausing to listen.

Scarlet had heard wild wolves before, prowling the country-side in search of easy prey on the farms.

But never had a wolf's howl sent a chill down her spine like that.

Nine

"ARGH, GET IT OFF, GET IT OFF!"

Cinder spun, steadying herself on the curved, slick concrete walls as she cast the flashlight behind her. Thorne was writhing and squirming in the cramped tunnel, swatting at his back and emitting an array of curses and unmanly shrieks.

She sent the beam of light to the ceiling and saw a thriving mass of cockroaches scuttling across it in all directions. She shuddered, but turned away and kept moving.

"It's only a cockroach," she called back to him. "It's not going to kill you."

"It's in my uniform!"

"Would you keep quiet? There's a manhole up ahead."

"Please tell me we'll be exiting through that manhole."

She scoffed, more preoccupied with the map of the sewer system in her head than on her companion's squeamishness. Even though the thought of a cockroach beneath her shirt did make her squirm, she figured it would still be preferable to walking through the ankle-deep sludge with one bare foot, and *she* wasn't whining.

They passed beneath the manhole and Cinder detected the steady sound of water growing louder. "We're almost to the combined main line," she said, at first eager to reach it—it was hot as Mars in this cramped tunnel and her thighs were burning from the crouch-walk routine. But then a gut-turning stench wafted toward her, so strong she almost gagged.

No longer would it just be surface water runoff they were trekking through.

"Oh, aces," said Thorne, groaning. "Tell me that's not what I think it is."

Cinder wrinkled her nose and focused on taking shallow, burning breaths.

The smell grew nearly unbearable as they traipsed through the sludge and came to the sewer connection, finding themselves on the lip of a concrete wall.

Cinder's imbedded flashlight searched the tunnel beneath them, darting up the slimy concrete walls. The main tunnel would be tall enough for them to stand in. The light bounced off a narrow metal grate that lined the far edge, stable enough for maintenance workers and covered in rat droppings. Between them and the grate, a river of sewage swelled and churned, at least two meters wide.

She fought off another bout of nausea as the pungent stink of the sewer clouded her nostrils, her throat, her lungs.

"Ready?" she said, inching forward.

"Wait—what are you doing?"

"What does it look like?"

Thorne blinked at her, then down at the sewage he could barely make out in the darkness. "Don't you have some tool in that fancy hand of yours that can get us across?"

Cinder glared, light-headed from her body's instinctively short breaths. "Oh, wow, how could I have forgotten about my *grappling hook?*"

Spinning away, she gobbled down another rank breath and lowered herself into the muck. Something smooshed between her toes. The current pounded against her legs as she made her way across, the water up to her thighs. Writhing on the inside, Cinder crossed as quickly as she could, choking down her gag reflex. The weight of her metal foot keeping her grounded so the current didn't knock her off balance and soon she was on the other side, pulling herself onto the grate. She flattened her back against the tunnel wall and peered back at the pretend captain.

He was staring at her legs with unbridled disgust.

Cinder looked down. The stark white jumper was now tinged greenish brown and clung, sopping, to her legs.

"Look," she yelled, aiming the flashlight at Thorne, "you can either get over here or you can go back and serve the rest of your sentence in peace. But you have to make a decision *now.*"

After a stream of curses and spitting, Thorne inched his way into the sludge, holding his arms aloft. He was grimacing the whole time as he slinked his way to the grate and hauled himself up beside Cinder.

"This is what I get for complaining about the soap," he muttered, pressing himself against the wall.

The grate was already digging into Cinder's bare foot and she shifted her weight onto her cyborg leg. "All right, Cadet. Which way?"

"Captain." He opened his eyes and peered down the tunnel in each direction, but beyond the pale light filtering in from the closest manhole, the sewers disappeared in blackness. Cinder adjusted the brightness of her flashlight, sending it darting over the frothy surface of the water and dripping concrete walls.

"It's near the old Beihai Park," Thorne said, scratching at his whiskered chin. "Which way is that?"

Cinder nodded and turned south.

Her internal clock told her they'd been walking for only twelve minutes, but it seemed like hours. The grate dug into her foot with each step. Her wet pants were plastered to her calves and sweat dripped down the back of her neck, sometimes tricking her into thinking it was a spider fallen down her jumpsuit and making her feel guilty for giving Thorne a hard time before. Though they didn't see any rats, she could hear them scurrying away from her light, down countless tunnels that fanned out beneath the city.

Thorne talked to himself as they walked, working through his clogged memory. His ship was definitely near Beihai Park. In the industrial district. Not six blocks south of the maglev tracks . . . well, maybe eight blocks.

"We're about a block away from the park," Cinder said,

pausing at a metal ladder. A spot of light drifted down toward them. "This goes up to West Yunxin."

"Yunxin sounds familiar. Sort of."

She pleaded for patience and started to climb.

The ladder rungs bit into her foot, but the air was blissfully fresh as she neared the top. The sound of the rushing water was replaced with the hum of maglev tracks. Reaching the manhole cover, Cinder paused to listen for signs of humanity, before pushing the cover off to the side.

A hover glided overhead.

Cinder ducked, heart racing. Daring to inch her head up, she spotted silent lights atop the white vehicle. It was an emergency hover. Visions of androids armed with brain-interface-overriding tasers sent a shudder through her, before the hover turned a corner and she saw a red cross on one side. It was a medical hover, not law enforcement. Cinder nearly collapsed from relief.

They were in the old warehouse district, near the plague quarantines. Medical hovers were to be expected.

She glanced both ways down the deserted street. Though it was still early, the day was already hot and whimsical mirages were rising from the pavement, having forgotten the drenching summer storm from two nights before.

"Clear." She hauled herself up onto the road and sucked in a deep breath of the city's humidity. Thorne followed, his uniform glaringly bright in the sun, except for the legs, which were still murky green and smelled of sewage. "Which way?"

Shielding his eyes with his forearm, Thorne squinted at the

concrete buildings and rotated in a full circle. Faced north. Scratched his neck.

Cinder's optimism crumbled. "Tell me you recognize something."

"Yeah, yeah, I do," he said, waving her away. "I just haven't been here in a while."

"Think faster. We aren't exactly blending in with our surroundings out here."

With a nod, Thorne started down the street. "This way."

Five steps later he paused, pondered, turned around. "No, no, this way."

"We're dead."

"No, I've got it now. It's this way."

"Don't you have an address?"

"A captain always knows where his ship is. It's like a psychic bond."

"If only we had a captain here."

He ignored her, marching down the street with spectacular confidence. Cinder followed three steps behind him, jumping at each sound—trash skidding across the road, a hover crossing an intersection two streets away. The sun glistened off the dusty warehouse windows.

Three empty blocks later, Thorne slowed his pace and peered up at the facade of each building they passed, rubbing his chin.

Cinder began desperately searching her brain for Plan B.

"There!" Thorne jotted across the street to a warehouse that was identical to every other warehouse, with giant rolling doors and years of colorful graffiti. Rounding the building's corner, he tested the main door. "Locked."

Spotting the ID scanner beside the door, Cinder cursed. "Figures." Kneeling down, she pried the plastic face off the scanner. "I might be able to disable it. Do you think there's an alarm?"

"There'd better be. I haven't been paying rent all this time for my darling to sit in an unprotected warehouse."

Cinder had just downloaded the programming manual for the scanner's product number when the door beside them swung open and a plump man with a thin black goatee stepped out into the sunlight. Cinder froze.

"Carswell!" the man barked. "Just saw the news! I thought you might be showing up here."

"Alak, how are you?" A grin broke across Thorne's face. "Am I really on the news? How do I look?"

Without answering, Alak swerved his attention toward Cinder. His friendliness froze over, buried beneath a trace of discomfort. Gulping, Cinder shut the scanner's panel and stood. Her netlink was already connecting to the newsfeed she'd abandoned during their escape, and sure enough, there was a stream of warnings flashing across her own picture, the one they'd taken when she'd been admitted into the prison. ESCAPED CONVICT. CONSIDERED ARMED AND DANGEROUS. IF SEEN, COMM THIS LINK IMMEDIATELY.

"Seen you on the news too," Alak said, glancing at her steel foot.

"Alak, I'm here to pick up my ship. We're in a bit of a hurry."

As sympathetic wrinkles creased the corners of Alak's mouth, he shook his head. "I can't help you, Carswell. The feds watch me close enough as it is. Storing a stolen ship is one thing, I can always claim ignorance to that. But assisting a convicted felon ... and assisting ... one of *them*." His nose wrinkled at Cinder, but he simultaneously took a step back as if afraid of her retaliation. "If they track you here and find out I helped, it's more trouble than even I can risk. You'd better just hang low for a time. I won't tell I saw you. But I won't let you take your ship. Not now. Not until all this blows over. You understand, right?"

Thorne flushed with disbelief. "But—she's my ship! I'm a paying customer! You can't just keep her from me."

"Each man for himself. You know how it is well as anyone." Alak slid his gaze back toward Cinder, his fear easing more and more into revulsion. "Get on your way now, and I won't comm the police. If they come around, I'll tell them I haven't seen you since you dropped off the ship last year. But if you stay here much longer, I'll comm them myself, I swear I will."

No sooner had he finished speaking than Cinder heard a hover down the street. Her heart skipped at the sight of a white emergency hover—this one without the red cross on its side—but it disappeared down another street. She spun back toward Alak. "We don't have anywhere else to go. We need that ship!"

He stepped back from her again, his body framed in the doorway. "Look here, little girl," he said, his tone determined despite the way his attention kept swooping down to her metal hand. "I'm trying to help you out because Carswell's been a good customer of mine, and I don't rat out my customers. But it's no favor to you. I wouldn't blink twice before sending you off to rot. It's the best your kind deserve. Now get away from my warehouse before I change my mind."

Desperation welled inside Cinder. She clenched her fists as a surge of electricity lashed out, blinding her. White-hot pain flared up from the base of her neck, flooding her skull, but it was blessedly brief and left bright spots sparking in her vision.

Panting, she reeled back the burning energy, just in time to see Alak's eyes roll back. He toppled forward, landing in Thorne's arms.

Cinder staggered against the wall, dizzy. "Oh stars—is he dead?"

Thorne groaned from the weight. "No, but I think he's having a heart attack!"

"It's not a heart attack," she murmured. "He'll . . . he'll be fine." She said it as much to convince herself as him, having to believe these accidental flares of her Lunar gift weren't dangerous, that she wasn't becoming the terror to society that everyone believed her to be.

"Aces, he weighs a ton."

Cinder grabbed Alak's feet and together they dragged him into the building. An office to their left had two netscreens—one with a security feed showing the warehouse's exterior, just as the door closed behind two white-clad fugitives and the unconscious man. The other screen showed a muted news anchor.

"He may be a selfish jerk, but he sure does have good taste in jewelry." Thorne held up Alak's hand by the thumb, fiddling with a silver-plated band around his wrist—a miniature portwatch.

"Would you *focus*?" Cinder hauled Thorne to his feet. Turning, she scanned the massive warehouse. It stretched out the full length of the city block, filled with dozens of spaceships, large and small, new and old. Cargo ships, podships, personal fliers, raceships, ferries, cruisers.

"Which one is it?"

"Hey, look, there was another jailbreak."

Cinder glanced at the netscreen, which now showed the chairman of national security talking to a crowd of journalists. On the bottom of the screen scrolled the words: *LUNAR ESCAPES FROM NEW BEIJING PRISON, CONSIDERED EXTREMELY DANGEROUS.*

"This is great!" said Thorne, nearly knocking her over with a slap on her back. "They're not going to worry about us if they have a Lunar to track down."

Cinder dragged her attention away from the broadcast, just as his grin fell.

"Wait. You're Lunar?"

"*You're* a criminal mastermind?" Spinning on her heels, she stalked into the warehouse. "Where's this ship?"

"Hold on there, little traitor. Breaking out of jail is one thing, but assisting a psychotic Lunar is a bit out of my league."

Cinder rounded on him. "First, I'm not psychotic. And second, if it wasn't for me, you would still be sitting in that jail cell ogling your portscreen, so you owe me. Besides, they've already got you pegged as my accomplice. You look like an idiot in that picture, by the way."

Thorne followed her gesture to the screen. His own jail picture was blown up beside hers.

"I think I look pretty good . . ."

"Thorne. *Captain*. Please."

He blinked at her, a touch of smugness wiped quickly away by a brisk nod. "Right. Let's get out of here."

Cinder sighed in relief, following Thorne as he marched into the maze of ships. "I hope it's not one in the middle."

"Doesn't matter," he said, pointing up. "The roof opens."

Cinder glanced up at the seam in the middle of the ceiling. "That's convenient."

"And there she is."

Cinder followed Thorne's gesture. His ship was larger than she'd expected—much larger. A 214 Rampion, Class 11.3 cargo ship. Cinder pulled up her retina scanner and downloaded the ship's blueprint, speechless at everything it could claim. The engine room and a fully stocked dock with two satellite podships took up the underbelly, while the main level housed the cargo bay, cockpit, galley kitchen, six crew quarters, and a shared washroom.

She rounded to the main entry hatch and saw that the seal of the American Republic had been hastily painted over with the silhouette of a lounging naked lady.

"Nice touch."

"Thanks. Did it myself."

Despite her worries that the painting could make them more easily identified, she couldn't help being faintly impressed. "It's bigger than I expected."

"There was a time when she housed a twelve-man crew," Thorne said, petting her hull.

"Should be plenty of room for avoiding each other then." Cinder paced beneath the hatch, waiting for Thorne to open it, but when she glanced back she found him lovingly rubbing his temple against the ship's underside and cooing about how much he'd missed her.

Cinder was in the middle of rolling her eyes when an unfamiliar voice ricocheted through the warehouse. "Over here!"

Turning, she saw someone crouched over Alak's body, haloed in a square of light. They wore the unmistakable uniform of the Eastern Commonwealth military.

Cinder swore. "Time to go. *Now.*"

Thorne ducked toward the hatch. "Rampion, code word: Captain is king. Open hatch."

They waited, but nothing happened.

Cinder raised panicked eyebrows.

"Captain is king. Captain is king! Rampion, wake up. It's Thorne, Captain Carswell Thorne. What the—"

Cinder shushed him. Beyond the ship's hull, four men were making their way through the crowded warehouse, flashlights shining off the assorted landing gear.

"Maybe the power cell is dead," said Cinder.

"How? It's just been sitting here."

"Did you leave the headlights on?" she snapped.

Thorne harrumphed and crouched against the ship. Footsteps grew louder.

"Or it could be the auto-control system," Cinder mused, racking her brain. She'd never worked on anything larger than a podship before, but how different could they be? "Do you have the override key?"

He blinked at her. "Yeah, let me just pull it out of my prison-issued pocket and we'll be on our way."

Cinder glared, but was silent as an officer passed two aisles away.

"Stay here," she whispered. "Keep trying to get in and take off as fast as possible."

"Where are you going?"

Without answering, she slinked around the side of the ship, a blueprint already streaming to her retina display. She found the access hatch and pried it open as quietly as she could, before crawling up into the ship undercarriage, contorting her body to avoid the wires and cables that crammed the space. She pulled the hatch shut behind her with a dull click, and found herself encased in darkness. The second interior door was more difficult to break into, but between the flashlight and her screwdriver she was soon wriggling out of the insulating layer and into the engine room.

Her flashlight beam zipped across the massive engine. She found the computer motherboard on the blue lines overlaying her vision and squirmed toward it. Pulling the universal connector cable from her hand, she snapped it into the main computer terminal.

Her flashlight dimmed as her own power was diverted. Pale green text scrawled across her eyesight.

```
DIAGNOSING COMPUTER SYSTEM, MODEL
135v8.2
5% . . . 12% . . . 16% . . .
```

Ten

THORNE JUMPED AT A CLANG OVERHEAD.

A man's voice followed—"Hear that?"

Thorne crouched down between the ship's landing feet and flattened himself against a metal beam. "Captain is king," he whispered. "Captain is king, captain is ki—"

A subtle hum pulsed over his head. Pale running lights flickered on near the ship's nose.

"Captain is—?"

Gears started to rattle before he could finish. The hatch opened, the ramp lowering onto the concrete. Heart leaping, Thorne dodged out beneath it, just in time to avoid being squashed.

"Over there!"

A flashlight beam fell over Thorne as he swung himself up onto the descending ramp. "Rampion, close hatch!"

The ship didn't respond.

A gun fired. The bullet pinged off the ship's overhead light.

Thorne ducked behind one of the plastic crates that filled the cargo bay. "Rampion, *close hatch!*"

"I'm working on it!"

He froze, glancing up at the pipes and tubes that lined the ship's ceiling. "Rampion?"

The following silence was punctuated by the clang of the ramp on the outside concrete, the thumping of booted feet, then the ramp creaked again and started to rise back up. A shower of bullets lodged into the plastic storage crates, pinging off the metal walls. Thorne covered his head and waited until the ramp was closed enough to block the bullets' path before shoving himself away from the crate and running toward the cockpit.

The ship vibrated as the ramp slammed shut. A volley of bullets pinged against the hull.

Thorne scrambled toward the emergency lights that framed the cockpit, shoving aside unopened crates. His knee smacked something hard and he let out a string of curses as he collapsed into the pilot seat. The windows were dirty and all he could see in the dark warehouse were the faint lights of Alak's office and the flashlight beams darting around the Rampion, searching for another way in.

"Rampion, ready for liftoff!"

The dash lit up with controls and screens—only the most important ones.

The same sterile feminine voice came over the ship's speakers. *"Thorne, I can't set the automatic lift. You're going to have to take off manually."*

He gaped at the controls. "Why is my ship talking back to me?"

"*It's me, you idiot!*"

He cocked his ear toward the speaker. "Cinder?"

"*Listen, the auto-control system has a bug. The power cell is on the fritz too. I think it can make it, but you're going to have to take off without computer assistance.*"

The words, too dry in the computer's tone, were punctuated by another round of bullets against the ship's closed hatch.

Thorne gulped. "Without computer assistance? Are you sure?"

A short silence was followed by the voice again, and Thorne thought he could detect Cinder's screeching despite its monotone. "*You do know how to fly, right?*"

"Uh." Thorne scanned the controls before him. "Yes?"

He squared his shoulders and reached for the controller that was attached to the ceiling. A moment later, a slash of sunlight cut across the warehouse as the roof opened down the middle.

Something pounded against the ship's side.

"Yeah, yeah, I hear you." Thorne jabbed the ignition.

The lights across the dash dimmed as the engine thrummed to life.

"Here we go."

Another crash echoed from outside the hatch. He jogged a few switches, engaging hover mode, and eased the ship off the ground. She rose up smoothly, the magnets beneath the city pushing the ship easily as a dandelion seed, and Thorne exhaled a long breath.

Then the ship warbled and began to tilt.

"Whoa, whoa, whoa, don't do that!" Thorne's pulse raced as he leveled the ship.

"*The power cell is going to die. You have to engage the backup thrusters.*"

"Engage the backup wha—oh, never mind, I found them."

The engine flared again. With the sudden jolt of power, the ship lurched to the opposite side and Thorne heard a crunch as she rammed into the next ship. The Rampion shuddered and started to slip back toward the ground. Another rainfall of bullets beat against the starboard side. A drop of sweat slid down Thorne's back.

"*What are you doing up there?*"

"Stop distracting me!" he yelled, gripping the controls and righting the ship. Overcompensated. The ship tilted too far to the right.

"*We're going to die.*"

"This isn't as easy as it looks!" Thorne leveled her out again. "I usually have an automated stabilizer to take care of this!"

To his surprise, no sarcastic comment was spat back at him.

A moment later, another panel lit up. MAGNETIC CONDUCTORS STABILIZING. POWER OUTPUT: 37/63 . . . 38/62 . . . 42/58 . . .

The ship settled calmly beneath him, once again trembling in midair. "Right! Like that!"

Thorne's knuckles whitened on the controls as he arched the ship's nose up toward the open roof. The engine's purr became a roar as the ship soared upward. He heard the last ricochet of bullets and then they fell away as the ship broke free of the warehouse and was flooded with the light from the yellow sun.

"Come on, darling," he murmured, squeezing his eyes shut as, without resistance, without wavering, the ship left the protective magnetic field of the city behind, drew on the full power of her thrusters, and speared through the wispy clouds that lingered in the morning sky. The towering skyscrapers of downtown New Beijing dropped away and then it was only him and the sky and the endless landscape of space.

Thorne's fingers stayed clamped like iron shackles around the controls until the ship had erupted from Earth's atmosphere. Light-headed, he adjusted the thruster output as the ship slipped into natural orbit before prying his hands away from the controls.

He slumped, shaking, back in the chair. It took him a long time to speak, waiting for his heartbeat to slow to a manageable pace. "Good work, cyborg girl," he said. "If you were hoping for a permanent position on my crew, you're hired."

The speakers were silent.

"I don't mean a lowly position, either. First mate is available. Well, I mean, pretty much every position is available. Mechanic . . . cook . . . a pilot would be nice so I don't have to go through *that* again." He waited. "Cinder? Are you there?"

When still there was no response, he pushed himself out of his chair and stumbled out of the cockpit, past the cargo bay, and into the corridor that split off to the crew's quarters. His legs were weak as he reached for the hatch that led into the ship's lower level. He clomped down the ladder into the tiny hall between the engine room and the podship dock. The screen beside the engine room didn't offer any warnings of space vacuums or unsafe compressions. It also didn't say anything about a living girl inside.

Thorne tapped the unlock icon on the screen and twisted the door's manual bolt, then shoved the door open.

The engine was loud and hot and smelled like melted rubber.

"Hello?" he called into the dark. "Cyborg girl? Are you in here?"

If she responded, the words were lost in the engine's thrumming. Thorne gulped. "Lights, on?"

A red emergency light brightened above the doorway, casting gloomy shadows over the enormous revolving engine and the masses of cords and coils that sprawled out beneath it.

Thorne squinted, spotting something almost white.

Sinking to his hands and knees, he crawled toward her. "Cyborg girl?"

She didn't move.

As Thorne came closer, he saw that she was on her back, dark hair sprawled across her face. Her robotic hand was plugged into the port of an exposed computer panel.

"Hey, you," he said, hovering over her. He peeled up her eyelids, but her gaze was dark and empty. Craning down, Thorne placed an ear against her chest, but if there was a heartbeat it was drowned out by the roaring engine.

"Come on," he growled, reaching for her hand and working the connector out of the port. The nearest computer panel went dark.

"Auto-control system disconnected," lilted a robotic voice

overhead, startling Thorne. "Engaging default system procedures."

"Good plan," he muttered, grabbing her ankles. Thorne dragged her slowly into the hallway and propped her up against the corridor wall. Whatever her cyborg parts were made of, it was a lot heavier than flesh and bone.

He pressed an ear to her chest again. This time he was met with a faint beat.

"Wake up," he said, shaking her. Cinder's head slumped forward.

Sitting back on his heels, Thorne screwed up his lips. The girl was horribly pale and filthy from their trek through the sewers, but in the hallway's brightness he could tell she was breathing, if barely. "What, do you have a power button or something?"

His attention fell on her metal hand with the cord and plug still dangling from her knuckle. Grabbing her hand, he peered at it from every angle. He remembered a flashlight, a screwdriver, and a knife in three of the fingers, but he wasn't yet sure what her pointer finger was hiding. If it was a power button, he couldn't see any way of getting at it.

The connector cable though . . .

"Right!" Thorne jumped up, nearly toppling into the wall. He jabbed at the screen that opened the door to the podship dock. White lights flared overhead as he entered.

He grasped Cinder's wrists and tugged her into the dock, dropping her in between the two small satellite ships that sat like toadstools among a mess of cables and service tools.

Panting, he reeled the podship's charging cord out of the wall, then froze, staring at the girl's cable, at the ship's cable, at the girl.... He cursed again and dropped them both. Two males. Even he could tell that they wouldn't connect.

Knocking his knuckles against his temple, Thorne forced himself to think, think, think.

Another idea flashed and he squinted down at the girl. She seemed to be growing paler still, but maybe that was a trick of the lighting.

"Oh...," he said, a new idea dropping into his brain. "Oh, boy. You don't think ... oh, that's disgusting."

Shoving away his squeamishness, he gently pulled the girl toward him so that she collapsed over one arm. With his free hand, he searched around her tangled hair until he discovered the tiny latch just above her neck.

He looked away as he opened it, before daring to peer inside from the corner of his eye.

A jumble of wires and computer chips and switches that made absolutely no sense to Thorne filled a shallow compartment in the back of her skull. He let out a breath, glad that the control panel completely hid any brain tissue from sight. At its base, he spotted what appeared to be a small outlet, the same size as the plugs.

"Ouch," Thorne muttered, reaching for the podship cable again and hoping that he wasn't about to make a huge mistake.

He wiggled the plug of the recharging cord into her control panel. It snapped into place.

He swallowed a breath.

Nothing happened.

Sitting back, Thorne held Cinder at arm's length. He pushed her hair back from her face and waited.

Twelve heartbeats later, something hummed inside her skull. It grew louder, and then fell silent altogether.

Thorne gulped.

The girl's left shoulder jerked out of Thorne's grip. He dropped her onto the floor, letting her head lull to one side. Her leg flailed, nearly catching Thorne in the groin, and he shoved himself away from her, planting his back against the podship's landing treads.

The girl sucked in a quick breath—held it for a couple seconds, then released it with a groan.

"Cinder? Are you alive?"

A series of milder spasms worked their way out of her robotic limbs, then she scrunched up her whole face as if biting into a lemon. Eyelids twitching, she managed to squint up at him.

"Cinder?"

She eased herself up to sitting. Her jaw and tongue worked silently for a moment and when she spoke, the words were heavily slurred. "Auto-control defaults ... almost drained my power system."

"I think it did drain your power system."

She frowned and seemed momentarily uncertain, before reaching for the cord still plugged into her brain. Yanking it out, she slammed the panel shut. "You opened my control panel?" she said, her words a little clearer with anger behind them.

He scowled. "I didn't *want* to."

Her expression was sour as she peered at him—not entirely angry, but not grateful either. They stared at each other for a long time, as the engine hummed across the hallway and a light in the corner started to go out, flickering at random intervals.

"Well," Cinder finally grumbled. "I guess that was pretty fast thinking."

A relieved grin filled up Thorne's face. "We're having another moment, aren't we?"

"If by a moment, you mean me not wanting to strangle you for the first time since we met, then I guess we are." Cinder slumped back on the floor. "Although maybe I'm just too exhausted to want to strangle anybody."

"I'll take it," said Thorne, stretching out on the floor beside her and enjoying the cold hardness of the dock's floor, the obnoxiously glaring lights overhead, the stink of sewage on their clothes, and the perfect sensation of freedom.

BOOK
Two

Little Red was a tender young morsel,

and the wolf knew she would be even

tastier than the old woman.

Eleven

THE EGG HISSED AS IT SLID INTO THE MELTED BUTTER, ITS vivid yolk drizzling into the white. Scarlet brushed a tufted feather off the next egg before cracking it open with one hand, simultaneously pushing the spatula across the bottom of the pan. The oozing whites grew opaque, fluffed up, developed a crackling film near the pan's edges.

Otherwise, the house was silent. She'd checked in on her dad when she'd gotten home from the fight and found him comatose in her grandma's bed, a bottle of whiskey stolen from the kitchen left open on the dresser.

She'd emptied the rest of the whiskey into the garden, along with every other bottle of liquor she could find, then spent four hours tossing in her own bed. Her head was full with the previous evening: the burn marks on her dad's arm, the terror in his face, his desperation to find whatever her grand-mère had hidden.

And Wolf, with his tattoo and his intense looks and his almost-convincing tone: *It wasn't me.*

Letting the spatula balance on the edge of the pan, Scarlet pulled a plate from the cabinet and sliced a hunk of stale bread from the loaf on the counter. The horizon was glowing and a clear sky promised another sunny day, but a wind had kicked up in the night, tossing the cornstalks and whistling past the chimney. A rooster crowed in the yard.

Sighing, she spooned the eggs onto the plate before sitting down at the dining table. She shoveled the food into her mouth while her hunger was stronger than her nerves. With her free hand, she reached for the portscreen on the table and established a netlink. "Search," she muttered through a half-full mouth. "Tattoo L-S-O-P."

UNABLE TO IDENTIFY COMMAND.

Grumbling, she typed in the terms and swallowed the last of the eggs while a stream of links came up: Extreme tattoos. Tattoo designs. Virtual tattoo models. The science behind tattoo removal. The latest in tattoo technology, virtually painless!

She tried: TATTOO LSOP962

No matches found.

She picked up the bread and ripped out a hunk with her teeth.

FOREARM TATTOO NUMBERS

A collection of images filled the screen, arms skinny and bulky, pale and dark, covered with garish drawings or displaying small, tiny symbols on their wrists. Thirteens and Roman numerals, birthdates and geographical coordinates. The first year of peace, "1 t.e.," was popular.

Jaw beginning to ache, Scarlet dropped the rest of the bread down on the plate and rubbed her palms into her eyes. *Street fighter tattoos? Kidnapper tattoos? Mafia tattoos?*

Who were these people?

She stood up and started a pot of coffee.

"Wolf," she whispered to herself as the water began to percolate. She let the word linger, feeling it on her lips. To some, a wild beast, a predator, a nuisance. To others, a shy animal who was too often misunderstood by humanity.

An uneasiness still lingered in the pit of her stomach. She couldn't get the memory of him out of her head, nearly killing his opponent amid all those spectators, before running out into the fields like a man possessed. At the time, she'd believed that the howl she'd heard minutes later had been a true wolf prowling the farms—they certainly weren't uncommon, not after the species protection act that had been enforced centuries ago—but her certainty was failing.

They call me Wolf at the fights.

She put her plate and the empty fry pan into the sink, running cool water over them while she scanned the fields' swaying shadows through the window. Soon the farm would be filled with life—androids and workers and genetically enhanced honeybees.

She poured the coffee before it was finished, topping her mug with a splash of fresh milk, and sat back at the table.

An image of a gray wolf filled the screen, fangs bared, ears flattened. Snowflakes clung to its thick coat.

Scarlet dragged her finger across the screen, sending the picture away. The images that followed were more peaceful: wolves tumbling with their mates, cubs sleeping piled on top of one another, regal white-and-gray-pelted wolves creeping through autumn woods. She chose a link from one of the species preservation societies and scanned the text, pausing when she came to the section on howling.

WOLVES HOWL IN ORDER TO GAIN THE ATTENTION OF THEIR PACK OR SEND TERRITORIAL WARNINGS. LONE WOLVES WHO HAVE BECOME SEPARATED FROM THEIR PACK WILL HOWL IN ORDER TO FIND THEIR COMPANIONS. OFTEN, THE ALPHA MALE IS THE MOST AGGRESSIVE HOWLER OF THE PACK. HIS AGGRESSIVENESS CAN BE DETECTED IN HIS LOW-PITCHED, ROUGH HOWLS WHEN HE APPROACHES A STRANGER.

A chill shook Scarlet so hard her coffee splashed up over the rim of her mug. Cursing, she stood to grab a towel and mopped it up, annoyed at being spooked by a stupid article. Did she honestly think the crazy street fighter had been trying to communicate with his *pack*?

She threw the towel into the sink and grabbed the port-screen, skimming through the rest of the article before following a link about pack hierarchy.

WOLVES TRAVEL IN PACKS, GROUPS THAT RANGE FROM SIX TO FIFTEEN MEMBERS AND HAVE AN ESTABLISHED HIERARCHY. AT THE TOP OF THE SOCIAL STRUCTURE ARE THE ALPHA MALE AND ALPHA FEMALE, A MATED PAIR. THOUGH THEY ARE FREQUENTLY THE ONLY WOLVES IN THE PACK WHO WILL BREED AND PRODUCE A LITTER, ALL OTHER PACK MEMBERS ASSIST IN FEEDING AND RAISING THE PUPS.

MALES WILL ESTABLISH THEIR ALPHA RANK THROUGH RITUAL COMBAT: ONE WOLF MAY CHALLENGE ANOTHER, RESULTING IN A FIGHT THAT DETERMINES WHICH WOLF IS SUPERIOR. REPEATED VICTORIES WILL EARN RESPECT FOR THE MALE WOLF, AND ULTIMATELY DECIDE THE PACK LEADER.

THE NEXT STEP IN THE PACK HIERARCHY ARE THE BETA WOLVES, WHO OFTEN HUNT AND PROVIDE PROTECTION TO THE CUBS.

THE OMEGA WOLF IS THE LOWEST RANKING IN THE PACK. OFTEN TREATED AS A SCAPEGOAT, THE OMEGAS ARE OCCASIONALLY PICKED ON BY THE REST OF THE PACK. THIS CAN LEAD TO THE OMEGA

A flurry of clucking startled Scarlet.

Setting the port on the counter, she peered out the window. Her stomach flipped.

The shadow of a man stretched across the yard, the gathered hens skittering away from him toward their coop.

As if sensing her, Wolf glanced up and spotted Scarlet in the window.

She spun away. Swallowing the rising panic, she ran into the foyer and snatched her grandmother's shotgun from its corner beneath the stairs.

Wolf hadn't moved by the time she'd thrown open the front door. The chickens were already growing familiar with the stranger, pecking around his feet in search of falling seed.

Scarlet settled the gun in her arms and released the safety.

If he was surprised, he didn't show it.

"What do you want?" she yelled, startling the hens away from him. The light from the house spilled around her onto the gravel. Her shadow shifted across the drive, almost brushing Wolf's feet.

The madness from the fight was gone, and the bruises on his face were nearly invisible. He seemed calm and unconcerned with the gun, though he didn't move toward her.

After a long silence, he raised both hands to either side of his head, open palmed. "I'm sorry. I've frightened you again." As if to make amends, he backed away. Two, three steps.

"You have a gift," she deadpanned. "Keep your hands up."

His fingers twitched in acknowledgment.

Scarlet paced out from the door, but she stopped when the gravel bit into her bare feet. Her senses prickled, waiting for Wolf to make any sudden movement, but he was as still as the stone house behind her.

"I've already commed the police," she lied, her thoughts stretching back to the portscreen left on the kitchen counter.

His eyes caught the light, and Scarlet suddenly remembered her dad sleeping upstairs. Was it too much to hope that her raised voice could dislodge him from his stupor?

"How did you get here?"

"Walked. Well, ran, mostly," he said, hands still raised. The wind was making messy patterns in his hair. "Would you like me to leave?"

The question took her off guard. "I want you to tell me what you're doing here. If you think I'm afraid of you—"

"I'm not trying to scare you."

With a glare, she peered down the barrel to make sure she still had him in line.

"I wanted to talk about what you said at the fight. About the tattoo . . . and what happened to your grandmother. And your father."

Scarlet clenched her jaw. "How did you find out where I live?"

His brow furrowed, as if in confusion. "Your ship has the

name of your farm on it, so I looked it up. I don't mean you any harm. It just seemed like you needed help."

"*Help?*" Heat flared in her cheeks. "From the psychopath who tortured my dad? Who kidnapped my grandmother?"

"It wasn't me," he said, his tone unwavering. "There are other tattoos like mine. It was someone else."

"Oh, really? Like you're part of some cult or something?" The feathered body of one of the chickens pressed against her leg and she started, barely managing to keep the gun level.

"Or something," he said with a flinching shrug. One foot crunched against the gravel.

"Don't come any closer!" Scarlet yelled. The chicken clucked and dawdled away. "I will shoot, you know."

"I know." A flicker of kindness passed over him and he pointed at his temple. "You'll want to aim for the head. That usually makes for a fatal shot. Or, if you're feeling shaky, the torso. It's a larger target."

"Your head looks pretty big from here."

He laughed—the expression changing everything about him. His stance relaxed, his face warmed.

A disgusted growl vibrated in Scarlet's throat. This man had no right to be laughing, not when her grandmother was still out there.

Wolf dropped his arms and folded them over his chest. Before Scarlet could order them up again, he was speaking. "I'd been hoping to impress you last night, but it seemed to backfire on me."

"I'm not usually impressed by men with anger management issues who kidnap my grandmother and follow me around and—"

"I didn't kidnap your grandmother." For the first time, his words were sharp, stealing the tirade out of Scarlet's mouth. His attention fell down to the gaggle of chickens as they tramped around the door. "But if it really was someone with a tattoo like mine, I may be able to help figure out who did."

"Why should I believe you?"

He took the question seriously, contemplating for a long while. "I have no proof other than what I told you last night. I've been in Rieux for nearly two weeks—they know me at the tavern, they know me at the fights. If your father were to see me, he wouldn't recognize me. Nor would your grandmother." He shifted his weight, like he was growing anxious from too long standing still. "I want to help."

Frowning, Scarlet squinted down the double barrels. If he was lying, then this was one of the men who had taken her grandmother from her. He was cruel. He was evil. He deserved a bullet between his eyes.

But he was her only lead.

"You'll tell me everything. *Everything.*" Pulling her finger off the trigger, she lowered the shotgun so that it pointed instead at his thigh. A nonfatal target. "And you'll keep your hands where I can see them at all times. Just because I'm letting you into this house doesn't mean I trust you."

"Of course." He nodded, all compliance. "I wouldn't trust me either."

Twelve

SCARLET GESTURED WITH THE GUN FOR WOLF TO COME inside, glowering as he crept toward the landing. He seemed to brace himself, taking in the stucco walls and dark-stained staircase, before passing by her into the hallway. He had to duck so his head wouldn't hit the door frame.

Scarlet kicked the door shut, refusing to take her eyes from Wolf, who stood still and hunched, his body compacting itself as well as it could. His attention shifted to the rotating digital photos on the wall that showed Scarlet as a child munching on raw peas from the garden, golden autumnal fields, her grandmother forty years younger in her first military uniform.

"This way."

He followed her gesture into the kitchen. Scarlet glanced at the picture just as her grandmother vanished, before marching in after him.

She spotted her portscreen on the counter, still displaying a picture of an alpha male with his mate, and slipped it into her pocket.

Without turning her back on the street fighter, she propped the gun into a corner of cabinets and grabbed her red hoodie from the back of one of the chairs. She felt less vulnerable as she shoved her arms into the sleeves. Even more so when she snatched a carving knife from its block on the counter.

Wolf's eyes flickered once to the knife, before taking in the rest of the kitchen. They landed on the wire basket beside the sink, his pupils widening with hunger.

Six glossy red tomatoes filled the basket.

Scarlet frowned as Wolf dropped his gaze.

"You must be hungry," she muttered. "After all that *running*."

"I'm fine."

"Have a seat," she said, gesturing at the table with the knife.

Wolf hesitated only for a moment before pulling out a chair. He didn't scoot it back in as he sat, as if he wanted to give himself enough space to jump up and run if he had to.

"Hands where I can see them."

He looked a breath away from amusement as he leaned forward and splayed his fingers on the edge of the table. "I can't imagine what you must think of me, after last night."

She scoffed. "Really, you can't imagine?" She grabbed the cutting board and slammed it down on the table opposite from Wolf. "Would you like me to clue you in?"

He lowered his gaze, rubbing a finger into an ancient scratch in the wood. "It's been a long time since I lost control like that. I don't know what happened."

"I hope you didn't come here for sympathy." Refusing to set down the knife or turn her back on him, she had to make two more trips from counter to table—grabbing first a loaf of bread, then two tomatoes.

"No—I told you why I'm here. It's just that I spent all night trying to figure out what went wrong."

"Perhaps you should go back to the moment you decided that street fighting was a valid career choice."

A long silence went unbroken as Scarlet, still standing, sliced a hunk off the bread and tossed it at Wolf, who caught it easily.

"You're right," he said, picking at the crust. "That's probably where it started." He sank his teeth into the bread, barely chewing before he swallowed.

Baffled that he had no argument, no excuse, Scarlet grabbed one of the tomatoes and set it on the cutting board, feeling the need to keep her hands busy. She ruthlessly pushed the knife into its flesh, ignoring the seeds that oozed out onto the board.

Skewering the tomato slices, she held them out to him, not bothering with a plate. A mess of bread crumbs on the table were quickly joined with watery red juice.

His gaze was distant as he took the slices from her. "Thank you."

Scarlet threw the tomato's vine into the sink and wiped her hands on her jeans. Outside, the sun was rising fast and the chickens were growing restless with their clucking, wondering why Scarlet hadn't fed them breakfast when she'd been out.

"It's so peaceful here," Wolf said.

"I'm not going to hire you." Grabbing the mug of cold and forgotten coffee, Scarlet finally sat down opposite Wolf. The knife lingered on the cutting board, just beyond her fingers. She waited until he was licking the last of the tomato's juices from his fingers.

"So. What's the story with the tattoo?"

Wolf glanced down at his forearm. The kitchen light was making his eyes sparkle like gems, but this time they weren't making Scarlet flustered. All she cared about now were the answers those eyes were hiding.

He extended his arm across the table so that the tattoo was fully in the light and pulled the skin taut, like he was seeing it for the first time. LSOP962.

"Loyal Soldier to the Order of the Pack," he said. "Member 962." He released the skin and curled his shoulders, hunkering down in the chair. "The biggest mistake I have ever made."

Scarlet's skin tingled. "And what exactly is the Order of the Pack?"

"A gang, more commonly referred to as the Wolves. They like to call themselves vigilantes and rebels and harbingers of change, but . . . they're not much better than criminals, really. If I can ever afford it, I'll have this awful thing removed."

A gust of wind rattled the oak tree outside the front door and a flurry of leaves swished against the window.

"So you're not a part of it anymore?"

He shook his head.

Scarlet glared across the table, unable to read him. Unable to decipher if he was telling the truth. "The Wolves," she murmured, letting the name sink into her brain. "And do they do this often? Take innocent people out of their homes for absolutely no reason?"

"They have a reason."

Scarlet pulled the drawstring of her hood until it was almost strangling her, before tugging the material back out again. "Why? What would they want with my grandmother?"

"I don't know."

"Don't tell me that. Is it ransom money? What?"

His fingers flexed in and out on the table. "She was in the military," he said, gesturing toward the hallway. "In those pictures, she was in uniform."

"She was a pilot for the EF, but that was years ago. Before I was born."

"Then maybe she knows something. Or they think she does."

"About *what*?"

"Military secrets? Top-secret weaponry?"

Scarlet scooted forward until her stomach pressed against the table's edge. "I thought you said they were common criminals. What do they care about that?"

Wolf sighed. "Criminals who think of themselves as . . ."

"Harbingers of change." Scarlet gnawed on her lip. "Right. So, what? Are they trying to take down the government or something? Start a war?"

Wolf glanced out the window as the lights of a small passenger ship skirted along the edge of the field—the first workers arriving for their shift. "I don't know."

"No, you *do* know. You're one of them!"

Wolf smiled, humorlessly. "I was nothing to them, hardly more than an errand boy. I wasn't let in on any executive plans."

Scarlet folded her arms. "Then take an educated guess."

"I know they stole a lot of weapons. They want people to be afraid of them." He shook his head. "Maybe they want to get their hands on military weaponry."

"My grandma wouldn't know anything about that. And even if she did before, when she was a pilot, she wouldn't know now."

Wolf opened his palms wide to her. "I'm sorry. I don't know what else it could be. Unless *you* can think of something she may have been involved with."

"No, I've been racking my brain since she disappeared, but there's nothing. She was just—she's my grandma." She gestured out toward the fields. "She owns a farm. She speaks her mind and she doesn't like being told what to think, but she doesn't have any enemies, not that I know of. Sure, people in town think she's a little eccentric, but there's no one who doesn't like her. And she's just an old woman." She clasped both hands around the coffee mug and sighed. "You must know how to find them, at least?"

"Find them? No—it would be suicide."

She tensed. "It's not for you to decide."

Wolf scratched behind his neck. "How long ago did they take her?"

"Eighteen days." Hysteria worked its way up her throat. "They've had her for *eighteen days.*"

His attention was plastered to the table, troubled lines drawn into his brow. "It's too dangerous."

The chair slammed against the floor as Scarlet bolted up. "I asked for information, not a lecture. I don't care how dangerous they are—that's just one more reason I need to find them! Do you know what they could be doing to her right now while you're wasting my time? What they did to my father?"

A slam echoed through the house and Scarlet jumped, barely catching herself before she tripped over the fallen chair. She glanced past Wolf, but the hall was empty. Her heart hiccupped. "Dad?" She bolted into the foyer and thrust open the front door. "Dad!"

But outside, the drive was already empty.

Thirteen

SCARLET SPRINTED INTO THE DRIVE, THE GRAVEL BITING into her feet. The wind kicked at her curls, throwing them across her face.

"Where did he go?" she said, tucking her hair into her hood. The sun was fully over the horizon already, flecking the crops with gold and filling the drive with swaying shadows.

"Perhaps to feed your birds?" Wolf pointed as a rooster pecked his way back around the side of the house, meandering toward the vegetable patch.

Ignoring the biting gravel, Scarlet jogged around the corner. Oak leaves spun on the wind. The hangar and barn and chicken coop all stood silent in the buffeting dawn. There was no trace of her father.

"He must have been looking for something, or—" Scarlet's heart skipped. "My ship!"

She ran, ignoring the rocky drive, the prickly weeds. She nearly plowed into the hangar's door but managed to grasp the handle and yank it open just as a crash shook the building.

"Dad!"

But he was not inside the ship, preparing to fly off with it as she'd feared. Instead, he was standing on top of the cabinets that ran the length of the far wall, reaching into the overhead cupboards and tossing their contents onto the floor. Paint cans, extension cords, drill bits.

An entire standing toolbox had been tipped over, flooding the concrete with screws and bolts, and two metal cabinets on the back wall stood wide-open, showing an assortment of military pilot uniforms, coveralls, and a single straw gardening hat shoved into a corner.

"What are you doing?" Scarlet strode toward him, then ducked and froze as a wrench sailed by her head. When a crash didn't follow, she glanced back to see Wolf gripping the wrench a foot from his face, blinking in surprise. Scarlet spun back. "Dad, what—"

"There's something here!" he said, yanking open another cupboard. He snatched up a tin can and tipped it over, mesmerized as hundreds of rusted nails crashed and clanged on the floor.

"Dad, stop! There's nothing here!" She picked her way through the mess, more aware of rusty sharp bits than she had been of the jagged rocks outside. "Stop it!"

"There is something here, Scar." Tucking a metal barrel under one arm, her dad hopped off the counter and crouched, working the plug out from the hole in the top. Though he was also barefoot, the jumble of nails and screws didn't appear to bother him. "She has something and they want it. It's got to be here. Somewhere ... but where ..."

The air filled with the pungent fumes of engine lubricant as her dad tipped over the barrel, letting the yellowish grease gurgle and spill out over his mess.

"Dad, put it down!" She grabbed a hammer off the floor and held it overhead. "I will hit you, I swear it!"

He finally looked at her with that same haunted madness. This was not her father. This man was not vain and charming and self-indulgent, all the things she'd admired as a child and despised as a teenager. This man was broken.

The stream of oil became a light drizzle.

"Dad. Put down the barrel. Now."

His lips trembled as his attention shifted away, focused on the small delivery ship not a body's length away from him. "She loved flying," he murmured. "She loved her ships."

"Dad. *Dad*—!"

Standing, her dad heaved the barrel into the back window of the ship. A hairline fracture cobwebbed out on the glass.

"Not my ship!" Scarlet dropped the hammer and ran for him, stumbling her way over tools and debris.

The glass shattered with the second hit and her dad was already hauling himself through the shards.

"*Stop it!*" Scarlet grabbed him around the waist and dragged him out of the ship. "Leave it alone!"

He thrashed in her hold, his knee catching Scarlet in the side, and they both fell onto the floor. A canister bit into Scarlet's thigh but all she could think about was tightening her hold on her dad, trying to lock his swinging arms to his sides. Blood was on his hands where he'd grabbed the broken glass, and a gash in his side was already turning crimson.

"Let me go, Scar. I'm going to find it. I'm going to—"

He cried out as he was lifted away from her. Instinctively, Scarlet clung, still trying to subdue him until she realized that Wolf was there, dragging her dad to his feet. She let go, panting. One hand went to rub her throbbing hip.

"Let go of me!" Craning his head, her dad snapped his teeth at the air.

Ignoring his struggles, Wolf bound his wrists with one hand and stretched the other out toward Scarlet.

No sooner had her palm sunk onto his than her dad's screams renewed.

"He's one of them! One of *them*!"

Wolf yanked Scarlet to her feet and released her, using both arms to restrain her struggling father. Scarlet almost expected to see foam at the corners of her dad's mouth.

"The tattoo, Scar! It's them! It's them!"

She pushed her hair off her face. "I know, Dad. Just calm down! I can explain—"

"You can't take me back! I'm still looking! I need more time! Please, no more. No more . . ." He dissolved into sobs.

Wolf's eyebrows drew together as he peered at the back of her father's drooped head, then he grabbed a thin chain around his neck and pulled, snapping it.

Her dad flinched and, when Wolf released him, sank heavily to the floor.

Scarlet gawked at the necklace hanging from Wolf's fist—a

small, unfamiliar charm dangling from it. She couldn't remember her father wearing any jewelry, other than the monogamy band that he'd taken off within days of her mother figuring out the ring hadn't served its purpose and leaving him.

"Transmitter," Wolf said, holding the charm up so that its silver sheen blinked in the light. It was no larger than Scarlet's pinkie nail. "They've been tracking him, and, I would guess, listening in on everything as well."

Scarlet's dad hugged his knees, rocking.

"Do you think they're listening right now?" Scarlet asked.

"Most likely."

A firework exploded in her rib cage and she launched forward, grabbing Wolf's fist in both hands. "There's nothing here!" she screamed at the charm. "We're not hiding anything and you have the wrong woman! You'd better bring my grandmother back, and I swear on the house I was born in if you've hurt one hair, one wrinkle, *one freckle on her body* I am going to hunt every last one of you down and snap your necks like the chickens you are, do you understand me? BRING HER BACK!"

Throat hoarse, she fell back and released Wolf's hand.

"Finished?"

Trembling with anger, Scarlet nodded.

Wolf dropped the transmitter on the floor, grabbed the hammer, and smashed it with a single, clean strike. Scarlet jumped as metal crunched against the concrete.

"Do you think they knew he would come here?" Wolf said, standing.

"They left him in our cornfield."

Her father's voice rose between them, dry and empty. "They told me to find it."

"Find what?" Scarlet asked.

"I don't know. They didn't say. Just . . . that she's hiding something. Something valuable and secret and they want it."

"Wait . . . you knew?" said Scarlet. "You knew all along that you were bugged and you didn't try to tell me? Dad, what if I'd said something or done something that made them suspect me? What if they *do* come after me next?"

"I didn't have a choice," he said. "It was the only way they would let me go. They said I could only have my freedom if I found what your grandmother was hiding. If I found some clue that would help . . . I had to get out of there, Scar, you don't know what it was like—"

"I know they still have her! And I know that you're coward enough to save your own skin and not worry about what's happening to her, or what could happen to me."

Scarlet held her breath, waiting for him to deny it. To give some twisted excuse like he'd always had, but he stayed perfectly still. Perfectly silent.

Her skin flushed with anger. "You're a disgrace to her—to everything she's ever stood for. She would risk her life to protect either one of us! She would risk her life for a stranger if it was the right thing to do. But all you care about is yourself. I can't believe you're her son. I can't believe you're my *father.*"

He raised his haunted eyes to her. "You're wrong, Scarlet. She watched them torture me. *Me.* And still she kept her secrets." A spark of defiance flickered over his face. "There's something your grandmother never told us, Scar, and it's put both of us in danger. She's the selfish one."

"You don't know anything about her!"

"No, *you* don't! You've been idolizing her since you were four years old and it's blinded you to the truth! She's betrayed us both, Scarlet."

Blood pounding against her temples, Scarlet pointed out the door. "Get out. Get off my farm, and never come back. I hope I never see you again."

He paled, the circles like bruises under his eyes. Slowly, he peeled himself off the floor. "You're going to abandon me too? My own daughter and my own mother, both turning against me?"

"You abandoned us first."

Scarlet realized that in the five years since last she'd seen him, she'd come to match her father's height. They stood eye to eye; she burning up on the inside, he frowning as though he wanted to be sorry but couldn't quite grasp the emotion.

"Good-bye, Luc."

His jaw flexed. "They'll come for me again, Scarlet. And it will be on your hands."

"Don't you dare. You're the one who was wearing that transmitter, you're the one who was willing to sell *me* out."

He held her eyes for a long, slow count, like he was waiting for her to change her mind. Waiting for her to welcome him back to the house, back into her life. But all Scarlet could hear was the crunch of the hammer against the transmitter. She thought of the burn marks on his arm and knew he would just as soon give her over for torture, if it would have saved his own skin.

Finally, his gaze fell, and without looking at her, without looking at Wolf, her dad shuffled through the debris and out of the hangar.

Scarlet's fists settled against her sides. She would have to wait. He would go into the house to collect his shoes. She imagined him rummaging through the kitchen for food before he went—or trying to hunt down some stray liquor bottles. She dared not run the risk of their paths crossing again before he was gone for good.

The coward. The traitor.

"I'll help you."

She crossed her arms, protecting her anger against the gentleness of Wolf's voice. She scanned the chaos all around her, the mess that would take weeks to put right. "I don't need your help."

"I meant, I'll help get your grandmother back." Wolf ducked away, like he was surprised he'd made the offer.

It took a pathetically long time for her thinking to change directions, from the internal rant against her traitorous father, to the hefty meaning behind Wolf's words. She blinked up at him and held her breath, imagining his words captured in a bubble that might blow away. "You will?"

His head jerked in what could have been a nod. "The Wolves are headquartered in Paris. That's probably where they're keeping her."

Paris. The word filled her up. A clue. A promise.

She glanced at her ship and its shattered window. Renewed hatred flared for her father, but it deflated quickly—there wasn't time. Not now. Not when she had her first taste of hope in two endless weeks.

"Paris," she murmured. "We can take the train from Toulouse—it's, what, eight hours?" She hated the thought of being without her ship, but even the obnoxiously slow maglev train would be quicker than getting the window replaced. "Someone will have to look after the farm while I'm gone. Maybe Èmilie, after her shift. I'll send her a comm, then I just need to grab some clothes and . . ."

"Scarlet, wait. We can't just rush up there. We need to think this through."

"Rush? We can't *rush*? They've had her for more than two weeks! This isn't rushing!"

Wolf's gaze darkened and Scarlet paused, for the first time recognizing his unease.

"Look," she said, wetting her tongue, "we'll have eight hours on the train to think up something. But I can't stay here a moment longer."

"But what if your father is right?" His shoulders stayed stiff. "What if she has hidden something here? What if they come looking for it?"

She roughly shook her head. "They can look all they want, but they won't find anything. My dad is wrong. Grand-mère and I don't keep secrets."

Fourteen

"YOUR MAJESTY."

Kai turned away from the window that he'd been staring out half the morning, listening to the drone of the news anchors and military officials reporting on the escape of the most-wanted convict in the Eastern Commonwealth. Chairman Huy stood in the doorway, Torin beside him. Both looked supremely unhappy.

He gulped. "Well?"

Huy stepped forward. "They've gotten away."

Kai's pulse hiccupped. He took a tentative step toward his father's desk and gripped the back of the chair.

"I've given the order to deploy our reserve fleets immediately. I am confident we'll have the fugitives found and taken into custody by sunset."

"With all respect, Chairman, you don't *sound* particularly confident."

Though Huy puffed his chest out, his face took on a tinge of pink. "I am, Your Majesty. We can find them. It's only that . . . it's complicated by it being a stolen ship. All the tracking equipment has been stripped."

Torin let out an irritated sigh. "The girl has proven herself to be more clever than I would have given her credit for."

Kai dragged his hand through his hair, extinguishing an unexpected spark of pride.

"There is also the issue of the girl being Lunar," Huy added.

"Whoever captures her will just have to be alert," said Kai. "They should all be made well aware that she'll no doubt try to turn their minds against them."

"There is that too, but not what I was referring to. In the past, we've had difficulty tracking Lunar ships. It seems that they've learned how to disable our radar systems. I'm afraid we're not sure how they do it."

"Disable our radar systems?" Kai glanced at Torin. "Did you know about this?"

"I've heard rumors," said Torin. "Your father and I chose to believe that's all they were."

"Not all my contemporaries agree with me on this matter," said Huy. "But I myself am convinced it is the Lunars disabling our equipment. Whether it's through their mental abilities or some other talent, I can't tell. Regardless, Linh Cinder won't get far. We'll have every resource searching for her."

Tempering his inner turmoil, Kai molded his face into stone. "Keep me informed."

"Of course, Your Majesty. There is one other thing I thought you might want to see. We've finished going over our security footage from the prison." Huy gestured to the inlaid screen in Kai's desk.

Rounding his chair, Kai tugged on his long sleeves, suddenly warm, and sat down. A comm from the council of national security rotated in the corner. "Accept comm."

The screen brightened with footage of the prison, all white and glossy walls. It showed a long hallway lined with smooth doors and ID scanners. A prison guard moved into view and gestured at a door. He was followed by a short, old man wearing a gray cap.

Kai jerked upward. It was Dr. Erland. "Volume up."

Dr. Erland's familiar voice filtered through the screen. "I am the leading scientist of the royal letumosis research team, and this girl is my prime test subject. I require blood samples from her before she leaves the planet." Looking miffed, he reached into a bag and pulled something out—a syringe, but the bag still bulged. That wasn't all that was inside it.

"I have my orders, sir," said the guard. "You'll have to obtain an official release from the emperor to be allowed entrance."

Kai frowned as the doctor put the syringe back into the bag, knowing that Dr. Erland hadn't made such a request.

"All right. If that's protocol, I understand," said Dr. Erland. And then he just stood there, serene and patient. After the space of a few heartbeats, Kai glimpsed the doctor's smile. "There, you see? I have obtained the necessary release from the emperor. You may open the door."

Kai's jaw dropped as, amazingly, the guard turned toward the cell door, swiped his wrist across the scanner, and punched in a code. A green light flashed and the door opened.

"Thank you kindly," said Dr. Erland, passing the guard. "I'll ask that you give us a bit of privacy. I won't be but a minute."

The guard complied without argument, shutting the door and meandering in the direction they'd come from, leaving the screen empty.

Kai glanced up at Huy. "Has that guard been questioned?"

"Yes, sir, and his statement is that he remembers denying access to the girl, and then the doctor left. He was confounded when we showed him this footage. He claims to not remember any of it."

"How is that possible?"

Huy busied his hands by buttoning his suit jacket. "It appears, Your Majesty, that Dr. Dmitri Erland glamoured the guard into allowing him access to the prisoner's cell."

Hairs prickling beneath his collar, Kai slumped back in his chair. "Glamoured? You think he's Lunar?"

"That is our theory."

Kai stared up at the ceiling. Cinder, Lunar. Dr. Erland, Lunar. "Is it a *conspiracy*?"

Torin cleared his throat, as he did whenever Kai mentioned some off-the-wall theory—although it seemed like a perfectly legitimate question to Kai. "We're in the process of investigating all possibilities," said Torin. "At least now we know how she escaped."

e have other video that shows the prisoner glamouring me guard on the next shift," said Huy, "and being shown to a new cell. In that footage she has two feet, and a different left hand from the one she entered the prison with."

Kai shoved himself out of his chair. "The bag," he said, pacing toward the windows.

"Yes. Dr. Erland was bringing her these tools, we must assume with the intention of assisting her escape."

"That's why he left." Kai shook his head, wondering how Cinder really knew Dr. Erland—what they'd really been doing all those times she'd come to see him at the hospital. Plotting, conniving, conspiring? "I thought she was just fixing a med-droid," he murmured to himself. "I didn't even question—stars, I've been so stupid."

"Your Majesty," said Huy, "our few resources not searching for Linh Cinder have been dedicated to finding Dmitri Erland. He will be arrested as a traitor to the crown."

"Please excuse the interruption," said Nainsi, the android who had once tutored Kai as a child, but had now taken on the more significant role of personal assistant. The android who had malfunctioned—was it not even four weeks ago?—and led him to his first meeting with Linh Cinder, back when she was nothing more to him than a renowned mechanic. "Her Majesty, Lunar Queen Levana, has requested an immediate appoint—"

"I will not be announced by an android!"

Huy and Torin spun around as Queen Levana swooped in and backhanded Nainsi across her single blue sensor, eyes flaming. The android no doubt would have toppled onto her back if her stabilizing hydraulics hadn't kicked in just in time to catch her.

The queen's usual entourage followed—Sybil Mira, head thaumaturge, whose role in the Lunar court seemed to be a cross between a doting lapdog and a gleeful servant who delighted in seeing to Levana's cruelest requests. Kai had once seen her attack and nearly blind an innocent servant at the queen's bidding, without a hint of hesitation.

She was followed by another thaumaturge, one rank beneath Sybil, who had dark skin and piercing eyes and no purpose, it seemed to Kai, other than to stand behind his queen and look smug.

Sybil's personal guard followed, the blond man who had held Cinder during the ball when Levana first threatened her life. Even after a month of their being guests in his palace, Kai didn't know his name. A second guard, his hair flaming red, had been the one to jump in between a bullet and Levana at the ball, taking it squarely in the shoulder. It seemed that bullet wounds weren't enough to let one off royal guard duty, though, and the only indication of the wound was the lump of a bandage beneath his uniform.

"Your Majesty," Kai said, addressing the queen with, he thought, an admirable lack of contempt. "What a pleasant surprise."

"One more patronizing comment and I will have you slice off and nail your own tongue to the palace gate."

Kai blanched. Levana's voice, usually so melodious and sweet, was rigid as steel, and though he'd seen her angry many times before, it had never been enough for her to drop the thin veneer of diplomacy. "Your Majesty—"

"You let her escape! *My* prisoner!"

"I assure you, we're doing everything we can—"

"Aimery, silence him."

Kai's tongue fell limp. Eyes widening, he reached a hand to his lips, realizing it wasn't only his tongue, but his throat, his jaw. The muscles had gone useless. Which perhaps was better than having his tongue nailed to the palace gate, but still . . .

His gaze darted to the male thaumaturge in his pristine red coat, who grinned charmingly back. Rage flared inside him.

"You're doing everything you can?" Levana flattened her palms on Kai's desk. Their glares battled over the netscreen that still showed the empty prison hallway, frozen in time. "You're telling me, young emperor, that you didn't assist her escape? That your intention from the start hasn't been to humiliate me on your soil?"

Kai sensed that she wanted him to fall to his knees and silently plead for forgiveness, to promise to move the Earth and heavens to satisfy her—but his anger overwhelmed his fear. With his ability to speak removed, he folded his arms over the back of his chair and waited.

From the corner of his eye he could see Torin and Huy, still as statues but for dark scowls. Sybil Mira, with her hands innocently tucked into her ivory sleeves, must have been holding them at bay with her Lunar mind magic.

Nainsi, the only being in the room that the Lunars couldn't control with mind tricks, was being physically held by the blond guard, turned so that her sensor—and built-in camera—couldn't capture the proceedings.

The queen's fingertips whitened against the desk. "You expect me to believe that you didn't encourage this escape? That you had nothing to do with it?" Her expression tightened. "You certainly don't seem too *upset* about it, Your Majesty."

Bewilderment stirred in Kai's gut, but his face remained neutral. Years of rumors and superstitions circulated in his thoughts—rumors that Levana knew whenever anyone was talking about her, anywhere on Luna, even on Earth—but he suspected a much more plausible reason for her uncanny ability to know what she shouldn't know.

She'd been spying on him, and his father before. He knew it—he just didn't know how.

Realizing that she was waiting for a response, Kai quirked an eyebrow and flourished a hand toward his mouth.

Levana seethed and pushed herself back from the desk. She stretched her neck until she was staring down her nose at him. "Speak."

Sensation returned to his tongue and Kai threw a thankless smile at Aimery. He then proceeded to do the most disrespectful thing he could think of—he pulled his chair back from his desk and sat down. Tipping back, he folded his hands over his stomach.

Anger sizzled behind Levana's charcoal eyes until she was almost—briefly—unbeautiful.

"No," Kai said. "I did not encourage the fugitive to escape or assist her in any way."

"What reason do I have to believe that, after you seemed so *enchanted* with her at the ball?"

His brow twitched. "If you're going to refuse to take my word, why don't you just force a full confession out of me and be done with it?"

"Oh, I could, Your Majesty. I could put any words into that mouth of yours that I wanted to hear. But, unfortunately, we are not mind *readers,* and I am concerned only with truth."

"Then allow me to give it to you." Kai hoped he seemed more indulgent than annoyed. "Our preliminary investigation has shown that she used both her Lunar and cyborg abilities to escape from her cell, and while she may have had assistance from within the palace, it was done without my knowledge. I'm afraid we were unequipped to keep a prisoner who is both cyborg and Lunar. We will, of course, be working on strengthening our prison system for the future. In the meantime, we are doing everything in our power to track down the fugitive and apprehend her. I made a bargain with you, Your Majesty, and I do intend to keep my end."

"You've already failed your end of the bargain," she spat, but then her face softened. "Young emperor, I certainly hope you didn't fancy yourself in love with this girl."

Kai's grip tightened until his knuckles screamed. "Any feelings I may have imagined for Linh Cinder were clearly nothing more than a Lunar trick."

"Clearly. I am glad you recognize that." Levana folded her own hands demurely before her. "I am done with this charade and am returning to Luna, immediately. You have three days to find the girl and deliver her to me. If you fail, I will send my own army to find her, and they will tear apart every spaceship, every docking station, and every home on this pathetic planet until she is found."

White spots flashed in Kai's vision and he shoved himself back to his feet. "Why don't you say what you mean? You've been wanting a reason to invade Earth for ten years and now you're using this one escaped Lunar, this *nobody*, to accomplish it."

The corners of Levana's lips tilted. "You seem to misunderstand my motives, so I will say precisely what I mean. I will someday rule the Commonwealth, and it is your decision whether that is to be through a war or through a peaceful and diplomatic marriage union. But *this* has nothing to do with war and politics. I want this girl, or I want her corpse. I will burn your country to the ground looking for her if I must."

Levana pulled away from the desk and drifted out of the office, her entourage falling in step behind her with neither expression nor comment.

When they had gone, Huy and Torin each melted in front of Kai, looking like they hadn't taken a breath since the queen's entrance. And perhaps they hadn't—Kai didn't know what Sybil had been doing to them, but he could guess it hadn't been comfortable.

Nainsi swiveled on her treads. "I am so sorry, Your Majesty. I never would have given her access, but the door was already open."

Kai silenced her with a wave. "Yes, how coincidental that she chose the one time when the door wasn't shut and coded to barge in here, isn't it?"

Nainsi's processor whirred, no doubt running the odds.

Kai rubbed one hand down his face. "It doesn't matter. Everyone, out. Please."

Nainsi vanished out the door, but Huy and Torin lingered.

"Your Majesty," Huy said. "With all due respect, I need your permission—"

"Yes, fine, whatever you need to do. Just, I need a moment. Please."

Huy clicked his heels. "Of course, Your Majesty." Though Torin looked more apt to argue, he didn't, and soon the door was hissing behind them both.

With the click of the latch, Kai let himself crumble into his chair. His entire body was shaking.

It was suddenly so clear that he wasn't ready for this. He wasn't strong enough or smart enough to fill his father's shoes. He couldn't even keep Levana out of his own office—how was he going to protect an entire country from her—an entire planet?

Spinning his chair around, he raked his hands back through his hair. His attention swept over the city below, but was soon pulled up to the glaring blue sky, cloudless. Somewhere beyond it was the moon and the stars and tens of thousands of cargo ships, passenger ships, military ships, delivery ships, vying for space beyond the ozone. And Cinder was in one of them.

He couldn't help it, but a part of him—maybe a large part of him—hoped Cinder would just disappear, like a fading comet's tail. Just to spite the queen, to keep from her this one thing she so desperately wanted. It was only her vanity, after all, that had set off this tirade. Because Cinder had made that one foolish comment at the ball, suggesting that Levana wasn't beautiful after all.

Kai massaged his temple, knowing that he had to give up these thoughts. Cinder had to be found, and soon, before millions were murdered in her place.

It was all politics now. Pros and cons, give and take, trades and agreements. Cinder had to be found, Levana had to be appeased, Kai had to stop acting cheated and indignant and start acting like an emperor.

Whatever he'd once felt for Cinder—or thought he'd felt for her—was over.

Fifteen

CINDER TURNED OFF THE SHOWER AND PROPPED HERSELF
against the fiberglass wall while the nozzle dripped onto her
head. She would have liked to stay in longer but was worried
about using up the water supply, and judging from the half-hour
shower Thorne had taken, she clearly couldn't rely on him for
conservation.

Nevertheless, she was clean. The smell of sewage was gone,
the salty sweat rinsed away. Stepping out of the communal
shower, she rubbed her hair with a starchy towel, then spent a
moment drying all the crevices and joints of her prosthetics to
protect against rust. It was habit, even though her new limbs already had a protective coating. Dr. Erland, it seemed, hadn't
skimped on anything.

Her soiled prison uniform was balled in a corner on the tiled
floor. She'd found a discarded military uniform in the crew
quarters—oversize charcoal-gray pants that had to be belted in
at her waist and a plain white undershirt, which wasn't much

different from the cargos and T-shirts she was used to, back before she'd become a fugitive of the law. All that was missing were her ever-present gloves. She felt naked without them.

She threw the towel and prison uniform into the laundry chute and unlatched the shower room door. The thin corridor revealed an open doorway to the galley on her right, and the cargo bay packed full with plastic crates to her left.

"Home sweet home," she murmured, wringing droplets from her hair as she ambled toward the cargo bay.

There was no sign of the so-called captain. Only the faint running lights along the floor were on, and the darkness and the silence and the knowledge of all the empty space around the ship, stretching out for eternity, gave Cinder the peculiar sensation that she was a phantom haunting a shipwreck. She picked her way through the obstacle course of storage bins and sank into the pilot's seat in the cockpit.

Through the window she could see Earth—the shores of the American Republic and most of the African Union visible beneath the swirling cloud cover. And beyond it—stars, so many stars swirling and misting into countless galaxies. They were both beautiful and terrifying, billions of light-years away, and yet seeming so bright and close it was almost suffocating.

All Cinder had ever wanted was freedom. Freedom from her stepmother and her overbearing rules. Freedom from a life of constant work with nothing to show for it. Freedom from the sneers and hateful words of strangers who didn't trust the cyborg girl who was too strong and too smart and too freakishly good with machines to ever be *normal.*

Now she had her freedom—but it wasn't anything like she'd envisioned.

Sighing, Cinder pulled her left foot onto her knee, shoved up her pant leg, and opened the hollow compartment inside her calf. The compartment had been searched and emptied when she'd been admitted into prison—just one more invasion—but the most valuable contents had been ignored. No doubt the guard performing her search had thought the chips nestled into the wiring were a part of Cinder's own programming.

Three chips. She plucked them out, one by one, laying them out on the arm of her chair.

There was the shimmering white D-COMM chip. It was a Lunar chip, made from some material Cinder hadn't seen before. Levana had ordered it to be installed in Nainsi, Kai's android, and used it to gather confidential information. The girl who had programmed the chip, supposedly the queen's personal programmer, had later used it to contact Cinder and tell her that Levana was planning to marry Kai . . . and then kill him and use the power of the Eastern Commonwealth to invade the rest of the Earthen Union. It was this information that had sent Cinder running to the ball only a few short days ago—what seemed like a lifetime ago.

She couldn't regret it. She knew she would do it all over again, despite what a mess her life had become since that single rash decision.

Then there was Iko's personality chip. It was the largest and most abused of the three. One side showed a distinct greasy thumbprint, probably Cinder's, and one corner had a hairline fracture. Nevertheless, Cinder was confident it would still function. Iko, a servant android who had belonged to Cinder's stepmother, had long been one of her closest friends. But in a fit of anger and desperation, Adri had dismantled Iko and sold off her parts, leaving only the most useless pieces behind. Including her personality chip.

The third chip in Cinder's stash made her heart cramp as she picked it up.

Peony's ID chip.

Her younger stepsister had died almost two weeks ago. The plague had claimed her, because Cinder couldn't get the antidote to her in time. Because Cinder had been too late.

What would Peony think now? That Cinder was Lunar. That Cinder was Princess Selene. That Cinder had danced with Kai, kissed Kai . . .

"*Eww*, is that an ID chip?"

She jumped, enclosing the chip in her fist as Thorne sank into the second chair. "Don't sneak up on me like that."

"Why do you have an ID chip?" he said, peering suspiciously at the other two chips on the arm of her chair. "It'd better not be yours, after you made me cut mine out."

She shook her head. "It's my sister's." Gulping, she unfurled her fingers. A bit of dried blood had crackled off in her palm.

"Don't tell me she's a runaway convict too. Doesn't she need it?"

Cinder held her breath, waiting for the aching in her chest to fade, and glared at Thorne.

He met the look, and realization gradually expanded over his face. "Oh. I'm sorry."

She fidgeted with the chip, passing it from one metal knuckle to the next.

"How long ago?"

"A couple of weeks." She tucked the chip into her fist. "She was only fourteen."

"The plague?"

Cinder nodded. "The androids who run the quarantines have been harvesting ID chips from the deceased. I think they're giving them to convicts and escaped Lunars . . . people wanting a new identity." She set the chip down beside the others. "I couldn't let them take hers."

Thorne settled back in his chair. He'd cleaned up well—his hair was neatly trimmed, he was clean shaven, and he smelled of very expensive soap. He was sporting a well-worn leather jacket with a single medallion pinned onto the collar, the rank of captain.

"Aren't the androids that work at the quarantines government property?" he said, staring at Earth through the window.

"Yeah, I think so." Cinder frowned. She'd never given it any thought before, but saying it aloud brought on a flurry of suspicion.

Thorne voiced the thought first. "Why would the government program androids to harvest ID chips?"

"Maybe it's not to sell on the black market," Cinder said, pressing Peony's chip into the arm of the chair. "Maybe they just wipe them clean and recirculate them."

But she didn't believe that. ID chips were cheap to make and if the public ever found out their loved one's identities were being erased, there would be an uproar.

She bit her lip. Was there another reason then? Something else the government was using the chips for? Or had someone managed to reprogram the quarantine androids without the government even knowing?

Her gut tightened. How she wished she could talk to Kai . . .

"What are those other two?"

She glanced down. "Direct communication chip, and a personality chip that used to belong to an android, a friend of mine."

"Are you some sort of chip hoarder or something?"

She scowled. "I'm just keeping them safe until I figure out what to do with them. Eventually I'll need to find a new body for Iko, something she can . . ." She trailed off, then gasped. "That's it!"

She hurriedly stashed the other two chips in her calf again. Grabbing Iko's personality chip, she sped off to the cargo bay. Thorne followed her—into the hall, down the hatch to the sub-level, into the engine room, lingering in the doorway while Cinder crawled beneath the ductwork and popped up beside the computer mainframe.

"We need a new auto-control system," she said, opening a panel and running her finger along the labels. "Iko *is* an auto-control system. All androids are! Of course, she's used to the functionality of a much smaller body, but ... how different can it be?"

"I'm going to guess, really different?"

She shook her head and plugged the chip into the system's mainframe. "No, no, this is going to work. It just needs an adapter." She worked while she talked, twisting live wires out of their connections, rearranging, reconnecting.

"And we have an adapter?"

"We're about to."

Turning, she scanned the control panel behind her. "We're never going to use the dust-vacuum module are we?"

"The dust what?"

She yanked a connector cord from the panel and snapped one end into the mainframe, the other into the inlet for the auto-control system—the same that had nearly fried her own circuitry.

"And that should do it," she said, sitting back on her heels.

The system lit up, the sound of an internal diagnostics check familiar to Cinder's ear. Her heart was palpitating—to think that she wouldn't be alone anymore, that she could succeed in rescuing at least one person who mattered to her ...

The mainframe fell quiet again.

Thorne stared up at the ship's ceiling as if he expected it to cave in on him.

"Iko?" Cinder said, facing the computer. Were the speakers on? The sound and data input settings correct? She'd been able to communicate with Thorne just fine when they were in the warehouse, but . . .

"Cinder?"

Her relieved gasp nearly knocked her backward. "Iko! Yes, it's me, it's Cinder!" She grabbed hold of a cooling tube that hung overhead—a part of the engine, a part of the ship.

And Iko was all of it.

"Cinder. Something's wrong with my vision sensor. I can't see you, and I feel funny."

Tongue jutting from her mouth, Cinder bent over to analyze the slot where Iko's personality chip had found a new home. It seemed to fit perfectly, protected and functional. There was no hint of any compatibility issues. Her smile split from ear to ear.

"I know, Iko. Things are going to be a little different for a while. I've had to install you as the auto-control system of a spaceship. A 214 Rampion, Class 11.3. Do you have net connectivity? You should be able to download the specs."

"A Rampion? A *spaceship*?"

Cinder ducked. Though there was only one speaker in the engine room, Iko's voice echoed from every corner.

"What are we doing on a spaceship?"

"It's a long, long story, but it's all I could think to do with your—"

"Oh, Cinder! *Cinder!*" Iko's voice came out as a wail, sending a chill down Cinder's spine. "Where were you all day? Adri is furious, and Peony . . . *Peony.*"

Cinder's words dried up.

"She's dead, Cinder. Adri received a comm from the quarantines."

Cinder stared dumbly at the wall. "I know, Iko. That was two weeks ago. It's been two weeks since Adri disabled you. This is the first . . . body . . . I've been able to find."

Iko fell silent. Cinder glanced around, sensing Iko all around her. The engine rotated faster for a moment, then reduced to normal speed. The temperature barely dropped. A light flickered in the hallway behind Thorne, who was stiff and uncomfortable in the doorway, looking like a poltergeist had just taken over his beloved Rampion.

"Cinder," Iko said after a few silent minutes of explorations. "I'm *enormous.*" There was a distinct whine in her metallic tone.

"You're a ship, Iko."

"But I'm . . . how can I . . . no hands, no visual sensor, humongous landing gear—are those supposed to be my feet?"

"Well, no. It's supposed to be landing gear."

"Oh, what's to become of me? I'm hideous!"

"Iko, it's only tempor—"

"Now, hold on just one minute there, little miss disembodied voice." Thorne strode into the engine room and crossed his arms over his chest. "What do you mean, 'hideous'?"

This time, the temperature spiked. "Who's that? Who's speaking?"

"I am Captain Carswell Thorne, the owner of this fine ship, and I will not stand to have her insulted in my presence!"

Cinder rolled her eyes.

"Captain Carswell Thorne?"

"That's right."

A brief silence. "My net search is finding only a Cadet Carswell Thorne, of the American Republic, imprisoned in New Beijing prison on—"

"That's him," said Cinder, ignoring Thorne's glare.

Another silence as the heat in the engine room hovered just upside of comfortable. Then, "You're ... rather handsome, Captain Thorne."

Cinder groaned.

"And you, my fine lady, are the most gorgeous ship in these skies, and don't let anyone ever tell you different."

The temperature drifted upward, until Cinder dropped her arms with a sigh. "Iko, are you *intentionally* blushing?"

The temperature dropped back down to pleasant. "No," Iko said. Then, "But am I really pretty? Even as a ship?"

"The prettiest," said Thorne.

"You do have a naked lady painted on your port side," added Cinder.

"Painted her myself."

A series of inset ceiling lights flickered and released a dim glow.

"And really, Iko, this is only temporary. We'll get a new auto-control system, and we'll get you a new body. Eventually. But I need you to watch over the ship, check the reports, maybe run a diagnostics—"

"The power cell is almost dead."

Cinder nodded. "Right. I knew that part already. Anything else?"

The engine hummed all around her. "I guess I could run a full system check ..."

Beaming, Cinder crawled toward the door, meeting a pleased-looking Thorne when she stood back up. "Thank you, Iko."

The lights flickered out again as Iko diverted her energy. "But why are we on this spaceship again? And with a convicted felon? No offense, Captain Thorne."

Cinder grimaced, too exhausted to tell the story, but knowing she couldn't keep it from her companions forever. "All right," she said, sidling past Thorne and into the hallway. "Let's go back to the cockpit. We might as well be comfortable."

Sixteen

SCARLET CALLED A HOVER TO TAKE THEM INTO TOULOUSE, nearly draining her account of Gilles's latest deposit. She sat opposite Wolf during the ride, her pistol digging into her back as she watched him. In such close quarters, she knew the pistol was all but useless to her. After all, she'd witnessed Wolf's speed more than once. He could have her pinned and half choked before she'd loosened the gun from her waistband.

But it was impossible to feel threatened by the semi-stranger across from her. Wolf was entranced by the rolling farmlands passing by, gaping at tractors and cattle and decrepit, crumbling barns. His legs jogged ceaselessly the whole time, though she doubted he realized it.

The almost child-like fascination was at odds with him in every way. The fading black eye, the pale scars, the broad shoulders, the calm composure he'd had as he nearly strangled Roland, the fierce brutality in his gaze as he'd nearly killed his opponent in the fight.

Scarlet chewed the inside of her cheek, wondering which side of him was an act, and which was real.

"Where are you from?" she asked.

Wolf swung his gaze around to meet hers, the curiosity vanishing. Like he'd forgotten she was there. "Here. France."

Her lips twitched. "Interesting. You look like you've never seen a cow before."

"Oh—no, not here. Not Rieux. I'm from the city."

"Paris?"

He nodded and his ticking legs switched to a new rhythm, alternating in time with each other. Unable to take it, Scarlet reached over and firmly pressed her palm onto one knee, forcing his bouncing leg to still. Wolf skittered at the touch.

"You're driving me crazy," she said, pulling back. His legs stayed still—for the time, at least—but his surprise lingered on her. "So how did you end up in Rieux of all places?"

His attention swept back to the window. "At first I just wanted to get away. I took a maglev to Lyon, and started following the fights from there. Rieux is small, but it draws a good crowd."

"I noticed." Scarlet leaned her head back against the seat. "I lived in Paris for a while, when I was a kid. Before I came down here to live with Grand-mère." She shrugged. "I've never really missed it."

They'd passed through the farms and olive groves, the vineyards and suburbs, and were swooping into the heart of Toulouse when she heard Wolf respond.

"I haven't missed it either."

THE SUBLEVEL OF THE MAGLEV STATION WAS OBNOXIOUSLY bright as they descended on the escalator, the fluorescents overcompensating for the lack of sun. Two androids and a weapons detector were waiting at the bottom, and one beeped the second Scarlet's feet touched the platform.

"Leo 1272 TCP 380 personal handgun detected. Please extend your ID chip and stand by for clearance."

"I have a permit," Scarlet said, holding out her wrist.

A flash of red. "Weapon cleared. Thank you for riding the European Federation Maglev Train," said the android, rolling back to its post.

Scarlet brushed past the androids, and found an empty bench just off the rails. Despite half a dozen small, spherical cameras orbiting near the ceiling, the walls were scribbled with years of elaborate graffiti and the ghost images of torn concert posters.

Wolf claimed the seat beside her, and within moments his frenetic energy had started up again. Though he'd left space in between them, Scarlet found herself attuned to the fidgeting fingers, jogging knees, shoulders rolling out their kinks. His energy was almost tangible.

Scarlet was exhausted just from watching him.

Trying to ignore him, she dug her portscreen from her pocket and checked her comms, though nothing but junk and ads had come in.

Three trains came and went. Lisbon. Rome. West Munich.

Scarlet grew anxious, and didn't realize that her own foot had started tapping to the same beat until Wolf placed the pad of a finger against her knee.

She froze, and Wolf instantly pulled away. "Sorry," he whispered, gripping his hands together in his lap.

Scarlet had no response, unsure what he was apologizing for. Unable to tell if his ears had just gone pink or if it was the flickering lights from a nearby ad.

She saw him let out a measured breath before, without warning, Wolf stiffened and whipped his head toward the escalators.

Instantly on edge, Scarlet craned her neck to see what had startled him. A man in a business suit was passing through the detectors at the base of the escalator. He was followed by another man in torn jeans and a sweater. Then a mother guiding a hovering carriage with one hand while checking her port with the other.

"What's wrong?" she asked, but the words were drowned out by the blaring speakers, announcing the train to Paris via Montpellier.

The strain in Wolf's muscles fell away and he bounded to his feet. The track's magnets started to hum and he went to join the other passengers rustling toward the platform's edge. The unease had already vanished from his face.

Scarlet hefted her bag onto her shoulder and glanced back once more before joining him.

The train's bullet-nose glided past, a blur at first before

coming to an easy stop. In one fluid movement, the cars lowered themselves onto the track with a clang and the doors all down the train hissed open. Androids deboarded from each car, their monotone voices speaking in unison. "Welcome aboard the European Federation Maglev Train. Please extend your ID for ticket scanning. Welcome aboard the European . . ."

A weight released from Scarlet's chest as the scanner passed over her wrist and she stepped onto the train. Finally, *finally* she was on her way. No more standing still. No more doing nothing.

She found an empty privacy room with bunk beds and a desk and a netscreen on the wall. The car had the musty smell of rooms sprayed with too much air freshener. "It's going to be a long trip," she said, depositing her bag on the desk. "We can watch the net for a while. Do you have a favorite feed?"

Standing just inside the room, Wolf looked from the floor to the screen to the walls, trying to find new places to land his eyes. Anywhere but on her. "Not really," he said, crossing to the window.

Scarlet perched on the edge of the bed, able to make out the flicker of netscreens on the glass, highlighting a collection of fingerprint smudges. "Me either. Who has time to watch it, right?"

When he didn't respond, she leaned back on her palms and pretended not to notice the sudden awkwardness. "Screen, on."

A panel of gossip reporters were seated around a desk. Their empty, catty words flew in and out of Scarlet's ears, her thoughts too distracted, before she realized they were critiquing the Lunar girl at the New Beijing ball—her atrocious hair, the embarrassing state of her gown, and were those *grease* stains on her gloves? Tragic.

One of the women cackled. "Too bad they don't have any department stores in space, because that girl could use a serious makeover!"

The other hosts tittered.

Scarlet shook her head. "That poor girl's going to be executed, and everyone's just making jokes about her."

Wolf glanced back at the screen. "That's the second time I've heard you defend her."

"Yeah, well, I try to think for myself once in a while, rather than buy in to the ridiculous propaganda the media would have us believe." She frowned, realizing that she sounded exactly like her grandmother. She tempered her annoyance with a sigh. "People are just so quick to accuse and criticize, but they don't know what she's been through or what led her to do the things she did. Do we even know for sure that she *did* anything?"

An automated voice warned that the train doors were closing and she heard them whistle shut seconds later. The train rose off the tracks and slithered out of the station, plunging them into a darkness only broken by the corridor lights and the blue netscreen. It picked up speed, a bullet coasting down the tracks, and broke ground all at once, sunlight spilling through the windows.

"Shots were fired at the ball," said Wolf, as the talking heads on the screen jabbered on. "Some believe the girl meant to start a massacre, and that it's a miracle no one was hurt."

"Some people have also said she was there to assassinate Queen Levana, and wouldn't that have made her a hero?" Scarlet mindlessly flipped through the channels. "I just think we shouldn't judge her, or anyone, without trying to understand them first. That maybe we should get the full story before jumping to conclusions. Crazy notion, I know."

She huffed, irritated to find heat rushing up to her cheeks. The channels ticked by. Ads. Ads. News. Celebrity gossip. A reality show about a group of children attempting to run their own small country. More ads.

"Besides," she muttered, half to herself, "the girl's only sixteen. It seems to me that everyone is overreacting."

Scratching behind his ear, Wolf sank onto the bed, as far from Scarlet as possible. "There have been cases of Lunars as young as seven years old being found guilty of murder."

She scowled. "As far as I know, *that* girl hasn't murdered anybody."

"I didn't murder Hunter last night. But that doesn't make me harmless."

Scarlet hesitated. "No. I guess it doesn't."

After a heavy silence, she changed the netscreen back to the reality show and feigned interest in it.

"I started fighting when I was twelve."

She slid her attention back to him. Wolf was staring at the wall, at nothing.

"For money?"

"No. For status. I'd only been in the pack for a few weeks,

but it became clear very fast that if you don't fight, if you can't defend yourself, then you're nothing. You're tormented and ridiculed . . . you practically become a servant, and there's nothing you can do about it. The only way to prevent becoming an omega is to fight. And to win. That's why I do it. That's why I'm good at it."

Her brow had knit together so tight it was beginning to ache, but Scarlet couldn't relax as she listened. "'Omega,'" she said. "Just like a real wolf pack."

He nodded, picking nervously at his blunt fingernails. "I saw how afraid of me you were—not even just afraid, but . . . revolted. And you were right to be. But you said that you like to have the full story before judging, to try to understand first. So that's my story. That's how I learned to fight. Without mercy."

"But you're not in the gang anymore. You don't have to fight anymore."

"What else would I do?" he said, with a humorless laugh. "It's all I know, all I'm good at. Until yesterday, I didn't even know what a tomato was."

Scarlet smothered the start of a grin. His frustration was almost endearing. "And now you do," she said. "Who knows? Tomorrow you might learn about broccoli. By next week, you could know the difference between summer squash and zucchini."

Wolf glared at her.

"I mean it. You're not a dog who can't be taught new tricks. You can learn to be good at something other than fighting. We'll find something else you can do."

Wolf ruffled his hair with a fist, making it even messier than usual. "That isn't why I'm telling you this," he said, his tone calmer now, but still discouraged. "It won't even matter once we get to Paris, but it seemed important for you to know that I don't enjoy it. I hate losing control like that. I've always hated it."

The fight flashed through Scarlet's memories. How Wolf had released the other fighter so quickly. How he'd hurled himself off the stage as if trying to outrun himself.

She gulped. "Were you ever the . . . the omega?"

A flash of insult passed over his face. "Of course not."

Scarlet quirked an eyebrow, and Wolf seemed to recognize the arrogance in his tone a moment too late. Evidently, the craving for status hadn't left him yet.

"No," he said, softer now. "I made sure that I was never the omega." Standing, he marched again to the window and peered out at rolling vineyard hills.

Scarlet pursed her lips, feeling something akin to guilt. It was easy to forget the risk Wolf was taking when all she could think of was getting her grandma back. Sure, Wolf may have gotten out of the gang, but now he was going right back to them.

"Thank you for agreeing to help me," she said after a long silence. "No one else was exactly lining up to help."

He shrugged stiffly, and when it was clear he wasn't going to respond, Scarlet sighed and started clicking the channels again. She stopped on a newsfeed.

SEARCH CONTINUES FOR ESCAPED LUNAR
FUGITIVE LINH CINDER.

She jerked upward. "Escaped?"

Wolf turned and read the ticker before frowning at her. "You hadn't heard?"

"No. When?"

"A day or two ago."

Scarlet cupped her chin, entranced by the unfolding news. "I had no idea. How is that possible?"

The screen started to replay the footage from the ball.

"They say someone helped her. A government employee." Wolf pressed a hand against the windowsill. "It makes one wonder what they would do in such a situation. If a Lunar needed help and you had the ability to help them, even though it would put you and your family at risk, would you do it?"

Scarlet frowned, barely listening. "I wouldn't risk my family for anyone."

Wolf dropped his gaze to the cheap carpet. "Your family? Or your grandmother?"

Rage came to her like a spigot turned to full, remembering her father. How he'd come to her farm wearing that transmitter. How he'd torn her hangar apart.

"Grand-mère's the only family I have left." Rubbing her clammy palms on her pants, Scarlet stood. "I could use an espresso."

She hesitated, not sure what she wanted his response to be when she asked, "Do you want to come to the dining car with me?"

His gaze slipped past her shoulder, to the door, looking torn.

Scarlet met his indecision with a smile, both teasing and friendly. Perhaps a little flirtatious. "It has been almost a full two hours since you ate. You must be famished."

Something flickered across Wolf's face, something bordering on panic. "No, thank you," he said quickly. "I'll stay here."

"Oh." The brief rush of her pulse slipped away. "All right. I'll be back soon."

As she was shutting the door behind her, she saw Wolf push his hand roughly through his hair with a relieved sigh—like he'd narrowly avoided a trap.

Seventeen

THE TRAIN'S CORRIDOR WAS BUZZING WITH ACTIVITY.
Making her way to the dining car, Scarlet passed servant androids delivering boxed lunches, a woman in a stiff business suit talking sternly at her port, a waddling toddler curiously opening every door he passed.

Scarlet dodged them all, through half a dozen identical cars, past the myriad passengers who were on their way to normal jobs, normal vacations, normal shopping trips, perhaps even going back to normal homes. Her emotions gradually started to fall away from her—her irritation with the media for demonizing a sixteen-year-old girl, only to discover that girl had escaped from prison and was still on the loose. Her sympathy for Wolf's violent childhood, followed by the unexpected rejection when he chose not to come with her. The fluctuating terror over her grandmother and what could be happening to her now, while the train careened too slowly through the countryside, tempered only by the knowledge that at least she was on her way. At least she was getting closer.

Her mind still spinning like a kaleidoscope, she was glad to find the dining car relatively empty. A bored-looking bartender stood inside a circular bar, watching a netscreen talk show that Scarlet had never liked. Two women were drinking mimosas at a small table. A young man was sitting with his legs up in a booth, tapping furiously on his port. Four androids loitered beside the wall, waiting to make deliveries out to the private cars.

Scarlet sat down at the bar, setting her port beside a glass of green olives.

"What will you have?" asked the bartender, still focused on the interview between the host and a washed-up action star.

"Espresso, one sugar, please."

She settled her chin on her palm as he punched her order into the dispenser. Sliding her finger across the portscreen, she typed,

THE ORDER OF THE PACK

A listing of music bands and netgroups spilled down the page, all calling themselves wolf packs and secret societies.

LOYAL SOLDIER TO THE ORDER OF THE PACK

Zero hits.

THE WOLVES

She knew as soon as she'd entered it that the term was far too broad. She quickly amended it to THE WOLVES GANG.

Then, when 20,400 hits blinked back up at her, she added PARIS.

One music band who had toured in Paris two summers ago.

WOLF STREET GANG. WOLF VIGILANTES. SADISTIC KIDNAPPERS PARADING AS RIGHTEOUS LUPINE WANNABES.

Nothing. Nothing. Nothing.

Frustrated, she tucked her hair into her hood. Her espresso had appeared in front of her without her notice and she brought the small cup to her mouth, blowing away the steam before taking a sip.

Surely if this Order of the Pack had been around long enough to recruit 962 members, there must be some record of them. Crimes, trials, murders, general mayhem against society. She strained to think of another search term, wishing she would have questioned Wolf more.

"That's quite the specific search."

She swiveled her head toward the man seated two stools away, who she hadn't heard sit down. He was giving her a teasing, droopy-eyed smile that hinted at a dimple in one cheek. He struck her as vaguely familiar, which startled her until she realized she'd only seen him an hour ago on the station's platform at Toulouse.

"I'm looking for something very specific," she said.

"I should say. 'Righteous Lupine Wannabes'—I can't even begin to imagine what that entails."

The bartender frowned at them. "What'll you have?"

The stranger swiveled his gaze. "Chocolate milk, please."

Scarlet chuckled as the bartender, unimpressed, took down an empty glass. "Would not have been my first guess."

"No? What would you have guessed?"

She scrutinized him. He couldn't have been much older than she was and, though not classically handsome, with that much confidence he undoubtedly had never had much trouble with women. His build was stocky but muscular, his hair combed neatly back. There was a keenness in the way he carried himself, a certainty that bordered on arrogance. "Cognac," she said. "It was always my father's favorite."

"I'm afraid I've never tried it." The dimple deepened as a tall glass of frothing chocolate milk was set in front of him.

Scarlet clicked off her port and picked up her espresso. The scent seemed suddenly too strong, too bitter. "That actually looks pretty good."

"Surprisingly high in protein," he said, taking a drink.

Scarlet took another sip from her cup and found that her taste buds disapproved. She set it back down on the saucer. "If you were a gentleman, you would offer to buy me one as well."

"If you were a lady, you would have waited for me to make the offer."

Scarlet smirked, but the man was already beckoning to the bartender and ordering a second chocolate milk.

"I'm Ran, by the way."

"Scarlet."

"Like your hair?"

"Oh, wow, I'd never heard that one before."

The bartender set the new drink on the bar, then turned away and upped the volume on the screen.

"And where are you traveling to, Mademoiselle Scarlet?"

Paris.

The word clunked into her head, filling up her thoughts with its weight. Her attention danced to the netscreen on the wall, checking the time, calculating their distance, their arrival.

"Paris." She took a long drink. It wasn't fresh like the milk she was used to, but the thick sweetness was a rare treat. "I'm going to visit my grandmother."

"That so? I'm heading to Paris too."

Scarlet nodded vaguely, suddenly wanting the conversation to be over. Sipping at the thick beverage, it occurred to her that she'd gotten it through manipulation, subconscious as it may have been. She wasn't interested in this man, had no curiosity about why he was going to Paris or if she would ever see him again after this moment. She had only needed to prove that she could garner *his* interest, and now she was annoyed that she'd captured it so easily.

It was just like something her father would do, and that realization turned her stomach. Made her want to shove the chocolate milk away.

"Are you traveling alone?"

She tilted her head toward him and smiled apologetically. "No. In fact, I should be getting back to him." She emphasized *him* more than was necessary, but he didn't flinch.

"Of course," he said.

They finished their drinks at the same time and Scarlet swished her wrist over the scanner on the bar before the stranger could object, paying for her own.

"Bartender," she said, sliding off the stool. "Do you have orders to go? Some sandwiches or anything?"

The bartender jerked his thumb at the screens inset into the bar. "Menus."

Scarlet frowned. "Never mind, I'll order something back at the room."

The bartender showed no sign of having heard her.

"It was nice to meet you, Ran."

He propped an elbow on the counter, twisting his stool toward her. "Perhaps our paths will cross again. In Paris."

Hair prickled on her neck as he settled his chin onto his palm. She noticed with a jolt of disgust that each of his fingernails had been filed into a sharp, perfect point.

"Perhaps," she said, her tone suffused with politeness.

The instinctual alarm hung with her for two whole cars as she made her way back through the train, a warning buzzing in the air. She tried to shake it off. This was her own nerves playing tricks on her, paranoia finally catching up to her after what had happened to her grandmother, and her father. It was amazing she could carry on a conversation at all with all the panic that was residing just beneath the surface of her skin.

He'd been polite. He'd been a gentleman. Maybe talon-like nails were a growing trend in the city.

Just as she'd determined that nothing about Ran had been deserving of the sudden, ardent distrust, she remembered.

She had seen him on the platform in Toulouse, stepping off the escalator in his ratty jeans and no luggage, when Wolf had become so on edge. When it seemed like Wolf had heard something, or recognized someone.

A coincidence?

The speaker overhead crackled. Scarlet barely heard it over the noise of the corridor, until the repeated words gradually silenced the chatter around her. "—experiencing a temporary delay. All passengers are to return to their private quarters immediately and stay clear of the corridors until further notice is given. This is not a test. We are experiencing a temporary delay . . ."

Eighteen

SCARLET SHUT THE DOOR BEHIND HER, RELIEVED THAT WOLF
was still there. Pacing. He swiveled toward her.

"I just heard the announcement," she said. "Do you know
what's going on?"

"No. I wondered if you might."

She wrapped her fingers around the portscreen in her
pocket. "Some sort of delay. It seems odd to clear the corridors,
though."

He didn't respond. His scowl became fierce, almost angry.
"You smell . . ."

When he didn't continue, an offended laugh erupted out of
her. "I smell?"

Wolf roughly shook his head, hair whipping across his
creased brow. "Not like that. Who did you talk to out there?"

Frowning, she fell back against the door. If Ran had been
wearing cologne, it had been too faint for her to pick up.

"Why?" she snapped, annoyed as much with his accusation

as with the unexpected sting of guilt it caused. "Is it any of your business?"

His jaw tensed. "No, that's not what I—" He paused, eyes flickering past her.

A knock startled Scarlet away from the wall. She turned and yanked open the door.

An android rolled into the room, scanner at the end of its wiry arm. "We are performing an identity check for the safety of all passengers. Please show your ID for scanning."

Scarlet raised her hand on instinct. She didn't think to question the order until a red light passed over her skin, beeped, and the android turned to Wolf.

"What's going on?" she said. "We scanned our tickets when we boarded."

Another beep. "You are not to leave this room until further instructions are given."

"That wasn't an answer," said Scarlet.

A panel opened in the android's torso and a third limb reached out to greet them, this one fitted with a slender syringe. "I must now conduct a mandatory blood check. Please extend your right arm."

Scarlet gawked down at the gleaming needle. "You're running blood tests? That's ridiculous. We're just going to Paris."

"Please extend your right arm," the android repeated, "or I will be forced to report you for failure to comply with maglev rail safety regulations. Your tickets will be considered invalid and you will be escorted off the train at the next station."

Scarlet bristled and glanced at Wolf, but he had eyes only for the syringe. For a moment Scarlet thought he was going to smash in the robot's sensor, before he reluctantly stretched out his arm. Wolf's expression became distant while the needle punctured his skin.

The moment the android had withdrawn a blood sample and retracted the skeletal limb, Wolf backed away and folded his arm against his chest.

A fear of needles? Scarlet squinted at him, holding out her own elbow as the android produced another syringe. She couldn't imagine it hurt any more than that tattoo had.

Scowling, she watched as the syringe filled with her own blood. "What exactly are you looking for?" she said as the android finished and both syringes disappeared into its body.

"Initiating blood scan," said the android, followed by a clatter of humming and beeps. Wolf had just tucked his arm against his side when the android pronounced, "Scan complete. Please shut the door and remain in this room until further instructions are given."

"You already said that," Scarlet said to the android's back as it retreated into the hall.

Pressing a thumb against the small puncture wound, Scarlet slammed the door shut with her foot. "What was that all about? I have half a mind to comm the maglev customer service and issue a complaint."

Turning, she found Wolf already at the window—his steps had been soundless. "We're slowing down."

It was a silent, agonizing moment before Scarlet felt it too.

Through the window, she could see a thick canopy of forest choking off the midday sun. There were no roads, no buildings. They weren't stopping at a station.

She opened her mouth, but Wolf's expression stopped her question before it could form. "Do you hear that?"

Scarlet tugged the zipper of her hoodie down to let air on her neck, and listened. The hum of the magnets. The whistle of air passing through an open window in the next cabin. The rattle of luggage.

Wailing. So distant it sounded like a fading nightmare.

Cold goose bumps grazed her arms. "What's going on out there?"

The wall speaker clattered. "Passengers, this is your conductor speaking. There has been a medical emergency aboard the train. We will be experiencing a delay while we wait for medical authorities. We ask that all passengers remain in their private quarters and comply with any requests from the staff androids. Thank you for your patience."

The speaker fell silent, leaving Scarlet and Wolf staring at each other.

Scarlet's throat constricted.

A blood test. Crying. A delay.

"The plague."

Wolf said nothing.

"They'll put the whole train on lockdown," she said. "We'll all be quarantined."

Out in the hall, doors were slamming, neighbors yelling questions and speculations at each other, ignoring the conductor's request to stay in their own rooms. The android must have moved on to the next car.

Scarlet heard the rushed words: *letumosis outbreak*, posed as a question, a fear.

"No." She spat the word like a bullet. "They can't keep us here. My grandma—!" Her voice hitched, a tide of panic overwhelming her.

Someone down the hall pounded erratically on a door. The distant wailing grew louder.

"Get your things," said Wolf.

She and Wolf moved at the same time. She threw her portscreen into her pack while Wolf crossed to the window and flung it open. The ground raced beneath them. Beyond the tracks, a dense forest stretched out, dissolving into shadows.

Scarlet checked the pistol in her waistband. "Are we jumping?"

"Yes. But they might be expecting it, so we have to do it before the train slows too much. They're probably prepping enforcement androids right now to round up runaways."

Scarlet nodded. "If it is letumosis, we've probably already become a quarantine."

Wolf thrust his head out the window, looking both ways down the length of the train. "Now's our best chance."

Pulling inside, he heaved the bag onto one shoulder. Scarlet peered down at the ground fleeing beneath them, dizzied by a moment of vertigo. It was impossible to focus on any one spot as the speckled sun flashed against the trees. "Well. This seems dangerous."

"We'll be fine."

She peered up at him, for a moment expecting to meet that crazed madman again, but his expression was stone-cold and clinical. He was focused hard on the landscape that whizzed by them. "They're braking," he said. "We'll start slowing down faster now." Again, it was a few seconds before Scarlet sensed it too, the subtle shift of speed, the way they were decelerating fast, no longer just coasting to a steady stop.

Wolf inclined his head. "Climb onto my back."

"I can jump myself."

"*Scarlet.*"

She met his eyes. His youthful curiosity from before was gone, replaced with a sternness she hadn't expected.

"What? It'll be just like jumping off the barn into a haystack. I've done that a hundred times."

"A haystack? Honestly, Scarlet, it'll be nothing like that."

Before she could argue, before she could cement her defiance, he bent over her and scooped her into both arms.

She gasped and had just enough time to open her mouth, ready to demand he put her down, before Wolf was on the windowsill, the wind whipping Scarlet's curls against her neck.

He jumped. Scarlet yelped and grabbed on to him, her stomach somersaulting, and then the shock of landing jogged up her spine.

She dug her fingers into his shoulders. Every limb trembled.

Wolf had landed in a clearing eight steps beyond the tracks. He staggered into the tree line and hunkered into the shadows.

"All right?" he asked.

"Just like"—she caught her breath—"a haystack."

A laugh reverberated through his chest, into her, and before she was ready Wolf settled her feet onto a patch of squishy moss. She scrambled out of his hold, caught her balance, then punched him squarely in the arm. "Never do that again."

He looked almost pleased with himself, before he tilted his head toward the forest. "We should move farther in, in case someone saw us."

She listened to the train zipping by, her pulse heavy and erratic, and followed Wolf into the trees. They hadn't gone a dozen steps when the thrumming of the train disappeared, fading away down the tracks.

Scarlet dug her port out of the bag on Wolf's shoulder and checked their location.

"Great. The nearest town is twenty miles east of here. It's out of our way, but maybe someone can give us a ride to the next maglev station."

"Because we seem so trustworthy?"

Scarlet peered up at him, noting the pale, scattered scars and the faded black eye. "What's your idea?"

"We should stay on the tracks. Another train will be by eventually."

"And *they'll* give us a lift?"

"Sure."

This time, she was sure she caught mischief in his eye as he started back down the rails. But they hadn't gone a dozen steps when he halted mid-step.

"What—"

Wolf spun on her, clamping one hand behind her head, the other firmly over her mouth.

Tensing, Scarlet moved to shove him away, but something gave her pause. He was staring off into the forest, brow furrowed. Tilting his nose up, he sniffed the air.

When he was sure she wouldn't make a sound, he snatched his hands away as if something had stung him. Scarlet stumbled back, surprised by the sudden release.

They lingered, still and silent, Scarlet straining to listen for what had Wolf on edge. Slowly reaching behind her, she pulled the gun from her waistband. The click as she released the safety echoed off the trees.

Off in the woods, a wolf howled. The lonely cry sent a shiver down Scarlet's spine.

Wolf didn't seem surprised.

Then, behind them, another howl, this one farther away. Then another to the north.

Silence crept around them as the howls faded longingly into the air.

"Friends of yours?" Scarlet asked.

Clarity returned to Wolf's expression and he glanced at her, then down at the gun. It struck her as odd that he could be startled by it, when the howls had garnered no reaction at all.

"They won't bother us," he said finally, turning and heading down the tracks.

With a snort, Scarlet trotted after him. "Well, isn't that a re-lief. We're stranded in wild wolf territory, but as long as you say they're not going to bother us..." She clicked the gun's safety back on and was tucking it back in her waistband when Wolf's gesture gave her pause.

"They won't bother us," he said again, almost smiling. "But you might want to keep that out anyway, just in case."

Nineteen

"WHAT IS ALL THIS JUNK?" CINDER LOCKED HER JAW, straining to push a plastic crate that was almost as tall as she was.

Thorne grunted beside her. "It's—not—junk." The tendons in his neck bulged as the crate collided with the cargo bay wall.

Thorne tossed his arms over the top with a groan and Cinder collapsed against it. Her shoulders ached, as tense as the metal that made up her left leg, and her arms felt like they were about to fall off. But when she allowed herself to look around the cargo bay, a sense of accomplishment settled around her.

All the crates had been slid to the walls, clearing an actual path from the cockpit to the living quarters. The smaller, lighter ones had been stacked on top of one another and some were left out as makeshift furniture in front of the main netscreen.

It bordered on cozy.

The next job would be to actually unpack the crates—the ones that were worth unpacking—but that would be a job for another day. "No, really," she said when she'd found her breath. "What is all this?"

Thorne slid down beside her and wiped his brow with his sleeve. "I don't know," he said, eyeing the stamped labels on the side of the nearest crate: an unhelpful code. "Supplies. Food. I think there are some guns in one of them. And I know I had a few sculptures from this really collectible second-era artist—I was going to make a fortune off of them, but I got arrested before I had a chance." He sighed.

Cinder squinted at him. Sure that the sculptures were stolen, she found it difficult to muster any sympathy. "Shame," she muttered, thumping her head back against the crate.

Thorne pointed at something on the far wall, his forearm jutting beneath Cinder's nose. "What's that?"

She followed his gesture, frowned, and with a cranky moan pushed herself back to her feet. The corner of a metal frame could be seen behind a tall stack of crates they'd left against the wall. "A door." She drew up the ship's blueprint on her retina display. "The medbay?"

Realization brightened Thorne's face. "Oh, right. This ship does have one of those."

Cinder settled her fists on her hips. "You covered up the *medbay*?"

Thorne pulled himself up. "Never needed it."

"Don't you think it might be good to have access to, just in case?"

Thorne shrugged. "We'll see."

Rolling her eyes, Cinder reached for the uppermost crate and hauled it down onto the floor, already disrupting their hard-won pathway. "How can we be sure there's nothing in these boxes that can be tracked?"

"What do you think I am, an amateur? Nothing entered this ship without being thoroughly inspected. Otherwise the Republic would have reclaimed it all a long time ago rather than let it idle in that warehouse."

"There may not be any trackers," said Iko, making Cinder and Thorne both jump. They still weren't used to their invisible, omnipresent companion. "But we can still be detected on radar. I'm doing my best to keep us out of the path of any satellites or ships, but it's surprisingly crowded up here."

Thorne unrolled his sleeves. "And it's next to impossible to re-enter Earth's atmosphere without detection. That's how they nabbed me last time."

"I thought there was a trick to it," said Cinder. "I'm sure I heard once about a way people could sneak into Earth's atmosphere without notice. Where did I hear that?"

"News to me. I got pretty good at sweet-talking my way into public hangars, but I don't think that's going to work with such a high-profile convict on the loose."

Having found an old rubber band in the galley, Cinder fished it from her pocket and tossed her hair up in a ponytail. Her brain ticked through her memories until, with a snap, it came to her. Dr. Erland had told her that there were more Lunars on Earth than people suspected, and that they had a way of getting to Earth without the government taking notice.

"Lunars know how to cloak their spacecrafts."

"Huh?"

She pulled herself from the daze, blinking at Thorne. "Lunars can cloak their spacecrafts. Keep Earthen radars from picking up on them. That's how so many are able to make it to Earth, if they manage to get away from Luna in the first place."

"That's terrifying," said Iko, who had acknowledged the truth of Cinder's race much as she'd acknowledged Thorne's convict status: with loyalty and acceptance, but without changing her opinion that Lunars and convicts remained untrustworthy and unredeemable as a general rule.

Cinder had not yet figured out how to tell her that she also happened to be the missing Princess Selene.

"I know it is," said Cinder, "but it would be awfully convenient if I knew how they did it."

"Do you think it's with their"—Thorne rolled his wrist toward her—"crazy Lunar magic stuff?"

"Bioelectricity," she said, quoting Dr. Erland. "Calling it magic only empowers them."

"Whatever."

"I don't know. It could be some special technology they install on their ships."

"Optimistically hoping it's magic, maybe you should start practicing?"

Cinder bit the inside of her cheek. Start practicing *what*?

"I guess I can try." Turning her attention back to the crate, she pulled up the lid and was met with a box of packing chips. She stuffed her metal hand into it and emerged with a skinny wooden doll bedecked in feathers and painted with six eyes. "What *is* this?"

"Venezuelan dream doll."

"It's hideous."

"It's worth about twelve thousand univs."

Heart skipping, Cinder lowered the doll back into the protective packaging. "You don't think you might have something useful in all of these? Like, I don't know, a fully charged power cell?"

"Doubtful," said Thorne. "How much longer will ours hold out?"

Iko chimed, "Approximately thirty-seven hours."

Thorne gave Cinder a thumbs-up. "Plenty of time to learn a new Lunar trick, right?"

Cinder shut the crate's lid and slid it back against the others, trying not to show panic at having to use her new gift for *anything*, much less something as huge as disguising a cargo ship.

"In the meantime, I'll do a little research, try to determine the best place for us to land. Not the Commonwealth, obviously. I hear Fiji's nice this time of year."

"Or Los Angeles!" Iko practically sang. "They have a huge escort-droid outlet store there. I wouldn't mind having an escort-droid body. Some of the newer models come with color-changing fiber-optic hair."

Cinder slumped onto the floor again and scratched at her wrist—a tic that was becoming awkward now that she had no gloves to fiddle with. "We're not landing a stolen American ship in the American Republic," she said, fixing her attention on the netscreen, where her own prison picture hovered in the corner. She was so sick of that picture.

"Do you have any suggestions?" said Thorne.

Africa.

She heard herself saying it, but nothing came out.

That's where she was supposed to go. To meet Dr. Erland, so that he could tell her what to do next. He had plans for her. Plans to make her a hero, a savior, a princess. Plans to overthrow Levana and instate Cinder as the true queen.

Her right hand started to shake. Dr. Erland had set up the cyborg draft and treated dozens, perhaps hundreds of cyborgs like throwaways, all for the sake of finding *her.* And then, when he found her, he kept the secret of her identity until he had no other choice but to tell her, all the while planning out the rest of her life. He had made his need for revenge the highest priority.

But what the doctor hadn't considered was that Cinder had no desire to be queen. She didn't want to be a princess or an heir to anything. All her life—at least, all the life she could remember—all she'd ever wanted was freedom. And now, for the first time, she had it, however tenuous it was. There was no one telling her what to do. No one to judge or criticize.

But if she went to Dr. Erland, she would lose all that. He would expect her to reclaim her rightful place as the queen of Luna, and that struck her as the most binding shackles of all.

Cinder gripped her shaking hand with the steady cyborg

one. She was tired of everyone deciding her life for her. She was ready to figure out who she really was—not what anyone else told her to be.

"Uh . . . Cinder?"

"Europe." She pressed her back into the crate, forcing herself to sit straight, to feign certainty. "We're going to Europe."

A brief silence. "Any reason in particular?"

She met his gaze and pondered a long moment, before choosing her words. "Do you believe in the Lunar heir?"

Thorne propped his chin on both palms. "Of course."

"No, I mean, do you believe she's still alive?"

He peered at her as if she were being cute. "Because it was so vague the first time. Yes, of course I think she's alive."

Cinder drew back. "You do?"

"Sure. I know some people think it's all conspiracy theories, but I've heard that Queen Levana was really paranoid for months after that fire, when she should have been ecstatic because she was finally queen, right? It's like she knew the princess had gotten away."

"Yeah, but . . . those could only be stories," Cinder said, not knowing why she was trying to dissuade him. Perhaps because she'd never believed any of it, until she'd known the truth.

He shrugged. "What does this have to do with Europe?"

Cinder shifted to face him more fully, crisscrossing her legs. "There's a woman who lives there, or at least, she used to live there. She used to be in their military. Her name is Michelle Benoit, and I think she might be connected to the missing princess." She took in a slow breath, hoping she hadn't said anything that could give her secret away.

"Where did you hear this?"

"An android told me. A royal android."

"Oh! Kai's android?" Iko said, excitedly changing the screen to one of Kai's fan pages.

Cinder sighed. "Yes, *His Majesty's* android."

Unbeknownst to her at the time, her cyborg brain had recorded every word that the android, Nainsi, had spoken, as if it had known that Cinder would someday need to draw on this information again.

According to Nainsi's research, a Lunar doctor named Logan Tanner had brought Cinder to Earth when she was still a child, after Levana's murder attempt had failed. He'd eventually been incarcerated in a psychiatric hospital and committed suicide, but not before passing her off to someone else. Nainsi had thought that someone else was an ex–military pilot from the European Federation.

Wing Commander Michelle Benoit.

"A royal android," Thorne said, showing the first sign of speculation. "And how did it get this information?"

"That, I have no idea. But I want to find this Michelle Benoit and see if it was right."

And hope that Michelle Benoit had some answers that Dr. Erland didn't. Perhaps she could tell Cinder about her history, about those eleven long years lost to her memory, about her surgery and the surgeons and Linh Garan's invention that had kept Cinder from using her Lunar gift until Dr. Erland had disabled it.

Perhaps she had her own ideas about what Cinder should do next. Ideas that left her some choices for the rest of her life.

"I'm in."

She started. "You are?"

"Sure. This is the biggest unsolved mystery of the third era. There's got to be someone out there offering a reward for finding this princess, right?"

"Yeah, Queen Levana."

Thorne tilted toward her, nudging her with his elbow. "In that case, we already have something in common with the princess, don't we?" He winked, setting Cinder's nerves on edge. "I just hope she's cute."

"Could you at least try to focus on the important things?"

"That would be important." Thorne pulled himself up with a groan, still sore from all the rearranging. "Hungry? I think there's a can of beans in there calling my name."

"No, I'm fine. Thank you."

When he had gone, Cinder hefted herself up onto the nearest crate and rolled out her shoulders. The news was still broadcasting on the screen, muted. A ticker read, "*Hunt continues for Lunar fugitive Linh Cinder and crown traitor Dmitri Erland.*"

Her throat constricted—crown traitor?

She shouldn't have been surprised. How long had she expected it to take them to figure out who had helped her escape?

Cinder sank onto her back, feet dangling off the crate, and

stared at the maze of pipes and bundled wires that cluttered the ship's rafters. Was she making a mistake by going to Europe? It was a draw she didn't think she could resist. Not only because of what Nainsi had said, but because of Cinder's own jumbled memories too. She'd always known that she'd been adopted in Europe and she had the faintest recollection of it. Only drug-muddled memories that she'd always thought might be part dream. A barn. A snow-covered field. A gray sky that never ended. And then a long, long train ride bringing her to New Beijing and her new family.

She felt compelled to go there now. To figure out where she had been during all those lost years and who had taken care of her, who else knew her biggest secret.

But what if she was only avoiding the inevitable? What if this was just a distraction to keep her from going to Dr. Erland and accepting her fate? At least the doctor could teach her how to be Lunar. How to protect herself from Queen Levana.

She didn't even know how to use her glamour. Not properly anyway.

Pursing her lip, she held her cyborg hand up over her face. Its metal plating shone almost mirror-like beneath the ship's dim lights. It was so pristine, so well crafted—it did not seem like *her* hand. Not yet.

Tilting her head, Cinder held up her other, human hand beside it and tried to imagine what it would be like to be fully human. Two limbs made of skin and tissue and bones. Blood pumping in faintly blue veins beneath the surface. All ten fingernails.

An electric current traipsed down her nerves and her cyborg hand began to morph in her vision. Little wrinkles appeared in her knuckles. Tendons stretched beneath her skin. The edges softened. Warmed. Turned to flesh.

She was looking at two hands, two human hands. Small and dainty with perfectly sculpted fingers and delicate, rounded nails. She flexed the fingers of her left hand, forming a fist, then stretched them out again.

An almost giddy laugh fell out of her. She was doing it. She was using her glamour.

She did not need gloves anymore. She could convince everyone that *this* was real.

No one would ever know she was cyborg again.

The realization was stark and sudden and overwhelming.

And then—too soon—an orange light flickered in the corner of her vision, her brain warning her that what she was seeing was a lie. That this was not real, would never be real.

She sat up with a gasp and squeezed her eyes shut before her retina scanner could start to pick up on all the little inaccuracies and falsehoods like it had done with Levana's glamour when Cinder had begun to see through it. She was annoyed with herself—disgusted at how easily the desire had come to her.

This was how Levana did it. She kept a hold on her people by tricking both their eyes and their hearts. She ruled with fear, yes, but also with adoration. It would be easy to abuse a person when they never recognized it as abuse.

It was not so different from when she'd glamoured Thorne.

She'd owned his mind without even trying to and he'd jumped at the chance to do her bidding.

She sat shivering for a while, listening to Thorne banging around in the galley and humming to himself.

If this was her chance to decide who she was, who she wanted to be, then the first decision was an easy one.

She would never be like Queen Levana.

Twenty

THE TRACK'S MAGNETS HAD GONE SILENT, REPLACED WITH the sounds of their own footsteps in the brush and the caws of migrating birds. Only a suggestion of sun filtered down through the thick tree cover, and the forest smelled of tree sap and the coming of autumn.

Time seemed to stretch on for eons, although Scarlet's portscreen indicated that not even an hour had passed when they came across the stopped train. Scarlet first noticed sounds that didn't belong to the forest—the crunching of treads on dirt and gravel as dozens of androids circled the perimeter.

Wolf abandoned the tracks, pushing through the brush and leading them into the security of the woods. Scarlet tucked away the port so she could use both hands to climb fallen logs and keep twigs and spiderwebs out of her hair. After a while, she tugged her hood over her head, lessening her vision but feeling better protected from the things that reached and jabbed at her.

They climbed up an embankment, using the roots of a pine

tree that looked about to topple over onto the tracks. On higher ground, Scarlet could see the dappled glint of sunlight off the train's metal roof. The occasional passenger cast a shadow against the windows. Scarlet could not imagine being among them. Surely everyone knew what the "medical emergency" was by now. How long would it take to test every passenger for the plague and determine who could be let go? How long could they keep healthy people quarantined?

Or would they let them go at all?

To prevent escapees, a small army of androids patrolled around the train, their yellow sensors shuffling over the windows and doors, occasionally darting toward the forest. Though Scarlet didn't think they could see her so high above the tracks, she nevertheless crept back from the embankment and slowly, slowly unzipped her hoodie. Wolf glanced back just as she was pulling her arms from the sleeves, glad she was wearing a much more camouflage-worthy black tank top underneath. She cinched the hoodie tight around her waist.

Better? she mouthed, but Wolf only glanced away.

"They'll have noticed we're missing," he whispered.

The nearest android spun toward them and Scarlet ducked, worried that even her hair could draw attention.

When the android rolled away again, Wolf slinked forward, holding back a tree branch for Scarlet to pass beneath.

They moved at a tractor's pace, crouched low to keep out of sight. It seemed every step Scarlet took sent another creature scurrying away for cover—a squirrel, a tiny swallow—and she feared that the androids would be able to track them by the disturbed wildlife alone, but no warning alarm came from the tracks.

They stopped only once, when a streak of blue light danced on the trunks over their heads. Scarlet followed Wolf's lead and pressed herself nearly to the ground, listening to the pounding of her heart, the rush of adrenaline in her ears.

With a start, she felt Wolf's warm fingers pressing into her back. They were steady against her, calming, as she watched the android's light scan back and forth, darting into the forest canopy. She risked the slightest tilt of her head until she could see Wolf beside her, immobile, every muscle taut—except the fingers of his other hand, which were tapping, tapping, tapping against a large rock, expelling the nervous energy that had nowhere else to go.

She watched the fingers, half mesmerized, and didn't realize that the light had flickered away until the pressure of Wolf's touch lifted from her back.

They prowled on.

Soon the train was behind them, the noise of lost civilization fading in the chatter of crickets and toads. When Wolf seemed satisfied they weren't being followed, he led them out of the forest and back down to the tracks.

Despite the growing distance between them and the train, neither spoke.

Just as the sun was kissing the horizon, almost blindingly bright in those rare moments when it could be glimpsed through the trees, Wolf stopped and turned back. Scarlet halted a few steps ahead of him and followed his gaze, but she saw nothing but overgrown sticker bushes and long shadows that had no end.

Her ears were perked, listening for another howl, but she couldn't pick up anything but bird chatter and, overhead, the squeaks of a colony of bats. "More wolves?" she finally asked.

A long silence, followed by a terse nod. "More wolves."

It wasn't until he started walking again that Scarlet released a captured breath. They'd been walking for hours without sign of another train, a cross-section of tracks, or civilization. On one hand, it was beautiful here—the fresh air, the wildflowers, the critters that came to the edge of the brush to watch Scarlet and Wolf before scurrying back into the ferns.

But on the other hand, her feet and back were sore, her stomach was growling, and now Wolf was telling her that the less loveable creatures of the forest were prowling nearby.

A chill rushed up her arms. Untying her hoodie from her waist, she tugged it on and yanked the zipper up to her neck. Pulling out her portscreen, she deflated to see that they'd gone a mere eighteen miles; they had another thirty to go before they reached the nearest station.

"There's a junction coming up, in about a half mile."

"Good," said Wolf. "Whatever trains were scheduled to come through on these tracks won't be making it through any time soon. We should start seeing some trains after the junction."

"And when this train comes," she said, "how do you plan on getting us onto it?"

"Same way we got off the last one." He sent a sly grin toward her. "Like jumping off a barn, was it?"

She glared. "The comparison doesn't work as well for jumping back *onto* a train."

His response was that same teasing smile, and Scarlet turned away, thinking that maybe she didn't want to know what his plan was, so long as he had one. A late-flowering shrub trembled just off the path and Scarlet's heart thumped—until a harmless pine marten crawled out and disappeared into the trees.

She sighed, annoyed at her restlessness. "So," she said, disrupting Wolf in another backward glance. "Who would win in a fight—you or a pack of wolves?"

He frowned at her, all seriousness. "Depends," he said, slowly, like he was trying to figure out her motive for asking. "How big is the pack?"

"I don't know, what's normal? Six?"

"I could win against six," he said. "Any more than that and it could be a close call."

Scarlet smirked. "You're not in danger of low self-esteem, at least."

"What do you mean?"

"Nothing at all." She kicked a stone from their path. "How about you and . . . a lion?"

"A cat? Don't insult me."

She laughed, the sound sharp and surprising. "How about a bear?"

"Why, do you see one out there?"

"Not yet, but I want to be prepared in case I have to rescue you."

The smile she'd been waiting for warmed his face, a glint of white teeth flashing. "I'm not sure. I've never had to fight a bear before." He cocked his head toward the east. "There's a lake that way, maybe a hundred yards. We should refill the water."

"Wait."

Wolf paused, glanced at her.

Scarlet's brow was creased as she inched toward him. "Do that again."

He took half a step back, eyes glinting with sudden nerves. "Do what?"

"Smile."

The order was met with the opposite response. Wolf shrank back, his jaw tense as if to be sure his lips stayed locked together.

Scarlet hesitated only a moment before reaching for him. He winced, but didn't move as she cupped his chin and gently pulled open his lips with her thumb. He took in a hissing breath, before touching his tongue to the point of his right tooth.

But they were not normal. They were almost fang-like, with sharp, elongated canines.

She realized, too slowly, they were like wolf teeth.

Wolf turned his face away, locking his jaw again. His whole body stayed tense, uncomfortable. She saw him gulp.

"Implants?"

He scratched the back of his neck, unable to look at her.

"That Order of the Pack sure takes this wolf thing seriously, don't they?" Finding her hand still hovering in midair, her fingers dangerously close to tilting Wolf's face back toward her, she let it fall and tucked it into her front pocket. Her heart was suddenly racing. "So are there any other oddities I should know about? A tail, perhaps?"

Finally, he met her gaze, flushed with insult until he found her smiling up at him.

"I'm joking," she said, offering an apologetic grin. "They're only teeth. At least they're not implanted on your scalp like that guy at the fights had."

It took a moment, but soon his embarrassment started to melt, his scowl softening around the edges. His lips turned up again, but it was not another true smile.

She nudged his foot with her toes. "All right, I'll accept that smile for now. You said you heard a river nearby?"

Seemingly grateful to be released from the conversation, Wolf ducked back from her. "A lake," he said. "I can smell it."

Scarlet squinted in the direction he'd gestured, seeing nothing but more trees, the same old trees. "Of course you can," she said, following as he pushed into the undergrowth.

And he was right, though it was more a pond than a lake—kept fresh by a creek that flowed in and out on the far side. The shore changed from grass to rocks before disappearing beneath the surface, and a cluster of beech trees hung their branches toward the water.

Rolling up her sleeves, Scarlet splashed some water on her face and slurped up big handfuls. She hadn't realized how thirsty she was until she found that she couldn't stop drinking it. Wolf busied himself dunking his hands and pulling his wet fingers through his hair, making it stand in each direction again as if it had gotten too tame during their trek.

Refreshed, Scarlet sat back on her heels and glanced across at Wolf. "I don't believe it."

He met her gaze.

"Your hands aren't twitching," she said, gesturing at the palm set loosely on his knee—it instantly flexed into a fist, his fingers uncomfortable beneath her scrutiny. "Maybe the forest is having a good effect on you."

Wolf seemed to consider this, his brow drawn as he topped off the water bottle and nestled it into the bag. "Maybe so," he said, then, "Is there any more food?"

"No. I didn't realize we'd be living off our own reserves." Scarlet laughed. "Now that you mention it—here I am thinking the fresh air must be working a miracle, when you're probably just suffering from low blood sugar. Come on, maybe we'll come across some wild berries or something."

She moved to stand when she heard quacking on the other side of the lake. Half a dozen ducks were making their way into the water, paddling out and dipping their heads beneath the surface.

Scarlet bit her lip. "Or . . . do you think you could catch one of those?"

As he shifted his attention to the ducks, a daring grin spread over his face.

He made it look easy, prowling up to the unsuspecting birds like a born predator. But if Scarlet was impressed, and perhaps she was, it was nothing compared to his awe as he watched her de-feather the dead fowl like a trained expert, pricking holes in its skin to allow for the outer layer of fat to drain out while it cooked.

The trickiest part was lighting a fire, but with a quick search on her portscreen and a clever use of the gunpowder in one of her gun's cartridges, Scarlet was soon mesmerized by the gray plumes of a small fire winding their way toward the forest canopy.

Wolf's attention was off in the woods as he stretched his long legs in front of him. "How long have you lived on the farm?" he asked, digging his heel into the dirt.

Scarlet settled her elbows over her knees and stared impatiently at the duck. "Since I was seven."

"Why did you leave Paris?"

She peered up at him, but his attention was caught on the tranquil water. "I was miserable there. After my mom left, my dad preferred to spend his time at the bar instead of with me. So I came to live with Grand-mère."

"And were you happier there?"

She shrugged. "It took some getting used to. I went from being a pretty spoiled city kid to getting up at dawn and being expected to finish my chores. I had my share of rebellions. But it wasn't the same . . . when I lived with my dad, I used to throw fits and tantrums, break things and make up stories and anything I could, just to get his attention. To get him to *care*. But I never did any of that with Grand-mère. We would sit in the garden on warm nights and just talk, and she would actually listen to what I said. She treated my opinions like they were valid, like I had something worthwhile to say." Her eyes fogged as she stared into the ashes beneath the flames. "Half the time we'd end up fighting with each other, because we both have such big opinions and are too stubborn to ever admit we're wrong about something, but there would always reach this point, every single time, when one of us would be yelling or just about ready to stomp away and slam the door, and then my grandma would just start laughing. And then of course I would start laughing. And she'd say that I was just like her." She gulped, tightening her arms around her knees. "She'd say that I was bound to have a tough life, because I was just like her." Scarlet rubbed her palms against her lashes, smearing away the tears before they could fall.

Wolf waited for her breaths to steady, before asking, "Was it always just the two of you?"

She nodded and when she was sure she'd stifled the tears, peeled her hands away. She sniffed and reached forward to flip the wings, their skin already blackened. "Yep, just the two of us. Grand-mère never married. Whoever my grandpa was, he's been out of the picture for a long time. She never really talked about it."

"And you didn't have any siblings? Or . . . adopted siblings? Wards?"

"Wards?" Scarlet swiped her sleeve across her nose and squinted at him. "No, it was just me." She added a branch to the fire. "How about you? Any siblings?"

Wolf curled his fingers into the rocks. "One. A younger brother."

Scarlet barely heard him over the crackle of the flames. She felt the weight of those three words. *A younger brother.* Wolf's expression showed neither affection nor coldness. He struck her as someone who would be protective of a younger sibling, but his face seemed hardened against that instinct.

"Where's he now?" she asked. "Does he still live with your parents?"

Leaning forward, Wolf adjusted the nearest duck leg. "No. Neither of us have spoken to our parents in a very long time."

Scarlet refocused on the cooking bird. "Not getting along with your parents. I guess that's something we have in common, then."

Wolf's grip locked around the drumstick, and only when a spark lanced out at him from the fire did he retract his arm. "I loved my parents," he said with the tenderness that had been missing when he'd mentioned his brother.

"Oh," she said dumbly. "Are they dead?"

She flinched at her crudeness, wishing just once she knew when to hold her tongue. But Wolf seemed more resigned than hurt as he picked through the rocks beside him. "I don't know. There are rules that come with being a member of the pack. One is that you'll cut all ties with people from your past, including your family. Especially your family."

She shook her head, baffled. "But if you had a good home life, why did you even join them in the first place?"

"I wasn't given a choice." He scratched behind his ear. "My brother wasn't given one either when they came for him, a few years after they took me, but that never seemed to bother him like it bothered me . . ." He trailed off, tossing a stone into the water. "It's complicated. And it doesn't matter anymore."

She frowned. It was unfathomable to her that you wouldn't have a choice to live that lifestyle, to leave your home and family, to join a violent gang—but before she could press him further, Wolf's attention swiveled back toward the train tracks and he leaped to his feet.

Scarlet turned, her heart landing in her throat.

The man from the dining car crept out of the shadows, quiet as a cat. He was still smiling, but it was nothing like that teasing, flirtatious grin she'd seen on him before.

It took her a slow, blank moment to recall his name. *Ran.*

Tipping his head back, Ran sniffed longingly at the air.

"Lovely," he said. "It seems I'm just in time for supper."

Twenty-One

"I'M SO SORRY IF I'VE INTERRUPTED YOU," RAN SAID, lingering beneath the forest canopy. "The scent was simply too enticing to pass up." His eyes were on Wolf as he said this and the twinkle behind them made Scarlet's toes curl in her shoes. Grasping the handle of her pistol, she dragged it in toward her hip.

"Of course," Wolf said after a long silence, his voice dark with warning. "We have plenty."

"Thank you, friend."

The man walked around the fire, passing by so close to Scarlet that she had to shrink away to keep her elbow from brushing his leg. The hairs stood up on her forearms.

Ran sprawled out opposite the fire from her, lounging as if the shore were his own private beach. After a moment, Wolf settled down between them. Not lounging.

"Wolf, this is Ran," said Scarlet, flushing from the awkwardness. "I met him on the train." Wishing she could restructure her emotions into nonchalance, she busied her hands with turning the duck pieces. Wolf inched closer to her, keeping himself as a block between her and Ran even though his face was tinged red from being so close to the flames.

"We had a lovely conversation in the dining car," said Ran. "About . . . what was it? 'Righteous lupine wannabes?'"

Scarlet glared at him. "A topic that never ceases to fascinate me," she said, tone even as she pulled the duck wings and legs out of the pit. "These are done."

She took a drumstick for herself and handed the other to Wolf. Ran didn't complain about the two bony wings, and Scarlet grimaced when he pulled the first apart, cartilage popping loudly at the joints.

"*Bon appétit,*" said Ran, picking at the meat with his eerily sharp nails, juices dripping down his arms.

Scarlet nibbled at the meat, while her two companions attacked their shares like animals, each keeping a wary eye on the other. She leaned forward. "So, Ran. How did you get away from the train?"

Ran tossed the clean bones of one wing into the lake. "I might ask you the same."

She pretended that her heart wasn't pulsating erratically. "We jumped."

"Risky," said Ran with a smirk.

Wolf bristled. The relaxation that had graced his features before was gone, replaced by the simmering temper Scarlet had seen at the street fight. The tapping fingers, the jostling foot.

"We're still a long way from Paris," said Ran, ignoring

Scarlet's question. "How unfortunate this turn of events has been. For the plague victim, of course."

Scarlet adjusted the breast meat. "It's awful. I'm grateful that Wolf was with me or I'd probably still be stuck there."

"Wolf," said Ran, enunciating it very carefully. "What an unusual name. Did your parents give it to you?"

"Does it matter?" said Wolf, tossing away his bone.

"I'm only making conversation."

"I'd prefer silence," Wolf said, a growl in his tone.

After a moment in which the distrust was palpable between them, Ran faked a gasp. "I'm so sorry," he said, picking the last bit of meat from the bones. "Have I stumbled upon a honeymoon? What a lucky man you are." His face taunted as he pushed the shredded meat into his mouth.

Wolf curled his fingers into the sand.

Squinting at the man through the haze of smoke and heat, Scarlet leaned forward. "Is it my imagination, or do you two *know* each other?"

Neither denied it. Wolf's focus was pinned to Ran, a twitch away from attacking him.

Suspicion sliced through Scarlet's thoughts and she gripped the gun. "Roll up your sleeve."

"I beg your pardon," said Ran, licking the juices as they dripped down his wrist.

Clambering to her feet, she leveled the barrel at him. "Now."

He hesitated only a moment. Expression unreadable, he reached for his left wrist and rolled the sleeve past his elbow. LSOP1126 was tattooed across the muscle of his forearm.

Anger boiled up inside Scarlet, every bit as hot as the coals beneath the fire. "Why didn't you tell me he was one of them?" she hissed without taking her focus or the gun off the tattoo.

For the first time, Ran's composure stiffened.

"I was hoping to determine why he's here and why he'd approached you on the train, without alarming you," said Wolf. "Scarlet, this is Ran Kesley, a Loyal Soldier to the Order of the Pack. Don't worry, he is only an omega."

Ran's nose wrinkled at what Scarlet could tell had been a low insult.

She swapped her attention between the two. "You could *smell* him on me," she said. "When I came back to the car, you knew—and you knew he was following us, all this time! How—?" She gaped at Wolf. The unnatural eyes. The uncanny senses. The teeth. The howls. The idea that he'd never had a tomato before. "Who are you people?"

Hurt flinched across Wolf's face, but it was Ran who spoke. "What exactly have you told her, brother?"

Wolf stood, forcing Ran to tilt back his head to hold his stare. "She knows I'm no longer a brother to you," he said. "And she knows that no one with that mark can be trusted."

Ran smiled at the irony. "Is that all?"

"I know you have my grandmother!" she yelled, startling a flock of swallows out of the nearest tree. Once their flapping had gone quiet, the woods settled into a thick hush, Scarlet's words still ringing. Her hand started to shake and she forced it to be still, though Ran continued to sit sprawled and at ease on the shore.

"You have my grandmother," she said, more slowly this time. "Don't you?"

"Well. Not *with* me . . ."

White sparks flashed across Scarlet's vision, and it took all her willpower not to pull the trigger and erase his smugness. "Why are you following us?" she said when the throbbing rage had become a manageable simmer.

She could see him calculating his response. Planting his palm on the rocky shore, Ran pushed himself to standing and brushed the dirt from his hands. "I've been sent to retrieve my brother," he said, as casually as if he'd been sent to the store for milk and bread. "Perhaps he did not tell you that he and I are part of an elite pack given a special assignment. That assignment has been canceled, and Master Jael wants us to return. *All* of us."

Scarlet's stomach tightened at Ran's meaningful look, but Wolf's expression was filled with more distrust and shadows than it had ever been.

"I'm not coming back," he said. "Jael no longer controls me."

Ran sniffed. "I doubt that. And you know as well as anyone that we don't allow our brothers to leave us." He rolled his sleeve down over the tattoo. "Though I confess, I haven't missed having one less alpha around."

The wind shifted, sending sparks from the fire into Scarlet's face and she stumbled back, blinking them away.

"Did you really think it wise to come here, without Jael to protect you?" said Wolf.

"I don't need Jael's protection."

"That would be a first."

With a snarl, Ran leaped forward, but Wolf danced out of his reach and retaliated with a fist aimed at Ran's jaw. Ran blocked, grasping Wolf's fist and using the momentum to spin Wolf around and lock his elbow around Wolf's neck. Wolf reached back, grasped Ran's shoulder, and flipped Ran over his head. Ran landed with a solid grunt, his feet smacking the water.

He was up again in a blink.

Scarlet's hand trembled, the gun dancing between the two, her pulse galloping. Ran was shaking with smothered rage, while Wolf was carved from rock, shrewd and calculating.

"I really do think it's time for you to return, brother," Ran said through clenched teeth.

Wolf shook his head, damp spikes of hair flopping onto his forehead. "You never were a match for me."

"I think you'll find me somewhat improved, *Alpha*."

Wolf snorted and Scarlet sensed he didn't believe Ran could ever be a genuine opponent. "Is this why you followed us? You saw your chance to improve your rank—to defeat me away from the pack?"

"I told you why I'm here. Jael sent for you. The assignment is canceled. When he finds out about this rebellion of yours—"

Wolf launched at Ran, knocking him onto his back. Ran's head landed in the water and Scarlet heard a sickening crunch as it collided with the hard stones beneath the surface. She screamed and ran toward them, digging her nails into Wolf's arm.

"No, stop! He might be able to tell us something!"

Wolf's sharp canines were bared as he pulled a fist back and landed a punch to Ran's face.

"WOLF! Stop it! My grandmother! He knows about—*Wolf, let him go!*"

When he didn't relent, Scarlet fired a warning shot into the air. The echo filled the clearing—but Wolf was unfazed. Ran's arms stopped flailing, slipped weakly down Wolf's forearms, and dropped into the water.

"You're going to kill him!" she shrieked. "Wolf! WOLF!"

As a last burst of bubbles rose up from Ran's mouth, Scarlet stepped back, let out a breath, and pulled the trigger again.

Wolf hissed and fell onto his side. He clasped his hand over his left arm, where blood was already seeping into the cloth of his sleeve. But it wasn't a deep wound. The bullet had barely grazed him.

He blinked up at Scarlet. "Did you just shoot me?"

"You didn't leave me much choice." With ringing ears, Scarlet fell to her knees and heaved Ran up by his shoulders, laying him back down at an awkward angle on the shore. He rolled onto his side, left eye already swelling shut and watered-down blood dripping down his nose and jaw. With a rattling cough, more blood and water spilled out of his mouth, puddling onto the sand.

Releasing a strangled breath, Scarlet glanced back up at Wolf. He hadn't moved, but his expression had shed the maniacal anger for something akin to admiration.

"When you greeted me with a gun on your doorstep," he said, "it's nice to know you meant it."

Scarlet scowled at him. "Honestly, Wolf. What are you *thinking*? He could tell us something. He could help get my grandma back!"

His half smile softened, and for a moment he looked sorry. For her. "He won't talk."

"How do you know?"

"I know."

"That's not a good enough answer!"

"Watch your gun."

"Wha—" She dropped her gaze to the shore beside her, just in time to see Ran wrap his fingers around the gun's handle. She grasped the barrel and snatched it away from him.

An exhausted chuckle brought more bloodied spittle to Ran's lips. "I will kill you one day, brother. If Jael doesn't first."

"Stop provoking him!" Scarlet yelled. Climbing to her feet, out of Ran's reach, she reset the safety and shoved the gun back into the waist of her jeans. "You're not exactly in any position to be making threats right now, anyway."

Ran said nothing. His eyes had closed, his lips left hanging open with a smear of blood on his cheek, taking in slow, rattling breaths.

Disgusted, she turned back to Wolf, watching as he peeled his hand away from his wound and stared with surprise at the blood coating his palm. He leaned over on his elbow and swished his hand around in the water to get the stain off.

With a sigh, she scrambled to her forgotten bag and pulled out a small first-aid kit. Wolf didn't argue as she ripped open the tear in his sleeve caused by the bullet and took over the job of washing and bandaging the wound. The bullet had just grazed his bicep.

"I'm sorry I shot you," she said, "but you were going to kill him."

"I still might," Wolf said, watching her hands.

She shook her head, taping off the bandage. "He's not your real brother, is he? That's just a gang thing, isn't it?"

Wolf grunted. Said nothing.

"Wolf?"

"I never said we got along."

Scarlet peered up at the wild contempt filling Wolf's face. His green eyes were burning, staring at Ran's prone body behind her.

"Good."

The ferocity in her voice startled away some of his hatred and Wolf turned his attention back to her.

"You must know his weaknesses. You'll know how best to question him."

That sympathetic look again. "We're trained to withstand questioning. He won't help us."

"But he already gave us some information." Packing up the remains of the kit, she tossed it toward her bag. It missed the opening and slid down to the ground. "He obviously knew something when I asked about my grandma. And then this assignment that was canceled—what's that about? Does it have something to do with her?"

Wolf shook his head, but she detected a clouding in his eyes. "He told us what he wanted us—me—to know. Or to believe. I wouldn't put stock in any of it."

"How can you be sure?"

His fingers started up again—clench, release, clench. "I know Ran. He would do anything to improve his standing. By tracking me down and forcing me to return—or even showing proof that he'd fought me and won—he hoped to do just that. As for the assignment I'd been a part of when I left . . . they wouldn't cancel it. It was too important to them."

"What about my grandmother?"

He shook off a troubled frown. "Right. We should keep moving." He tested the strength in his injured arm before using it to push himself to his feet. The fire had burned down to smoldering coals and soon he had stamped them out, ignoring the duck breast that had shriveled up into a chunk of coal.

"That's not what I meant," said Scarlet, staying put on the shore. "Shouldn't we at least *try* to question him?"

"Scarlet, listen to me. Does he know something that would help? Yes, probably. But he won't give it to us. Unless you plan on torturing it out of him, and even then there's nothing you could do that would frighten him more than what the pack will do if he talks. We already know where your grandmother is. Dealing with him is a waste of time."

"What if we brought him with us and offered him as a trade?" she suggested, watching as Wolf reloaded their bag.

Wolf laughed. "A trade? For an omega?" He gestured at Ran.

"He's worth *nothing.*" Though his temper could be heard just beneath the surface, Scarlet was glad that the temporary insanity was gone from his eyes.

"He'll go back to them," she said, "and tell them you're with me."

"Doesn't matter." Slinging the pack over his shoulder, Wolf spared a final scornful look at his brother. "We'll get there before he does."

Twenty-Two

NIGHT CREPT UP FAST. THE FOREST LEANED IN TOWARD them, a solid wall of shadows beneath the dim spotlight of a waning moon. They'd passed only one junction and continued wordlessly north. Seeing another set of tracks combining with theirs had given Scarlet a beat of hope—at least now there was a chance of crossing paths with a new train. But the maglev tracks remained silent. Scarlet's portscreen light was enough to see by for a time, but she worried about killing the battery and knew they should probably stop soon.

Wolf was no longer looking back every few minutes and Scarlet suspected he'd known they were being followed all along.

Wolf stopped suddenly and Scarlet's heart leaped, for a moment sure he'd heard wolves again. "Here. This will work." He peered upward at a log that had fallen across the embankments on either side of them, creating a bridge over the tracks. "What do you think?"

Scarlet followed him through the waist-high brush. "I

thought maybe you were kidding before. You really think you can jump onto a moving train from there?"

He nodded.

"Without breaking a leg?"

"Or anything else."

He met her speculative look with a hint of arrogance.

She shrugged. "Anything to be out of these woods."

The ledge was a few feet over her head, but she clambered up with little trouble, grasping onto roots and jutting rocks. She heard a hiss from below and turned to see a shot of pain cross Wolf's face as he hauled himself up after her. She held her breath, feeling guilty, as he dusted off his hands.

"Let me see," she said, grasping Wolf's forearm and holding up her portscreen to shine a light on the bandage. No blood had leaked through yet. "I really am sorry about shooting you."

"Are you?"

Her touch lingered as it reached the end of the bandage, checking that it was still securely tied. "What does that mean?"

"I suspect you would shoot me all over again if you thought it would help your grandmother."

She blinked up at him, almost surprised to discover how close they were standing. "I would," she said. "But that doesn't mean I wouldn't be sorry about it afterward."

"I'm just glad you didn't take my advice and shoot me in the head," he said, his teeth showing in the portscreen's brightness. His fingers barely fluttered across her sweater's pocket, making her jump.

Then his fingers were gone and Wolf was squinting against the bright light of the portscreen.

"Sorry," Scarlet stammered, angling it toward the ground.

Wolf moved around her, pressing on the fallen log with his foot. "It appears trustworthy."

Scarlet discovered a strange irony in his choice of words. "Wolf," she said, testing the way her voice echoed in the forest's emptiness. He stiffened, though he didn't turn around. "When you first told me about leaving the pack, I thought maybe it had been months, or even years, but Ran made it sound like you'd just left."

One hand came up to ruffle his hair as he turned back toward her.

"Wolf?"

"It's been three weeks," he whispered. Then, "Less than three weeks."

She sucked in a breath, held it, released it all at once. "About the time my grandmother disappeared."

He ducked his head, unable to meet her gaze.

Scarlet shivered. "You told me that you were a nobody, barely more than an errand boy. But Ran called you an 'alpha.' Isn't that a pretty high rank?"

She saw his chest rise with a slow, tense breath.

"And now you tell me that you left them around the same time my grandmother was kidnapped."

He rubbed absently at the tattoo, still saying nothing. Scarlet waited, blood beginning to simmer, until he dared to look at her.

The portscreen cast a wash of bluish white light at their feet, but it did little to illuminate him. In the dark, she could see only the vaguest outline of his cheekbones and jaw, his hair like a clump of pine needles sticking out from his scalp.

"You told me that you had no idea why they would take my grandmother. But that was a lie, wasn't it?"

"Scarlet—"

"So what *was* true? Did you really leave them or is this all some story to get me to—" Gasping, she stumbled back. Her thoughts turned, a cascade of doubts and questions rushing through them. "Am *I* the mission that Ran was talking about? The one that was supposedly canceled?"

"No—"

"And after my dad warned me about this! He said one of you would come for me and there you were, and I even knew you were one of them. I knew I couldn't trust you and still I let myself believe—"

"Scarlet, *stop.*"

She wrapped her fist around her hood's cords, tightening them against her throat. Her heart was pulsating now, blood running hot beneath her skin.

She heard Wolf inhale, saw his hands spread out in the beam of the portscreen. "You're right, I lied to you about not knowing why they took your grandmother. But you *aren't* the mission that Ran was talking about."

She tilted the port upward, shining it into his face. Wolf flinched, but didn't look away.

"But it has something to do with my grandmother."

"It has everything to do with your grandmother."

She bit down hard on her lower lip, trying to still the tide of rage rising inside her.

"I'm sorry. I knew that if I told you, you wouldn't trust me. I know I should have anyway, but . . . I couldn't."

The hand holding her port began to shake. "Tell me *everything.*"

There was a long pause.

A sickeningly long pause.

"You're going to despise me," he murmured. His chest sank in, trying to make himself small again, like he had in the alleyway, in the headlights of her ship.

Scarlet pressed her hands so hard onto her hips, her bones began to ache.

"Ran and I were both in the pack sent to retrieve your grandmother."

Scarlet's stomach curdled. *The pack sent to retrieve her.*

"I wasn't with them when she was taken," he added quickly. "As soon as we arrived in Rieux, I saw my chance to escape. I knew I could disappear there without the grid of the city to find me. So I took it. That was the morning she was taken." He crossed his arms, like he was protecting himself from her hatred. "I could have stopped them. I was stronger than all of them—I could have kept it from happening. I could have warned her, or you. But I didn't. I just ran."

Scarlet's eyes started to burn. Inhaling sharply, she turned her back on him, tilting her head up toward the black sky to keep the sudden tears in without having to swipe at them. She waited until she was sure she could speak before pivoting back toward him. "That's when you started going to the fights?"

"And the tavern," he said with a nod.

"And then what? You felt guilty, so you thought you'd follow me around for a while, maybe help out on the farm, like that would *make up* for it?"

He winced. "Of course not. I knew that getting mixed up with you would be suicide, that eventually they would find me if I didn't leave Rieux, but I…but you…" He seemed frustrated with the words that wouldn't come. "I couldn't just leave."

Scarlet heard the crunch of plastic and forced her grip to loosen on the portscreen. "Why did they take her? What do they want with her?"

He opened his mouth, but was silent.

Scarlet raised both eyebrows. Her pulse was thundering. "Well?"

"They're trying to find Princess Selene."

The ringing in her ears made her think for a moment she hadn't heard him correctly. "They're trying to find *who*?"

"The Lunar Princess Selene."

She drew back. It occurred to her that maybe Wolf was playing some kind of cruel joke, but his expression was too serious, too horrified. "*What?*"

He started to sway uncomfortably from foot to foot. "They've been searching for the princess for years, and they believe your grandmother has information on her where-abouts."

Scarlet squinted at him, baffled, sure she misunderstood. Sure he must be mistaken. But Wolf's attention held her, penetrating and sure.

"Why would my grandmother—" She shook her head. "The Lunar princess is dead!"

"There's evidence that she survived the fire, and that someone rescued her and brought her to Earth," said Wolf. "And, Scarlet . . ."

"What?"

"Are you sure your grandma doesn't know anything?"

Her jaw hung for so long her tongue turned dry and sticky in her mouth. "She's a *farmer*! She's lived in France her whole life. How would she know anything?"

"She was in the military before she was a farmer. She traveled then."

"That was over twenty years ago. How long has the princess been missing? Ten, fifteen years? That doesn't even make sense."

"You can't discount it."

"Sure I can!"

"What if she does know something?"

She frowned, but her disbelief faded upon seeing Wolf's growing desperation.

"Scarlet," he said, "Ran said that the assignment had been called off—he could only have meant the search for the princess. I can't imagine why, after so many years . . . but if it's true, then it may mean they have no more use of your grandmother."

A pang in her stomach. "So they would let her go?"

Wrinkles formed around Wolf's lips, and a weight dropped onto Scarlet's chest. He didn't need to speak for her to see his answer.

No. No, they would not let her go.

She sucked in a dizzying breath, dropping her attention to the streaks of moonlight on the tracks below.

"If I'd known . . . if I'd met you before . . . I want to help you, Scarlet. I want to try and make this better, but they want information that I don't have. The best thing for your grandmother is to be useful. Even if they have stopped looking for Selene, there may still be something she knows, or something in her past, anything that would make her valuable to them. That's why, if there's anything *you* know, any information you have . . . It's the best chance you have of saving her. You can barter for her. Give them the information they want."

Her frustration nearly enveloped her. "I don't know what they want."

"*Think.* Has there ever been anything suspicious? Anything your grandma has said or done that struck you as peculiar?"

"She does peculiar things all the time."

"That's related to Lunars? Or the princess?"

"No, she's . . ." She paused. "I mean, she's always been more sympathetic to them than most people. She's not quick to judge."

"What else?"

"Nothing. Nothing else. She has nothing to do with the Lunars."

"There's evidence that that's not true."

"What evidence? What are you talking about?"

Wolf scratched at his hair. "She must have told you that she's been to Luna."

Scarlet pressed her palms against her eyelids, sucking in a shaky breath. "You're insane. Why would my grandmother have ever gone to *Luna*?"

"She was part of the only diplomatic mission to be sent from Earth to Luna in the last fifty years. She was the pilot that brought the Earthen officials. The visit lasted almost two weeks, so she must have had *some* interaction with Lunars...." He frowned. "She never told you any of this?"

"*No!* No, she never told me any of this! When was this?"

Wolf looked away, and she could see his hesitation.

"Wolf. When was this?"

He gulped. "Forty years ago," he said, his tone going quiet again. "Nine months before your father was born."

Twenty-Three

THE WORLD SPUN. SCARLET SEARCHED WOLF'S FACE FOR A joke that never came. "My father."

"I'm sorry," he murmured. "I thought she must have told you . . . *something* about this."

"But . . . how do you know all this?"

"It all ties back to the princess. Evidence suggests she was taken off Luna by a man named Logan Tanner, a doctor." He searched her for some recognition, but the name meant nothing to Scarlet. Wolf continued, "The only Earthens Dr. Tanner would have had contact with prior to taking the princess were those who had been on the same mission as your grandmother. People who knew him suspected that Dr. Tanner had had a liaison with Michelle Benoit during her stay. Those theories became more plausible when we learned that Michelle had given birth to a son, with no record of the father, nine months later."

Unable to stay standing, Scarlet sank to the ground. If Wolf was telling the truth . . . if these theories were correct . . . then her grandfather was *Lunar.*

A flurry of thoughts passed before her. Clues she'd never known she was collecting settled into place. Why her grandma was so sympathetic to Lunars. Why she never talked about Scarlet's grandfather. Why she had insisted that neither Scarlet nor her father be born in a hospital—the mandatory blood tests would have shown their ancestry.

How could she have kept it secret for so long?

It occurred to her with a jolt that it was always her grandmother's intention to keep it a secret. She had never meant to tell Scarlet the truth to begin with.

Something so big. Something so important. And her grandma had kept it from her.

"We don't keep secrets," she whispered to herself, head sinking as tears started to well in her eyes again. "We don't keep secrets from each other."

"I'm sorry," said Wolf, kneeling before her. "I thought for sure you would have known about this."

"I didn't." She rubbed the tears away. Why wouldn't her grandmother have told her about this Logan Tanner? Was it to protect her from the distrust and prejudice that could come from being part Lunar, or was there something else? An even more unlikely secret she'd been protecting . . .

Her chest ached as she wondered how many secrets had been kept from her.

Wolf's attention darted to the south, one ear cocked to the sky.

Instantly, Scarlet's thoughts settled. She listened, but there was only a breeze in the forest, a charming chorus of crickets.

Though she heard nothing, Wolf whispered, "A train is coming." He fixated on her again, concern etched across his brow. She could see that he believed he'd said too much, but she thirsted for more.

With a nod, she planted a hand on the ground and pushed herself to standing. "And these people think my grandmother knows something about the princess because . . . ?"

Wolf skirted to the edge of the short cliff, peering off down the rails. "They believe Dr. Tanner asked your grandmother for assistance when he brought the princess to Earth."

"They believe, but they can't know that for sure."

"Perhaps not, but that's why they took her," he said, testing the fallen log with his foot again. "To find out what she knew."

"And did they ever consider that maybe she doesn't know anything?"

"They're convinced that she does. Or at least, they were when I left them, though I don't know what they've learned since—"

"Well, why don't they find this Dr. Tanner and ask him?"

Wolf clenched his jaw. "Because he's dead." Stooping, he grabbed their forgotten pack and draped it over his elbow. "He killed himself, earlier this year. In an insane asylum in the Eastern Commonwealth."

Some of Scarlet's anger fizzled out, replaced with pity for a man who had not existed to her minutes before. "An asylum?"

"He was a patient there. Self-admitted."

"How? He was Lunar. Why wasn't he captured and sent back to Luna?"

"He must have figured out how to blend in with Earthen society."

Wolf held out his hand and Scarlet took it instinctively, starting when his hot fingers enclosed hers. After a heartbeat, his hold relaxed as he stepped out onto the tree trunk.

Scarlet angled her portscreen toward their treacherous footings and struggled to find her train of thought over the pounding in her ears. "There must be someone else he had contact with on Earth. The trail can't end with my grandma. According to my dad, she hadn't told them anything, after *weeks* of . . . of who knows what they've been doing to her. They must realize they've got the wrong person!"

There was a peculiar restraint when Wolf responded. "Are you sure they have?"

She glared. The Lunar heir was a myth, a conspiracy, a legend . . . how could her diligent, proud grandmother, living in small-town Rieux, possibly be involved?

But she couldn't be entirely sure of anything anymore. Not if her grandmother had kept something so big from her already.

A faint hum cut through the forest's whispers. The magnets waking up.

A squeeze of her fingers sent a shock up Scarlet's spine.

"Scarlet," said Wolf, "it's in her best interest, and yours, to give them something. Please, think. If you know anything at all, we may be able to use it to our advantage."

"About Princess Selene."

He nodded.

"I don't know anything." Scarlet shrugged, helpless. "I don't know anything."

She felt captured beneath his stare, until, with a deep frown, he released her. His hand slipped away, hanging at his sides. "It's all right. We'll figure out something else."

Scarlet knew he was wrong. It wasn't all right. These monsters were chasing a ghost, and her grandma was caught in the middle of it, all because of some fling that had allegedly happened forty years ago . . . and there was nothing Scarlet could do.

She glanced down—her stomach flipped at seeing how high up they were. With the encroaching darkness, it felt like she was standing at the edge of an abyss.

"We have maybe thirty seconds," said Wolf. "Once it's here, we'll need to act fast. No hesitation. Can you do that?"

Scarlet tried to wet her parched tongue, but it was as dry as the crackled bark beneath her. She tried to calm her heartbeat. Seconds were counting off in her head. Going by too fast. The magnets were growing louder. She heard the whistle of air down the tracks.

"You're going to let me jump on my own this time?" she asked, spotting a bright glow around the nearest bend. Lights blared across the treetops, echoing endlessly through the gathered trunks. The magnets directly beneath them crackled.

"Do you *want* to jump on your own?" He set the bag between them.

Scarlet studied the tracks, imagining a racing train beneath them. Subtle vibrations tickled her feet. Her knees seized up.

She tossed the portscreen into the bag and stepped onto a knot that protruded from the trunk. "Turn around."

He started to grin, but there was still a crease between his eyebrows, a lingering distraction. He let her climb onto his back, hitching her legs higher until she had a firm grip around him.

Tying her arms around Wolf's shoulders, it occurred to Scarlet that she had every right to despise him. He'd had the chance to rescue her grandmother, but he'd run away instead. He'd lied to her and kept these enormous secrets that she had every right to know. . . .

But that didn't change the fact that he was still here. Still risking his life and facing his own tormenters to help her. Still taking her to find her grandmother.

Biting her lip, she leaned forward. "I'm glad you told me everything."

His body seemed to deflate beneath her. "I should have told you sooner."

"Yes, you should have." She tilted her head, temple to temple. "But I still don't despise you." She swept a kiss against his cheek and felt his body lock up. His heartbeat thundered against her wrist as she clasped her hands together.

The train rounded the corner, smooth as a snake. Its glossy white body rushed toward them, the vacuum creating a gust of wind that buffeted the trees to either side of the gully.

Peeling her head off Wolf's shoulder, Scarlet glanced aside at him, noticed yet another scar, this one on his neck. Unlike the others, it was small and perfectly straight—more the work of a scalpel than a brawl.

Then Wolf was crouching and her heart jumped, tearing her attention back to the train. Wolf braced his hands on the bag. His muscles were still rigid, his pulse galloping, and she couldn't help but contrast it with the uncanny calm he'd had when they'd jumped out of the train window before.

Then the train was beneath them, shaking the log and rattling Scarlet's teeth.

Wolf shoved the bag off the trunk, and leaped. Digging her nails into Wolf's shirt, Scarlet clenched her jaw against a scream.

They landed heavily on the glass-smooth roof, the levitating train barely dipping from the impact, and Scarlet felt it instantly. The wrongness. Wolf slipped, his shoulders tilting too heavy to the left, his balance rocking beneath her weight.

Scarlet cried out, the momentum of the jump sending her spinning away from him toward the ledge. She dug her fingernails into his shoulders but his shirt ripped out from beneath her and then she was falling, the world tumbling around her.

A hand gripped her wrist, her fall stopped with a painful yank on her shoulder. She screamed, thrashing her feet as the ground whipped by beneath her. Blinded by the wind-thrown hair in her face, she flailed her free hand up toward him and grasped on to his forearm, squeezing as desperately as she could with slick fingers.

She heard his grunt—bordering on a roar—and felt herself being hauled up. She beat her feet against the train's side, struggling for any traction, before she was heaved onto the roof. Wolf rolled her away from the edge, landing on top of her. His hands hastily brushed the curls from her face, gripped her shoulders, rubbed her bruised wrist, every ounce of his frenetic energy devoted to checking that she was there. That she was all right.

"I'm sorry. I'm so sorry. I lost focus, I slipped—I'm sorry. Scarlet. Are you all right?"

Her breaths shuddered. The world slowly stopped spinning, but every nerve hummed with the rush of adrenaline, every bit of her trembling down to her core. Gaping up at Wolf, she wrapped her fingers around his, stilling them. "I'm all right," she panted, attempting a weary smile. He didn't return the look. His eyes were full of horror. "I may have pulled something in my shoulder, but—" She paused, noting a splotch of red on Wolf's bandage. He'd caught her with his injured arm, reopening the wound. "You're bleeding."

She reached for the bandage, but he caught her hand, gripping it almost too tight. Scarlet found herself pinned beneath his gaze, intense and terrified. He was still breathing hard. She was still shaking, couldn't stop shaking.

Her mind emptied of everything but the gusting wind and how fragile Wolf looked in that heartbeat, like one movement could break him open.

"I'm all right," she assured him again, wrapping her free arm around his back and pulling him toward her until she could curl up beneath the shelter of his body, burying her head against his neck. She felt his gulp, then his arms were around her, crushing her against his chest.

The train angled toward the west, the forest blurring on either side of them. It seemed ages before the adrenaline drained out of Scarlet's limbs, before she could breathe without her lungs hiccupping at the effort. Wolf's embrace never relaxed. The sensation of his breath against her ear the only proof he was living flesh, not stone.

When finally she had stopped trembling, Scarlet peeled herself away from him. The vice of his arms reluctantly let her go and she dared to meet his gaze again.

The shocked horror had left him, replaced with heat and longing and uncertainty. And fear, so much fear, but she didn't think it had anything to do with her nearly falling off the train.

Lips tingling, she arched her neck toward him.

But then he was pulling away from her, the space between them filling with harsh, cold wind. "We need to get down before we run into any tunnels," he said, his voice shaky and rough.

Scarlet sat up, heat rushing to her face as she was struck with an almost irresistible yearning to crawl toward him—not to get off the train's roof, but to be wrapped up against him again. To feel warm and safe and content, just for another moment.

She smashed the desire down into her gut. Wolf wasn't looking at her, and she knew he was right. They weren't safe up here.

Not trusting herself to stand, she half slid, half crawled toward the front of the car, adjusting to the subtle movements of the train. Wolf hovered by her side, not touching her, but never too far to grab her should she get too close to the ledge.

When they reached the end, Wolf swung himself down onto the platform between the cars. Scarlet peered down after him and spotted the bag at his feet. She'd all but forgotten it, but now a surprised laugh fell out of her. His aim had been perfect.

And perhaps if she hadn't kissed his cheek right before the jump, his balance would have been too.

Her nerves fluttered at the thought, wondering if she had been the cause of his distraction.

She sat down with her legs dangling over the side. "Showoff," she said, reaching out and letting him catch her as she jumped down. His hands were achingly gentle as he lowered her to the platform, and lingered a second too long after her feet were firmly planted, or not nearly long enough.

His expression had become haunted and confused, his brow tense. Without meeting her gaze, he grabbed the bag and disappeared into the car.

Scarlet gaped at the doorway, waiting for the gusting wind to take down her temperature, burningly aware of the memory of his hands on her waist, her shoulders, her wrists. Her head was too full of the memory, the too-recent agony of wanting to kiss him.

Slumping against the rail, she tucked her hair into the hood. She dimly tried to tell herself it was a good thing Wolf had pulled away. She was always rushing into things without thinking them through, and it always got her into trouble. This was just one more example of her emotions carrying her away, all over a guy she'd known for only . . . she strained to count back and realized with some shock they'd barely known each other for a day.

Only a day. Could that be right? Had that awful street fight happened just the night before? Had her father's fit in the hangar been only that morning?

But even knowing it, her feelings didn't change. Her skin didn't cool. The fantasy of being tucked in his arms didn't fade.

She'd wanted him to kiss him. She still did.

She let out a sigh and, when her legs were solid again, ducked into the car.

It was a storage car, wide-open and stacked with plastic shipping crates. A square of moonlight fell in through the open doorway. Wolf had climbed onto a stack of crates and was busy shuffling them around to make more room.

Scarlet climbed up to join him. Though the silence was painful, anything she could think to say sounded trite and artificial. Instead, she pulled a comb out of her bag and started picking the knots out of her windblown curls. Finally Wolf stopped shifting crates and sat down beside her. Legs folded. Hands gripped in his lap. Shoulders hunched. Not touching her.

Scarlet scrutinized him from the corner of her eye, tempted to close the gap between them, even just to rest her head on his shoulder. Instead, she reached out and traced a finger across the tattoo that she could make out in the dimness. He went rigid.

"Was Ran telling the truth? Do you think they'll kill you for leaving them?"

A momentary silence had her pulse pounding in her finger-tip against his arm.

"No," he said finally. "You don't have to worry about me."

She trailed her finger down a long scar that had once been a gash from wrist to elbow. "I'll stop worrying when this is all over. When we're all safely away from them."

His eyes flicked to hers, then down to the scar and her fingers resting on his wrist.

"What's this scar from?" she asked. "One of the fights?"

His head shifted, almost imperceptibly. "Stupidity."

Chewing her lip, she inched closer and grazed a fainter scar across his temple. "How about this one?"

He ducked back, forced to lift his head to pull away from her. "That was a bad one," he said, but didn't elaborate.

Scarlet hummed thoughtfully, then dragged her knuckle against the tiniest scar on his lip. "What about—"

His hand snatched at her, stilling her caresses. His grip was not harsh, but unforgiving all the same. "Please stop," he said, even as his gaze fell to her lips.

Scarlet licked them instinctively, saw his eyes grow frantic. "What's wrong?"

A heartbeat.

"Wolf?"

He didn't release her.

Scarlet reached her other hand toward him, brushing her thumb over his knuckles.

He sucked in a quick breath.

Her fingers traveled up his arm, along the bandage and its spot of dried blood. He was taut as a bowstring, plastered against the wall. The fingers grasping her hand twitched. "They're just ... they're what I'm used to," he said, voice strained.

"What do you mean?"

She saw him gulp. No explanation came.

Leaning forward, she found his jawline. The pronounced cheekbones. His hair, every bit as wild and soft to the touch as it had looked. Finally, he leaned his head into her touch, gently nuzzling her fingers.

"It came from a fight," he murmured. "Just another pointless fight. All of them." His eyes lingered on her lips again.

She hesitated. When he still didn't move, Scarlet leaned forward and kissed him. Softly. Just once.

Barely able to breathe around her hammering heart, Scarlet drew back enough for warm air to slip between them, and Wolf dissolved before her, a resigned sigh brushing against her mouth.

Then he was pulling her toward him and bundling her up in his arms. Scarlet gasped as Wolf buried one hand into her mess of curls and kissed her back.

"Oh, Grandmother,

what terribly big teeth you have!"

Twenty-four

"*HIDE.*" CINDER SAID THE WORD SLOWLY. TENDERLY. A breathy plea ending in the soft, careful *d*. "*Hide.* Rampion, hide. Hide, Rampion. Disappear . . . Fade away . . . You do not exist. . . . You cannot be seen. . . ."

She was sitting cross-legged on her bunk, in the dark, envisioning the ship that surrounded her. The steel walls, the churning engine, the screws and soldered seals that held everything together, the computer mainframe, the thick glass of the cockpit windows, the closed exit ramp in the cargo bay, the podship dock beneath her feet.

Then she imagined it invisible.

Swimming past radars, and the radars remaining silent.

Dissolving into blackness under the watchful eye of satellite stations.

Gracefully dancing between all the other ships that cluttered the solar system. Drawing no attention. Not existing.

Her vertebrae tingled, beginning at the top of her neck and running down to her tailbone. A warmth radiated outward, filling every muscle and every joint, seeping through her fingers and back into her knees. Recirculating.

She released the air from her lungs, let her muscles release with her breath, and started the chant again. "Hide, Rampion. Rampion, hide. *Hide.*"

"Is it working?"

Her eyes popped open. In the darkness, all she could see were pinpoints of stars beyond her window. They were on the side of Earth opposite from the sun, leaving the ship cloaked in shadow and the vastness of space.

Cloaked. Hiding. Invisible.

"Good question," she said, turning her attention up toward the ceiling as had already become habit, even though she knew it was ridiculous. Iko was not some spot on the ceiling, was not even the speakers that projected her chipper voice. She was every computer wire, every chip, every system. She was everything but the steel and bolts holding the ship together.

It was a little disconcerting.

"I have no idea what I'm doing," Cinder said. She glanced out the window. There were no ships visible through the small portal, only stars and stars and stars. In the distance, a vague purple haze, perhaps some gas left off the tail of a comet. "Do *you* feel any different?"

Something rumbled beneath her feet, soft as a kitten's purr. It reminded her of the way Iko's fan used to spin extra fast when she was processing information.

"No," Iko said after a minute, and the thrumming died down. "Still gargantuan."

Cinder untucked her legs, allowing blood back into her foot. "That's what worries me. I feel like it shouldn't be this easy. The entire Commonwealth military is after us. For all we know, they could have elicited the help of other Union militaries by this point too, not to mention Lunars and bounty hunters. How many ships have you picked up on *our* radars?"

"Seventy-one."

"Right—and not one of them noticed us or got suspicious? Does that seem possible?"

"Maybe what you're doing is working after all. Maybe you're a natural at this Lunar thing."

Cinder shook her head, forgetting that Iko couldn't see her. She wanted to believe she was having an effect, but it felt wrong. Lunars had control over bioelectricity, not radio waves. She had a suspicious feeling that all this chanting and visualizing was an enormous waste of time.

Which left the question: Why hadn't they been spotted yet?

"Cinder, how long will I have to stay like this?"

Cinder sighed. "I don't know. Until we can install another auto-control system."

"And until you find me a new body."

"That too." She rubbed her hands together. The subtle warmth that had filled up her right fingers had faded, and for once they were colder than the hard metal ones.

"I don't like being a ship. It's awful." There was a distinct whine in Iko's tone. "It makes me feel less alive than ever."

Falling back on her cot, Cinder studied the black shadows of the bunk. She knew exactly how Iko felt—for the brief time she'd been acting as the auto-control system herself, it had seemed like her brain was being stretched in every direction. Like she'd lost touch with her physical body, had detached her brain and was hovering in a nonexistent space between the real and the digital. Pity welled up in her for Iko, who had never wanted anything but to become more human.

"It's only temporary," she said, pushing the hair off her forehead. "As soon as it's safe to get back to Earth, we'll—"

"Hey, Cinder! Are you watching the net?" Thorne crowded into the doorway, outlined by the energy-saving lights in the hallway. "What is this, nap time? Turn some lights on."

Cinder's muscles knotted across her shoulders. "Can't you see I'm busy?"

Thorne surveyed the small, dark room. "Yeah, good one."

Throwing her feet off the bed, Cinder sat up. "I'm trying to concentrate."

"Well. Keep up the good work, mate. In the meantime, you should come watch this. They're talking about us on all the channels. We're famous."

"No, thank you. I'd rather not see myself acting like a maniac at the most important social event of the year." She'd only watched the footage from the ball once—of when she'd lost her foot and crashed down the stairs, landing in a heap of wrinkled silk and muddied gloves—and that one viewing had been plenty.

Thorne waved his hand. "They already showed the clips. And now you've achieved the dream of every red-blooded girl under the age of twenty-five."

"Right, my life is a real dream come true."

Thorne wiggled his eyebrow. "Maybe not, but at least dreamy Prince Kai knows your name."

"*Emperor* Kai," she said, frowning at him.

"Precisely." Thorne cocked his head toward the front of the ship. "They're starting a press conference, to talk about *you*. Thought you wouldn't want to miss"—Thorne fanned himself, swooning—"his heavenly, chocolate-brown eyes, and perfectly tousled hair, and—"

Cinder sprang off the bed, shoving Thorne into the door frame as she marched past him.

"Ow," he said, rubbing his arm. "What's got your wires crossed?"

"I'm adjusting the channel now." Iko's voice followed Cinder through the cargo bay and into the cockpit, where the main screen was showing Emperor Kai at a podium before an audience of journalists. "The conference is just starting, and he looks so *handsome* today!"

"Thanks, Iko," said Cinder, claiming the pilot's seat.

"Hey, that's my—"

She silenced Thorne with a wave and adjusted the screen's volume.

"—thing we can to find the escaped convicts," Kai was saying. The circles beneath his eyes suggested that it had been a long time since he'd experienced a proper night's rest. Nevertheless, seeing him made Cinder both warm with longing and miserable when she thought of the last few moments she'd seen him. Her, having just tripped on the garden steps and lying sprawled on the gravel pathway with her wires sparking out of her ankle.

He—disgusted, baffled, disappointed.

Betrayed.

"We've deployed our fastest ships with the most advanced search technology and the best pilots in order to track down the fugitives. They've been lucky in their evasion of us so far, but we don't expect that luck to last. The class of ship they're inhabiting is not meant for extended periods of orbit. Eventually they will have to return to Earth, and we'll be ready for them."

"What kind of ship are they on?" asked a lady in the front row.

Kai checked his notes. "It's a stolen military cargo ship from the American Republic—a 214 Rampion, Class 11.3. Its tracking devices have been stripped, which is largely responsible for the difficulties we've had in apprehending them."

Thorne proudly poked Cinder in the back.

On the screen, Kai nodded at another journalist near the back.

"You said our military would be waiting for them when they return to Earth. How long do you suspect that to be, and are you abandoning the space search in the meantime?"

"Absolutely not. Our primary objective is to find them as soon as possible, and we plan to continue the search in space until they're found. However, my experts project the ship will be returning to Earth anytime from two days to two weeks, depending on their fuel and power reserves, and we will be prepared for that return if necessary. Yes?"

"My sources have told me that this cyborg, this Linh Cinder—"

"That's you," Thorne whispered with another jab. She batted him away.

"—was given a VIP invitation to the annual ball and was, in fact, an invited guest of *yours*, Your Majesty. Do you refute that claim?"

"A what?" Thorne asked.

"VIP invitation?" said Iko.

Cinder scrunched up her shoulders, ignoring them both.

On the screen, Kai shifted back from the podium, arms fully extended as if to give himself space to breathe, before clearing his throat and nearing the mic again. "I do not refute the claim. I met Linh Cinder two weeks prior to the ball. As many of you know, she was a renowned mechanic here in the city and I had hired her to fix a malfunctioning android. And, yes, I did invite her to the ball as a personal guest."

"*What?*"

Cinder flinched from the shriek that pierced through the cockpit's speakers.

"When did this happen? It better have happened after Adri dismantled me because if he asked you to the ball and you didn't tell me—"

"Iko, I'm trying to listen!" Cinder squirmed in her seat. Kai *had* asked her to the ball before Iko's body had been taken apart and sold off. Cinder had had the chance to tell her, but at the time she'd been determined not to accept the invitation, so it hadn't seemed that important.

When Kai called on another journalist, Cinder realized she'd missed an entire question.

"Did you know that she was cyborg?" asked a woman in an unhidden tone of disgust.

Kai stared at her, appearing confused, then let his gaze dance over the crowd. He shuffled his feet closer to the podium, a wrinkle forming on the bridge of his nose.

Cinder bit the inside of her cheek and braced herself for adamant disgust. Who would ever invite a cyborg to the ball?

But instead, Kai said simply, "I don't see that her being cyborg is relevant. Next question?"

Cinder's metal fingers jolted.

"Your Majesty, did you know that she was *Lunar* when you extended this invitation?"

Looking like he might keel over from exhaustion, Kai shook his head. "No. Of course not. I—naively, it seems—was under the impression that there were no Lunars in the Commonwealth. Other than our diplomatic guests here at the palace, of course. Now that it's been brought to my attention how easy it is for them to blend in with the populace, we will be taking additional security measures to both keep Lunars from emigrating here, as well as to find and export any that may be within our borders. I have every intention to comply with the statutes of the Interplanetary Agreement of 54 T.E. on this matter. Yes, second row."

"Regarding Her Majesty, Queen Levana, has she or any of the Lunar court commented on the escape of the convict?"

Kai's jaw tensed. "Oh, she's had a thing or two to say about it."

Behind Kai, a government official cleared his throat. The irritation quickly evaporated from Kai's face, replaced with tactful vacancy.

"Queen Levana wants Linh Cinder to be found," he amended, "and brought to justice."

"Your Majesty, do you think these events may have harmed the diplomatic proceedings between Earth and Luna?"

"I don't think they helped."

"Your Majesty." A man stood, three rows back. "Witness accounts from the ball seem to indicate that Linh Cinder's arrest was part of an agreement between yourself and the queen, and that letting her go could be cause for war. Is there reason to believe the cyborg's escape could lead to a greater threat to our national security?"

Kai moved to scratch behind his ear, but caught the nervous tic and placed his hand back on the podium. "The word *war* has been thrown around between Earth and Luna for generations. It is my prerogative, as it was always my father's, to avoid that at all costs. I assure you, I am doing everything in my power not to further unravel our fragile relationship with Luna, starting with finding Linh Cinder. That's all, thank you."

He stepped off the stage to a wave of unanswered questions, and was pulled into a whispered conversation with a group of officials.

Pouting, Thorne slumped into the copilot's seat. "He didn't mention me. Not once."

"Me either," said Iko, without pity.

"You're not an escaped convict."

"True, but His Majesty and I met once, at the market. I felt like we had a really strong connection. Didn't you think so, Cinder?"

The words slipped meaninglessly through Cinder's audio interface. She didn't respond, unable to tear her focus away from Kai.

He was being forced to take responsibility for her actions. He was being unfairly faced with the repercussions of her decisions. In the aftermath of her escape, he alone had to deal with Queen Levana.

Shutting her eyes against the sight of him, she rubbed her throbbing temple.

"But I'm a wanted fugitive, like Cinder," Thorne continued. "They do realize I'm missing, don't they?"

"Maybe they're grateful," Cinder muttered.

Thorne grumbled something incoherent, followed by a long silence during which Cinder massaged her brow and tried to convince herself she'd done the right thing.

Spinning, Thorne kicked his feet onto the armrest of Cinder's chair, nudging her elbow off it. "Now I understand why you've been so immune to my charms. I had no idea I was competing with an emperor. That's a tough hand to beat, even for me."

She snorted. "Don't be ridiculous. I hardly know him, and now he despises me."

Thorne laughed, hooking his thumbs behind his belt loops. "I have great instincts when it comes to *amore*, and he does not despise you. Plus, he asked a cyborg to the ball? That takes guts. I generally dislike royalty and government officials on principle, but I have to give him credit for that."

Standing, Cinder shoved Thorne's feet off her chair, freeing her path to the door. "He didn't know I was cyborg."

Thorne tilted his head as she passed. "He didn't?"

"Of course not," she said, marching out of the small cockpit.

"But he knows you're cyborg now and he still likes you."

She spun back to him, pointing toward the screen. "You got *that* from a ten-minute conference in which he said he's doing everything in his power to hunt me down and turn me over for execution?"

Thorne smirked. In a terrible, snotty voice that Cinder guessed was meant to be a Kai impersonation, he said, "'I don't see that her being cyborg is relevant.'"

Rolling her eyes, Cinder spun away.

"Hey, come back!" Thorne's boots hit the ground behind her. "I have something else to show you."

"I'm busy."

"I promise not to make fun of your boyfriend anymore."

"He's not my boyfriend!"

"It's about Michelle Benoit."

Cinder sucked down a slow breath, and turned back around. "What?"

Thorne hesitated, as if afraid to move in case he set her off again, before inclining his head toward the cockpit's dash behind him. "Come take a look at this."

Heaving a sigh, Cinder trudged back toward him. She settled her elbows on the back of Thorne's chair.

Thorne dismissed the news channel. "Did you know that Michelle Benoit has a teenage granddaughter?"

"No," said Cinder, bored.

"Well, she does. Miss Scarlet Benoit. Supposedly she just turned eighteen, but—brace yourself—she doesn't have any hospital records. Get it? Holy spades, I'm a genius."

Cinder scowled. "I don't get it."

Tilting back, Thorne peered at her upside down. "She doesn't have any *hospital records.*"

"So?"

He spun the chair to face her. "Do you know a single person who wasn't born in a hospital?"

Cinder considered. "Are you suggesting that she could be the princess?"

"That's precisely what I'm suggesting."

The netscreen turned to a profile and picture of Scarlet Benoit. She was pretty, with pronounced curves and fiery red curls.

Cinder squinted at the image. A teenage girl without a birth record. A ward of Michelle Benoit.

How convenient.

"Well, then. Excellent detective work, Captain."

Twenty-Five

SCARLET DREAMT THAT A BLIZZARD HAD COVERED ALL OF Europe in neck-deep snow. A child again, she came downstairs to find her grandmother kneeling in front of the wood stove. "I thought I'd found someone who would take you in," her grandma said. "But they'll never come for you in all this snow. I guess I'll have to wait until spring now to be rid of you."

She stoked the fire. The sparks flew into Scarlet's eyes, stinging, and she woke up with wetness on her cheeks, her fingers like ice. For a long time she couldn't sort out what was a dream and what was a memory. Snow, but not so much snow. Her grandmother wanting to send her away, but not when she was a child. A teenager. Thirteen.

Had it been January, or later still in the winter? She struggled to piece together thawing memories. She'd been sent out to milk the cow, a chore she'd despised, and her hands were so numb she was afraid she would squeeze the udders too tight.

Why hadn't she been in school that day? Was it a weekend? A vacation?

Oh—right. She'd been visiting her father, just come back the day before. She was supposed to stay with him for a full month, but she couldn't stand it. The drinking, the coming back to the apartment in the middle of the night. Scarlet had taken the train home without telling anyone, surprising her grandmother with her arrival. Rather than happy to see her, her grandmother had been angry that Scarlet hadn't commed to tell her what was happening. They'd had a fight. Scarlet was still mad at her, milking the cow, fingers freezing.

It was the last time she'd ridden the maglev. The last time she'd seen her father.

She remembered hurrying through her chores, desperate to be finished with them so she could go inside and get warm. It wasn't until she was rushing back to the house that she saw the hover out front. She'd seen plenty hovers when she lived in the city, but they were rare out in the country, where the farmers preferred larger, faster ships.

She'd sneaked in through the back door and heard her grandmother in the kitchen, and a man, their voices muffled. She inched her way around the staircase, her feet silent on the terra-cotta tiles.

"I can't imagine what a burden she's been for you all these years," said the man in an eastern accent.

Scarlet frowned, sensing the kitchen's warmth upon her cheeks as she peered through the cracked door. He was at the table, a mug in his hands. He had silk-black hair and a long face. Scarlet had never seen him before.

"She hasn't been as much trouble as I expected her to be," said her grandmother, who she couldn't see. "I've almost grown attached to her after all these years. But I must say, I'll be glad when she's gone. No more panicking each time an unfamiliar ship flies by."

Scarlet's throat constricted.

"You said she'd be ready to go in a week's time? Can that be so?"

"Logan seems to think so. This device of yours is all we were waiting for. If the procedure goes smoothly it could even be sooner. But you'll have to be patient with her. She'll be quite weak, and more than a little bewildered."

"Understandably so. I can't imagine what this must be like for her."

Scarlet clamped a palm over her mouth to smother her breathing.

"You have accommodations set up?"

"Yes, we're quite prepared. It will take some getting used to for us as well, but I'm sure it will all work out once she's settled in. I have two girls of my own about her age—twelve and nine. I'm sure they'll adore each other, and I will treat her as if she were my own."

"And what about Madame Linh? Is she prepared?"

"Prepared?" The man chuckled, but the sound was rough and uncomfortable. "She could not have been more astounded when I brought up the idea of adopting a third girl, but she's a good mother. I'm sorry she wasn't able to come with me, but I wanted to draw as little attention to this trip as possible. Of course, she doesn't *know* about the girl. Not . . . everything."

Scarlet must have made a sound, because the man suddenly looked up and saw her. He stiffened.

Her grandmother's chair scratched against the floor and the door swung open. She was furious. Scarlet was furious right back at her.

"Scarlet, you know better than to eavesdrop. Go to your room!"

She wanted to scream, to stomp, to tell her that she couldn't just send her away like she was nothing, not again—but the words wouldn't come. They were choked off at the base of her tongue.

So she did as she was told, her feet pounding up the stairs and into her room before her grandma could see the tears.

It wasn't only realizing that she wasn't wanted, or that she could be passed off to any stranger that came for her. It was that, after six long years, she'd just begun to feel like she belonged. Like maybe her grandma loved her—more than her mother had, more than her father. Like maybe the two of them were a team.

After that morning, she'd lived in fear for a week. Two weeks. A month.

But the man never came for her, and she and her grandmother never spoke of it again.

"Scarlet?"

The tightening of Wolf's arm around her waist dragged Scarlet back into the present, into a train car that was slowing down around her. She was curled up like a child with her back against him, and though her eyes were squeezed shut, a few hot tears had escaped, rolled over the bridge of her nose, dripped across her temples. She hastily brushed them away.

Wolf stirred and propped himself up behind her. "Scarlet?" His tone was nervous.

"I had a bad dream," she said, not wanting him to think the tears had anything to do with him. Already they were stopping and she rolled onto her back. It must have still been night for the darkness that took up the train car, but the unnatural glimmer of city neon targeted the crates just inside the door, sending splashes of pink and green over the stacked boxes.

"I remembered something," she whispered. "I think it might have to do with the princess."

He tensed.

"I remember my grandma mentioning Logan now, but she didn't want me to overhear. I was eavesdropping. And there was another man . . ." She told him the story as well as she could, piecing the memory back together again as her brain threatened to fog over.

When she was done, she lay still, listening to the whistle of wind outside the train cars. Her side was stiff from sleeping on the hard crate.

Rather than look relieved or hopeful, Wolf peered down at her, terrified.

"That's what they're looking for, isn't it? I mean—it *must* have been the princess that they were talking about. I don't know where she was, who was taking care of her . . . I never saw her. All this time I thought she'd been planning on sending *me* away, but now . . . after what you told me about Logan Tanner and Grand-mère and Princess Selene . . ."

Wolf pulled away from her, sitting up and curling his knees against his chest. He stared blankly at the stacks of crates surrounding them.

"This man had an accent. I think he was from the Eastern Commonwealth." Scarlet pushed herself up beside him, combing her hair to one side. "And I'm pretty sure my grandma called his wife 'Madame Linh.' I don't know how common of a name it is, but . . . I would recognize him if I saw him again. I'm sure I would."

"Don't say that." Wolf pressed his hands over his ears. "I didn't hear that."

Scarlet blinked, stunned by his grimace. "Wolf?" Reaching forward, she tugged his hands down. "This is good, isn't it? They want information, I have information. We'll barter. We'll trade for my grandmother's safety. Isn't that—"

"Don't go."

His gaze trapped her in the darkness. Tousled hair, faint scars, flecks of sleep in his eyelashes. Wolf twisted a curl of her hair around his fingers.

"Don't go looking for your grandmother."

A streak of orange light flashed through the door and vanished.

"I have to."

"No, Scarlet, you don't have to." He grasped her hand,

engulfing it in both of his. "There's nothing you can do for her. If you go, you'll only be putting yourself in danger. Would your grandmother want that?"

Scarlet yanked her hand out of Wolf's grip.

"We can run away," he continued, his fingers scrambling for contact, knotting themselves around her pockets. "We'll disappear in the forest. Go to Africa, or the Commonwealth. We can survive and they'll never find us. I can keep you safe, Scarlet. I can protect you."

"What are you talking about? Just last night you said that if I had any information it could help, it could be my grandma's only chance, and now I have information. I thought that's what you wanted."

"*Maybe,*" he said. "Maybe, if you had a full name, an address, something specific. But a last name and a country—an enormous country—and a description? Scarlet, if you tell them this, they'll only take *you* captive, in hopes that you'll be able to identify this man."

Tugging at her zipper, she studied him, how his eyes were more crazed with every breath he took.

"Good," she said. "Then we'll offer to trade me for my grandmother."

He shrank back, shaking his head, but Scarlet was bolstered. "We'll go together. You can tell them that you have information, but you'll only give it to them on the condition that they let you walk away free, and that you take my grandmother with you. And they can have me."

Wolf shuddered.

"Wolf, you have to promise me you'll take care of her. We don't know what kind of condition she'll be in. If they've . . . if she's hurt . . . you'll have to take care of her." Her voice hitched, but there were no more tears. Her resolve was complete.

Until—"What if she's already dead, Scarlet?"

Dread settled in her stomach at the words she'd refused to speak, for fear it could make them real. The train was still slowing and Scarlet could make out the furious noise of the city: hovers and netscreens and buzzers warning to stay off the tracks. It was the middle of the night, but in the city there was never silence.

"Do you think she is?" Her voice trembled. Her heart throbbed as she waited for him to answer. "You think they've killed her?"

Every moment wrapped around Scarlet's neck, strangling her, until the only possible word from Wolf's lips had to be *yes*. Yes, she was dead. Yes, she was gone. They'd murdered her. These monsters had murdered her.

Scarlet pressed her palms into the crate, trying to push through the plastic. "Say it."

"No," he murmured, shoulders sinking. "No, I don't think they've killed her. Not yet."

Scarlet shivered with relief. She covered her face with both hands, dizzy with the hurricane of emotions. "Thank the stars," she whispered. "Thank you."

His tone hardened. "Don't thank me for telling the truth when it would have been mercy to lie to you."

"Mercy? To tell me she's dead? To break my heart?"

"Making you believe she was dead was the only chance I had to convince you not to go looking for her. We both know that. I should have lied."

The hum of the tracks deepened as the train crawled into a station. Voices yelled. Machinery clanked and hissed.

"It's not your decision to make," she said, grabbing the portscreen and checking their location. They'd made it to Paris. "I have to go after her. But you don't have to come with me."

"Scarlet—"

"No, listen. I appreciate your help. How far you've brought me. But I can go on alone. Just tell me where to go and I'll find it myself."

"Maybe I won't."

Scarlet shoved the port into her pocket, anger burning in her cheeks. But then she met Wolf's gaze and saw, not stubbornness, but panic. His fingers curling and uncurling, again and again.

She released her mounting resentment. Scooting toward Wolf, she cupped his face in her hands. He flinched, but didn't pull away. "They'll want this information, won't they?"

His expression was stone.

"We'll offer me as a trade. You and Grand-mère can go somewhere safe, take care of each other, and when they let me go, I'll come find you. They can't keep me forever."

She smiled as warmly as she could, and waited for him to return it. When he didn't, she rubbed her thumbs across his cheeks and kissed him. Though he instantly pulled her against him, he didn't let the kiss linger.

"There's no guarantee they'll let you go. When they're done with you, they might kill you. You're sacrificing your life for hers."

"It's a chance I have to take."

The train came to a steady stop and sank down onto the tracks.

Wolf's eyes saddened. "I know. You'll do what you have to do." Peeling her hands off his shoulders, he placed a sweet kiss against her wrist, where the blood pulsed beneath her skin. "And so will I."

Twenty-Six

THE UNDERGROUND PLATFORM WAS WELL LIT AND FILLED
with androids and hovering carts ready to unload the train's
cargo. Scarlet followed Wolf into the shadows of another freight
train. They waited until an android turned away before crawling
up onto the platform.

Wolf grabbed her wrist and pulled her across the platform,
ducking behind a cart loaded with crates. A moment later Scarlet saw an android roll into the car she and Wolf had just abandoned, its blue light seeping back out the door.

"Be ready to run when that train leaves," Wolf said, adjusting
the bag on his shoulder. Not seconds later, the train lifted up off
the tracks and began gliding back into the tunnel.

Scarlet sprang toward the tracks, only to find herself being
pulled back by her hood. She let out a strangled cry and slammed
back into Wolf.

"Wha—"

He placed a finger to his mouth.

Scarlet glared and ripped her hood from his grasp, but then she heard it too. The hum of an approaching train.

It was on the third track out and blew past them without any indication of slowing, vanishing into the darkness again as quickly as it had come.

Wolf grinned. "Now we can go."

They reached the other platform without any further run-ins, spotted only by a middle-aged man who watched them curiously over his port.

Scarlet checked her own port when they reached street level. The city was quiet in the still of morning. They were at the Gare de Lyon, surrounded by avenues of shops and offices. Though Wolf tried to hide it, Scarlet could tell he was sniffing for something.

All she could smell was city. Metal and asphalt and baking bread from a closed patisserie on the corner.

Wolf headed northwest.

The street was lined with imposing second-era Beaux-Arts structures and flower boxes hanging from stone-wrapped windows. An ornate clock tower stood in the distance, its face lit up and showing two broad pointed hands and roman numerals; below it stood a digital screen that read 04:26 beside an ad for the newest model of house android.

"How far are we?" Scarlet asked.

"Not far. We can walk."

They turned left at a traffic circle, Wolf half a step ahead of her, hunched over like he was barricading himself. Scarlet's gaze traveled down his arm, over the bandaged wound that no longer seemed to be bothering him, to his fidgeting fingers. She wanted to reach out to him, but found it impossible. She tucked both of her hands into her hoodie's pockets instead.

There was an abyss opening up between them, cutting through whatever they'd shared on the train. They were almost there—almost to her grandmother, almost to the Order of the Pack.

Maybe he was leading her to her death.

Maybe Wolf was marching toward his.

She tilted her chin up, refusing to frighten herself with her own morose thoughts. All that mattered now was rescuing her grandmother, and she was so close. So close.

The ancient residences drew in closer to the road as they left the busy intersection behind. There was only the occasional sign of life—a cat cleaning itself in the window of a hat shop, a man in a suit darting from a hotel into a waiting hover. They passed a netscreen that showed a commercial for a shampoo that claimed to change the color of one's hair based on their moods.

She already yearned for the solitude of the farm. That was the only reality she knew. The farm and her grandmother and her weekly deliveries. And now, Wolf. That was the reality she wanted.

Wolf quickened his pace, but his shoulders were squeezing inward again. Locking her jaw, Scarlet reached forward and grasped his wrist.

"I can't let you do this," she said, angrier than she'd intended.

"Just tell me where it is and I'll go on by myself. Just tell me what to do. Give me some indication of what I'm dealing with and I'll figure something out, but I can't let you go with me."

He stared down at her for a long moment and she tried to see softness in his stark green eyes, but the warmth and desperation that had been so apparent on the train were now replaced with a cold resolve. He pried his arm away.

"Do you see the man sitting in front of the closed café on the other side of the street?"

She slid her attention off him and found the man sitting at one of the outdoor tables. One ankle was propped on his knee, his elbow dangling off the back of his chair. He was staring at them, and he didn't try to hide it. When Scarlet caught his eye, he winked.

A chill crawled over her skin.

"Pack member," said Wolf. "We passed another at the magrail station two blocks back. And ..." He craned his head. "If the stench is any indication, we're about to cross paths with another when we turn this next corner."

Her heart was suddenly stomping. "How did they know we were here?"

"I suspect they've been waiting for us. They've probably been tracking your ID."

That's what people did when they ran away and didn't want to be found—they cut out their ID chips.

"Or yours," she murmured. "If they do have access to an ID tracker, then maybe they've been following you."

"Maybe." His voice was nonchalant and she realized this

wasn't news to him. Had he thought this could be possible? Was that how Ran had found them?

"We might as well go find out what they want." Wolf turned away and she had to race to keep up with him.

"But there's only three of them. You can fight three of them, can't you? You said you could take—" She hesitated. Wolf had told her he would win in a fight against six wolves. When had those wild animals become synonymous with these men, this Order of the Pack?

"You could still get away. There's still a chance," she finished.

"I said I would protect you and that's what I'm going to do. It's pointless to discuss this any further."

"I don't need your protection."

"Yes," he said, the word biting over the synthesized noise of a music video on a nearby billboard. "Yes, *you do*."

Scarlet darted in front of him, planting her feet. He stopped just shy of plowing into her.

"No," she said. "What I need is to know that I'm not responsible for whatever they'll do to you. You need to stop being stupid and get out of here. At least give yourself a chance!"

He peered over her head at some place in the distance. Scarlet tensed, wondering if he'd picked up on the presence of a fourth pack member, or even more. Gulping, she glanced at the man by the café, who was stroking his ear and watching them with obvious amusement.

"What's stupid is not that I'm going to try and protect you," Wolf said, pulling his focus back down to her. "What's stupid is that I almost believe it will make a difference."

He stepped around her, shrugging off the hand that reached out to stop him. Her thoughts teetered, knowing she had a choice. She could run away with him, leave the city, and never come back. She could choose not to go in search of her grandmother after all, and maybe save his life.

But it was not really a choice. She barely knew him. Despite the ache in her heart, despite everything. She would never be able to live with herself knowing that she'd abandoned her grandmother when she was this close.

She turned back only once, as they were rounding a corner, and saw that the man by the café was gone.

A block later, the memory of the Fourth World War caught up to them all at once. The scorch marks and crumbling facades of a city pummeled by war. There weren't enough of the beautiful old buildings left to draw the interest of the conservationists, and the sheer amount of destruction must have been too overwhelming for reconstruction. Unable to demolish the city's history, the government had left this quarter alone. The districts, though separated by only a few streets, seemed worlds apart.

With a gasp, Scarlet recognized the massive building stretching along the opposite side of the street, with its shattered arched windows and the statues of men in old-fashioned clothing, many with broken limbs and some alcoves missing their statues altogether. The Musée du Louvre, one of the few sights her father had taken her to as a child. The building, half collapsed on the west end, was too unstable to go inside, but she and her father had stood together on the sidewalk while he told her about the priceless artworks that had been destroyed in the bombings, or the lucky few that had become spoils of war.

Many had still not been found, over a century later.

It was one of the few pleasant memories she had of her father, and she'd forgotten it until now.

"Scarlet."

She snapped her head around.

"This way." Wolf angled his head toward another street.

She nodded and followed him without looking back.

Despite the district's tarnish, it was clear that these ancient streets weren't entirely abandoned. A small motel advertised "come stay the night with the ghosts of fallen civilians" in the window. A thrift store displayed headless mannequins garbed in a rush of vibrant fabrics.

At an intersection, Wolf paused on a concrete city square with a boarded-up entrance to the subway and a sign that indicated the platform was closed; the nearest could be found on the Boulevard des Italiens.

"Are you ready?"

She followed his transfixed gaze up to a towering, gorgeous building before them. Angels and cherubim stood guard at massive arched doorways.

"What is this?"

Wolf followed her gaze. "Once it was an opera house and an architectural marvel. Then the war came and it was converted into storage for artillery and, eventually, prisoners of war. Then, when no one else wanted it, we took over."

Scarlet frowned at that word. *We.* "Seems a little conspicuous for a secret street gang, don't you think?"

"Would *you* ever suspect something horrible was living inside?"

When she didn't answer, he backed away, scrutinizing her as he approached the massive theater. Again, he asked, "Are you ready?"

Catching her breath, she examined the carvings—faces grim and beautiful, the chalky busts of men staring down at her, a long balcony missing half its balusters. Clenching her jaw, she crossed the street and marched up the steps that spanned the length of the building, past the silent, unpreserved angels, beneath the shadowed portico.

"I'm ready," she said, eyeing the mess of graffiti across the doors.

"Scarlet."

She turned to face him, surprised by the gruffness in his voice.

"I'm sorry."

He was careful not to touch her as he passed.

Her mouth went dry, warnings cluttering her head as Wolf pulled the nearest door open and stepped into the shadows.

Twenty-Seven

THE DOOR THUDDED SHUT BEHIND THEM. SCARLET FOUND herself in the immense foyer of the opera house, almost pitch-black but for warm, flickering candlelight beyond the arches. The lobby was full of silence and dust and chunks of broken marble along the floor. The dust clogged Scarlet's throat and she struggled not to cough as she moved toward the light. Her footsteps were shockingly loud in the empty, hollow building as she passed between two massive columns.

She gasped. The light was coming from one of two statues that flanked a grand double staircase. It depicted two women draped in billowing fabric atop a pedestal, each holding aloft a bouquet of torches. Dozens of wax candles glowed and flickered, casting a haunting orange film over the lobby. The staircase, carved from red-and-white marble, was missing random balustrades, and a companion statue to the first was missing her head and the arm that had once held her own candelabra.

Scarlet's foot splashed into a puddle and she drew back, first looking down at the broken marble floor, then up. Three stories of balconies rose above and in their center, where the light barely reached, was a painted ceiling with a square window in its center. The window, it seemed, had long been missing.

Hugging herself, Scarlet turned back to Wolf. He lingered between the columns.

"Maybe they're sleeping," she said, attempting nonchalance.

Wolf peeled himself out of the shadows and prowled toward the staircase. His body was as tense as the statues that watched them.

Scarlet's gaze darted over the railings above, but she saw no movement, no sign of life. No garbage. No smell of food. No sound of talking or netscreens. Even the sounds of the street had disappeared beyond the massive entry doors.

She clenched her jaw, anger flaring up inside her at the sickening sensation of being trapped like a mouse to be preyed upon. Stomping past Wolf, she marched toward the stairs until her toes pressed against the first riser.

"*Hello?*" she yelled, craning her head. "You have visitors!"

Her words echoed back to her, harsh and defiant.

No sound. No alarm.

Then, from the silence, a familiar chime. Scarlet jumped at the sound that echoed between the marble pillars, despite being muffled within her pocket.

Heart racing, she pulled out the portscreen just as the computerized voice began to speak. "*Comm received for Mademoiselle Scarlet Benoit from L'hôpital Joseph Ducuing in Toulouse.*"

Scarlet blinked. A hospital?

Hand shaking, she pulled up the comm.

30 AUG 126 T.E.

THIS COMMUNICATION IS TO INFORM SCARLET
BENOIT OF RIEUX, FRANCE, EF, THAT AT 05:09 ON
30 AUG 126, LUC RAOUL BENOIT OF PARIS,
FRANCE, EF, WAS PRONOUNCED DEAD BY
ON-STAFF MEDICAL PRACTITIONER ID #58279.
PRESUMED CAUSE OF DEATH: ALCOHOL
POISONING
PLEASE RESPOND WITHIN 24 HOURS IF YOU
WOULD LIKE AN AUTOPSY TO BE PERFORMED FOR
THE COST OF 4500 UNIVS.
WITH SYMPATHIES,
THE STAFF OF L'HÔPITAL JOSEPH DUCUING,
TOULOUSE

Confusion reigned, her heart thumping erratically. The message didn't want to compute, her brain turning it over and over. She pictured him the last time she'd seen him, raving and tortured and afraid. How she'd screamed at him. Told him she never wanted to see him again.

How could he be dead, only twenty-four hours later? Shouldn't she have received a comm when he'd been admitted into the hospital? Shouldn't there have been a warning?

Swaying on her feet, she peered up at Wolf. "My dad's dead," she said, her whisper barely filling the enormous space. "Alcohol poisoning."

His jaw flexed. "Are they sure about that?"

His suspicion was slow to filter through her encroaching numbness. "You think they sent the comm by mistake?"

A touch of sympathy flickered in his eyes. "No, Scarlet. But I do think he was in danger of something much worse than a fondness for drinking."

She didn't understand. He'd been tortured, but the burn marks wouldn't have killed him. The insanity wouldn't have killed him.

Through the fog in her brain, a gentle, caressing instinct told her to look up. So she did.

Behind Wolf, framed by two pillars that held unlit sconces, was a man. He was willowy and lean, with wavy dark hair and near-black eyes that burned in the candlelight. He would have had a pleasant smile if Scarlet hadn't been so startled—by his presence, his silence, the fact that Wolf did not seem surprised he was there, did not even bother to face him though he un-doubtedly felt him too.

More terrifying than all that was his clothing. He wore a crimson red coat that flared at his waist and had long, bell-shaped sleeves. Gold-embroidered runes sparkled along the hems. It was almost like a child's costume, an imitation of the horrible Lunar court.

Fear thumped against Scarlet's rib cage. This was not a cos-tume. This was the stuff of nightmares and horror stories told to keep children from misbehaving.

A thaumaturge. A Lunar thaumaturge.

"Hello," the man said, in a voice as sweet and smooth as melted caramel. "You must be Mademoiselle Benoit."

She stumbled back onto the first step, catching the rail for balance. In front of her, Wolf dipped his eyes and turned around. The man acknowledged him with a polite nod.

"Alpha Kesley, so glad you've made it back safely. And if I am to correctly understand the comm the lady just received, Beta Wynn's task in Toulouse must be finished as well. It seems we will soon be a full pack again."

Wolf clamped a fist to his chest and gave a slight bow. "I am glad to hear it, Master Jael."

Gulping, Scarlet pushed her hip into the rail. "No," she said, finding her voice on the second try. "He brought me here to find my grandmother. He's not one of you anymore."

The man's smile was warm and understanding. "I see. I'm sure you are quite eager to see your grandmother. I hope to reunite you shortly."

Scarlet clenched her fists. "Where is she? *If you've hurt her—*"

"She is quite alive, I assure you," said the man. Without any change in expression, he slid his attention back to Wolf. "Tell me, Alpha, were you able to meet your objectives?"

Wolf lowered his hand to his side. Obedience hung from him like a thin, absurd disguise.

A headache pounded at Scarlet's temples. Her nerves hummed as she waited, hoping and wishing he was going to tell this man that he'd left their ridiculous pack and he was never coming back.

But the hope couldn't be entertained for long. It was being shucked off before Wolf even opened his mouth.

This man was not a rebellious criminal, some member of a vigilante gang. If he was truly a thaumaturge, a real thaumaturge standing before her, then he worked for the Lunar crown.

And Wolf—what did that make Wolf?

"I have questioned her to the best of my ability," Wolf said. "She has a single, vague memory, but I doubt both its usefulness and its reliability. Time and stress seem to have had an effect on her recollections, and at this point I have no doubt she would create falsehoods if she believed they would benefit her grand-mother."

The thaumaturge tilted his chin up, considering him. *Alpha Kesley.*

Scarlet's heart hammered against her collarbone, ready to choke her.

I have questioned her to the best of my ability.

"Wolf."

He did not turn to her. Did not flinch or sigh or respond. He was a statue. He was a pawn.

The thaumaturge made a sad sound. "No matter." Then, after a silence in which Scarlet felt the stairs crumbling beneath her, he said, "Omega Kesley was to inform you that our objectives have changed. Her Majesty is no longer concerned with identifying Selene."

Wolf's fingers twitched.

"Nevertheless, it has become clear to me that Madame Benoit has not yet given up all her secrets. Perhaps we can find another use for the mademoiselle."

Wolf's chin lifted, just slightly. "If she'd had any additional information, she would have told me. I am sure her trust was complete."

Scarlet half slumped onto the marble rail, grasping the base of the headless statue to keep from sinking to the ground.

"I'm sure you've done very well," said the thaumaturge. "Don't be alarmed. I will see that your efforts are given proper recognition."

"Who's Beta Wynn?" said Scarlet. "What was his task in Toulouse?" Her voice was weak, filled with disbelief as she teetered on the stairs. She struggled to believe this was all a nightmare. Soon she would wake up on the train, in Wolf's arms, and this would all happen very differently. But she did not wake up, and the thaumaturge was eyeing her with dark, sympathetic eyes.

"Beta Wynn's task was to kill your father in a manner that would not raise suspicions," he said, with no more reservation than if he were giving her the time of day. "I did offer your father a chance. If he had found something useful on Madame Benoit's property, I think I truly would have considered letting him live, perhaps kept him as a slave. But he failed in the time we gave him, so I was forced to have him silenced. He knew too much about us, you see, and he had served his usefulness. I'm afraid we have little tolerance for useless Earthens."

He grinned, the look twisting Scarlet's gut—not because it

was a cruel smile, but because it was a kind one. "You appear to be ill, Mademoiselle. Perhaps you will need some rest before you're fit to see your grandmother. Rafe, Troya, won't you see the lady to her prepared room?"

They emerged from the shadows, two men who were nothing but blurs in Scarlet's consciousness. They lifted her by her elbows, not bothering with ties or cuffs.

Her mind flashed and before she knew it, she was reaching for her waistband.

Wolf's hand was there first, one arm brushing against her side. Her breath caught and she was frozen, staring wide-eyed into his face. His emerald eyes hollow as his fingers lifted the back of her sweatshirt and pulled out the gun.

He was going to kill them.

He was going to protect her.

Flipping the gun around so that he gripped the barrel, Wolf held it out to one of her captors.

When his severity melted, hinting at something like regret, Scarlet set her jaw. "A Loyal Soldier to the Order of the Pack?"

She saw the pain in his gulp. "No. Lunar Special Operative."

The room spun.

Lunar. He was Lunar. He worked for them.

He worked for the queen.

Scarlet turned her head away and forced her legs to be strong, refusing to be carried away like a child as they guided her to another set of stairs, stairs that led down to the opera house's sublevels. She refused to give them the pleasure of a struggle.

The thaumaturge's voice followed behind her, all benevolence. "You have my leave to rest until sunset, Alpha Kesley. I can see that your trials have wearied you."

Twenty-Eight

KAI PACED THE LENGTH OF HIS OFFICE FROM DOOR TO DESK, desk to door. Two days had passed since Levana had issued her ultimatum: Find the cyborg girl, or she would attack.

Time was running out and every hour filled Kai with growing dread. He hadn't slept for over forty-eight hours. With the exception of five press conferences in which he still had nothing new to report, he hadn't left his office in that time either.

Still, no sign of Linh Cinder.

No sign of Dr. Erland.

Like they'd simply vanished.

"Gah!" He pulled his hands back through his hair until his scalp stung. "*Lunars.*"

The speaker on his desk hummed. "Royal android Nainsi has requested entrance."

Kai released his hair with a deflated groan. Nainsi had been good to him the past few days, bringing vast amounts of tea and saying nothing when she took the still-full-but-now-cold cups back out hours later. She encouraged him to eat and reminded him when a press conference was coming up or that he'd neglected to return the Australian Governor-General's comms. If it weren't for the title, "Royal android Nainsi," he almost would have expected a human to walk through the doors every time she was summoned.

He wondered if his father had felt the same way toward his android assistants. Or maybe Kai was just delirious.

Shooing away the unhelpful thoughts, he rounded to the back of his desk. "Yes, enter."

The door opened and Nainsi's treads rolled across the carpet. She was not carrying the tray of snacks he'd expected.

"Your Majesty, a woman by the name of Linh Adri and her daughter, Linh Pearl, have requested an immediate appointment. Linh-jiĕ says she has important information on the Lunar fugitive. I encouraged her to contact Chairman Huy but she insisted she speak with you directly. I scanned her ID and she appears to be who she claims. I wasn't sure if I should turn her away."

"That's fine. Thank you, Nainsi. Send her in."

Nainsi rolled back out. Kai glanced down at his shirt and buttoned the collar, but determined there was nothing he could do about the wrinkles.

A moment later, two strangers entered his office. The first was a middle-aged woman with hair just beginning to gray, and the other was a teenage girl with thick hair that hung straight down her back. Kai frowned as the two bowed deeply before him, and it wasn't until the girl attempted a shy grin that he felt like an idiot for his exhaustion-muddled brain not picking up on their names when Nainsi had first announced them. Linh Adri. Linh Pearl.

They were not entirely strangers. He'd seen the girl twice before, once at Cinder's booth at the market, then again at the ball. This was Cinder's stepsister.

And the woman.

The woman.

His blood curdled with the memory of her, made worse by the almost bashful, girlish look she was giving him now. He had seen her at the ball too. When she'd been about to strike Cinder for daring to attend in the first place.

"Your Majesty," said Nainsi, returning behind them. "May I introduce Linh Adri-jiě and her daughter, Linh Pearl-mèi."

They each bowed again.

"Yes, hello," said Kai. "You are—"

"I *was* the legal guardian of Linh Cinder," said Adri. "Please forgive the intrusion, Your Imperial Majesty. I understand you are quite busy."

He cleared his throat, wishing now he'd left the collar alone. It was already strangling him. "Please, sit down," he said, gesturing to the sitting area around the holographic fire. "That will be all, Nainsi. Thank you."

Kai moved to claim the chair, determined not to sit beside either of the women. They in turn perched straight-backed on the sofa so as not to crumple the bows on their kimono-style dresses, and folded their hands demurely atop their laps. The resemblance between the two was remarkable—and of course, nothing at all like Cinder, whose skin had been always sun darkened, whose hair was straighter and finer, and who had carried an understated confidence with her even when she was shy and stammering.

Kai caught himself before he could smile at the memory of Cinder, shy and stammering.

"I'm afraid we were not formally introduced when our paths crossed at the ball last week, Linh-jiě."

"Oh, Your Imperial Majesty is too kind. Adri, please. Truth be told, I am attempting to distance myself from the ward who now carries my husband's name. And you will, I am sure, remember my lovely daughter."

He turned his attention to Pearl. "Yes, we met at the market. You had some packages you wished Cinder to store for you."

He was glad the girl flushed, and he hoped she was remembering how rude she'd been that day.

"We also met at the ball, Your Majesty," said Pearl. "We discussed my poor sister—my real sister—who recently fell ill and passed away from the same disease that claimed your illustrious father."

"Yes, I recall. My condolences on your loss."

He waited for the expected return of sympathy, but it did not come. The mother was too busy examining the office's lacquered woodwork; the daughter was too busy examining Kai with faux timidity.

He tapped his fingers against the chair's arm. "My android tells me you have information to impart? Regarding Linh Cinder?"

"Yes, Your Majesty." Adri drew her attention back to him. "Thank you for seeing us on such short notice, but I do have some information that I think could be helpful in your search for my ward. As a concerned citizen, I of course want to do anything I can to assist with the search, and ensure she is apprehended before she can do further damage."

"Of course you do. But forgive me, Linh-jiě, I was under the impression you'd already been contacted and questioned by the authorities as a part of the investigation?"

"Oh yes, we both spoke at length with some very nice men," said Adri, "but since then, something new has come to my attention."

Kai settled his elbows on his knees.

"Your Majesty, I trust you are familiar with the recorded footage from the quarantines, about two weeks ago, in which a girl attacked two med-droids?"

He nodded. "Of course. The girl who spoke to Chang Sunto, the boy who recovered from the plague."

"Well, at the time I was very distracted, having just lost my youngest daughter, but since then I've taken a closer look at the video and I'm convinced that the girl is Cinder."

Kai's brow drew together, already replaying the video in his mind. The girl was never clearly seen—the recording was grainy and shaky and only showed glimpses of her back. "Really," he mused, trying not to sound speculative. "What makes you think that?"

"It's difficult to tell on the video itself, and I would not know for sure, except I was having Cinder's ID tracked that day, as she'd been behaving suspiciously for some time. I know she was near the quarantines that day. Before, I'd thought she was merely attempting to run away from her household duties, but I now see that the little aberration had a much more sinister motive in mind."

His eyebrows rose. "Aberration?"

Adri's cheeks tinted pink. "Even that is too kind for her, Your Majesty. Are you aware that she can't even *cry*?"

Kai sat back. After a moment he found that, rather than being disgusted as Adri clearly expected, he was left merely curious. "Really? Is that normal for ... for cyborgs?"

"I wouldn't know, Your Majesty. She is the first and hopefully the last cyborg I'll ever have the misfortune of knowing. I can't understand why we make cyborgs in the first place. They're dangerous and proud creatures, parading around like they think they're better than everyone else. Like they deserve special treatment for their ... eccentricities. They're nothing but a drain on our hardworking society."

Collar beginning to itch, Kai cleared his throat. "I see. You said something earlier about evidence that Cinder had been near the quarantines? And ... done something sinister?"

"Yes, Your Majesty. If you'd be so kind as to refer to my ID page, you'll see I've uploaded a video that is rather incriminating."

Kai unlatched his portscreen from his belt, thinking about the footage from the quarantines as he searched for Adri's page. The video was at the top—a low-quality image tagged with the symbol of the Commonwealth's law enforcement androids. "What is this?"

"When Cinder wouldn't respond to my comms that day, and I was sure she was fleeing the country, I enacted my right to have her forcibly retrieved. This is the footage from when they found her."

Holding his breath, Kai played the video. It was shot from a hovercar, peering down on a dusty street surrounded by abandoned warehouses. And there was Cinder, panting and angry. She raised a clenched fist toward the android. "I didn't steal it! It belongs to her family, not to you or anyone else!"

The camera shook as the hover landed and the android approached her.

Scowling, Cinder took half a step back. "I haven't done anything wrong. That med-droid was attacking me. It was self-defense."

Kai watched, shoulders tense, as the android rambled on in its monotone voice about the rights of her legal guardian and the Cyborg Protection Act, until finally Cinder assented to come with them and the video ended.

It took a mere four seconds for Kai to pull up the footage of the girl attacking the quarantine med-droid, and his grip tightened around the device as he fit the puzzle pieces together. He found himself feeling like a fool, for the hundredth time that week.

It made sense that it was Cinder. *Of course* it was Cinder. He had given the antidote just hours before to Dr. Erland, right in front of her. Erland must have passed it to her, and she then gave it to Chang Sunto. And though the cameras had never got a good shot of her, the hasty ponytail and baggy cargo pants matched perfectly.

Gulping, he shut off the video and reattached the port to his belt. "What was she talking about, that she didn't steal? What belongs to her family?"

Adri set her mouth in a firm line, deep wrinkles cutting into her upper lip. "Something that did indeed belong with her family—with those who would have given proper respect to the deceased. And Cinder mutilated that which was once most precious to me in order to get it."

"She what?"

"I believe she stole my daughter's ID chip, not minutes after her death." Adri placed a hand on the swath of silk over her abdomen. "It churns my stomach to think of, but I know I should have expected it. Cinder was always jealous of both my girls, and so spiteful. Although I could not have imagined her sinking to such a low before, now that I know her true nature, I cannot be surprised by it. She deserves to be found and punished for what she's done."

Kai drew away from the venom in her tone, and couldn't connect her accusations to his own memories of Cinder. He thought of their paths crossing in the elevator, of her eyes filling with sadness as she spoke of her dying sister. How she'd asked if Kai would save a dance for her in case she miraculously survived.

Or was every memory he had of Cinder truly nothing more than a Lunar trick? What did he know about her, really?

"Are you sure?"

"The reports claimed that the weapon used against the androids was a scalpel, and it all happened just moments after I received the comm telling me that my daughter . . . my daughter . . ." Her jaw trembled, her knuckles whitening in her lap. "And I can just *see* her trying to take Peony's identity in that *inhuman* head of hers." She grimaced. "It chills me to think, but it is precisely something she would have done."

"And you think she could still have the ID chip with her?"

"That, Your Majesty, I cannot say. But it is a possibility."

With a nod, Kai stood. Adri and Pearl gawked up at him, mute, before bolting to their own feet.

"Thank you for bringing this to my attention, Linh-jiĕ. I'll have a tracker set up for the ID immediately. If she has the chip, we will find her."

Even as he spoke, he found himself pleading to the stars that Linh Adri was wrong. That Cinder had not taken the ID chip. But that was a stupid wish, an immature wish. He had to find her, and he only had one more day to do it. He had no desire to find out what Levana would do if he failed.

"Thank you, Your Majesty," said Adri. "I only want to know that my daughter's memory won't be tarnished because I was once so generous as to allow that awful girl into my family."

"Thank you," he started, not sure what he was thanking her for, but it seemed the right thing to say. "If we have any further questions, I'll have someone contact you."

"Yes, of course, Your Majesty," Adri said with a bow. "I only wish to do well by my country, and see this horrid girl brought to justice."

Kai listed his head. "You do realize that once she's found, Queen Levana intends to have her executed, don't you?"

Adri folded her hands prettily before her. "I am sure the law is there for a reason, Your Majesty."

Pursing his lips, Kai stepped away from the sitting area and led them toward the door.

After two more bows apiece, Pearl glided out of the room with lashes fluttering at Kai until her neck could no longer crane toward him, but Adri paused in the doorway. Bowed one more time. "It was such an honor, Your Majesty."

He smiled tautly back.

"I do wonder—not that this matters one little bit, but only as a matter of curiosity—*should* this lead to any discoveries in the investigation . . . might I be able to expect any sort of reward for my assistance?"

Twenty-Nine

SCARLET'S PRISON CELL HAD BEGUN LIFE AS A DRESSING room. The vague outlines of mirrors and vanities were burned into the walls and the strips of lightbulbs that had surrounded them had been reduced to empty sockets. The carpet had been pulled up, revealing cold stone beneath, and the solid oak door had been taken off its hinges and left abandoned in the corner, replaced instead with welded iron bars and an ID-sensitive lock.

Scarlet's fury had kept her pacing and storming about the room, kicking the walls and growling at the bars, for all night and most of the day. At least, it seemed like nearly a full day had passed—it seemed like months had passed—but being trapped in the opera house's sublevel meant she had no indication of time other than the two meals that had been brought to her. The "soldier" who had made the delivery said nothing when she asked how long they were going to keep her there or demanded to see her grandmother immediately, only smirked at her through the bars in a way that made her skin crawl.

She had finally collapsed on the blanketless mattress, physically exhausted. She glared at the ceiling. Hating herself. Hating these men that kept her prisoner. Hating Wolf.

She gnashed her teeth and dug her fingernails into the worn, broken mattress.

Alpha Kesley.

If she ever saw him again she would scratch his eyes out. She would throttle him until his lips turned blue. She would—

"Finally wore yourself out?"

She jerked upward. One of the men who had first brought her to the cell stood on the other side—Rafe or Troya, she didn't know which.

"I'm not hungry," she spat.

He sneered. Every last one of them seemed to carry that same humorless smile, like it had been bred into them. "I'm not offering food," he said, and swiped his wrist past the scanner. Grasping the bars, he lugged the door open. "I'm taking you to see your precious grand-mère."

Scarlet scrambled off the mattress, all exhaustion flooding away. "Really?"

"Those are my orders. Am I going to have to bind you or do you intend to come willingly?"

"I'll come. Just take me to her."

His gaze dipped over her. Evidently determining she didn't pose a threat, he stepped back and gestured toward the long, dim corridor. "Then after you."

As soon as she stepped into the hallway, he grasped her

wrist and lowered his face so that his breath steamed against her neck. "Do anything stupid and I'll take my displeasure out on the old hag, do you understand?"

She shuddered.

Without waiting for a response, he released her and nudged her between her shoulder blades, prodding her down the hallway.

Her heart raced. She was near delirium with fatigue and the promise of seeing her grandmother, but it didn't keep her from scoping out her prison. Half a dozen barred doorways lined this basement corridor, all dark. The man urged her around a corner, up a thin stairwell, through a doorway.

They were backstage. Dusty old props filled the rafters and black curtains hung like phantoms in the darkness. The only light came from runners along the aisles in the audience and Scarlet had to squint as the soldier led her out onto the stage, then down the steps into the empty audience. An entire section of seats had been removed, leaving holes where they'd once been bolted to the sloped floor. Another group of soldiers was standing there, in the shadows, like they'd been having a jovial conversation before Scarlet and her captor had interrupted them. Scarlet kept her eyes firmly glued to the end of the aisle. She didn't think any of them were Wolf, but she didn't want to know if she was wrong.

They reached the back of the theater and Scarlet pushed open one of the huge doors.

They were on a balcony overlooking the lobby and the grand staircase. Still no sunlight came through the hole in the ceiling—clearly she'd missed the whole day.

Her captor grabbed her elbow, pulling her away from the stairs, past more haunting statues of cherubs and angels. She yanked her arm from his grip and tried to commit their journey to memory, creating a blueprint of the opera house in her mind, but it was difficult when she knew that she was going to see her grandmother. Finally.

The thought of being held by these monsters for nearly three long weeks curdled her stomach.

He guided her up a staircase to the first balcony and continued to the second. Closed doors led back into the theater, to the higher tiers of seats, but the soldier bypassed them and moved to another hallway. Finally he stopped before a closed door, grasped the handle, and shoved it open.

They had reached one of the private balconies that overlooked the stage, holding only four red velvet chairs in two rows.

Her grandma was sitting alone in the front row, her thick gray braid dangling over the back of the seat. The tears Scarlet had been fighting for so long came at her in a rush.

"Grand-mère!"

Her grandma started, but Scarlet was already barreling toward her. She collapsed to her knees in the space between the chairs and the railing and draped herself over her grandma's lap, crying into her jeans. The same dirt-covered jeans she always gardened in. The familiar aroma of dirt and hay peeled up from the fabric, making Scarlet cry harder.

"Scarlet! What are you doing here?" her grandma asked, settling her hands down on Scarlet's back. She sounded stern and angry, but not unkind. "Stop that. You're making a fool of your-self." She pulled Scarlet off her lap. "There, there, calm down. What are you doing here?"

Scarlet sat back on her heels and stared bleary-eyed into her grandma's face. Bloodshot eyes belied her exhaustion, no matter how her jaw was set. She was on the verge of crying too, but hadn't yet succumbed to the tears. Scarlet took her hands, squeezing them. Her grandmother's hands were soft, as if three weeks away from the farm had rubbed away years of calluses.

"I came for you," she said. "After Dad told me what happened, what they were doing to you, I had to come find you. Are you all right? Are you hurt?"

"I'm fine, I'm fine." She rubbed her thumbs over Scarlet's knuckles. "But I don't like seeing you here. You shouldn't have come. These men—they—you shouldn't be here. It's dangerous."

"I'm going to get us both out of here. I promise. Stars, I missed you so much." Sobbing, she pressed her forehead to their entwined fingers, ignoring the hot tears that dripped off her jaw. "I found you, Grand-mère. I found you."

Slipping one hand out of Scarlet's grip, her grandma brushed a cluster of messy curls off Scarlet's brow. "I knew you would. I knew you would come. Here, sit down next to me."

Stifling the tears, Scarlet pulled herself off her grandma's lap. A tray sat on the seat beside her grandma, holding a cup of tea, half a baguette, and a small bowl of red grapes that seemed untouched. Her grandma took the tray and held it out to the soldier in the doorway. His lips curled, but he took the tray and left, letting the door shut behind him. Scarlet's heart expanded—she did not hear a lock being put on the door. They were alone.

"Sit here, Scarlet. I've missed you so much—but I'm so angry with you. You shouldn't have come. It's too dangerous...but now that you're here. Oh, darling, you're exhausted."

"Grand-mère, don't they monitor you? Aren't they afraid you'll escape?"

The old woman's face softened and she pet the empty seat. "Of course they monitor me. We are never truly alone here."

Scarlet considered the wall that separated them from the next private balcony, covered in flaking red wallpaper. Perhaps someone was there now, listening to them. Or the group of soldiers she'd seen down in the first-floor audience—if their senses were nearly as attuned as Wolf's, they could probably hear them even from down there. Ignoring the urge to scream obscenities across the void, she lifted herself into the chair and reached for her grandma's hands again, holding them tight. Soft as they may have become, they were also deathly cold.

"You're sure you're all right? They haven't hurt you?"

Her grandma smiled, wearily. "They haven't hurt me. Not yet. Although I don't know what they have planned, and I don't trust them a hair, not after what they did to Luc. And they've mentioned you. I was terrified that they would go after you too, darling. I wish you hadn't come. I should have been more prepared for this. I should have known this would happen."

"But what do they want?"

Her grandma dragged her attention down to the dark stage. "They want information that I can't give them, though I would in a heartbeat if I could. I would have weeks ago. Anything to come home to you. Anything to keep you safe."

"Information about what?"

Her grandma took in a slow breath. "They want to know about Princess Selene."

Scarlet's pulse skipped. "Is it true, then? Do you really know something about her?"

Her grandma's eyebrows jumped upward. "Have they told you why, then? Why they suspect me?"

She nodded, feeling guilty for knowing the secret her grandma had so long harbored. "They told me about Logan Tanner. How they think he brought Selene to Earth, and how he may have sought out your help. They told me they think he's my . . . my grandfather."

The wrinkles on her grandma's forehead deepened and she cast a concerned look at the wall behind Scarlet, toward the other balcony, before drawing her attention back. "Scarlet. My love." Her expression was gentle, but she didn't continue.

Scarlet gulped, wondering if, after all these years, her grandma couldn't stand to dig up the past. The romance that had been so brief, but had been clinging to her for so long.

Did she even know that Logan Tanner was dead?

"Grand-mère, I remember the man that came to the house. The man from the Eastern Commonwealth."

Her grandma tilted her head up, patient.

"I thought he was coming to take *me* away, but he wasn't, was he? You two were talking about the princess."

"Very good, Scarlet, dear."

"Why don't you just tell them his name? You must remember what it was, and then they could go to him. Won't he know where the princess is?"

"They no longer want to know about the princess."

She bit down on her lip. Frustration welled up inside her. She was shaking. "Then why don't they let us go?"

Her grandma squeezed Scarlet's fingers. Years of pulling weeds and chopping vegetables had made them strong, despite their age. "They can't control me, Scarlet."

She scrutinized her grandma's lined face. "What do you mean?"

"They're Lunar. The thaumaturge—he has the Lunar gift. But it doesn't work on me. That's why they're keeping me here. They want to know why."

Scarlet grasped for figments in her mind. All those bits and pieces she'd learned about Lunars—impossible ever to tell which were true and which were exaggerated tales. It was believed that their queen ruled through mind control, and that her thaumaturges were almost as strong as she was. That they could manipulate people's thoughts and emotions. That they could even control people's bodies if they chose, like puppets on strings.

Scarlet gulped. "Are there a lot of people who can't be ... controlled?"

"Very few. Some Lunars are born that way. They call them

shells. But they've never known of an Earthen who could resist before. I'm the first."

"How? Is it genetic?" She hesitated. "Can *I* be controlled?"

"Oh yes, dear. Whatever makes me like this, you do not have it. They'll use that against us, mark my words. I imagine they'll want to experiment on us both as they attempt to find out where this abnormality comes from. Whether or not they should be worried about other Earthens being able to resist them as well." In the darkness, her grandmother's jaw hardened. "It must not be hereditary. Your father was weak also."

Scarlet was lost in warm brown eyes that had always been soothing, and yet struck her as harsh now in the darkness of the theater. Something gnawed at the back of her thoughts. The faintest suspicion.

Her father *was* weak. Weak for women. Weak for booze. A weak father, a weak man.

But her grandmother had never suggested she could think the same of Scarlet. *You'll be fine,* she always said, after a skinned knee, after a broken arm, after her first youthful heartbreak. *You'll be fine because you're strong, like me.*

Heart thumping, Scarlet lowered her gaze to their intertwined fingers. Her grandmother's very wrinkled, very frail, very soft hands.

Her chest constricted.

Lunars could manipulate people's thoughts and emotions. Manipulate the way they experienced the very world around them.

Gulping, Scarlet pulled away. Her grandma's fingers clenched in a brief effort to restrict her, but then let go.

Scarlet staggered out of her seat and backed against the rail, staring at her grandmother. The familiar unkempt hair in its always crooked braid. The familiar eyes, growing colder as they peered up at her. Growing wider.

She blinked rapidly against the hallucination, and her grandmother's hands grew larger.

Repulsion ripped through Scarlet. She gripped the railing to hold herself steady.

"Who are you?"

The door at the back of the balcony opened, but instead of her guard, Scarlet saw the thaumaturge's silhouette in the hallway. "Very well, Omega. We have learned as much as we can from her."

Scarlet faced her grandmother again. A startled cry was wrenched out of her.

Her grandmother was gone, replaced by Wolf's brother. Omega Ran Kesley sat staring up at her, perfectly at ease. He wore the same shirt she'd seen him in last, wrinkled and flecked with dried mud. "Hello, dear. How nice to see you again."

Scarlet glared up at the thaumaturge. She could make out the whites of his eyes, the draping of his fancy tunic. "Where is she?"

"She is alive, for now, and unfortunately remains a mystery." He squinted at Scarlet. "Her mind remains impenetrable, but whatever her secret is, she has not passed it on to her son or her grandchild. I would think if it was a mental trick she were using, she would have at least tried to teach it to *you,* if not to that pathetic drunkard. And yet, if it is genetic, could it be a random trait? Or is there a shell in your ancestry?" He touched a finger to his lips, analyzing Scarlet like a frog he was about to dissect. "Perhaps you won't be entirely useless, though. I wonder how lubricated the old lady's tongue would become if she were to watch as you hammered needles into your own flesh."

Fury clawed up her throat and Scarlet hurled herself at him with a ragged cry, nails scratching at his face.

She froze with her fingertips millimeters from his eye sockets. The fury drained away all at once and she collapsed, sobbing uncontrollably on the floor. Wondering what was wrong with her. She reached for her hatred again but it slipped continuously from her mind, like trying to hold on to an eel. The harder she tried, the faster and harder the tears came. Choking her. Blinding her. All her anger dissolving into hopelessness and misery.

Her head filled with self-loathing. She was useless. Weak and stupid and insignificant.

She folded in on herself, her cries nearly drowning out the thaumaturge's unimpressed chuckle above her.

"How unfortunate your grandmother hasn't been so easy to manipulate. It would make this all so much simpler."

Her mind hushed, the destructive words slipping back to a far, quiet corner of her thoughts, and the tears faded away with them. Like turning a faucet on and off.

Like toying with a puppet.

Scarlet lay crumpled on the floor, gasping. She swiped the mucus from her face.

Digging her hands into the carpet, she forced her body to stop trembling and pushed herself up, using the doorjamb for support. The thaumaturge's face twisted in that sickeningly charming way he had.

"I'll have you escorted back to your quarters," he said, his tone all syrupy kindness. "Thank you most humbly for your cooperation."

Thirty

ALPHA ZE'EV KESLEY'S HARD-SOLED BOOTS CLIPPED HARSH against the marble floor as he marched through the lobby, ignoring a handful of soldiers that nodded to him in respect, or perhaps fear. Perhaps even curiosity at the officer who had spent weeks out in the midst of humans, pretending to be one of them.

He tried not to think of it. Being back at the headquarters felt like he'd awoken from a dream. A dream that had once sounded like a nightmare, but not quite so anymore. He had woken up to a reality much darker. He had remembered who he really was. *What* he really was.

He reached the Lunar Rotunda—an ironic name that had pleased Master Jael greatly. He passed a mirror, pocked and darkened with age, almost not recognizing his reflection with its clean uniform and hair combed neatly back. He snatched his gaze away.

He smelled his brother as soon as he stepped into the

library and the hairs on his neck prickled. His pace faltered briefly as he made his way through the wood-paneled gallery and into the thaumaturge's private office. It had once been suited for royalty—a room for important, high-society Earthens to muse over the philosophical works of their ancestors. Display cases had once held priceless art and bookshelves climbed two stories over his head. But the books were all gone now, rescued when the opera house had been taken over by the military, and a musty, mildew scent had settled into the pores of the surrounding wood.

Jael was seated at a wide desk. Made of plastic and metal, it stood stark and dull against the extravagant décor. Ran was there too, leaning against the wall of empty shelves.

His brother smiled. Almost.

Jael stood. "Alpha Kesley, thank you for coming at such short notice. I wanted you to be the first to know your brother had made it back safely."

"I'm glad to see it," he said. "Hello, Ran. You were not looking too well last I saw you."

"Likewise, Ze'ev. Your smell is much improved now that you've washed that human off."

Every muscle tightened. "I hope there are no hard feelings about what happened in the forest."

"None at all. You were playing a role. I understand you did what you had to. I should not have interfered."

"No. You shouldn't have."

Ran hooked his thumbs over the wide sash around his

waist. "I was worried about you, brother. You seemed almost . . . *confused.*"

"As you said," said Ze'ev, tilting his chin up. "I was playing a role."

"Yes. I should never have doubted you. Nonetheless, it is nice to see you returned to your normal self, and that her bullet didn't go deeper. I'd worried when I heard it go off that she may have hit your heart." Ran grinned and turned back to Jael. "If we are through here, I'd like to request permission to report to command."

"Permission granted," said Jael, nodding as Ran saluted him, a fist to his chest.

Ze'ev caught a trace of Scarlet's scent on Ran as he brushed past, and his stomach squeezed. He urged his body to relax, burying the animal instinct to tear out his brother's throat if he found out he'd laid one finger on her.

Ran listed his head, expression darkening with a withheld secret. "Welcome home, brother."

Ze'ev remained expressionless as Ran continued on, waiting until he heard the door close at the other end of the gallery. He saluted the thaumaturge. "If there's nothing else—"

"Actually, there is something else. A few things, actually, that I wish to discuss with you." Jael sank back into his seat. "I received a comm from Her Majesty this morning. She's asked that all packs stationed on Earth be prepared to attack tomorrow."

His jaw tightened. "Tomorrow?"

"Her negotiations with the Eastern Commonwealth have

not gone according to her desires, and she's quite finished offering compromises that they refuse to accept. She has offered a temporary continuation of peace should the cyborg girl, Linh Cinder, be captured and handed over to her, but that has not happened. The attack will be centered in New Beijing, beginning at midnight their local time. We will attack at 18:00." He tucked his hands into his wide crimson sleeves, their embroidered runes catching the light of self-sustained bulbs overhead. "I'm glad you've returned in time to lead your men. I want you positioned at the heart of our Paris attack. Will you accept this role?"

Ze'ev clasped his hands behind his back, gripping his wrists until they ached. "I do not wish to question Her Majesty's motives, but I cannot understand why she is calling us away from our initial objective of finding the princess in order to teach a petty lesson to the Commonwealth. Why the change of priorities?"

Jael leaned back, studying him. "It is not for you to question Her Majesty's priorities. However, I would hate for your mind to be clouded as we head into this important first battle." He shrugged. "She is enraged with the escape of this Linh Cinder. Though she may be a mere civilian, she was able to see beyond Her Majesty's glamour. And yet, she is not a shell."

Ze'ev couldn't keep the surprise from his face.

"We are not sure yet if this unusual ability is due to something in her cyborg programming, or if her own Lunar gift is exceptionally strong."

"Stronger than Her Majesty's?"

"We do not know." Jael sighed. "What is strange is that this ability of hers to resist our queen is not unlike Madame Benoit's ability to resist *me*. To find two nonshells with the same skill in such a short period of time is quite remarkable. Unfortunately, I am no closer to determining the reason for Michelle Benoit's ability. I tested her granddaughter an hour ago—she is as malleable as clay, so she has not inherited the trait."

Behind his back, Alpha Kesley's fists clenched. Still, he couldn't shake her scent from the room, the faintest breath of her dancing beneath his nostrils. So Jael had questioned her, and Ran must have been there too. What had they done? Had she been hurt?

"Alpha?"

"Yes," he said, quickly. "I apologize. I thought I'd sensed the girl."

Jael started to laugh. A clear, amused laugh. It was Jael's peculiar warmth that Ze'ev had always distrusted most—at least the other thaumaturges made no pretense of their ruthlessness, their haughty control of the lesser Lunar citizens . . . and of their soldiers.

"Your senses are remarkable, Alpha. Without doubt, one of our best." He tapped at his chair, before pushing himself up. "And your strength of character is unequaled. Your loyalty. Your willingness to make sacrifices. I'm sure none of my other men would have gone to the lengths you did to obtain information from Miss Benoit, gone so above the call of duty. That is precisely why I've chosen you to lead tomorrow's attack."

Jael paced to the row of shelves and ran a finger along them, dust collecting pale and gray against his skin. Ze'ev kept his expression blank, trying not to think what sacrifices Jael thought he had made, so far above the call of duty.

But she was there in his mind. The pad of her thumb brushing against his scars. Her arms wrapping around his neck.

He swallowed hard. Every muscle drew tight against his bones in an effort to block out the memory.

"Now it is only a question of what to do with the girl. How frustrating that we finally find someone who might lead us closer to Princess Selene, just when we no longer have use of the information."

Ze'ev's fingernails bit into his palms. *Frustrating* seemed laughable. If Her Majesty had changed her focus away from the princess three weeks ago, Scarlet and her grandmother never would have been involved in any of it.

And he never would have known the difference.

A clamp squeezed in on his chest.

"But I am optimistic," Jael continued, speaking absently. "We may still find a use for the girl, if she can persuade her grandmother to talk. The madame tries to play at ignorance, but she knows why she is able to resist control. I'm sure of it." He fidgeted with the cuff of his sleeve. "Which do you suppose will be more important to the old lady? Her granddaughter's life, or her own secrets?"

Ze'ev had no response.

"I guess we will see," said Jael, returning to his desk. "At least now I'll have some power over her." His lips parted, showing perfect white teeth in a pleasant smile. "You still have not answered my question, Alpha. Will you accept the role of leading our most important battle in the European Federation?"

Ze'ev's lungs burned. He wanted to ask more, to know more—about Scarlet, her grandmother, what Jael would do to her.

But the questions would not be acceptable. His mission was complete. He no longer had any tie to Mademoiselle Benoit.

He clasped a fist to his chest. "Of course, Master Jael. It would be an honor."

"Good." Opening a drawer, Jael pulled out a plain white box and slid it across the desk. "On that, we've just received this shipment of ID chips from the Paris quarantines. I hope it won't be too out of your way to take them down for wiping and reprogramming? I want them to be ready for the new recruits I expect to arrive tomorrow morning." He tilted back in his chair. "We will want as many soldiers available as we can manage. It is imperative that the people of Earth be too terrified to even consider fighting back."

Thirty-One

CINDER PEERED OUT THE COCKPIT WINDOW AT A CROP OF leafy plants. The fields stretched out in every direction, the view of the flat horizon broken only by a stone farmhouse nearly a mile away.

A house. A lot of vegetables. And a giant spaceship.

"This isn't conspicuous at all."

"At least we're in the middle of nowhere," said Thorne, peeling himself out of the pilot seat and sliding on his leather jacket. "If anyone calls the police, it will take them a while to get here."

"Unless they're already on their way," Cinder muttered. Her heart had been drumming throughout their eons-long descent down to Earth, her brain skimming over a thousand different fates that could await them. Though she'd kept up the ridiculous chanting as long as she could, they still had no way of knowing how effective she was being, and she still had the sinking feeling that her attempts to disguise their ship using Lunar magic were pathetically futile. She couldn't understand how she could manipulate radars and radio waves with nothing but her own muddled thoughts.

Nevertheless—the fact remained that no one had discovered them in space, and so far their luck was holding. Benoit Farms and Gardens appeared to be wholly deserted.

The ramp began to lower off the cargo bay and Iko chirped, "You two go off and have fun now. I'll be sitting here, by myself, all alone, checking for radar interference and running diagnostics. It's going to be *fantastic*."

"You're getting really good at your sarcasm," said Cinder, joining Thorne at the top of the ramp as it smashed a very fine row of hearty foliage.

Thorne squinted at the glare on his portscreen. "Bingo," he said, pointing at the two-story house that had to be old enough to have survived the Fourth World War. "She's here."

"Bring me back a souvenir!" Iko yelled as Thorne stomped down into the field. The ground was soggy from a recent watering and mud clung to the hem of his pants as he cut through the crop, making his own direct route to the house.

Cinder followed, drinking in the wide-open farmland and the fresh air, so sweet after being locked up inside the Rampion's recycled oxygen. Even with her audio interface turned off, it was the deepest silence she'd ever experienced. "It's so quiet here."

"Creepy, isn't it? I don't know how people can stand it."

"I think it's kind of nice."

"Yeah, like a morgue is nice."

A cluster of smaller buildings were thrown haphazardly

throughout the fields: a barn, a chicken coop, a shed, a hangar big enough to house a number of hovers or even a spaceship, though not one as big as the Rampion.

Cinder drew up short when she spotted it. She frowned, stretching for the gossamer memory that seemed to recognize the hangar. "Wait."

Thorne turned back to her. "Did you see someone?"

Without answering, she changed direction, squishing through the mud. Thorne trailed after her, silent as Cinder shoved open the hangar's door.

"I'm not sure that breaking into Michelle Benoit's outbuildings is the best way to introduce ourselves."

Cinder glanced back, scanning the house's empty windows. "I need to see something," she said, and stepped inside. "Lights, on."

The lights flickered to life and she gasped at the sight before her. Tools and parts, screws and bolts, clothes and grimy shop rags, all flung haphazardly around the space. Every cabinet hung open, every storage crate and toolbox had been tipped over. The glossy white floor could hardly be seen beneath the mess.

On the other side of the hangar, a small delivery ship sat with its back window busted out. Shards of glass glittered beneath the blazing lights. The hangar smelled of spilled fuel and toxic fumes, and a little bit like Cinder's market booth.

"What a sty," said Thorne, disgusted. "I'm not sure I can trust a pilot with such little respect for her ship."

Cinder ignored him, busy sending her scanner over the

shelves and walls. Despite the distraction of the chaos, her brain-machine interface was picking up on something. A general impression of familiarity, tinges of a long-lost memory. The way the sun angled in from the door. The combined smells of machinery and manure. The crisscrossed pattern of the exposed trusses.

She paced across the concrete, crunching through the debris. She moved slowly, lest the ghost of familiarity vanish.

"Uh, Cinder," said Thorne, glancing back toward the farm. "What are we doing in here?"

"Looking for something."

"In this mess? Good luck with that."

She found a small plot of empty concrete and stalled, thinking. Examining. Knowing she'd been there before. In a dream, in a daze.

She noticed a thin metal cabinet painted a putrid brown, where three jackets hung on a rod. They all had insignias from the EF military embroidered on their sleeves. Squaring her shoulders, Cinder picked her way toward it and pushed the jackets to the side.

"Really, Cinder?" said Thorne, coming up beside her. "This is not the time to be worried about a change of clothes."

Cinder barely heard him over the ticking in her head. The mess was no coincidence. Someone had been there, and they'd been looking for something.

They'd been looking for *her.*

She wished the realization hadn't struck, but there was no dismissing it.

Crouching in front of the cabinet, she slid her hand against the back corner until it brushed against the handle she'd known would be there. Painted the same brown color, it was invisible in the shadows. It would never be noticed unless a person knew to look. And she knew—because she'd been here. Five years ago, in a state of drugged-up delirium that she'd always mistaken for a dream, she'd emerged in this spot. Every joint and muscle aching from the recent surgeries. Crawling slowly out of endless darkness and blinking, as if for the first time, into a dizzily bright world.

Cinder braced herself against the cabinet and pulled.

The secret door was heavier than she'd expected, made of something much sturdier than tin. She heaved it up on hidden hinges and let it slam down on the concrete floor. A cloud of dust billowed up on all sides.

A square hole gaped up at them. A ladder of plastic rungs was drilled into the foundation, leading to a secret sublevel.

Thorne bent over, planting his hands on his knees. "How did you know that was there?"

Cinder couldn't tear her gaze away from the hidden passageway.

Unable to voice the truth, she said simply, "Cyborg vision."

She descended first, releasing her flashlight as she was hit with thick, stale air. The beam bounced around a room as big as the hangar above, with no doors and no windows. Almost afraid to know what she'd just stumbled into, she tentatively ventured, "Lights. On."

She heard the sound of an independent generator click on first, before three long overhead fluorescents gradually brightened, one after another. Thorne's shoes thumped on the hard floor as he skipped the last four rungs of the ladder. He spun around and froze.

"What—what *is* this?"

Cinder couldn't answer. She could barely breathe.

A tank sat in the center of the room, about two meters long with a domed glass lid. A collection of complex machines stood around it—life monitors, temperature gauges, bioelectricity scanners. Machines with dials and tubes, needles and screens, plugs and controls.

A long operating table against the far wall held an array of moveable lights sprouting from each end like a metal octopus, and beside it a small rolling table with a near-empty jug of sterilizer and an assortment of surgical tools—scalpels, syringes, bandages, face masks, towels. On the wall were two blank netscreens.

As much as that side of the secret chamber imitated an operating room, the opposite side more closely resembled Cinder's workshop in the basement of Adri's apartment building, complete with screwdrivers, fuse pullers, and a soldering iron. Discarded android parts and computer chips. An unfinished, three-fingered cyborg hand.

Cinder shuddered, chilled from the air that smelled like both a sterile hospital room and a damp underground cave.

Thorne crept toward the tank. It was empty, but the vague

imprint of a child could be seen in the goo-like lining beneath the glass dome. "What's this?"

Cinder went to fidget with her glove before remembering that it wasn't there.

"A suspended animation tank," she said, whispering as if the ghosts of unknown surgeons could be listening. "Designed to keep someone alive, but unconscious, for long periods of time."

"Aren't those illegal? Overpopulation laws or something?"

Cinder nodded. Nearing the tank, she pressed her fingers to the glass and tried to remember waking up here, but she couldn't. Only addled memories of the hangar and the farm came back to her—nothing about this dungeon. She hadn't been fully conscious until she'd been en route to New Beijing, ready to start her new life as a scared, confused orphan, and a cyborg.

The girl's outline in the goo seemed too small to have ever been hers, but she knew it was. The left leg appeared to have been significantly heavier than the right. She wondered how long she had lain there without any leg at all.

"What do you suppose it's doing down here?"

Cinder licked her lips. "I think it was hiding a princess."

Thirty-Two

CINDER'S FEET WERE CEMENTED TO THE GROUND AS SHE took in the underground room. She couldn't shake the vision of her eleven-year-old self lying on that operating table as unknown surgeons cut and sewed and pieced her body together with foreign steel limbs. Wires in her brain. Optobionics behind her retinas. Synthetic tissue in her heart, new vertebrae, grafted skin to cover the scar tissue.

How long had it taken? How long had she been unconscious, sleeping in this dark cellar?

Levana had tried to kill her when she was only three years old.

Her operation had been completed when she was eleven.

Eight years. In a tank, sleeping and dreaming and growing.

Not dead, but not alive either.

She peered down into the imprint of her own head beneath the tank's glass. Hundreds of tiny wires with neural transmitters were attached to the walls and a small netscreen was implanted on the side. No, not a netscreen, Cinder realized. No net access could infiltrate this room. Nothing that could ever get back to Queen Levana.

"I don't get it," said Thorne, examining the surgical tools on the other side of the room. "What do you think they did to her down here?"

She peered up at the captain, but there was no suspicion on his face, only curiosity.

"Well," she started, "programmed and implanted her ID chip, for starters."

Thorne shook the scalpel at her. "Good thinking. Of course she wouldn't have had her own when she came to Earth." He gestured at the tank. "What about all that?"

Cinder gripped the tank's edges to steady her hands. "Her burns would have been severe, even life threatening. Their priority would have been keeping her alive, and also keeping her hidden. Suspended animation would solve both problems." She tapped a finger on the glass. "These transmitters would have been used to stimulate her brain while she was sleeping. She couldn't receive life experience or learn like a normal child, so they had to make up for it with fake learning. Fake experiences."

She bit her lip, silencing herself before she mentioned the netlink they'd planted in the princess's brain that made for an efficient way to learn when she was finally awake, without being any the wiser that she should have known these things anyway.

It was easy to talk about the princess as if she were someone else. Cinder couldn't stop thinking that she *was* someone else.

The girl who had slept in this tank was someone different from the cyborg that had woken up in it.

It occurred to Cinder with a jolt that this was why she had no memories. Not because the surgeons had damaged her brain while inserting her control panel, but because she had never been awake to make memories in the first place.

If she thought back, could she grasp something from before the coma? Something from her childhood? And then she recalled her recurring dream. The bed of coals, the fire burning off her skin, and realized it may have been more memory than nightmare.

"Screen, on."

Both screens over the operating table brightened at Thorne's command—the one on the left output a holograph of a torso from the shoulders up, spinning and flickering in the air. Cinder's heart jolted, thinking it was *her*, until she took in the second screen.

PATIENT: MICHELLE BENOIT
OPERATION: SPINAL AND NERVOUS SYSTEM
BIOELECTRICITY SECURITY BLOCK.
PROTOTYPE 4.6
STATUS: COMPLETE

Cinder approached the holograph. The shoulders were slender and feminine, but nothing could be seen above the line of her jaw.

"What's a bioelectricity security block?"

Cinder pointed at the holograph as it spun away from her and a dark square spot appeared on the spine, just beneath her skull. "This. I had one implanted too, so I wouldn't accidentally use my Lunar gift when I was growing up. In an Earthen, it makes it so you can't be brainwashed by Lunars. If Michelle Benoit did have information about Princess Selene, she would have had to protect herself, in case she ever fell into Lunar hands."

"If we have the technology to nullify the Lunar's craziness, why doesn't everyone have one of these?"

A wave of sadness washed over her. Her stepfather, Linh Garan, had invented the bioelectricity block, but he'd died of the plague before seeing it past the prototype stage. Though she'd barely known him, she couldn't help feeling that his life had been cut far too short. How different things could have been if he'd survived—not only for Pearl and Peony, but for Cinder too.

She sighed, tired of thinking, and said simply, "I don't know why."

Thorne grunted. "Well, this proves it, doesn't it? The princess really was here."

Cinder scanned the room again, her attention catching on the table of mechanics. The tools that had made her cyborg. Thorne either hadn't noticed them, or hadn't yet figured out what they would have been used for. The confession settled on the tip of her tongue. Maybe he should know. If she was going to be stuck with him, he deserved to know who he was traveling with. The true danger she'd put him in.

But before she could speak, he said, "Screen, show Princess Selene."

Cinder spun back around, pulse rushing, but it was not an eleven-year-old version of herself that greeted her. What she saw was hardly recognizable as human at all.

Thorne stumbled back, clapping a hand to his mouth. "What the—"

Cinder's stomach heaved once before she shut her eyes, tempering the revulsion. She swallowed hard and dared to look at the screen again.

It was the photo of a child.

What was left of a child.

She was wrapped in bandages from her neck to the stump of her left thigh. Her right arm and shoulder were uncovered, showing the skin that was gouged bloody red in spots, bright pink and glossy in others. She had no hair and the burn marks continued up her neck and across her cheek. The left side of her face was swollen and disfigured, only the slit of her eye could be seen, and a line of stitches ran along her earlobe before cutting across to her lips.

Cinder raised trembling fingers to her mouth, smoothing them over the skin. There was no scar, no sign of these wounds. Only some scar tissue around her thigh and wrist, where the prostheses had been attached.

How had they fixed her? How could they possibly fix this?

But it was Thorne who asked the true question.

"Who would do this to a child?"

Goose bumps covered Cinder's skin. There was no memory

of the suffering those burns must have caused her. She couldn't connect the child with herself.

But Thorne's question lingered, haunting the cold room.

Queen Levana had done this.

To a child, barely more than a baby.

To her own niece.

And all so she could rule. So she could claim the throne. So she would be queen.

Cinder clenched her fists at her sides, her blood boiling. Thorne was watching her, his expression equally dark.

"We should go talk to Michelle Benoit," he said, setting down the scalpel.

Cinder blew a strand of hair out of her face. The ghost of her child self lingered in the air here, a victim struggling to stay alive. How many people had helped rescue and protect her, had kept her secrets? How many had risked their lives because they believed hers was worth more? Because they believed she could grow into someone powerful enough to stop Levana.

Nerves scratching at her stomach, she followed Thorne back up into the hangar, making sure to close the hidden door behind them.

As they walked back into the daylight, the house still towered eerily still and silent above a small garden. The Rampion stood enormous and out of place in the fields.

Thorne checked his portscreen, and his voice was tight when he spoke. "She hasn't moved since we got here."

He didn't try to hide his stomping footsteps across the

gravel. He pounded on the front door, every strike bouncing around the courtyard. They waited for the telltale footsteps within, but only the sound of chickens scratching in the yard greeted them.

Thorne checked the knob and the door swung open, unlocked.

Stepping into the foyer, Thorne peered up the wood-paneled stairway. To their right was a living room, filled with rugged furniture. To their left a kitchen with a couple dirty plates left at the table. All the lights were off.

"Hello?" Thorne called. "Miss Benoit?"

Cinder called up a netlink and traced the signal to Michelle Benoit's ID chip. "The signal is coming from upstairs," she whispered. The stairs groaned beneath the weight of her metal leg. Small screens lined the wall, alternating pictures of a middle-aged woman in a pilot uniform and a girl with flaming red hair. Though chubby and covered in freckles as a child, later pictures showed her quite stunning, and Thorne gave a low *"Hello,* Scarlet" as they passed.

"Miss Benoit?" Cinder called again. Either the woman was a very deep sleeper, or they were about to stumble across something that Cinder was sure she didn't want to see. Her hand shook as she pushed open the first door off the stairs, preparing herself not to scream if she spotted a decaying body sprawled across the bed.

But there was no body.

The room was in upheaval just as the hangar had been.

Clothes and shoes, trinkets and blankets, but no human being. No corpse.

"Hello?"

Glancing around the room, Cinder spotted the vanity beside the window and her heart fell. She paced to it and picked up the small chip and held it up for Thorne to see.

"What's that?" he asked.

"Michelle Benoit," she said. Sighing, she dismissed the netlink.

"You mean . . . she's not here?"

"Try to keep up," Cinder grumbled, and pushed past him into the hallway. She planted her fists on her hips and scanned the other closed door, no doubt another bedroom.

The house was abandoned. Michelle Benoit wasn't here, and neither was her granddaughter. No one with any answers.

"How do we track a person who doesn't have an ID chip?" Thorne said.

"We don't," she said. "That's the whole point of removing it."

"We should talk to the neighbors. They might know something."

Cinder groaned. "We're not talking to anyone. We're still fugitives, in case you've forgotten." She stared at the rotating pictures. Michelle Benoit and a young Scarlet kneeling proudly beside a freshly planted vegetable bed.

"Come on," she said, dusting her hands as if she was the one who had been digging in the dirt. "Let's get out of here before the Rampion attracts any attention." The floorboards clapped hollowly beneath her as she tromped down the stairs and rounded the first landing.

The front door swung open.

Cinder froze.

A pretty girl with honey-blonde curls froze in front of her.

Her eyes widened, first with surprise, then recognition. They fell to Cinder's cyborg hand and the color drained from her cheeks.

"*Bonjour,* mademoiselle," said Thorne.

The girl glanced up at him. Then her eyes rolled back into her head and she collapsed onto the tile floor.

Thirty-Three

CINDER CURSED AND GLANCED BACK AT THORNE, BUT HE only shrugged. She turned back to the fainted girl. Her head was bent at an awkward angle against an entry table, her feet splayed across the doorway.

"Is it her granddaughter?" Cinder asked, even as her scanner was connecting the measurements of the girl's face to the database in her brain and coming up with nothing. Scarlet Benoit it would have recognized. "Never mind," she said, and inched toward the girl's prone body. She nudged the table out of the way and the girl's head thumped onto the tiles.

Creeping over her, Cinder peered out the front door. A beat-up hover sat in the courtyard.

"What are you doing?" said Thorne.

"Looking." Cinder turned around to see Thorne stepping into the foyer, eyeing the girl with mild curiosity. "She seems to be alone."

A wicked grin spread across his face. "We should take her with us."

Cinder glared. "Are you crazy?"

"Crazy in love. She's gorgeous."

"You're an idiot. Help me carry her into the living room."

He made no argument, and a moment later the girl was swooped up in his arms without Cinder's help.

"Here, on the couch." Cinder bustled ahead of him and re-arranged a few faded pillows.

"I'm good like this." Thorne shifted his arms so the girl's head fell against his chest, her blonde curls clinging to the zipper of his leather jacket.

"Thorne. Put her down. Now."

Muttering something to himself, he laid the girl down and meticulously arranged her shirt to cover her bared stomach and then moved down to more comfortably position her legs when Cinder grabbed him by the back of his collar and hauled him to his feet. "Let's get out of here. She definitely recognized us. The moment she wakes up she'll have a comm to the police."

Thorne pulled a portscreen out of his jacket pocket and handed it to Cinder.

"What's that?"

"Her port. I took it off her while you were busy panicking."

Cinder snatched the portscreen away and shoved it into the side pocket of her military cargos. "Still, it won't be long before she tells *someone*. And they'll come to investigate and realize we were looking for Michelle Benoit and then *they'll* be looking for Michelle Benoit and—maybe I should disable her hover before we go."

"I think we should stay and talk to her. Maybe she'll know where to find Michelle."

"Stay and *talk* to her? And give her even more leads about how to track us? That's the stupidest thing I ever heard."

"Hey, I liked my idea of bringing her along, but you already vetoed that idea, so now I'm resorting to Plan B, which is to interrogate her. And I am really looking forward to it. I used to play a game called interrogation with one of my old girlfriends where we—"

"That's enough." Cinder raised her hand, silencing him. "This is a bad idea. I'm leaving now. You can stay here with your girlfriend if you like." She marched past him.

Thorne stayed on her heels. "Now *that* was definitely jealousy I just heard."

A whimper stopped them both halfway to the front door and they turned to see the girl's eyelashes fluttering open.

Cinder cursed again and tugged Thorne toward the entryway, but he didn't budge. After a moment, he peeled himself out of her grip and meandered back into the living room. Terror flashed over her face and she sat up, pushing herself against the arm of the sofa.

"Don't be alarmed," said Thorne. "We're not going to hurt you."

"You're those people from the netscreens. The fugitives," she said in an endearing European accent. She gaped at Cinder. "You're the . . . the . . ."

"Escaped Lunar cyborg fugitive?" Thorne offered.

The last bit of color drained from the girl's face. Cinder prayed for patience.

"A-are you going to kill me?"

"No! No, no, no, of course not." Thorne slid himself onto the other end of the sofa. "We just want to ask you a few questions."

The girl gulped.

"What's your name, love?"

She chewed on her lower lip, eyeing Thorne with a mixture of distrust and mild hope. "Émilie," she breathed, barely audible.

"Émilie. A beautiful name for a beautiful girl."

Fighting back the urge to gag, Cinder thumped her head against the door frame. It brought the girl's attention back to her and Émilie shriveled away in fear again.

"Sorry," said Cinder, holding out both hands. "Uh, it's really nice to meet—"

Émilie broke into hysterical crying, her focus latched on to Cinder's metal hand. "Please don't kill me. I won't tell anyone I saw you! I promise, just please don't kill me!"

Jaw dropping, Cinder stared at the offensive limb for a second, before realizing it wasn't her cyborg half that the girl was afraid of. It was the Lunar in her. She glanced at Thorne, who was glaring accusations at her, before throwing her arms into the air. "Fine, you take care of it," she said, and marched out of the room.

She sat down on the stairs, where she could hear Thorne trying to calm the girl while keeping an eye on the road through the front window. She folded her elbows on top of her knees and listened to Thorne's cooing and Émilie's sobs and tried to rub away an oncoming headache.

Once, people had looked at her with revulsion. Now, people were terrified of her.

She wasn't sure which was worse.

She wanted to scream to the world that it wasn't her fault she was this way. She'd had nothing to do with it.

It surely wouldn't have been her choice if one had been given to her.

Lunar.

Cyborg.

Fugitive.

Outlaw.

Outcast.

Cinder buried her face in her arms and urged the swirling injustices away. She would not get carried away with self-loathing. She had too many other things to worry about.

In the next room, she could hear Thorne mentioning Michelle Benoit, pleading with the girl to tell him something, anything useful, but all he got back were blubbery apologies.

Cinder sighed, wishing there were some way she could convince the girl they meant her no harm, that they were in fact the good guys.

Her body tensed.

She *could* convince the girl of that. Quite easily.

Guilt flooded her veins a moment later, but it didn't quite dispel the temptation. She scanned the horizon, still seeing no sign of civilization beyond the fields.

She folded her fingers together, debating.

"You do know Michelle Benoit, don't you?" Thorne said, his

tone taking on an edge of pleading. "I mean, you are in her house. This is her house, isn't it?"

Cinder massaged her thumbs over her temples.

She was not like Queen Levana and her thaumaturges and all the other Lunars who abused this gift—brainwashed and cajoled and controlled others for their own selfish gains.

But if controlling someone were for the greater good . . . and only for a short time . . .

"Émilie, please stop crying. It's just a simple question, really."

"Fine," Cinder muttered, pushing herself off the stairs. "It's for her own good, after all."

Taking in a breath to dispel the guilt, she stepped back into the living room.

The girl's gaze whipped toward her, eyes puffed. She cowered away.

Cinder forced herself to relax and let the gentle tingle slip down her nerves, thinking kind, friendly, welcoming thoughts. "We're your friends," she said. "We're here to help you."

Émilie's eyes brightened.

"Émilie, can you tell us where Michelle Benoit is?"

A last tear slipped unnoticed down Émilie's cheek. "I don't know where she is. She disappeared three weeks ago. The police never found anything."

"Do you know anything about her disappearance?"

"It happened in the middle of the day, when Scarling was out doing her deliveries. She didn't have a hover or a ship. She didn't seem to take any belongings with her. Her ID chip had been re-moved and left behind, along with her portscreen."

It took all of Cinder's focus to maintain the aura of friendli-ness and trust when disappointment started to settle in.

"But I think Scarlet may have known something."

Cinder perked up.

"She was going to look for her. She left a couple days ago and asked me to watch the farm. It seemed she had some lead, but she didn't tell me what it was. I'm so sorry."

"Have you heard from Scarlet since?" asked Thorne, leaning forward.

Émilie shook her head. "Nothing. I'm worried about her, but she's a tough girl. She'll be all right." Her expression brightened like a child's. "Have I helped? I want to help."

Cinder flinched at the girl's eagerness. "Yes, you helped. Thank you. If you think of anything else—"

"One more question," said Thorne, holding up a finger. "Our ship is in need of some repairs. Are there any good parts stores nearby?"

Thirty-Four

SCARLET'S SLEEP WAS RESTLESS, FILLED WITH THAUMATURGES and prowling wolves. When she managed to pull herself from the daze, she saw that two trays of food had been left for her. Her stomach growled upon seeing them, but she ignored it, instead rolling over and curling up on the filthy mattress. Many years ago, someone had sketched their initials on the dressing room wall and Scarlet traced her fingertips over them. Were they the work of a rising opera star in the second era or a prisoner of war?

Had they died in this room?

She leaned her forehead against the cool plaster.

The scanner beeped in the hallway and the door clanked open.

Scarlet rolled onto her back and froze.

Wolf was standing in the doorway, having to duck his head to keep from hitting the frame. His eyes pierced through the darkness but they were the only thing about him that hadn't changed. His once messy, spiky hair had been combed off his brow, making his handsome features appear too sharp, too cruel. He'd washed the dirt from his face and now wore the same uniform she'd seen on the other soldiers: a maroon shirt and rune-decorated guards on his shoulders and forearms. A series of belts and sashes held empty holsters—she briefly wondered if Wolf preferred to fight without weaponry, or if he simply hadn't been allowed to bring any guns into her cell.

She leaped off the bed, instantly regretting it as the world tilted beneath her and she had to brace herself against the wall. Wolf remained silent, watching, until their gazes clashed across the room—his dark and expressionless, hers growing more hateful, more angry by the second.

"Scarlet." A hint of a struggle crossed his face.

Her revulsion tore through her and she screamed. She had no memory of crossing the room, but the crunch of her fists as they struck his jaw, his ear, his chest thundered up her arms.

He allowed her five strikes with nothing more than a grimace before stopping her. He caught her wrists mid-swing, holding them fast against his stomach.

Scarlet reeled back and aimed her heel for his kneecap, but he whipped her around so fast she lost balance and found herself facing away from him, her arms locked in his grip.

"Let go of me!" she screeched, aiming her foot for his toes, stomping and screaming and thrashing, but if she hurt him, he showed no sign of it. She craned her neck and snapped her teeth, though she had no hope of actually biting him. Instead, with a painful twist of her neck, she managed to land a gob of spit on his jaw.

He flinched again, but didn't release her. Didn't even look at her.

"You traitor! You bastard! Let go of me!"

She'd lifted her knee for another backward kick when he obeyed, releasing her. She collapsed forward with a yelp.

Scarlet scurried away, clenching her jaw. Her knees throbbed and she had to use the wall to pull herself back to standing. She swung around to face him. Her stomach roiled and she was sure she would be sick with loathing and disgust and fury.

"What?" she yelled. "What do you want?"

Wolf scrubbed the spit from his chin with his wrist. "I had to see you."

"Why? So you could gloat over what a fool you made me out to be? How *easy* it was to convince me that you—" A shudder ripped through her. "I can't believe I let you *touch me*." She squirmed, wiping her hands down her arms to dispel the memory. "Go away! Just leave me alone!"

Wolf didn't move, and didn't speak again for a long time. Spinning away, Scarlet crossed her arms over her chest and glared at the wall, shaking.

"I lied to you about a lot of things," he finally said.

She snorted.

"But I meant every apology."

She scowled, seeing bright spots on the wall.

"I never wanted to lie to you, or frighten you, or . . . and I tried, in the train . . ."

"Don't you dare." She faced him again, digging her nails into her arms to keep from lashing out and making an idiot of herself again. "Don't you even *think* about bringing that up, or trying to justify what you did to me. What your people have done to my grandmother!"

"Scarlet—" He took a step toward her but she threw her hands up and backed away until her calves collided with the mattress.

"Don't come near me. I don't want to see you. I don't want to listen to you. I would rather die than ever be touched by you again."

She saw a gulp straining against his throat. Hurt flashed across his face but it only served to make her angrier.

Wolf cast a glance toward the door and Scarlet followed the look, noting that her usual guard was waiting outside, watching them as if they were a popular drama on the netscreens. Her stomach twisted.

"I'm sorry to hear that, Scarlet," Wolf said, turning back to her. His voice had lost the edge of regret and was all business and cruelty again. "Because I didn't come to apologize. I came for something else."

She straightened. "I don't care what you—"

He was at her in a single stride, his hands buried in her hair, pressing her against the wall. His mouth stifled her surprised cry, and then an angry scream. She tried to shove him off her but she'd have had no more luck against the iron bars on the door.

Her eyes went wide as she felt his tongue and in a flash of

rebellion she thought to bite him, but then there was something else. Something small and flat and hard being pressed into her mouth. Every muscle went taut.

Wolf pulled away. His grip softened, cradling her head. His scars were a blur in her vision. She couldn't find her breath.

And then he murmured, so quiet she could barely catch the words even as they steamed against her lips. "Wait until morning," he said. "The world won't be safe tonight."

Wolf focused on his own fingers as they took a red curl between them. He flinched, as if touching her pained him.

Indignation returning, Scarlet swiped him away and darted beneath his arm. She fled to the corner of the room and crouched down on the bed. Covering her mouth with one hand, she smashed the other against the wall for balance.

She waited, her entire body aflame, until Wolf slinked out of the room. The bars opened and shut.

Outside, the guard snickered. "I suppose we all have our thing," he said, and then their footsteps padded down the corridor.

Slumping against the wall, Scarlet spit the foreign object into her palm.

A small ID chip winked up at her.

BOOK
Four

"The better to eat you with, my dear."

Thirty-Five

"SHE'S GOING TO BE FINE, YOU KNOW."

Cinder jumped, startled from a reverie. Thorne was piloting the small podship into Rieux, France, and Cinder was somewhat amazed they hadn't crashed and died yet.

"Who's going to be fine?"

"That Émilie girl. You shouldn't feel bad about knocking her out with your Lunar mind-trick thing. She'll probably be extra refreshed when she wakes up."

Cinder screwed up her mouth. Her thoughts had been so preoccupied with finding a power cell and making it back to Iko before anyone else showed up on the farm that she'd hardly thought of the blonde girl they'd left behind. Oddly enough, once she'd made the decision to glamour the girl into trusting them, all the doubt and guilt she'd felt about it had faded away. It had seemed so natural, so easy, so clearly the right thing to do.

The ease of it frightened her more than the lack of guilt. If it was so natural for *her,* after only a few days of practicing her new gift, how could she ever survive against a thaumaturge? Or the queen herself?

"I just hope we're long gone before she wakes up," she muttered. Returning her focus to the window, Cinder redid her ponytail in the ghost reflection. She could vaguely make out her brown eyes and plain features. She tilted her head, wondering what she looked like with her glamour. She would never know, of course. Mirrors couldn't be fooled by glamours. But Thorne had sure seemed impressed, and Kai . . .

You're even more painful to look at than she is.

His words made her whole body feel heavy.

The town came into focus beneath them and Thorne made a too-fast descent. Jolting, Cinder grabbed for the harness around her waist.

Thorne straightened the ship and coughed. "There was a gust of wind."

"Sure there was." She let her head fall against the rest.

"You're extra gloomy today," Thorne said, nicking her chin. "Cheer up. We may not have found Michelle Benoit, but now we know for sure that she housed the princess. This is good. This is progress."

"We found a ransacked house and were identified by the first civilian who spotted us."

"Yeah, because we're *famous.*" He sang the word with a certain measure of pride. When Cinder rolled her eyes, he nudged her in the arm. "Oh, come on, it could be worse."

She quirked an eyebrow at him and his grin broadened.

"At least we have each other." He held out his arms, like he would have given her a huge hug if they hadn't been strapped into their seats. The nose of the ship tipped to the right and he quickly grasped the controls again, leveling it out just in time to dodge a flock of pigeons.

Cinder covered a laugh with her metal hand.

It wasn't until Thorne had landed, crookedly, on a cobble-stoned side street that Cinder began to realize what a bad idea this was. But they didn't have a choice—they needed a new power cell if they wanted to get the Rampion back into space.

"People are going to see us," she said, glancing around as she emerged from the podship. The street was empty, serenely overshadowed by centuries-old stone buildings and silver-leafed maples. But the tranquility did nothing to quell her nerves.

"And you are going to pull your very handy brainwashing magic on all of them and they won't even know they're seeing us. Well, I mean, I guess they'll still see us, they just won't recognize us. Or, hey, *can* you make us invisible? Because that would come in handy."

Cinder stuffed her hands into her pockets. "I don't know if I'm ready to trick a whole town. Besides, I don't like doing it. It makes me feel . . . evil."

She knew if her internal lie detector could see her, it would have recognized a lie. It felt all *too* right, and maybe that's what felt so horrendously wrong about it.

Blue eyes twinkling, Thorne hooked his thumbs behind his belt. He looked slightly ridiculous in his fancy leather jacket in this quaint rural town, and yet he had the swagger of a man who belonged there. Who belonged anywhere he wished to. "You might be a crazy Lunar, but you're not *evil*. As long as you're using your glamour to help people, and more important, to help *me*, then there's nothing to feel guilty about." He stopped to check his hair in the dirty window of a shoe store while Cinder gawked after him.

"I hope that wasn't your idea of a pep talk."

Smirking, he jerked his head toward the next store. "Here we are," he said, pushing open a creaking wooden door.

The hollow sound of digital bells greeted them, meshed with the smell of engine grease and burnt rubber. Cinder sucked in the scent of home. Mechanics. Machinery. This is where *she* belonged.

Though the shop had seemed prettily charming from outside, with its stone facade and aged wooden windowsills, she could see now that it was enormous, stretching back the length of the town block. Near the front, towering metal shelves held replacement parts for androids and screens. Toward the back, Cinder could make out parts for the bigger machines: hovers and tractors and ships.

"Perfect," she muttered, heading toward the back wall.

They passed a young, acne-faced clerk sitting behind a worktable, and though Cinder instantly called up her glamour, disguising her and Thorne as the first thing that came to mind—dirty, grungy farmhands—she doubted the ploy was necessary. The boy didn't even bother with a polite nod, his attention fixed on a portscreen that emanated the upbeat tune of a game app.

Cinder rounded the aisle of power converters and spotted a boulder of a man leaning against an engine lift, the only other customer in the store. His attention was focused on picking at his nails instead of browsing the shelves, and when he met Cinder's gaze it was with a taunting smirk.

Shoving her metal hand into her pocket, Cinder found the vibrations of his thoughts in the air and twisted them away. *You are not interested in us.*

But his smile only widened, sending a chill down her back.

When he turned away a moment later, Cinder crept into the aisle, her attention divided between maintaining the glamour and scouring the mishmashed parts until she found the power cell they'd come for. She snatched it off the shelf, gasping at its weight, and hurried back toward the front.

Thorne exhaled as soon as they were out of the stranger's sight. "He scared me."

Cinder nodded. "You should go start the podship, in case we need to make a quick getaway." She dropped the power cell onto the clerk's desk with a thunk.

The clerk didn't bother to look up, one hand still playing the game single-thumbed while the other held the scanner out to Cinder. The red laser flickered across the counter.

Dread settled in Cinder's stomach. "Um."

The kid managed to pull his attention away from the game and gave her an irritated glare.

Cinder gulped. Neither of them had an ID chip or any means of paying. Could she glamour her way out of that? She imagined Levana probably wouldn't have had any trouble . . .

Before she could speak, something sparkly dangled in the corner of her eye.

"Will this cover it?" said Thorne, holding out a gold-plated digital portscreen watch. Cinder recognized it as the one Alak had been wearing, the man who owned the spaceship hangar in New Beijing.

"Thorne!" she hissed.

"This isn't a pawn shop," said the boy, dropping the scanner gun on the counter. "Can you pay or not?"

Cinder glared at Thorne, but then spotted the strange man plodding out of the aisle near the back of the shop. Strolling toward them, he whistled a chirpy tune, then pulled a pair of thick work gloves out of one pocket and made a big show of pulling one onto his left hand.

Heart hammering, Cinder turned back to the kid. "You want the watch," she said. "It's a fine trade for this power cell and you're not going to report us for taking it."

The kid's eyes glazed over. He'd just started to nod when Thorne deposited the watch into his palm and Cinder grabbed the power cell off the counter. They marched out the door, leaving the ringing of fake bells behind.

"No more stealing!" she said as Thorne fell into step beside her.

"Hey, that watch saved us in there."

"No, *I* saved us in there and in case you already forgot, that is exactly the kind of mental trick that I *don't* want to pull on people."

"Even if it saves your skin?"

"Yes!"

A light flashed in Cinder's eye, indicating an incoming comm. A moment later, words began tracking across her vision.

WE'VE BEEN DETECTED—POLICE. WILL KEEP THEM OUT AS LONG AS POSSIBLE.

She stumbled in the middle of the street.

"What?" said Thorne.

"It's Iko. The police have found the ship."

Thorne paled. "No time to shop for new clothes then."

"Or an android body. Come on."

She took off running, Thorne keeping step, until they spun around the corner and both skidded to a halt.

Two policemen stood between them and their podship—one comparing the ship's model with something on his portscreen.

Something beeped on the other officer's belt. As he reached for it, Cinder and Thorne backed away, ducking around the building.

Pulse racing, Cinder glanced up at Thorne, but he was scanning the nearest window. RIEUX TAVERN was painted off center on the glass.

"Here," he said, dragging her around two wrought-iron tables and through the door.

The tavern stank of booze and fried fat, and was thrumming with sports on the netscreens and uproarious laughter.

Cinder took two steps inside, her breath caught, and she spun around to leave. Thorne blocked her path with an outstretched arm. "Where are you going?"

"There are too many people. We'll have better luck with the police." She pushed him away but froze when she spotted a green hover easing onto the cobblestones outside, the emblem of the Eastern Commonwealth military painted on its side. *"Thorne."*

His arm stiffened and then the tavern seemed to quiet. Cinder slowly faced the crowd. Dozens of strangers, gaping at her.

A cyborg.

"Stars," she whispered. "I need to find a new pair of gloves."

"No, you need to calm down and start using your brainwave witchery thing."

Cinder drew closer to Thorne and swallowed her growing panic. "We belong here," she murmured. Sweat beaded on the back of her neck, dripping down her spine. "We're not suspicious. You don't recognize us. You have no interest or curiosity or . . ." She trailed off as the attention of people around the room began to drift back to their food and drinks and the netscreens behind the bar. Cinder continued the mindless chanting in her head, *We belong here, we are not suspicious,* until the statements blurred together into a sensation of invisibility.

They weren't suspicious. They did belong there.

She forced herself to believe it.

Scanning the crowd, she saw that only one set of eyes was still on her—vibrant blue and filled with laughter. He was a muscular man sitting at a table near the back, a smile playing on his mouth. When Cinder's gaze held his, he sat back and lifted his attention to the screens.

"Come on, then," said Thorne, guiding her toward an open booth.

The sound of the door creaking behind them sent Cinder's stomach heaving like a dying motor. They slid into the booth.

"This was a bad idea," she whispered, tucking the power cell beside her on the bench. Thorne said nothing, both of them bending their necks over the table as three red uniforms brushed past. A scanner beeped, sending Cinder's pulse thrumming against her temples, and the last officer paused.

With her cyborg hand beneath the table, Cinder deftly opened the barrel of her imbedded tranquilizer gun, the first time she'd engaged that finger since Dr. Erland had given her the hand.

The officer remained beside their booth and Cinder forced herself to turn toward him, thinking *innocence, normal, indistinguishable from anyone else.*

The officer was holding a portscreen with a built-in ID scanner. Cinder gulped and looked up. He was young, perhaps in his early twenties, and his face was contorted in confusion.

"Is there a problem, monsieur?" she said, sickened to hear her own voice come out as saccharine sweet as she'd once heard Queen Levana's.

His eyes blinked wildly. The attention of the other officers, one man and one woman, was captured too, and Cinder could see them hovering nearby.

Heat spread out from the base of her neck, creeping

uncomfortably down her limbs. She clenched her fists. The wash of energy in the room was pulsing, almost visible. Her optobionics were beginning to panic, sending concerned warnings about hormones and chemical imbalances across her eyesight, and all the while she desperately grasped for control over her Lunar gift. *I am invisible. I am unimportant. You do not recognize me.* Please, *don't recognize me.*

"Officer?"

"You are...um." His eyes darted from the port to her face, and he shook his head to dispel the cobwebs. "We're looking for someone, and this says...you wouldn't happen to..."

Everyone was watching now. The waitresses, the customers, the eerie guy with the stormy eyes. No amount of internal pleading could make her invisible when a military officer from another country was speaking to her. She was becoming dizzy with the effort of it. Her body was warming, sweat beading on her brow.

She gulped. "Is everything all right, Officer?"

His brow drew together. "We're looking for a girl...a teenager, from the Eastern Commonwealth. You wouldn't happen to be...Linh..."

Cinder raised her eyebrows, feigning ignorance.

"Peony?"

Thirty-Six

CINDER'S SMILE FROZE TO HER FACE. PEONY'S NAME WAS like a stone on her chest, pressing the air out of her lungs as memories fell across her vision. Peony scared and alone in the quarantines. Peony dying, with the antidote still in Cinder's hand.

The pain was instant, fire ripping through her muscles. Cinder cried out and gripped the table, nearly falling out of the booth.

The officer stumbled back and his female comrade yelled, "It's her!"

Cinder felt the table being shoved toward her as Thorne jumped up. It took a moment for the burning to dwindle. The taste of salt lingered on her tongue and someone screamed and in the muddle of her brain she heard chair and table legs screeching across the floor. The woman's voice: "Linh Cinder, we are taking you into custody." Red text flashed across her retina.

INTERNAL TEMP ABOVE RECOMMENDED CON-
TROL TEMP. IF COOL DOWN PROCEDURE DOES
NOT ENGAGE, AUTOMATIC SHUTDOWN WILL
OCCUR IN ONE MINUTE.

"Linh Cinder, slowly place your hands on top of your head.
Do not make any sudden movements."

She blinked past the bright fog in her vision, barely making
out the officer with a gun pointed at her forehead. Behind her,
Thorne was swinging a punch at the nose of the young man with
the port, who ducked, then swung back. The third officer had his
gun on the two men as they collapsed in a brawl onto a nearby
table.

Cinder took in a deep breath, glad that only a residue of the
pain lingered beneath her skin.

FIFTY SECONDS UNTIL AUTOMATIC—

She released the breath, slowly.

SHUTDOWN COUNTDOWN PAUSED. TEMPERA-
TURES DROPPING. COOL DOWN PROCEDURE
ENGAGED.

"Linh Cinder," the woman said again. "Put your hands on top
of your head. I have been authorized to shoot to kill if necessary."

She forgot that one of her fingertips was open, ready with
a dart as it passed her gaze.

"Slowly come out of the booth and turn around." The woman stepped away to allow Cinder room to maneuver. Behind her, Thorne grunted as a punch collided with his stomach and he slumped over.

Cinder recoiled at the sound, but did as she was told, waiting for her guts to stop churning, for the weakness to pass. She tried to prepare her brain for the attempt, knowing she would only get one more chance at it.

She stood from the booth just as they were ratcheting handcuffs around Thorne's wrists. Cinder turned around. From the corner of her eye, she saw the officer reach for her belt.

"You don't want to do that," Cinder said, again cringing at the lovely serenity of her own voice. "You want to let us go."

The officer paused and stared at her with hollow eyes.

"You want to let us go." The command was directed at all the officers—at everyone in the tavern, even the frightened patrons who had pushed themselves against the back wall. Cinder's head buzzed with the return of strength and control and power. "You want to let us go."

The female officer dropped her arms to her sides. "We want to let you—"

A guttural cry ricocheted across the tavern. Beyond the officer, the man with the blue eyes moved to stand, but then collapsed over his table. The table legs snapped from the weight and he crashed to the floor. The other customers pulled away from him, everyone's attention diverted. Cinder glanced at Thorne, who was watching the spectacle with his hands locked behind his back.

The stranger snarled. He was crouching down on all fours, saliva dripping from his mouth. Beneath dark eyebrows, his eyes had taken on an eerie luminescence and a crazed, bloodthirsty expression that twisted Cinder's stomach. He curled his fingers, pulling his nails across the hard floor, and peered up at the terrified faces surrounding him.

A growl rolled up from his throat and his lips curled, revealing teeth that came to a fine point, more canine than human.

Cinder pressed herself against the bench, sure her momentary meltdown had fried something, that her optobionics were sending crossed messages to her brain. But her vision didn't clear.

In unison, the military officers rounded their guns on the man, but he showed no concern. He seemed pleased at the horrified cries, the way the crowd surged away from him.

He lunged for the nearest officer before he could pull the trigger. His hands wrapped around the officer's head—a loud snap and the officer fell lifeless to the ground. It happened so fast, every movement a blur.

Screaming filled the tavern. There was a stampede for the door, customers struggling over the crashed tables and chairs.

Ignoring the crowd, the man smirked at Cinder. She stumbled back into the booth, trembling.

"Hello, little girl," he said, his voice too human-like, too restrained. "I believe my queen has been looking for you."

He leaped for her. Cinder pulled back, unable to scream.

The female officer jumped between them, facing Cinder,

her arms spread out wide in protection. Her face completely, entirely blank. Her lifeless eyes peered down at Cinder, even as the man howled with rage and grabbed her from behind. He wrapped one arm around her head, yanking her back and sinking his fangs into her throat.

She didn't scream. Didn't fight.

A bloodied gurgle erupted from her mouth.

A gun fired.

The crazed man roared and picked up the officer, swinging her around like a dog would a toy and tossing her halfway across the tavern. She crumpled to the ground as another shot rang out, catching the man in the shoulder. Bellowing, he whipped forward, snatching the gun away from the remaining officer with one hand. He swiped with the other, his fingers curled into a claw that left four red gashes on the officer's face.

Heart hammering, Cinder gaped down at the woman as the life drained out of her eyes. Her gasps stuck in her throat. Her heart was pounding so hard it was sure to break out of her chest. White spots specked her vision. She couldn't breathe.

"*Cinder!*"

She searched the room, dazed, and found Thorne scrambling out from behind a toppled table with his hands still latched behind his back. He collapsed to his knees beside the bench.

"Come on, the cuffs!"

Her lungs burned. Her eyes stung. She was hyperventilating.

"I—I killed her—" she stammered.

"What?"

"I killed—she was—"

"This is not the time to go crazy, Cinder!"

"You don't understand. It was me. I—"

Thorne threw himself at her, his forehead hitting hers so hard she yelped and fell back onto the bench.

"Pull yourself together and help me unlock these things!"

She grabbed on to the table and hauled herself back up. Head aching, she blinked at Thorne, then at the officer who lay slumped against the wall, neck dangling at an odd angle.

Her brain struggling to grasp on to reality, she lurched forward, dragging Thorne with her through the toppled chairs. Crouching beside the first fallen officer, she grabbed his arm and held up his wrist. Thorne twisted his hands toward her and the cuffs blinked and fell open.

Cinder dropped the limp hand and stood. She bolted for the door—but something grabbed her ponytail and hauled her backward. She cried out, falling onto a table. Glass bottles shattered beneath her, water and alcohol soaking into the back of her shirt.

The crazed man hovered over her, leering. Blood was dripping out from his lips and his bullet wounds but he hardly seemed to notice.

Cinder tried to scramble backward, but she slipped—a shard of glass slicing through her palm. She gasped.

"I would ask what brought you to little Rieux, France, but I think I already know." He smiled, but it was haunting and unnatural with the jutting canines slicked with blood. "So sad for you that we found the old lady first, and now my pack has you both. I wonder what my reward will be when I bring your left-over pieces to my queen in a plastic box."

Thorne roared and heaved a chair upward, breaking it over the man's back.

The man spun around and Cinder used the distraction to roll off the table. She collapsed to the floor, looking up just as the man buried his teeth in Thorne's arm. A scream.

"Thorne!"

The man pulled away, chin dripping with blood, and let Thorne collapse to his knees.

His eyes glinted. "Your turn."

He took two sauntering steps toward her. Cinder upended the table, creating a blockade between them, but he kicked it aside with a laugh.

Standing, she raised her hand and fired a tranquilizer dart into his chest.

He snarled and yanked the dart out like a minor annoyance.

Cinder backed away. Tripping over a fallen chair, she cried out and collapsed backward onto the warm, unmoving body of the officer who had managed to get off two useless bullets.

The man grinned sickeningly, then paused again, paling. His cruel smile vanished and, with one more step, he crashed face-first on the ground.

Cinder stared, stomach in knots, at his still form amid the wreckage.

When he didn't move, she dared to glance at the dead officer whose blood was leaking onto her collarbone. Rolling off him, she grabbed the gun that had been tossed onto the floor and shoved herself back to her feet.

She seized Thorne's elbow and stuffed the gun into his hand. He moaned in pain but didn't fight her as she hauled him to his feet and shoved him toward the door. Rushing back to the booth, Cinder tucked the power cell under her arm before running after him.

The street was chaos, people screaming and barreling out of the buildings and crying hysterically.

Cinder spotted the two policemen who had been inspecting the podship, trying to direct a fleeing crowd. A window shattered as a man threw himself through the glass—the creepy man from the parts store—and tackled one of the police in the same movement. His jaws latched on to the officer's neck.

Nausea welled up in Cinder as the maniac released the officer and turned his bloodied face up to the sky.

He howled.

A long, proud, ominous howl.

Cinder's dart caught him in the neck, silencing him. He had time to turn his glower on her before he collapsed onto his side.

It didn't seem to matter. As Cinder and Thorne ran for their abandoned podship, the man's howl was picked up by another and another, half a dozen unearthly calls being sent up in every direction to greet the rising moon.

Thirty-Seven

"WHAT WAS THAT?" THORNE YELLED AS HE PEELED THE podship off the street. Flying lower and much faster than regulations suggested, they fled over the patchwork of crops that surrounded the town of Rieux.

Cinder shook her head, still panting. "They were Lunar. He mentioned his queen."

Thorne slammed his palm down on the podship's control board, cursing. "I know Lunars are supposed to have some screws loose—no offense—but those men were psychotic. He practically gnawed off my arm! And this is my favorite jacket!"

Cinder glanced over at Thorne, but his injured shoulder was the one turned away from her. She could, however, make out a red welt where he'd pounded his forehead into hers in order to snap her from her delirium.

She pressed her cool metal fingers to her own forehead, which was starting to throb, and noticed a skein of text in her vision that she'd been too terrified and distracted to notice before.

WHERE ARE YOU???

"Iko's panicking."

Thorne swerved around an abandoned tractor. "I forgot about the police! Is my ship all right?"

"Hold on." Sick to her stomach at the swerving, Cinder gripped her harness and called up a new comm.

ON OUR WAY. ARE THE POLICE STILL THERE?

Iko's response was almost instantaneous.

NO, THEY STUCK A TRACKING DEVICE TO THE BOTTOM OF THE SHIP AND LEFT. SOMETHING ABOUT A DISTURBANCE IN RIEUX. I'M LOOKING AT THE NETSCREENS NOW—CINDER, ARE YOU SEEING THIS?

She gulped, but didn't answer. "The police are gone. They left a tracker."

"Well, that's predictable." Thorne swooped down, catching the tip of a windmill on the landing gear. Cinder saw the Rampion only a few miles off, a large gray splotch amid the crops, barely discernible in the night.

IKO, OPEN THE PODSHIP DOCK.

By the time the pod dipped toward the Rampion, the dock was wide-open. Cinder squeezed her eyes shut, bracing herself against the seat as Thorne dove toward it too fast, but he released the thrusters just in time and soon they were coming to a very rocky, sudden stop. The podship shuddered and died—Cinder had tumbled out of the side door before the lights faded.

"Iko! Where's the tracker?"

"Stars, Cinder! Where have you been? What is going on out there?"

"No time—the tracker!"

"It's under the starboard landing gear."

"I'll get it," said Thorne, marching toward the wide-open doors. "Iko, seal the dock as soon as I'm out, then open the main hatch. Cinder, get that power cell installed!" He jumped down off the dock, and Cinder heard a squelch of mud when he landed. A moment later, the interlocking doors began to slide shut.

"Wait!"

The doors froze, leaving a space not larger than Cinder's pounding head between them.

"What?" cried Iko. "I thought he was out! Did I crush him?"

"No, no, he's fine. I just have to do something."

Chewing on her lip, she knelt on one knee. Yanking her pant leg up, she unlatched the compartment to her prosthetic leg and found two small chips lodged in the mess of bundled wires. The direct communication chip glittering with its peculiar iridescence, and Peony's ID chip, still caked with dried blood.

Those officers had tracked her through Peony's chip, and she wouldn't have been surprised if Levana's minions had found her the same way.

"I'm so stupid," she muttered, prying the chip loose. Her heart suddenly clamped up, but she did her best to ignore it as she brushed a quick kiss against the ID chip and threw it out into the field. It glinted once with moonlight before vanishing in the dark.

"All right. You can close the doors now."

As the doors clanged shut, she threw herself toward the podship and pulled the power cell off the floorboard.

The engine room glowed with red emergency lights. Her retina display had already pulled up the plans by the time she slithered on her stomach to the ship's exterior corner and unbolted the old power cell.

When she yanked it free, the whole ship went black.

She cursed to herself.

"*Cinder!*" came Thorne's distraught scream from somewhere overhead.

Cinder flicked on her flashlight and tore off the protective packaging of the new cell, her breaths coming in short, panicked gasps. It didn't take long for the engine room to grow stifling hot without the cooling system.

She plugged a cable into the cell's outlet, then bolted it to the engine. Already she was forgetting how she'd ever managed to survive without the screwdriver in her new hand as she secured the cell to the wall. The overlaid blueprint on her vision zoomed in as she connected the delicate wires.

Gulping, she punched the restart code into the mainframe. The engine hummed, grew louder, and soon purred like a contented cat. The red lights flickered back on, and were just as quickly replaced with bright whites.

"Iko?"

The response was almost instantaneous. "What just happened? Why won't anyone tell me what's going on?"

Exhaling, Cinder dropped to her stomach and wriggled back toward the door. She grasped the ladder rungs that led to the ship's main level, calling out, "Ready for takeoff!"

No sooner had the words left than the combustors flared beneath her and the ship lurched up off the ground. Cinder screamed and grasped the ladder, clinging tight to it as the Rampion hovered momentarily before shooting up into the sky, away from the destruction happening in Michelle Benoit's beautiful hometown.

When they'd entered orbit again, Cinder found Thorne in the cockpit, slumped in his chair with both arms draped toward the floor.

"We should clean our wounds," she said, seeing the dark spot of blood on his shoulder.

Thorne nodded without facing her. "Yeah, I definitely don't want to catch whatever he had."

Her right leg shaking under her own weight, Cinder made

her way awkwardly into the medbay, grateful she'd had the fore-thought to clear the crates away from it, and found an assort-ment of bandages and ointments.

"Nice takeoff back there," she said when she joined Thorne in the cockpit. "Captain."

He grunted, sulking as Cinder used her imbedded knife to cut open his sticky sleeve.

"How does it feel?" she asked, examining the bite marks on his arm.

"Like I was bit by a feral dog."

"Are you light-headed? Woozy? You lost a lot of blood."

"I'm fine," he said, glowering. "Pretty upset about my jacket."

"It could have been a lot worse." She ripped off a long band of medical tape. "I could have used you as a human shield, like that officer." Her voice hiccupped on the last word. A headache was coming on, starting in her desert-dry eyes, as she wrapped a bandage around Thorne's arm and taped it.

"What happened?"

She shook her head and peered down at the gash in her palm. "I don't know," she said, awkwardly wrapping the tape around it too.

"Cinder."

"I didn't mean to." She slumped back in her own chair. She felt sick, remembering the dead, blank stare of the woman as she put herself between Cinder and that man. "I just panicked, and the next thing I knew, she was there, in front of me. I didn't even think—I didn't try—it just happened." She shoved herself out of the chair and marched out into the cargo bay, needing room. To breathe, to move, to think. "This is exactly what 1 was talking about! Having this gift. It's turning me into a monster! Just like those men. Just like Levana."

She rubbed her temples, biting back her next confession.

Maybe it wasn't just being Lunar. Maybe it ran in her blood. Maybe she was just like her aunt . . . just like her mother, who had been no better.

"Or maybe," Thorne said, "it was an accident, and you're still learning."

"An accident!" She spun around. "I killed a woman!"

Thorne held up a finger. "No. That blood-sucking, howling wolf-man killed her. Cinder, you were scared. You didn't know what you were doing."

"He was coming after *me*, and 1 just used her."

"And you think he would have left the rest of us alone once he had you?"

Cinder clamped her jaw shut, stomach still churning.

"1 get that you feel like it was your fault, but let's try to put some of the blame where it belongs here."

Cinder frowned at Thorne, but she was seeing that man again, with his haunting blue eyes and sick smile.

"They have Michelle Benoit." She shuddered. "And that's my fault too. They're looking for *me*."

"Now what are you rambling on about?"

"He knew that's why we came to Rieux, but he said they'd already found her. The 'old lady,' he said. But they only came after her because they're trying to find me!"

Thorne pulled a palm down his face. "Cinder, you're being

delusional. Michelle Benoit housed Princess Selene. If they tracked her down, *that's* why. It has nothing to do with you."

She gulped, her entire body shaking. "She might still be alive. We have to try and find her."

"Since neither of you will tell me anything," said Iko, her voice taut, "I'll just have to guess. Were you by chance attacked by men who fought like starved wild animals?"

Thorne and Cinder traded glances. Cinder noticed that the cargo bay had grown abnormally warm during her tirade.

"Good guess," said Thorne.

"They're talking about it all over the newsfeeds," said Iko. "It's not just in France. It's happening all over the world, every country in the Union. Earth is under attack!"

Thirty-Eight

HOWLS FILLED THE THEATER'S BASEMENT. FROM THE CORNER of her bed, in the cell's near blackness, Scarlet held her breath and listened. The lonesome cries were muffled and distant, somewhere out on the streets. But they must have been loud indeed to reach all the way to her dungeon.

And there seemed to be dozens of them. Animals seeking one another in the night, eerie and haunting.

There shouldn't be wild animals in the city.

Peeling herself off the bed, Scarlet crept toward the bars. A light filtered down the hallway from the stairs that led up to the stage, but it was so faint she could barely make out the iron bars over her own door. She peered down the corridor. No movement. No sound. An EXIT sign that probably hadn't been lit up in a hundred years.

She peered the other direction. Only blackness.

She had the sinking sensation of being trapped all alone. Of being left to die in this underground prison.

Another howl echoed up, louder this time, though still stifled. Perhaps on the street just outside the theater.

Scarlet slicked her tongue over her lips. "Hello?" she started, tentatively. When there was no response—not even a distant howl—she tried again, louder. "Is anyone out there?"

She shut her eyes to listen. No footsteps.

"I'm hungry."

No shuffling.

"I need to use the bathroom."

No voices.

"I'm going to escape now."

But no one cared. She was alone.

She squeezed the bar, wondering if it was a trap. Perhaps they were luring her into a false security, testing her to see what she would do. Perhaps they wanted her to try to escape so they could use it against her.

Or perhaps—just perhaps—Wolf really had meant to help her.

She snarled. If it wasn't for him, she wouldn't be in this mess to begin with. If he'd told her the truth and explained to her what was going on, she would have come up with another plan to get her grandma out, rather than be led like a lamb to the feast.

The joints in her fingers started to burn from clenching the bars too tight.

Then, from the hollowness of the basement, she heard her name.

Weak and uncertain, posed as a delirious question. *Scarlet?*

Stomach clenching, Scarlet pushed her face into the bars, their coldness squeezing her cheekbones. "Hello?"

She started to shake as she waited.

Scar... Scarlet?

"Grand-mère? *Grand-mère?*"

The voice went silent, as if speaking had drained it.

Scarlet thrust herself away from the barred door and ran back to the bed, claiming the small chip she'd tucked beneath the mattress.

She returned to the door desperate, pleading, hoping. If Wolf had tricked her about this—

She reached through the bar and flicked the chip across the scanner. It chimed, the same sickeningly cheerful chime it had given when her guards brought her food, a sound she had despised until this moment.

The bars swung open without resistance.

Scarlet lingered in the open doorway, her pulse racing. Again she found herself straining to hear any sound of her guards, but the opera house seemed abandoned.

She stumbled away from the stairwell, into the blackness of the hallway. Her hands on the walls to either side were her only guides. When she came to another iron-barred door, she paused and leaned against the opening. "Grand-mère?"

Each cell was empty.

Three, four, five cells, all empty.

"Grand-mère?" she whispered.

At the sixth door, a whimper. "Scarlet?"

"Grand-mère!" She dropped the chip in her excitement and immediately fell to the floor in search of it. "Grand-mère, it's all right, I'm here. I'm going to get you—" Her fingers found the chip and she whipped it up before the scanner. A wash of relief covered her when it chimed, although a pained, terrified sound came from her grandmother upon hearing it.

Scarlet yanked the bars open and pushed into the cell, not bothering to stand lest she accidentally trip over her grandmother in the darkness. The cell was rank with the stench of urine and sweat and old, stale air. "Grand-mère?"

She found her huddled on the gritty stone ground against the back wall. "Grand-mère?"

"Scar? How—?"

"It's me. I'm here. I'm going to get you out of here." Her words dissolved into sobs and she grasped her grandma's frail arms, pulling her into an embrace.

Her grandma cried out, an awful, pitiable sound that cut through Scarlet's ears. She gasped and laid her back down.

"Don't," her grandma whimpered, her body sliding limply down to the ground. "Oh Scar—you shouldn't be here. You shouldn't be here. I can't stand you being here. Scarlet ..." She started crying, choking, wet sobs burbling up from her.

Scarlet hovered over her grandma's body, fear gripping every muscle. She couldn't remember hearing her grandmother cry before. "What did they do to you?" she whispered, drawing her hands over her grandmother's shoulders. Beneath a thin, tattered shirt, there were the lumps of bandages and something damp and sticky.

Biting back her own tears, she traced her grandmother's chest and ribs. The bandages were everywhere. She stroked the woman's arms and hands—her hands were shaped more like clubs now, so covered in bandages.

"No, don't touch them." Her grandma tried to pull away, but her limbs only twitched uncontrollably.

As tenderly as she could, Scarlet ran her thumb over her grandma's hands. Hot tears slipped down her cheeks. "What did they do to you?"

"Scar, you have to get out of here." Each word a struggle until she could barely talk, barely breathe.

Scarlet knelt over her, resting her head on her grandma's breast and stroking the sticky hair off her brow. "It's going to be all right. I'm going to get you out of here and we're going to go to the hospital and you're going to be fine. You're going to be fine." She forced herself to sit up. "Can you walk? Have they done anything to your legs?"

"I can't walk. I can't move. You have to leave me here, Scarlet. You have to get out."

"I'm not leaving you. They've all left, Grand-mère. We have time. We just need to figure out a way—I can carry you." Tears dripped off Scarlet's chin.

"Come here, my love. Come closer." Scarlet swiped at her nose and buried her face against her grandma's neck. Arms tried to encircle her, but served to only beat weakly against her sides. "I didn't want to involve you in this. I'm so sorry."

"Grand-mère."

"Hush. Listen. I need you to do something for me. Something important."

She shook her head. "Stop it. You're going to be all right."

"Listen to me, Scarlet." Even her grandmother's faint voice seemed to drop. "Princess Selene is alive."

Scarlet squeezed her eyes shut. "Stop talking, please. Save your strength."

"She went to live in the Eastern Commonwealth with a family by the name of Linh. A man named Linh Garan."

A sad, frustrated sigh. "I know, Grand-mère. I know you kept her, and I know you gave her to a man in the Commonwealth. But it doesn't matter anymore. It's not your problem anymore. I'm going to get you out of here, and I'll keep you safe."

"No, darling, you must find her. She'll be a teenager now . . . a cyborg."

Scarlet blinked, wishing she could see her grandmother in the blackness. "A cyborg?"

"Unless she changed her name, she's called Cinder now."

The name struck a chord of familiarity in the back of Scarlet's mind, but her brain was too clouded to pinpoint it. "Grand-mère, please stop talking. I have to—"

"You must find her. Logan and Garan are the only ones who know, and if the queen found me, she could find them. Someone must tell the girl who she is. Someone must find her. *You* must find her."

Scarlet shook her head. "I don't care about the stupid princess. I care about you. I'm going to protect *you*."

"I can't go with you." Her padded hands rubbed against Scarlet's arms. "Please, Scarlet. She could make all the difference."

Scarlet shrank down. "She'll just be a teenager," she managed between her renewed sobs. "What can she do?"

She remembered then, the name. The newsfeeds flashed through her thoughts—a girl running down palace steps, falling, landing in a heap on a gravel path.

Linh Cinder.

A teenager. A cyborg. A Lunar.

She gulped. So Levana had already found the girl. Found, but lost her again.

"It doesn't matter," she murmured, laying her head against her grandma's chest. "It's not our problem. I'm going to get you out of here. We're going to get away."

Her mind desperately searched for a way they could escape together. Something to use as a stretcher or a wheelchair or—

But there was nothing.

Nothing that could make it up the stairs. Nothing she could carry. Nothing her grandma could endure.

Her heart broke, the pain of it pushing a wail out of her throat.

She couldn't leave her like this. She couldn't let them hurt her anymore.

"My sweet girl."

She clamped her eyes shut, pushing out two more hot tears. "Grand-mère, who is Logan Tanner?"

Her grandma brushed a light kiss against Scarlet's forehead.

"He's a good man, Scarlet. He would have loved you. I hope you'll meet him someday. Tell him hello for me. Tell him good-bye."

A sob cut through Scarlet's heart. Her grandma's shirt was soaked through with her tears.

She couldn't bring herself to tell her that Logan Tanner was dead. Had gone crazy. Had killed himself.

Her grandfather.

"I love you, Grand-mère. You're everything to me."

The heavy bandaged limbs stroked her knees. "I love you too. My brave, stubborn girl."

She sniffed, and vowed to herself that she would stay until morning. She would stay forever. She wouldn't abandon her. If her captors came back, they would find them together—kill them together if they must.

She would never leave her again.

The vow was made, the promise determined, when she heard footsteps echoing down the corridor.

Thirty-Nine

HUNKERING DOWN OVER HER GRANDMOTHER, SCARLET turned toward the hallway. Old wires hummed overhead and pale light flooded the cell. The door still stood open, the bars casting skeletal shadows along the floor.

Her eyes adjusted slowly. She held her breath, listening, but the footsteps had stopped. Still, someone was there. Someone was coming.

Her grandmother's bandaged hand slipped into hers and she turned back. Her gut clamped. Streaks of dried blood were on the weathered face, her hair was tangled and matted. She was little more than a wasted skeleton now, though her brown eyes were still strong, still vibrant. Still filled with more love than was kept in all the rest of the world.

"Run," she whispered.

Scarlet shook her head. "I'm not leaving you."

"This is not your fight. Run, Scarlet. *Now.*"

Footsteps again, growing closer.

Clenching her jaw, Scarlet pulled herself onto shaking legs and faced the door. Her heart was galloping, waiting as the steps grew louder.

Maybe it was Wolf.

Come to help her, to help them.

She was dizzy from the fluttering of her pulse, unable to believe that she *wanted* to see him again, after everything he'd done to her.

But he'd given her the chip. And he was strong, strong enough to carry her grandmother. If it was Wolf, returned for her, they'd be saved...

She saw the shadow cross the floor before the man stepped into the threshold.

It was Ran, and he was smiling.

Scarlet gulped and solidified her knees, determined not to show her fear. But there was something different about Ran now. His eyes were no longer merely ruthless—now they were hungry, peering at Scarlet like she was a treat, one he'd been looking forward to for a long time.

"Ah, little fox. And just how did you get out of your cell?"

A shudder ripped through her.

"Leave my granddaughter alone." Her grandmother's raspy voice had gained an ounce of strength. She stirred, trying to sit up.

Scarlet dropped beside her, squeezed her grandmother's hand. "Grand-mère—no, don't."

"I remember you." Michelle stared at Ran. "You were with the ones who came for me."

"Grand-mère—"

Ran chuckled. "A sharp memory you have for such an ancient thing."

"Don't worry about him, Scarlet," said Michelle. "He is only the omega. He must have been left behind, because he is too weak to join the battle."

Ran snarled, baring his jutting canines, and Scarlet shrank back.

"I stayed behind," he growled, "because I have unfinished business here." His eyes flashed, practically glowing. There was nothing but hatred inside them—fiery and unrestrained.

Scarlet shifted so that her body better covered her grandmother.

"You are nothing," Michelle said, her lashes dipping from exhaustion. Terror clutched at Scarlet's heart. "Nothing but a puppet for that thaumaturge. They've taken away your gift and turned you all into monsters, but even with all the strength, all the senses, all the bloodlust—you remain the lowest of your peers, and you always will be."

Scarlet's mind whirred. Wanting the conversation to end, wanting her grandmother to stop goading him—knowing it made no difference. There was murder on Ran's face.

A rough laugh burst out of him. His hands gripped the doorjamb to either side, entirely blocking the exit. "You're wrong, you old hag. You know so much—you must know what becomes of a pack member who kills his alpha?" He didn't wait for her response. "He takes his alpha's place." His cheeks dimpled. "And I've found that my brother, my *alpha,* has a weakness." His words slipped off as his attention found Scarlet again.

"You are a naive young man." Her grandmother coughed. "You are weak. You will never be more than a lowly omega. Even *I* can see that."

Scarlet hissed. She could see the fury building inside Ran, feel the anger rolling off him. "Grand-mère!"

Then it became obvious, what her grandmother was trying to do.

"No! She doesn't mean it." She despised herself for pleading, but couldn't care. "She's old, she's delirious! Just leave her—"

Fuming into the cell, Ran snatched Scarlet up by her hair and pried her away from her grandmother.

She shrieked, clawing at his forearm, but he tossed her back into the corner. "*No!*"

Her grandma screamed in pain as Ran lifted her by the throat. In a blink she was pinned against the wall, too weak to flail, to fight, to put up any resistance.

"LEAVE HER ALONE!" Scarlet scrambled up and jumped onto Ran's back, locking her elbows around his neck, squeezing with all her might. When Ran didn't even flinch, she clawed at him, aiming for his eye sockets.

Ran howled and dropped her grandmother into a heap, then flung Scarlet off his back. She collapsed against the wall, but she barely felt the impact, her attention falling on her grandmother's limp, bandaged form.

"*Grand-mère!*"

Their gazes met and she could see, in an instant, that her

grandmother would not be moving again. Her dry lips managed to stammer—"Ru..." But nothing followed. Her eyes lingered open, eerily empty.

Scarlet shoved herself off the wall, but Ran was there first, his massive form crouching over her grandmother's body, scooping one hand beneath her back so that her head fell heavily onto the hard floor.

Like a starved animal having brought down his first kill, Ran leaned over and clamped his jaws over Michelle's neck.

Scarlet screamed and fell backward. The world spun with the sight of blood and Ran crouched on all fours.

Her grandmother's accusation echoed back to her. *They've turned you all into monsters.*

Still in shock, she forced her face away and rolled onto her side. Her stomach heaved, but there was nothing inside her but bile and saliva. She tasted iron and acid and blood and realized she'd bitten her tongue when Ran had thrown her at the wall, but there was no pain. Only hollowness and horror and a dark cloud creeping over her.

She was not here. This was not happening.

Stomach burning from trying to push up food that wasn't there, she crawled toward the far wall, putting as much distance between her and Ran as she could. Ran and her grandmother.

Her hand fell into the streak of light from the hallway. Her skin was sickly pale. She was trembling.

Run.

Lifting her head, she could see the start of a stairwell at the end of the hallway. Beside it, a painted sign long since faded. TO STAGE.

Run.

Her brain struggled to find the meaning of the words. TO STAGE. Stage. Stage.

Her grandmother's last words.

Run!

Reaching forward, she wrapped her fingers around the bars of the cell and used them as leverage. Straining to pull herself up. To stand. To push forward, into the hallway, into the light.

Her legs felt nonexistent at first as she hobbled to the bottom of the stairs, but as she climbed, she found strength in them. She pushed forward. She ran.

A closed door loomed at the top of the stairs, an old wooden door not even equipped with an ID scanner. It creaked when she shoved it open.

Then footsteps below, coming for her.

Scarlet emerged backstage. Old pillars stood clustered together to her right and a maze of fake stone walls and painted trees filled the shadows to her left. The door slammed behind her and she ran into the wooden forest, grabbing a wrought-iron candelabra.

She lifted it in both hands and waited, feet braced.

Ran burst through the door, chin covered in blood.

Scarlet swung as hard as she could. A roar was wrenched out of her as the iron bar collided with Ran's skull.

He cried out and stumbled back into the curtain. He tripped on the fabric and fell backward.

Scarlet thrust the candelabra at him, not sure she had the strength to heft it again. She heard fabric ripping, but she was already gone, dodging between the set pieces, scanning the creaking wooden floorboards as she lunged over coiled dusty power cords and toppled spotlights. She stumbled onto the stage, the empty expanse of wooden floorboards and trapdoors, and half jumped, half fell into the phantom orchestra. Ignoring a jolt of pain that burned across her knee, she shoved the music stands aside and bolted into the auditorium.

Footsteps thumped across the stage behind her. Inhumanly fast.

The rows of empty chairs flashed by and all she could see was the door looming ahead.

He grabbed her hood.

She let him pull her back, used the momentum to swing around and aim her knee for his groin.

He let out a cry of pain and staggered.

Scarlet darted through the crumbling marble arches, past the cherubs with their broken arms, past the shattered chandeliers and broken tile floors. She flew down the marble stairs, focusing on the huge doors that would lead to the street. If only she could get out of there. Into public. Into the real world.

As she hit the lobby floor, the silhouette of another man moved across the exit.

Her feet skidded to a stop, landing her in the square of pale sunlight from the hole in the ceiling.

Pivoting, she ran for the other staircase, the stairs that went back down to the depths of the opera house.

Above, a door slammed shut, and there were footsteps pounding and she couldn't tell if it was one set of footsteps or two.

Sweat coated the back of her shirt. Her legs ached, her burst of adrenaline fading.

She rounded a corner and barreled into darkness. The main room had once been used for important guests of the opera house and a series of doors and hallways led to every corner of the sublevel. Scarlet knew the halls to the right would take her back to the prison cells, so she veered left. A drained fountain basin filled the space between the two stairways that led to the upper level. The bronze statue of a half-dressed maiden lingered in an alcove atop a pedestal, one of the few statues that seemed to have survived so many years of neglect.

Scarlet ran for the opposite staircase, wondering if going back up to the lobby would be suicide—and yet knowing that to be trapped down here was no alternative.

She reached the bottom of the stairs and her foot hit the low ledge of the fountain. She stumbled, crying out.

Ran was on her before she hit the ground.

Fingernails dug into her shoulder, flipping her onto her back amid the tiny broken tiles of the dry basin. She peered up into his glowing eyes, the eyes of a madman, of a murderer, and she remembered Wolf onstage at the street fight.

Fear clamped her throat shut, strangling a scream.

He gripped her shirt and lifted her from the ground. She grabbed his wrists, but was too petrified to fight as he brought her face toward his. Scarlet nearly gagged on the stench of his breath, like rotten meat and blood—so much blood—her grandmother—

"If it wasn't such a repulsive thought, I might take advantage of you here, now that we're all alone," he said, and Scarlet shuddered. "Just to see the look on my brother's face when I told him about it." With a roar, he threw her at the statue.

Her back collided with the bronze pedestal and pain exploded through her head, knocking the wind from her. She collapsed to the ground, grasping her chest, trying to draw air back into her lungs.

Ran crouched before her, ready to spring. His tongue swiped out over his canines, coating them with strings of saliva.

Her stomach lurched. She kicked at the ground in an attempt to push herself into the small space between the statue and the wall. To disappear. To hide.

He sprang.

She cowered against the wall, but the impact didn't come.

Scarlet heard a battle cry, followed by a heavy thud. Snarling.

She lowered her trembling arms. In the center of the cavern, two forms tangled with each other. Jaws snapping. Blood dripping over taut muscles.

Eyesight blurring, she managed to ease in a breath, glad to feel her chest expand. Reaching overhead, she gripped the statue and tried to pull herself up, but the muscles in her back screamed at her.

Clenching her jaw, she worked on tucking her legs under her

and battled against the pain until she could stand, panting and sweating against the bronze goddess.

If she could just get away before the brawl was over—

Ran pulled the other man into a headlock. The opponent's glowing emerald eyes pierced Scarlet, for one heart-stopping moment, before he flipped Ran over his head.

The ground vibrated from the impact, but Scarlet barely felt it.

Wolf.

It was Wolf.

Forty

RAN REBOUNDED ONTO HIS FEET AND HE AND WOLF SPRANG apart, each straining against unburned energy. Scarlet could almost see it, simmering and seething beneath their skin. Wolf was covered in gashes and blood, but he didn't seem to notice as he stood slightly hunched, hands flexing.

Ran bared his fangs.

"Return to your post, Ran," Wolf said with a snarl. "This one is mine."

Ran snorted in disgust. "And let you embarrass me—embarrass our family—with all your newfound sympathy? You're a disgrace." He spat a glob of blood onto the broken concrete. "Our mission is to kill. Now, stand aside so I might kill her, if you're not willing to do it yourself."

Scarlet glanced behind her. The staircase was low enough that she could climb over the railing, but her body ached just thinking of it. Trying to shake off the helplessness, she struggled to crawl to the edge of the fountain.

"She is mine," Wolf repeated, his voice tinted with a low growl.

"I do not want to fight you over a human, brother," Ran said, though the loathing etched into his face made the endearment sound like a joke.

"Then you will leave her."

"She was left under my jurisdiction. You should not have abandoned your own post to come for her."

"She is *mine*!" Wolf's temper flared and he swiped at the nearest candelabra, tearing the bronze arm from the wall. Scarlet ducked as it crashed to the floor, sending wax candlesticks hurtling into the fountain's basin.

They both remained in their hunched stances. Panting. Glaring.

Finally, Ran snarled. "Then you've made your choice."

He pounced.

Wolf batted him from the air with an open palm, swiping him down onto the fountain wall.

Ran landed with a yelp, but quickly rolled back onto his feet. Wolf lunged, digging his teeth into Ran's forearm.

With a cry of pain, Ran swiped his sharp nails down Wolf's chest, leaving crimson gouges. Unlocking his jaw, Wolf backhanded Ran across the face, sending him reeling into the fountain's statue.

Scarlet screamed and stumbled back against a column at the base of the stairs.

Ran attacked again and Wolf, expectant, grasped him by the neck and used the momentum to throw him overhead. Ran rolled gracefully onto his feet. They were both panting, blood soaking through their shredded clothes. They paced, waiting, hunting for weaknesses.

Again, Ran made the first move. He threw his whole weight at Wolf, tackling him to the ground. His jaws went for the neck, snapping, but Wolf held him off, hands wrapped around his throat. He grunted beneath Ran's weight, struggling to avoid the dripping fangs, when Ran dug his fist into Wolf's shoulder—the bullet wound from Scarlet's gun.

Howling, Wolf curled his legs to gain purchase and shoved Ran off him with a kick to the stomach.

Ran rolled away and they both staggered to their feet again. Scarlet could see their energy dissolving as they stood, wobbling, gazes flashing murder. Neither moved to cover their wounds.

Ran swiped a bare arm across his mouth, streaking his chin with blood.

Wolf crouched and sprang, shoving Ran onto his back and landing on top of him. A fist clawed for him. Wolf ducked, catching the brunt of the damage on his ear.

Pushing his opponent into the marble, Wolf raised his face to the ceiling, and howled.

Scarlet forced her back into the column, petrified. The howl resounded off the walls and through her skull and joints, filling every empty space in her body.

When he stopped howling, Wolf dropped down and snapped his jaw around Ran's throat.

Scarlet hid behind her arms but couldn't bring herself to

look away. Blood gurgled up, coating Wolf's chin and neck, dribbling down onto the mosaic floor.

Ran shook and jerked, but the struggle was quick to drain out of him. A moment later, Wolf released him, letting the dead body slump onto the ground.

Reaching around the column, Scarlet grasped the stair railing and hauled herself up the flight. Running, half limping up the steps.

The lobby was still deserted. Her feet splashed through the puddle in the center of the room as she ran for the doors. Doors that would lead to the street. To freedom.

Then she heard Wolf, chasing her.

She shoved through the exit. The cool evening air engulfed her as she pounded down the stairs to the empty street, already scanning the open square for help.

She saw no one.

No one.

The door slammed open behind her before it had time to close and she stumbled blindly across the street. In the distance, she saw a woman running into a nearby alley. Hope flashed and Scarlet urged her feet to move faster, to fly. She suddenly felt like she could take off and soar over the concrete. If she could just reach the woman, just use her port to call for help—

And then another figure appeared. Another man, his gait abnormally fast. He sped into the alley and a moment later the woman's terrified scream screeched across the square, and was cut short.

A howl erupted from the same dark alley.

In the distance, another howl rose up to greet it, and another, and another, filling the twilight with bloodthirsty cries.

Terror and hopelessness choked Scarlet all at once and she fell, silt and concrete digging into her palms. Gasping, drenched with sweat, she rolled onto her back. Wolf had stopped running, but he still came for her. Prowling toward her with measured, patient steps.

He was panting almost as hard as she was.

Somewhere off in the city, another chorus of howling started.

Wolf did not join them.

His attention was all for Scarlet, cold and sharp and hungry. The pain was clear. The fury was clearer.

She scrambled away on her burning palms.

Wolf paused as he reached the center of the intersection. He was silhouetted by the moonlight, eyes gold and green and black and seething.

She saw him drag his tongue across his fangs. Watched as he curled and uncurled his fingers. His jaw worked as if to take in a bigger gulp of air.

She could see his fight. His struggle. As clearly as she could see the animal—the wolf—in him. As clearly as she could still see the man.

"Wolf." Her tongue was parched. She tried to wet her dry lips and tasted blood. "What have they done to you?"

"*You.*" The word was spat out at her, full of hatred. "What have *you* done to me?"

He took another stumbling step toward her and she scooted away, pushing at the ground with the heels of her shoes, but it was useless. In the blink of an eye he had crouched down over her, knocking her onto her elbows without even having to touch her. His hands hit the ground on either side of her head.

Scarlet gaped up at eyes that now seemed to glow in the dark. His mouth was ruby red, the front of his shirt black from the gore. She could smell blood on him, on his clothes, his hair, his skin.

If it was this pungent to her, she couldn't imagine how it must overwhelm him.

He growled and lowered his nose to her neck.

Sniffing.

"I know you don't want to hurt me, Wolf."

His nose bumped against her jaw. His breath caressed her collarbone.

"You helped me. You *rescued* me."

A steaming tear escaped down her cheek.

The tips of his hair, wild and messy again, brushed against her lips. "Things have changed."

Her heart fluttered like a firefly with a missing wing. Her pulse pounded through her veins, expecting the clamp of jaws on her throat at any moment. But something was holding him back. He could have killed her already, but he hadn't.

She gulped. "You protected me from Ran—it wasn't so you could kill me now."

"You don't know the thoughts going through my head."

"I know you're different from them." She attached her gaze

to the enormous moon over the skyline. Reminded herself that this was not a monster. This was Wolf, the man who had held her so tenderly on the train. The man who had given her the ID chip to help her escape. "You said you never wanted to scare me. Well, you're scaring me."

A growl vibrated against her. Scarlet shivered, but forced her body not to shrink away. Instead, she gulped and brought her hands up to his face. Stroking her thumbs over his cheeks, she placed a kiss against Wolf's temple.

His body tensed and she was able to angle his head back just far enough that she could see his eyes. His lips curled into a snarl, but she held his gaze.

"Stop this, Wolf. You're not one of them anymore."

His brow twitched, but his resentment seemed to fade. His expression held pain and desperation and mute anger—but not for her. "He's in my head," he said, his voice a rumbling growl. "Scarlet. I can't—"

He looked away, face scrunching.

Scarlet traced her fingers along his face. The same jaw, the same cheekbones, the same scars, all splattered with blood. She brushed her fingers through his wild hair. "Just stay with me. Protect me, like you said you would."

Something whooshed by her ear and thudded into Wolf's neck.

Wolf went rigid. He looked up, eyes wide and already brightening with bloodlust, but then they grew bleary. With a strangled gurgle in his throat, the strength left him and he collapsed on top of her.

Forty-One

"WOLF! *WOLF!*" CRANING HER NECK, SCARLET SAW A MAN and a woman sprinting toward her, the moonlight glinting off the woman's gun. Scarlet's terror was short-lived; they weren't crazed Lunars. She returned her attention to Wolf, searching out the dart imbedded in his neck. "Wolf!" she yelled again, prying the dart out of his flesh and dropping it to the ground.

"Are you all right?" the woman yelled as she got closer. Scarlet ignored her until her own name cut through her panic. "Scarlet? Scarlet Benoit?"

She glanced up again as the woman slowed—but no, not a woman. A girl, with messy hair and fine, vaguely familiar features. Scarlet frowned, sure she'd seen the girl before.

The man caught up, gasping for air.

"Who are you?" she asked, locking her arms around Wolf as the two stooped to pull him away from her. "What did you do to him?"

"Come on," said the man, grabbing Wolf. He tried to pry Wolf away but she held tight. "We have to get out of here."

"Stop it! Don't touch him! *Wolf!*"

She gripped the sides of Wolf's face and tilted him back. If it hadn't been for his fangs and the blood on his jaw, he would have looked peaceful.

"What did you do to him?"

"Scarlet, where's your grandmother? Is she with you?" said the girl.

This brought Scarlet's scattered attention back to her. "My grandmother?"

The girl knelt beside her. "Michelle Benoit? Do you know where she is?" The girl's words tripped over themselves in her rush to speak.

Scarlet blinked. Her memory shifted. She did know this girl. Light bounced off the girl's fingers and Scarlet realized what she had seen before wasn't a gun. It was her hand.

"Linh Cinder," she whispered.

"Don't worry," said the man. "We're the good guys."

"Scarlet," said Cinder, grasping Wolf by the shoulder to leverage some of the weight away from her. "I know how it looked on the netscreens, but I swear we're not here to hurt you. I just need to know where your grandmother is. Is she in danger?"

Scarlet gulped. This was Princess Selene. This was the girl they'd been searching for, the girl her grandmother had been questioned over.

The girl her grandmother had given everything to protect.

Together, she and the man heaved Wolf away, dropping him onto the concrete.

"*Please*," said Cinder. "Your grandmother?"

"She's in the opera house," Scarlet said. "She's dead."

The girl gaped at her, with pity or disappointment—Scarlet couldn't tell which. Sitting up, she flattened her palm against Wolf's chest, relieved to feel it rise beneath her touch. "They were looking for you."

Surprise quickly stole away the girl's sympathy.

"Come on," said the man from behind her, stooping and hooking his elbow beneath Scarlet's armpit. "Time to go."

"No! I'm not leaving him!" She scrambled out of his hold and crawled toward Wolf's unconscious body, tying her arms around his head. The strangers gawked at her like she was mad. "He's not like the rest."

"He's exactly like the rest!" said the man. "He was trying to eat you!"

"He saved my life!"

The strangers exchanged disbelieving glances, and the girl gave a baffled shrug.

"Fine," the man said. "You take the helm."

He pulled Scarlet off Wolf while the girl grabbed Wolf's wrist and hoisted him up over her shoulder, grunting with the effort.

The man skirted behind and grabbed Wolf's legs. "Holy spades," he muttered, already breathless. "What are these guys made of?"

Cinder started moving toward the opera house at a pace only barely slower than a jaunt. Scarlet ducked in between them, supporting Wolf's abdomen as well as she could as they awkwardly stumbled across the square.

Past the woman, the gleaming form of a military cargo ship poked out from the next street.

A howl nearly startled Scarlet into dropping Wolf's body. She could not imagine feeling more vulnerable, her arms wrapped around Wolf's torso, leaving her stomach and chest exposed, moving at this snail's pace, sweating, exhausted, in pain. Blood oozing down her side.

"You better have those tranquilizers ready," the man said.

"Can only . . . put in . . . one at a time . . ."

The man cursed beneath his breath, then gasped. "Cinder! Ten o'—"

There was a snap and a dart lodged itself into a man's chest on the sidewalk in front of the theater. He had crumpled to the ground before Scarlet even realized he was there.

"Let's pick it up," the man behind her said. "How many more of those do you have?"

"Just three," the girl panted.

"Gonna have to restock."

"Right. I'll just . . . head down . . . to the convenience store, and—" She didn't finish, the strain too much.

Cinder tripped and they all stumbled, Wolf's body landing on the ground with a thud. Scarlet pulled out from beneath him and her heart lurched to see blood gushing out of his wounds, made worse from the trek. "Wolf!"

An eerie howling rose up all around them. Much closer than it had seemed before.

"Open the ramp!" the girl yelled, startling the man.

"We need bandages," said Scarlet.

The girl got to her feet and grasped Wolf's wrists again. "There are bandages on the ship. Come *on*."

The man ran ahead, screaming, "Iko! Open the hatch!"

Scarlet heard the clicking of gears and the humming of electricity as the hatch began to open, revealing the welcoming interior of the ship. Pulling herself onto her feet, she'd just grabbed Wolf's ankles when she saw a man loping toward them at a sprint, his nostrils flaring, lips pulled taut against his fangs. He was one of the men who had first taken her to her cell.

A ping, a thunk, as a dart buried itself in his forearm. He roared and increased his speed for two steps before his anger faded and he fell forward, face slamming onto the pavement.

"Almost there," said Cinder through her teeth, picking up Wolf's dropped wrists.

More howling greeted them from the roads and alleys and shadows, great loping figures appearing out of the darkness.

Scarlet's back and legs ached and her palms were slick as she struggled to retain her grip on Wolf's ankles. "They're coming!"

"I noticed!"

Scarlet fell, crashing onto her knees. She looked up at Wolf's unconscious face, at the panicking girl, and frustration welled up inside her. She forced herself to stand again, though her legs were no stronger than unbaked dough.

Then the man was back, shoving her toward the ship. "Go!" he yelled, and grabbed Wolf's ankles.

"Thorne! You're supposed to be flying the ship, you dunce!"

Scarlet turned toward the ship's open hatch. "I can fly! Just get him inside!"

She ran, though her mind screamed at her for leaving Wolf behind. Her muscles burned, her head pounded with the rush of blood. She could only focus on putting one foot in front of another. Ignoring the burning. Ignoring the sharp stabbing pain in her side. Blinking away the sweat. One. More. Step.

Something sliced across her back. She heard the rip of fabric, a loud thump, and then something grabbed her ankle. She screamed and collapsed at the bottom of the ramp. Fingernails buried themselves into the flesh of her calf and she cried out in pain.

Whistle. Thud.

The hand released her.

Scarlet kicked the man in the jaw before scrambling up the rest of the ramp, into the gaping hull of the ship. She flew into the cockpit and stumbled into the pilot's seat. They hadn't bothered to stop the engines and the ship rumbled and purred around her. Her motions were automatic. She could barely see for the salty sting of sweat in her eyes. Her heartbeat felt like horse's hooves trampling her chest.

But her fingers knew what to do as they breezed over the panel.

"Captain? Cinder?"

Startled, she spun back toward the door, but there was no one there. "Who's there?"

A momentary silence, then: "Who are you?"

Scarlet swiped the sweat from her forehead. The ship. The ship was talking to her.

"I'm Scarlet. We need to get ready for takeoff. Can you—"

"Where are Thorne and Cinder?"

"Right behind me. Is this ship equipped with auto lift?"

A series of lights lit up on the panel. "Auto lift and auto magnetic stabilizers."

"Good." She reached for the thruster output control and waited to hear the sound of footsteps on the ramp.

A drop of sweat slid down to her temple. She gulped, harshly, failing in her attempt to wet her sandpaper throat.

"What's taking them so long?" Swiveling the chair around, she threw herself toward the cockpit entrance and peered past the cargo bay.

Wolf's prone body was laid out not a dozen steps from the end of the ramp, and there were Linh Cinder and her friend, standing back to back.

They were surrounded by seven Lunar operatives, and the thaumaturge.

Forty-Two

CINDER SENSED THE THAUMATURGE BEFORE SHE SAW HIM, like a snake slithering into her brain. Urging her to stop running. To stand still and be captured.

Her right leg obeyed—her left kept going.

With a yelp, she crashed to her hands and knees. The unconscious man—Wolf?—nearly crushed her before his body rolled away. Thorne cried out and tripped, barely able to catch himself before falling.

Cinder jumped back to her feet and spun around.

The men came out of the shadows, from the alleyways, around corners, from behind the ship, each with their glowing eyes and sharp canines bared. Seven in all.

She spotted the thaumaturge, handsome as they always were, with curly black hair and a chiseled face. He wore a red coat—a second level thaumaturge.

Backing up, she collided with Thorne.

"So . . . ," he murmured. "How many more darts do you have?"

The thaumaturge's dark irises sparkled with moonlight.

"One."

She doubted the thaumaturge could have heard her, but he smiled serenely and tucked his hands into his maroon sleeves.

"Right," said Thorne. "In that case."

He snatched the officer's stolen gun from his belt and spun, aiming for the thaumaturge. Then froze.

"Oh no."

From the corner of her eye, Cinder saw Thorne's arm curl back, change direction, until the barrel was aimed at her temple instead.

"Cinder ..." His voice nearly broke from panic.

The thaumaturge's expression remained complacent.

Cinder held her breath, stilling her nerves, and targeted her last tranquilizer at Thorne's leg. The thunk made her cringe, but within seconds the gun had clattered from Thorne's fingers and his body collapsed motionless on top of Wolf's.

A warm laugh spilled out of the thaumaturge. "Hello, Miss Linh. How pleasant to make your acquaintance."

She swooped her gaze over the seven men. They were all threatening, hungry, ready to pounce on her and tear her limb from limb at the slightest provocation.

Somehow, she preferred that to the thaumaturge's gleeful amusement. At least with these men there was no misinterpreting their intentions.

She'd taken three steps forward before she realized it. She braced herself and strained to keep her feet still, wobbling for a moment before finding balance and standing solid on the pavement, at the same time that her bionics picked up on the intrusion.

BIOELECTRICAL MANIPULATION DETECTED.
INITIALIZING RESISTANCE PROCED—

The text vanished as Cinder regained purchase of her own thoughts, her own body. Her brain was being stretched in two directions as the thaumaturge failed to control her, her own Lunar gift fighting against him.

"So it's true," he said.

The pressure released, her ears popped, and she was back in her own head again. She was panting, feeling like she'd just run across the whole continent.

"You will forgive me. I did have to try." His white teeth glinted. He didn't seem at all put off by the fact that she couldn't be controlled as easily as Thorne had been.

As easily as the seven men surrounding her.

Heart skipping, she glanced at the nearest man—one with shaggy dark blond hair and a scar that ran from temple to jaw. She forced herself to be calm, urged the desperation to subside, and reached her thoughts toward him.

His mind wasn't like any of those she'd touched with her Lunar gift yet. Not open and focused like Thorne's, not cold and determined like Alak's, not petrified like Émilie's, not anxious or proud like the military officers'.

This man had the mind of an animal. Scattered and wild and raging with primal instinct. The desire to kill, the need to feast, the constant awareness of where he stood in the pack and how he could improve his station. *Kill. Eat. Destroy.*

With a shudder, she pulled her thoughts away from him.

The thaumaturge was chuckling again. "What do you think of my pets? How easily they fit in with the humans, but how quickly they turn into beasts."

"You're controlling them," she said, finding her voice.

"You flatter me. I'm only encouraging their natural instincts."

"No. No person—not even animals have instincts like this. To hunt or defend, maybe, but you've turned them into monsters."

"Perhaps there were some genetic modifications involved." He finished the statement with another chuckle, like she'd caught him in a guilty pleasure. "But don't worry, Miss Linh. I won't let them hurt you. I want my queen to have that pleasure. Your friends, unfortunately ..."

In unison, two of the soldiers stepped forward and grasped Cinder by the elbows.

"Take her to the theater," said the thaumaturge. "I will inform Her Majesty that Michelle Benoit turned out to be useful for something after all."

But Cinder's captors hadn't taken her two steps when the roar of an engine rattled the pavement. They hesitated and Cinder glanced back as the Rampion started to rise, hovering chest height above the street. The ramp was still down and Cinder could see the metal vibrating, the storage crates rattling against one another.

"*Cinder!*" Iko's voice cut through her thundering pulse. "Get down!"

She sank to her knees, hanging limp between the two soldiers, as the ship surged forward. The lowered platform collided with the two men. They dropped Cinder onto all fours and she glanced up as the ramp cut through the rest of the soldiers, mowing down all but one who had the sense to dodge out of its way, before the ramp smashed into the thaumaturge.

He gasped, his legs dangling as he clung to the edge.

Staying low as the belly of the ship hovered overhead, Cinder spun around and scrambled for Thorne's dropped pistol. She waited until she was sure she had a clear shot before firing. The bullet lodged itself in the thaumaturge's thigh and he screamed, releasing the ramp and dropping onto the pavement.

His calmness was gone, his face contorted with rage.

The blond soldier came out of nowhere, tackling Cinder to the ground, sending the gun skidding across the pavement. She struggled to push him off, but he was too heavy, pinning her right arm to the ground. She swung a punch at him with her metal fist—heard the bones crunch on impact, but he didn't release her.

He snarled and opened his jaws wide.

Just as he brought his mouth toward her neck, the ship spun in the air. The landing gear took the soldier in his side, throwing him off Cinder. She rolled away, colliding with Thorne's and Wolf's prone bodies.

The ship swept back around, its running lights washing over the street. The ramp scraped against the road as it settled back to the ground, not half a dozen steps from where Cinder lay. Inside the ship, Scarlet Benoit's head appeared in the cockpit's doorway.

"Come on!"

Clambering to her feet, Cinder grabbed Thorne by the elbow and dragged him off Wolf, but she'd barely moved when a long howl ricocheted down her spine. It was quickly picked up by the rest of the soldiers, the sound deafening.

Cinder stumbled at the base of the ramp and looked back. Two of the soldiers were lying motionless—the two who had taken the brunt of the ship's impact. The rest were crouched down on all fours, their faces turned up to the sky as they howled.

The thaumaturge, farther away, picked himself up from the ground with a sneer. Though it was too dark to see any blood, Cinder could tell he was favoring the leg that had been shot.

Brushing the sweat from her eyes, Cinder focused on the soldier closest to her. She mentally reached out for the bioelectric waves that were rolling off him, frenzied and hungry, and clamped her thoughts around them.

One howl was cut off sharply from the rest.

A headache was already forming at her temples from the effort required to control him, but she sensed the change immediately. Still violent, still angry, but no longer a wild beast sent to rip apart anyone in his path.

You. She wasn't sure if she said it out loud or merely thought it. *You are mine now. Get these two men on board the ship.*

His eyes flickered, loathing but restrained.

"*Now.*"

As he moved to lumber toward her, the rest of the howling ceased. Four faces peered at Cinder and the traitor. The thaumaturge snarled, but Cinder could barely see him. Bright spots were dancing in her vision. Her legs were beginning to shake from the effort of keeping herself standing while maintaining her control on the man.

He grabbed on to Wolf and Thorne by their wrists and began dragging them up the ramp—a puppet under her strings.

But she could already feel the strings fraying.

Hissing, she fell to one knee.

"Impressive."

The thaumaturge's voice was muffled in her head. Behind her, her pawn dropped Wolf and Thorne onto the cargo bay floor.

"I can see why my queen fears you. But taking control of one of my pets will hardly save you now."

She was so close. Get the soldier out of the ship. Get herself inside.

She managed to bring him back to the edge, the very bottom of the ramp, before her hold on him snapped. She fell forward, clutching her temples, feeling as if a hundred needles were being jabbed into her brain. It hadn't hurt like this to control anyone else, had never hurt at all.

The pain began to ease. She squinted. The thaumaturge was snarling at her, one arm clutching his stomach where the ramp had hit him.

The rest of the soldiers were just standing there, their eyes still glowing but their expressions passive, and it occurred to Cinder that the thaumaturge was too hurt to keep control of them all. That even his hold on them was tenuous.

But it didn't matter. She had no more strength.

She sank back on her heels, letting her hands fall heavy at her sides. Her body swayed—she could feel unconsciousness calling to her, seeping into her brain.

A grin once again creased the thaumaturge's lips, but this time it showed more relief than amusement.

"Troya," he said, "go in and retrieve Mademoiselle Benoit. I will have to decide what is to be done with Alpha Kes—"

His eyes darted past Cinder at the same moment she heard a gunshot.

The thaumaturge stumbled back, clutching his chest.

Slipping onto her hip, Cinder glanced back to see Scarlet marching down the ramp, carrying a shotgun.

"Mademoiselle Benoit retrieved," she said, planting her heel on the back of the dazed, blank-faced soldier and shoving him off the ramp. "And don't worry, we'll take Alpha Kesley off your hands."

Sneering, the thaumaturge sank down to the ground. Blood began to dribble out between his fingers.

"Where did you get that?" Cinder wheezed.

"One of your storage crates," Scarlet said. "Come on, let's . . ."

A mix of emotions flickered through her eyes—writhing fury, startled confusion, emptiness.

She lowered the barrel of the gun.

Cinder cursed. "Iko, the ramp!" she said, crawling up onto the ramp and collapsing at Scarlet's feet. Reaching up, she snatched the gun away before the thaumaturge could turn it on either of them, and the ramp began to rise, dropping them both down into the cargo bay.

An angry scream reached them, and then another chorus of howls that faded quickly away. The thaumaturge's last fading effort to control his pets.

Cinder saw Scarlet shaking her head to rid herself of the fog, before hauling herself to her feet.

"Hold on to something if you can," Scarlet yelled as she hobbled into the cockpit. "Ship, engage magnet lifters and rear thrusters!"

Cinder sank exhausted onto the floor, still clutching the gun. Moments later, she felt the ship rising up away from the Earth and whipping toward the sky.

Forty-Three

KAI WAS SWEATING WITH THE EFFORT NOT TO THROW UP.
His eyes stung, but he couldn't look away from the netscreen. It
was like watching a terrible horror production—too gruesome
and fantastical to be real.

The vidlink was being transferred from the downtown city
square, where the weekly market and the annual festival had
been held only days before, the day of his coronation. Bodies
littered the square, their spilled blood black beneath the flickering billboards. Most of the corpses were concentrated near the
opening of a late-night restaurant, one of the few businesses
that had been open and crowded at midnight, when the attack
had started.

He'd been told only one assailant had been in the restaurant
at the time, but with the amount of carnage he felt certain it had
to be more. How could one man do so much damage?

The feed switched to a hotel in Tokyo just as a man with
crazed eyes threw a limp body against a pillar. Kai cringed at the

impact and turned away. "Turn it off. I can't watch anymore. *Where are the police?*"

"They're doing their best to stop the attacks, Your Majesty," said Torin from behind him, "but it takes time to mobilize them and make an organized attempt to fight back. This attack was so unprecedented. So . . . abnormal. These men move fast, rarely stay on a single block for more than a few minutes—just enough time to kill anyone within reach before moving to another area of the city . . ." Torin trailed off, as if he heard the panic rising in his own voice and had to stop talking before it overwhelmed him. He cleared his throat. "Screen, show major global feeds."

Noise buzzed in the room, six news anchors reporting the same stories: sudden attacks, murderous psychopaths, monsters, unknown fatalities, planet-wide mayhem . . .

Four cities had been struck inside the Commonwealth: New Beijing, Mumbai, Tokyo, and Manila. Ten more had fallen victim across the other five Earthen countries: Mexico City, New York, Sao Paulo, Cairo, Lagos, London, Moscow, Paris, Istanbul, and Sydney.

Fourteen cities in all, and though it was impossible to gain an exact number on the attackers, witness accounts noted that not more than twenty or thirty men seemed to be behind the attacks at each post.

Kai struggled to do the math in his head. Three hundred men, maybe four hundred.

It seemed impossible, as the death toll continued to rise, as the victimized cities began requesting assistance from their neighbors, shipping their injured to other hospitals.

As many as ten thousand dead, some were saying, in the course of not two hours, and at the hands of only three or four hundred men.

Three or four hundred Lunars. Because he knew, he *knew* that Levana was behind this. In two of the attacked cities, survivors claimed they'd seen a royal thaumaturge in their midst. Though both witnesses had been near delusional with loss of blood, Kai believed them. It made sense that the queen's most prized minions would be involved in this. It made equal sense that they themselves were removed from the bloodshed, merely orchestrating the attacks through their own pawns.

Kai paced away from the screen, rubbing his fingers into his eyes.

This was because of him. Levana had done this because of him.

Him, and Cinder.

"This is war," said Queen Camilla of the United Kingdom. "She's declared war on us."

Kai slumped against his desk. They'd all been so silent, entranced by the ongoing footage, that he'd forgotten he was still in a global conference with the other Union leaders.

The voice of Africa's Prime Minister Kamin sounded through the speakers, seething. "First fifteen years of the plague—and now this! And for what? Levana is upset that a single prisoner got away? A mere girl? No, she's using it as an excuse. She means to make a mockery of us."

"I'm having all of my major cities evacuated immediately," said President Vargas of America. "We can at least attempt to staunch the bleeding . . ."

European Prime Minister Bromstad chimed in, "Before you go that route, I'm afraid I have yet more unsettling news."

Kai's chin fell onto his chest, defeated. He was tempted to cover his ears and not listen. He didn't want to hear anymore, but he braced himself instead.

"The attack is not only in the major metropolises," said Bromstad. "I've just been informed that, in addition to Paris, Moscow, and Istanbul, we've had one small town attacked as well. Rieux, a farming community in southern France. Population three thousand, eight hundred."

"Three thousand, eight hundred!" said Queen Camilla. "Why would she attack such a small town?"

"To confuse us," said Governor-General Williams from Australia. "To make us believe there's no sense to these attacks—to make us afraid that she could strike anywhere, at any time. It is precisely something Levana would do."

Chairman Huy burst into Kai's office without knocking. Kai jumped, for a moment thinking that the chairman was a lunatic come to kill him, before his pulse began to subside again.

"Any news?"

Huy nodded. Kai noticed that his face had aged years in the last week. "Linh Cinder has been spotted."

Kai swallowed a gasp and shoved himself off the desk.

"What? Who was that speaking?" said Camilla. "What about Linh Cinder?"

"I must tend to other matters," said Kai. "End conference." Sounds of protests were immediately silenced, and Kai focused on the chairman, every nerve humming. "Well?"

"Three military officers managed to track her using a positive ID on her deceased stepsister, Linh Peony, just like her guardian said we would. We found her in a small town in southern France, minutes before the attack."

"Southern—" Kai glanced at Torin just as his adviser shut his eyes, wearied by the same realization. "Was it a town called Rieux?"

Huy's eyes widened. "How did you know?"

Kai groaned and rounded to the back of his desk. "Levana's men attacked Rieux, the only non-major city they went after. They must have been able to track her too. That's why they were there."

"We must alert the other Union leaders," said Torin. "At least we know she isn't attacking at random."

"But how did they find her? Her sister's ID chip was our only lead. How else could she be…" He trailed off, yanking both hands through his hair. "Of course. She knew about the chip. I'm such an *idiot.*"

"Your Majesty?"

He spun back toward Huy, but it was Torin that caught his eye. "Don't you say this is paranoia. She *is* listening. I don't know how she does it, but she is spying on us. This very office is probably bugged. That's how she knew about the chip, that's how she knew when my office was open and she could barge in here unannounced, that's how she knew when my father died!"

Torin's expression darkened, but for once he made no snide comment about Kai and his ridiculous theories.

"So—we've found her then? Cinder?"

Embarrassment flickered over Huy's brow. "I'm sorry, Your Majesty. Once the attack began, she managed to get away in the chaos. We found the ID chip on a farm outside of Rieux, next to signs of a ship's takeoff. We're working on rounding up anyone who might have seen her, but unfortunately ... all three officers who first identified her were killed in the attack."

Kai began to shake, his entire body burning up from the inside out. He cast furious eyes up to the ceiling, half screaming. "Well, see that, *Your Majesty*? If it wasn't for your attack, we would have had her! I hope you're pleased with yourself!"

Huffing, he crossed his arms over his chest and waited for his blood pressure to drop again. "Enough of this. Call off the search."

"Your Majesty?" said Torin.

"I want all available military and enforcement officers focused on finding these men who are attacking us and putting an end to this. That's our new priority."

As if relieved by the decision, Huy gave a curt bow and clipped out of the office, leaving the door open in his wake.

"Your Majesty," said Torin, "while I don't disagree with this course of action, we have to consider how Levana will react. We should consider the possibility that this attack, awful as it is, is only an annoyance compared to what she is truly capable of. Perhaps we should attempt to placate her before she can do any further damage."

"I know." Kai faced the screen and the muttering, frightened news anchors. "I haven't forgotten those pictures that the American Republic had."

The memory still sent a chill down his back—hundreds of soldiers standing in formation, each one a cross between a man and a beast. Protruding fangs and enormous claws, hunched shoulders and a fine layer of fur up their broad arms.

The men who were attacking all over Earth were vicious and wild and brutal, that much was clear. But they were still only men. Kai suspected they were just the precursor to what Levana's beast army could become.

And he'd thought he couldn't loathe her anymore. Not after she'd purposely withheld the letumosis antidote from him. Or attacked one of his servants to prove a political point. Or forced him to betray Cinder, for no other reason than she'd escaped from Luna years ago.

But he could not have fathomed this cruelty.

Which is why he would forever hate himself for what he was about to do.

"Torin, will you give me a moment?"

"Your Majesty?" Torin's eyes were wrinkled in the corner, as if carved into his skin. Perhaps they'd all aged unfairly this week. "You want me to leave?"

He bit the inside of his cheek and nodded.

Torin's lips perched, but it seemed a long time before he could form any words. Kai could see knowledge on his adviser's face—Torin knew what he was planning.

"Your Majesty, are you sure you don't wish to discuss this? Let me offer guidance. Let me help you."

Kai tried to smile, but it came out nothing more than a painful grimace. "I can't stand here, safe in this palace, and not do anything. I can't let her kill anyone else. Not with these monsters, not by withholding the letumosis antidote, not by . . . whatever she has planned next. We both know what she wants. We both know what will stop this."

"Then let me stay and support you, Your Majesty."

He shook his head. "This isn't a good choice for the Commonwealth. It may be the *only* choice, but it will never be a good one." He fidgeted with his collar. "The Commonwealth should not be able to blame anyone but me. Please, go."

He saw Torin take in a slow, painful breath, before bowing deeply. "I will be right outside should you need me, Your Majesty." Looking supremely unhappy about it, Torin left, shutting the door behind him.

Kai paced before the netscreen, his gut twisting with anxiety. He straightened his shirt, wrinkled from a long day, but at least he'd still been in his office when the alert had come. He believed he might never experience a full night of sleep again after this.

After what he was about to do.

In his frenzied thoughts, he couldn't help thinking of Cinder at the ball. How happy he'd been to see her descending the stairs into the ball room. How innocently amused he'd been at her rain-drenched hair and wrinkled dress, thinking it was a fitting look for the city's most renowned mechanic. He'd thought she must be immune to society's whims of fashion and decorum. So comfortable in her own skin that she could come to a royal ball as the emperor's own guest with messy hair and oil stains on her gloves and keep her head high as she did so.

That was before he knew that she'd rushed to the ball to give him a warning.

Cinder had sacrificed her own safety to plead with him not to accept the alliance. Not to marry Levana. Because after the marriage ceremony was done and she had ascended to the throne of the Eastern Commonwealth, Levana intended to kill him.

He felt sick to his stomach, knowing that Cinder was right. He knew that Levana wouldn't hesitate to dispose of him as soon as he'd served his purpose.

But he had to stop these murders. He had to stop this war.

Cinder was not the only one capable of sacrificing herself for something greater.

Inhaling, exhaling, he faced the screen.

"Establish vidlink to Queen Levana of Luna."

The small globe in the corner turned over only once before it brightened with the image of the Lunar queen, draped in her lacy white veil. He imagined her face old and haggard and decrepit beneath its sheath, and it didn't help.

Kai sensed she'd been waiting for his comm. He sensed she'd been listening in on everything, and already knew precisely what his intentions were. He sensed she was smirking behind the veil.

"My dear Emperor Kaito, what a pleasant surprise. It must be quite late in New Beijing. About two hours and twenty-four minutes past midnight, is that correct?"

He swallowed his disgust as best he could and opened his hands wide to her. "Your Majesty, I beg you. Please stop this attack. Please call off your soldiers."

The veil shifted as she listed her head to the side. "You *beg* me? How delightful. Do go on."

Heat flooded his face. "Innocent people are dying—women and children, bystanders, people who haven't done anything to you. You've won, and you know it. So *please*, end it now."

"You say I've won, but what is my prize, young emperor? Have you captured the cyborg girl who started all this? She is the one you should be appealing to. If she turns herself over to me then I will call off my men. That is my offer. Do let me know when you are prepared to bargain with me. Until then, good night."

"Wait!"

She folded her hands. "Yes?"

His pulse thrummed painfully against his temples. "I can't give you the girl—we thought we had her, but she's gotten away again, as I suspect you already know. But I can't let you continue to murder innocent Earthens while we try and find another way to track her."

"I'm afraid that's not my problem, Your Majesty."

"There's something else you want, something I *can* offer. We both know what that is."

"I'm sure I don't know what you speak of."

Kai didn't realize he was gripping his hands, practically pleading with her, until his knuckles started to ache. "If your offer of a marriage alliance still stands, I accept. Your prize for calling off your men will be the Commonwealth." His voice broke on the final word and he clamped his jaw shut.

He waited, breathless, knowing that every second that passed meant more bloodshed on the streets of Earth.

After an agonizing silence, Levana tittered. "My dear Emperor. How could I resist such a charming proposal?"

Forty-Four

AS THE SHIP ENTERED NEUTRAL ORBIT, SCARLET RELEASED the air from her burning lungs and slumped into the pilot's seat. Moaning, all the aches and wounds catching up to her at once, she turned herself around to face the ship's bay.

Linh Cinder was sitting on the floor with her legs splayed out before her. Wolf, unconscious, was spread-eagle on his back. A streak of blood followed him from the ramp where he'd been dragged. The other man was flopped onto his stomach.

"You're a pilot," said Cinder.

Linh Cinder.

Princess Selene.

"My grandma taught me. She was a pilot in—" The words evaporated, her heart aching. "But your ship does pretty well on its own."

"So glad to be of service," said the disembodied voice. "I'm Iko. Is anyone hurt?"

"Everyone's hurt," said Cinder, groaning.

Scarlet hobbled over to Wolf's body and sank down beside him.

"Are they going to be all right?"

"I hope so," said Cinder, "but I've never stuck around long enough to see the aftereffects of these darts."

Scarlet unzipped her shredded hoodie and tied it over the open wound on Wolf's arm. "You said you had bandages?"

She could see Cinder's dread at being forced into action again, but soon Cinder pushed herself up and disappeared through a door on the far side of the cargo bay.

A low moan drew her attention to the stranger. He rolled onto his back, cringing.

"Whererewe?" he muttered.

"Oh, you're awake already," said Cinder, returning with salve and gauze. "I was hoping you'd stay knocked out awhile longer. The peace and quiet was a pleasant change."

Despite her tone, Scarlet could sense the relief rolling off the girl as she dropped a tube of salve onto the man's stomach. She passed the gauze to Scarlet along with another tube of salve and a scalpel. "We need to cut out your ID chips and destroy them, before they track you."

Easing to a seated position, the man gave Scarlet a hazy, suspicious look and she thought for a moment he'd forgotten where she'd come from, before his attention dropped down to Wolf. "Managed to get the loon on board, huh? Maybe I can find a cage for him in one of these bins. I'd hate for him to kill us in our sleep after all that."

Scarlet scowled, unraveling a strip of gauze. "He's not an

animal," she said, focusing on the claw marks on the side of Wolf's face.

"Are you sure?"

"I hate to agree with Thorne," said Cinder, "I mean, I *really* hate to agree with him, but he's right. We don't know that he's on our side."

Scarlet pressed her lips and pulled out another strip of tape. "You'll see when he wakes up. He's not ..." She hesitated, and realized a moment later that she couldn't even convince herself that he was on their side.

"Well," said the man. "I feel much better." Tearing a hole in his pants, he dabbed the ointment on the puncture wound from the tranquilizer.

Pulling her hair out of her face, Scarlet ripped open Wolf's shirt and slathered the medical salve onto the deep gashes across his abdomen. "Who are you?"

"Captain Carswell Thorne." Recapping the salve, he propped himself against the cargo bay's wall. His hand landed on the shotgun. "Where did this come from?"

"Scarlet found it in one of the crates," said Cinder, facing the netscreen on the wall. "Screen, on."

The screen showed a shaking image of a bloodied man running full speed toward the camera. There was screaming, and then static. A male anchorman behind a desk replaced the video, his face pale. "This is footage fed to us from the attacks in Manhattan earlier tonight, and sources have confirmed that more than a dozen cities across the Union are also under siege."

Scarlet bent over to cut the ID chip from Wolf's wrist. She noticed he already had a scar there, as though it hadn't been very long ago when the ID chip had been put in him to begin with.

The anchorman continued, "Citizens are urged to stay in their homes and lock all doors and windows. We are now going to a live feed from Capitol City where President Vargas will be making an address."

A groan drew everyone's attention to Wolf. From the corner of her eye, Scarlet saw Captain Thorne cock the gun and level the barrel at Wolf's chest.

Scarlet set aside the scalpel and both their ID chips and tilted Wolf's face toward her. "Are you all right?"

He lifted bleary eyes to her, before suddenly wrenching away and rolling onto his side, vomiting onto the ship's floor. Scarlet winced.

"Sorry," said Cinder. "That's probably a side effect of the drugs."

Thorne gagged. "Aces, I'm glad that didn't happen to me. How embarrassing."

Swiping at his lips, Wolf collapsed again onto his back, cringing with every movement. He furrowed his brow, then squinted up at Scarlet. His eyes had returned to their normal vibrant green—no longer filled with animal hunger. "You're alive."

She tucked a curl behind her ear, baffled at her own relief. This was the man who had handed her over to those monsters. She should have hated him, but all she could think of was his desperation when he'd kissed her on the train, when he'd begged her not to go looking for her grandmother. "Thanks to you."

Thorne scoffed. "Thanks to *him?*"

Wolf tried to look at Thorne, but couldn't twist his neck enough. "Where are we?"

"You're aboard a cargo ship orbiting Earth," said Cinder. "Sorry about the whole tranquilizer thing. I thought you were going to eat her."

"I thought I was too." His expression darkened as he took in Cinder's metal hand. "I think my queen is looking for you."

Thorne quirked an eyebrow. "Was that supposed to make me feel better about having him on board?"

"He's better now," Scarlet said. "Aren't you?"

He shook his head. "You shouldn't have brought me here. I'll only put you all in danger. You should have left me down there. You should have killed me."

Thorne released the safety on the gun.

"Don't be ridiculous," said Scarlet. "They did this to you. It's not your fault."

Wolf eyed her like he was speaking to a stubborn child. "Scarlet . . . if anything happened to you because of me . . ."

"Do you intend to harm anyone aboard this ship or not?" said Cinder, cutting through their conversation.

Wolf blinked at her, at Thorne, then at Scarlet, his eyes lingering. "No," he whispered.

Three heartbeats later, Cinder's body relaxed. "He's telling the truth."

"What?" said Thorne. "And *that's* supposed to make me feel better?"

"Kai is going to make an announcement!" Iko's voice blared through the ship, then the volume of the netscreen rose.

An anchor was speaking again. "—appears that all attacks have ceased. We will keep you posted as news develops. Now, we connect you to the feed from the Eastern Commonwealth where we are expecting an emergency announcement from Emperor Kaito to begin—"

He was cut off, the screen turning to the EC's press room, where Kai stood behind a podium. Cinder bunched the material of her pants in both fists.

"Cinder has a bit of a crush on him," Thorne stage-whispered.

"Don't we all?" said Iko.

Kai seemed momentarily disconcerted beneath the bright lights, but it passed as he squared his shoulders. "You all know why I have called this press conference in the middle of the night, and I thank you for coming on such short notice. I hope to answer some of the questions that have been posed since these attacks began nearly three and a half hours ago."

Wolf hissed in pain as he sat up to see better. Scarlet's fingers tightened around his hand.

"I can confirm that these men are from Luna. Some of our scientists have already begun conducting tests on the body of one of these men, killed by a police officer in Tokyo, and have confirmed that they are genetically engineered soldiers. They appear to be Lunar males whose physical makeup has been combined with the neural circuitry of some sort of wolf hybrid. It seems clear that their surprise attack was orchestrated in a way to ensure terror, confusion, and chaos throughout Earth's major cities. In this, I feel it is safe to say they succeeded.

"Many of you are aware that Queen Levana has been threatening to declare war on Earth for nearly her entire rule. If you are wondering why Queen Levana chose now to initiate this attack after so many years of threats . . . it's because of me."

Scarlet noticed Cinder pulling her knees into her chest, squeezing them until her arms began to shake.

"Queen Levana is angry at my inability to adhere to a treaty between Luna and Earth that states that all Lunar fugitives be apprehended and returned to Luna. Queen Levana made her expectations quite clear in this regard, and I failed to meet them."

A strange sound escaped Cinder's throat—a squeak or a whimper—and she clamped her metal hand over her mouth to stifle it.

"Because of this, I feel it is my responsibility to end these attacks and prevent a full-scale war so long as it is within my power to do so. So that is what I've done, in the only way I could." His gaze pierced the back wall of the press room as if he were too mortified to look any of the journalists in the eye. "I have accepted an alliance of marriage with Queen Levana of Luna."

A shocked scream ripped from Cinder and she launched herself to her feet. "No. No!"

"In return," Kai continued, "Queen Levana has agreed to

withhold further attacks. The wedding has been scheduled for the next full moon, the twenty-fifth day of September, to be followed immediately by Queen Levana's coronation as empress of the Eastern Commonwealth. The removal of all Lunar soldiers from Earthen soil will begin the following day."

"*No!*" Cinder screeched. Grabbing the boot off her foot, she heaved it at the screen. "Idiot! You idiot!"

"My cabinet and I will have further updates in the coming days. I will not be taking any questions tonight. Thank you." The room filled with barking questions regardless, but Kai ignored them all, slinking off the platform like a defeated general.

Cinder spun away and kicked the nearest crate with her bare metal foot. "He knows this was her doing but he's still going to give her everything she wants! She is responsible for the deaths of thousands of Earthens, and now she's going to be *empress!*" She paced the floor, spotted the two bloodied ID chips beside Scarlet, and mercilessly stomped them to pieces, grinding them into the floor with her heel. "And how long will she be satisfied with that? A month? A week? I even told him! I told him she planned on using the Commonwealth as a stepping stone to wage war on the rest of Earth, and he's still going to marry her! She's going to have complete control over all of us, and it will be all his fault!"

Scarlet crossed her arms over her chest. "It sounds to me," she said, her voice rising to compete with Cinder's, "that it will be all *your* fault."

Cinder's tirade ceased and she gaped at Scarlet. Between

them, Thorne settled his chin on his palm as if watching a great show—though his free hand still held the shotgun aimed at Wolf's head.

"You know why she did this," said Scarlet, climbing to her feet despite the protests of her angry muscles. "You know why she's after you."

Cinder's fury simmered off. "Your grandmother told you."

"Yes, she did. What sickens me is that you let this happen in the first place!"

Glowering, Cinder bent down and ripped off her other boot. Scarlet shied away but Cinder only tossed it into a corner. "What would you rather I did? Just hand myself over? Sacrifice myself in hopes that would satisfy her? It would have come to this anyway."

"I'm not talking about when you were arrested at the ball. I mean before that. Why haven't you done anything to stop her? People are relying on you. People think you can make a differ-ence, and what are you doing? Running away and hiding! My grandmother didn't die so you could live as a fugitive, too much a coward to do something!"

"Uh, I'm confused," said Thorne, raising a finger in the air. "What are we talking about?"

Scarlet glanced at the captain. "Would you *stop pointing that gun at him?*"

Thorne tossed the gun to the side and folded his hands in his lap.

"He doesn't even know, does he?" Scarlet rounded on Cinder.

"You've put his life in danger—all of our lives in danger—and he doesn't even know why."

"It's more complicated than that."

"Is it?"

"I haven't even known for a week! I found out who I was the day after the ball, when I was sitting in a jail cell preparing to be handed over to Levana like a trophy. So between breaking out of prison and running from the entire Commonwealth military and trying to save *your* life, I haven't had much time to overthrow an entire regime. I'm sorry if I've disappointed you, but what do you want me to do?"

Scarlet drew back, a headache pounding at her temple. "How could you not have known?"

"Because your grandmother shipped me off to the Commonwealth without bothering to tell me."

"But isn't that why you were at the ball?"

"Stars, no. You think I would have been stupid enough to face Levana if I'd known the truth?" She hesitated. "Well. I don't know. For Kai, maybe, but ..." She grasped her head with both hands. "I don't know. I didn't know."

Scarlet was suddenly dizzy from the anger, the rush of blood, the exhaustion. The only response she could form was a baffled "Oh."

Thorne coughed. "I'm still confused."

With a sigh, Cinder wilted onto a crate, staring down at her mismatched hands. She scrunched her whole face up, like preparing for a blow, and muttered, "I'm Princess Selene."

Thorne snorted and they all turned to him.

He blinked. "What, really?"

"Really."

The joking smile froze on his lips.

A heavy silence was followed by a vibration beneath their feet and Iko's voice. "I don't compute."

"That makes two of us," said Thorne. "Since when?"

Cinder shrugged. "I'm sorry. I should have told you, but . . . I didn't know if I could trust you, and I thought if I could find Michelle Benoit and have her explain some things to me, tell me how I came to be here, how I came to be *this* . . ." She held up both hands before letting them fall limply back into her lap. ". . . then maybe I could start figuring things out." She sighed. "Iko, I'm really sorry. I swear I didn't know before."

Snapping his jaw shut, Thorne scratched at his chin. "*You're Princess Selene*," he said, testing the words. "The crazy cyborg girl is Princess Selene."

"Is your gift intact?" Wolf asked. He was sitting crookedly, trying not to put too much weight on his side.

"I think so," said Cinder, shifting uncomfortably. "I'm still learning how to use it."

"She controlled one of the . . . special operatives," said Scarlet. "I saw her do it."

Cinder glanced down. "Only barely. I couldn't maintain control."

"You were able to manipulate one of the pack? While Jael was there?"

"Yeah, but it was awful. I could only get to one of them and I nearly passed out—"

A sharp laugh silenced her, before Wolf coughed painfully. Still, an amused expression lingered on his face. "And this is why Levana wants you. You *are* stronger than she is. Or . . . you could be, with practice."

Cinder shook her head. "You don't understand. That thaumaturge had seven men under his control and I could barely manage one. I'm nowhere near as strong as them."

"No, *you* don't understand," said Wolf. "Each pack is ruled by a thaumaturge who controls when our animal instincts take over, when all we can think about is killing. They've manipulated our Lunar gift and used it to turn us into these monsters instead—with some physical modifications. But it's all connected to our master. Most Lunars couldn't control us at all—we might as well be shells to them—and even our masters, who could control hundreds of average citizens at once, can only keep hold of a dozen or so operatives. That's why our packs are kept so small. Do you see?"

"No," said Cinder and Thorne at once.

Wolf was still smiling. "Even the most talented of thaumaturges can only control a dozen operatives, fifteen at the most, and this after years of genetic modifications and training. And yet you manage to take one away from his master on your first attempt? With some practice . . ." He looked like he wanted to laugh. "I would not have thought it before, but now I think Her Majesty might actually have cause to be afraid of you, Princess."

Cinder flinched. "Don't call me that."

"I am assuming, of course, you do mean to fight against her," continued Wolf, "judging from your response to your emperor's announcement."

Cinder shook her head. "I don't have the first idea how to.... I don't know anything about being a ruler or a leader or—"

"But plenty of people think you can stop her," said Scarlet. "My grandmother died so you could have this chance. I'm not going to let her sacrifice be wasted."

"And I would help you," added Wolf. "You could practice your abilities, on me." He slumped, his body tired from sitting up for too long. "Besides, if you are who you claim to be, that makes you my true queen. Therefore, you have my loyalty."

Cinder shook her head and hopped off the crate again. "I don't want your loyalty."

Scarlet planted her hands on her hips. "What do you want?"

"I want—I want some time to think about this and figure out what to do next without everyone yapping in my ear!" Cinder stomped off toward the main corridor, every other step a loud clang as her metal foot struck the floor.

When she had gone, Thorne let out a low whistle. "I know, I know. She seems a little"—crossing his eyes, he swirled both fingers around his ears—"but it's really part of her charm, once you get to know her."

Forty-Five

SHE'D HAD THE BRIDGE BUILT FOR HERSELF OUT OF VERY special glass, so that she could watch her soldiers from above—watch them train, watch them fight, watch them adapt to their new mutations—all without being observed herself. She was intrigued now by a new pack who had just completed the genetic transformation a few days ago. They were still so young. Mere boys—not one older than twelve years.

They were almost precious, the way some of them stood off from the group, constantly checking the fine fur on their knuckles, bouncing back and forth on their restructured limbs, while others were already brawling and taunting one another.

Making their place. Choosing their hierarchy.

Just like the animals they were.

Each thaumaturge beckoned to their assigned subjects, leading them through various formations. This too always fascinated her. How some of them would force the control, while others tried to seduce it from their cubs, like tender mothers.

She watched the youngest faction with growing pleasure. Seven had lined up without question, leaving only one cub standing off from the rest. Crouched on all fours, he was snarling at his thaumaturge, fangs fully bared, more wolf-like than any of them. Rebellion and hatred glowed behind his golden eyes.

That one would make alpha. She could already tell.

"Your Majesty."

She listed her head but didn't take her eyes off the boy. "Sybil."

Her head thaumaturge's heels clicked on the glass floor. She detected the ruffle of fabric as Sybil bowed.

Down in the cave, the cub was prowling a circle around his mistress—a young, blonde-haired girl who looked ghastly pale in her black coat. Her expression held a trace of anxiety, a tinge of doubt that she would have the mental strength to control this one.

"All special operatives have been temporarily relieved from their missions and returned to concealment status. We estimate two hundred, sixty operative deaths."

"The Earthens will notice the tattoos soon, if they haven't already. Be sure they take care to mask them well."

"Of course, Your Majesty. I'm afraid I also have one thaumaturge death to report."

Levana looked up, for a moment expecting to catch Sybil's reflection in the glass, but there was none, not in this window. Not in any of the royal windows. She'd made sure of that. And yet, after all these years, she still wasn't entirely used to it.

She raised an eyebrow, prompting Sybil to continue.

"Thaumaturge Jael. He was shot in the chest."

"Jael? It isn't like him to abandon his sanctuary, even in battle."

"One of his betas has informed me that Linh Cinder presented herself—it seems he was attempting to apprehend her personally."

Levana's nostrils flared and she turned back toward the training grounds, just as the young cub lunged for his mistress. The girl screamed and fell onto her back, before her entire body seized up in concentration. Even from her overlook, Levana could see beads of sweat forming on the girl's brow, sliding across her temple.

The cub opened his mouth, teeth glinting, then hesitated.

Levana couldn't tell what was fighting his animal instinct— the thaumaturge grasping for control, or the remnants of a Lunar boy still clinging to the thoughts in his head.

"Jael's pack has already disbanded, except for the one beta who was found inside the Paris stronghold. I will send Thaumaturge Aimery to retrieve them."

The cub fell off his mistress, curling into a ball on his side. Trembling. Whimpering. In obvious pain.

Unsteady herself, the thaumaturge climbed to her feet and brushed the black regolith dust from her jacket. The regolith dust was everywhere in these caves—naturally created lava tubes that would never be clear, no matter how long they continued to develop and build within them. Levana hated the dust, the way it clung to her hair and nails, filled up her lungs. She avoided the tubes whenever she could, preferring to stay in the bright, glistening dome that housed Luna's capital and her palace.

"Your Majesty?" said Sybil.

"No, don't send Aimery," she said, her attention glued to the cub as he writhed in pain. Still fighting his mistress's control. Still struggling to keep his own mind. Still wanting to be a little boy. Not a soldier. Not a monster. Not a pawn. "Let Jael's pack go. The special operatives have served their purpose."

Finally, the cub stopped twitching. The fine fur on his cheeks was wet with tears as he lay there, panting.

His mistress's gaze was fierce, as animalistic as her charges. Levana could almost hear the woman's orders, even though no words were being spoken. Telling him to get up. To join the line. To obey her.

The boy did. Moving slowly, painfully, he lifted himself up onto his slender legs and shuffled into the line. Head bowed. Shoulders hunched.

Like a scolded dog.

"These soldiers are nearly ready," Levana said. "Their genetic modifications are complete, their thaumaturges are prepared. The next time we strike against Earth, these men will be leading the attack, and there will be no disguising them."

"Yes, Your Majesty." Sybil bowed—this time Levana felt the respect rolling off her as much as heard it. "And may I also wish you my warmest congratulations on your engagement, My Queen."

Levana's left hand curled, her thumb running over the

polished stone band on her finger. She always hid it in her glamour. She wasn't sure that anyone alive knew she still wore it. She herself so often forgot that it was there, but her finger was tingling tonight, since Emperor Kaito's acceptance of a marriage alliance.

"Thank you, Sybil. That will be all."

Another bow, then the retreating footsteps.

Below, the factions were beginning to disband, their training over for the day. The thaumaturges led them off through separate caves, into the natural labyrinth beneath Luna's surface.

It was peculiar to watch these men and boys, these creatures that had been only an experiment in her parents' time, but had become a reality under her rule. An army faster and stronger than any other army. The intelligence of men, the instincts of wolves, the pliability of children. They made her nervous, a feeling she hadn't experienced for many years. So many Lunars, with such peculiar brainwaves, that even she could not control them all. Not all at once.

These beasts—these scientific creations—would never love her.

Not like the people of Luna loved her.

Not like the people of Earth would soon come to.

Forty-Six

SCARLET CRIED FOR HOURS, CURLED UP ON THE BOTTOM
bunk of her new crew quarters. Each sob pulsed through her
aching muscles, but the pain only made her cry harder with the
memory of it all.

The adrenaline and anger and denial had fallen away while
she'd been digging through the dresser and had found a military
uniform folded neatly in the bottom drawer. Though the American uniform was all gray and white, instead of the mix of blues
found on European pilots, it still looked remarkably like the
clothes her grandma had worn in her military days.

She'd clutched the plain white T-shirt to her and cried into it
for so long it was almost as soiled as the clothes she was supposed to be changing out of.

Her entire body was throbbing as the tears finally began to
dry up. Gasping for breath, she rolled onto her back and wiped
the last streaks away with the cotton. Every time her crying
had started to subside before, the words would echo in her

head, *Grand-mère is gone,* and send her into another torrent. But the words were becoming hollow, the sting fading into numbness.

Her stomach growled.

Groaning, Scarlet settled a hand on top of it, wondering if she just shut her eyes and went to sleep, would her body forget that it hadn't eaten in more than a day? But as she lay there, willing the numbness to take over, her stomach rumbled again. Louder.

Scarlet sniffed, annoyed. Grabbing hold of the bunk overhead, she pulled herself to sitting. Her head swam with dizziness and dehydration, but she managed to stumble to the door.

She heard a crash from the galley as soon as she pulled it open. Peering down the hallway, she saw Wolf hunkered over a counter, holding a tin can.

Stepping into the galley's light, Scarlet saw that the can was labeled with a picture of cartoon-red tomatoes. Judging from the enormous dents in its side, Wolf had been trying to open it with a meat tenderizer.

He glanced up at her, and she was glad that she wasn't the only one red faced. "Why would they put food in here if they were going to make it so hard to open?"

She bit her lip against a weak smile, not sure if it was from pity or amusement. "Did you try a can opener?"

At Wolf's blank expression, she stepped around the table and riffled through the top drawer. "We Earthens have all sorts of special tools like this," she said, emerging with the can opener. She clamped it around the can's lid and slowly twisted it open.

Wolf's ears glowed pink as he curled back the lid and frowned down at the bright red goop. "That's not what I was expecting."

"They're not farm fresh like you've become accustomed to, but we're just going to have to make do." Digging through the cabinet, Scarlet cobbled together a can of olives and a jar of marinated artichoke hearts. "Here, we'll have an antipasto."

She felt the lightest touch against her hair and ducked away. Wolf's hand dropped down, gripping the edge of the counter. "I'm sorry. You had—your hair—"

Setting down the jars, Scarlet felt for the back of her hair, finding it knotted and tangled as a haystack. She shoved the olives at Wolf. "Why don't you give the can opener a try?"

Mindlessly picking at the tangles, she found a fork and sat down at the long table. It had years of military personnel's initials carved into the top, reminding her of her prison cell in the opera house. Though being on the ship was immeasurably better than being stuck in that basement, the confinement of it still pressed in around her, almost suffocating. She knew that her grandma had probably been stationed on a similar ship during her time in the military. No wonder she'd retired to a farm, with all the sky and horizon a person could want.

She hoped that Émilie was still taking care of the animals.

When she couldn't find any more knots, she smoothed down

her hair with both hands, then twisted open the jar of artichokes. Glancing up, she saw that Wolf was still standing with the olives and tomatoes clasped in each hand.

"Are you all right?"

His eyes flashed. Panic, she thought. Maybe fear.

"Why did you bring me here?" he said. "Why didn't you just leave me?"

Looking down, she speared an artichoke and watched the oil drizzle back into the jar. "I don't know. I didn't exactly stop to weigh the pros and cons." She let the artichoke heart plop back down into the marinade. "But it didn't feel right to leave you there."

He turned his back on her, setting the cans on the counter, and picked up the can opener. On the third try, he managed to clip it to the olive can's lid and twist it around the edge.

"Why didn't you tell me the truth?" said Scarlet. "Before we got to Paris?"

"It wouldn't have mattered." He set the opened cans on the table. "You still would have insisted on going after your grandmother. I thought I could plead your case with Jael and convince him that you were useless to us—that he should let you go. But I could only do that if I was still loyal to them."

Scarlet stabbed the artichoke heart again and slipped it into her mouth. She didn't want to go over the what-ifs. She didn't want to linger on all the choices that could have ended with her and her grandmother safely back on the farm. She didn't even know if such choices had existed.

Dropping his gaze, Wolf eased himself onto the bench opposite her, grimacing in pain at each movement. Settled, he picked a tomato from the can and stuffed it into his mouth. His nose crinkled. He looked like he was choking down a worm as he swallowed.

Scarlet pressed her lips against a chuckle. "Makes you appreciate my garden tomatoes, doesn't it?"

"I appreciated everything you gave me." He picked up the can of olives and sniffed at them, wary of being tricked again. "Although I didn't deserve any of it."

Scarlet bit her lip. She didn't think he was referring to the produce.

Dipping her head, she dunked her fork into the can of olives Wolf was holding, managing to spear two on its tines.

They ate in silence, Wolf discovering he liked the olives and suffering through two more soppy tomatoes before Scarlet offered him an artichoke. The combination of the two, they discovered, bordered on acceptable.

"Some bread would be nice," Scarlet said, scanning the open shelves behind Wolf that showed mismatched plates and coffee mugs painted with the American Republic insignia.

"I'm so sorry."

Goose bumps scattering across her arms, she dared to look at him, but he was staring at the can of tomatoes, nearly crunching it in his fists.

"I took you away from everything you cared about. And your grandmother . . ."

"Don't, Wolf. Don't do this. We can't change what happened and . . . you did give me that chip. You did save me from Ran."

He hunched his shoulders. Half his hair was messy and wild and normal, the other half still matted down with dried blood. "Jael told me he was going to torture you. He thought it would make your grandmother talk. And I just couldn't . . ."

Scarlet shuddered, closing her eyes.

"I knew they would kill me when they found out, but . . ." He struggled for words, releasing a sharp breath. "I think I realized that I would rather die because I betrayed them, than live because I betrayed you."

Scarlet wiped her oily fingers on her jeans.

"I was going back for you and your grandmother when I saw you being chased by Ran. My head was so jumbled, I couldn't think straight—I honestly don't know if I meant to help you both, or kill you. Then when Ran threw you at that statue, something just . . ." His knuckles whitened. He shook his head, spikes of hair flailing. "It doesn't matter. I was too late."

"You saved me."

"You wouldn't have needed saving if it wasn't for me."

"Oh? So if you hadn't been chosen to bring me to them or find out what information I had, they would have left me alone? No. If it had been anyone but you, I would be dead now."

Wolf frowned at the table.

"And I don't believe for a second you were coming back to kill us. No matter how much control that thaumaturge had over you, it was still you in there. You weren't going to hurt me."

Wolf met her gaze, sad and bewildered. "I honestly hope we never have to test that theory again. Because you don't know how close I was."

"You still fought it."

His face contorted, but she was glad when he didn't argue with her. "It shouldn't have been possible to resist him like that. What they did to us . . . to our brains . . . it changed the way we think about things. Anger and violence come so quickly, but other things . . . it shouldn't even be possible." His hand started to move toward hers, but halted halfway. He quickly withdrew, fiddling with the battered tomato label instead.

"Well, what if . . ." Scarlet listed her head. "You said they control when your animal instincts will overpower your own thoughts, right? But fighting and hunting aren't the only instincts wolves have. Aren't wolves . . . monogamous, for starters?" Her cheeks started to burn and she had to look away, scratching her fork into a set of initials. "And isn't the alpha male the one who's responsible for protecting everyone? Not only the pack, but his mate too?" Dropping the fork, she threw her hands into the air. "I'm not saying I think you and I are—after just—I know we just met and that's . . . but it's not out of the question, is it? That your instincts to protect me could be as strong as your instincts to kill?"

She held her breath and dared to look up. Wolf was gaping at her openly and for a second he seemed almost mortified—but then he grinned, the look warm and bewildered. Scarlet caught a glimpse of his sharp canines, her stomach flipping at the sight of them.

"You could be right," he said. "That makes some sense. On Luna, we're kept so far removed from the rest of the citizenry that there's never any chance of falling in ..."

Scarlet was glad when he started to blush too.

He scratched his ear. "Maybe that's it. Maybe Jael's control worked *against* him, because my instincts were telling me to protect you."

Scarlet attempted a nonchalant smile. "There you have it. As long as there's an alpha female nearby, you should be just fine. That shouldn't be hard to find, right?"

Wolf's expression iced over and he looked away. His tone became uneasy again. "I know you must want nothing to do with me. I don't blame you." Wolf scrunched up his shoulders, and met her with an expression full of regret. "But you're the only one, Scarlet. You'll always be the only one."

Her pulse fluttered. "Wolf—"

"I know. We met less than a week ago and in that time I've done nothing but lie and cheat and betray you. I know. But if you give me a chance ... all I want is to protect you. To be near you. For as long as I'm able."

Biting her lip, she reached forward, pulling his fingers away from the can. She found that the label had been shredded beneath his mindless fidgeting. "Wolf, are you asking me to be ... your alpha female?"

He hesitated.

Scarlet couldn't help it—she burst into laughter. "Oh—I'm sorry. That was mean. I know I shouldn't tease you about this."

Still grinning, she made to retract her hand, but he was suddenly gripping it, refusing to relinquish the touch. "You just look so scared, like I'm going to disappear at any minute. We're stuck on a *spaceship*, Wolf. I'm not going anywhere."

His lips twitched, his nervousness beginning to ease away, though his hand stayed tense over hers.

"Alpha female," he murmured. "I sort of like that."

Beaming, Scarlet gave a mild shrug. "It could grow on me."

Forty-Seven

CINDER LAY ON HER BACK, STARING UP INTO THE GUTS OF the Rampion's engine. Only her cyborg hand moved, flipping the small, shimmering D-COMM chip up and over her fingers, one by one. She was mesmerized by how the chip's odd material caught the lights from the motherboard on the wall and reflected them, sending rubies and emeralds twinkling across all the wires and fans and humming power converters. Mesmerized, but without really seeing them. Her thoughts were stretched between thousands of miles.

Earth. The Eastern Commonwealth. New Beijing and Kai, who was now engaged to Queen Levana. Her stomach turned, and she kept recalling the venom in his voice when he'd talked to her about the queen. She tried to imagine what he was going through now. *Did* he have any other choice? She couldn't be sure. She wanted to say yes, that anything—war, pestilence, slavery— would be better than choosing Levana as empress, but she didn't know if it was true. She didn't know if he'd ever had a choice, or if this decision had always been inevitable.

Her thoughts turned away from Earth, toward Luna. A country she didn't remember, a home she'd never known. Queen Levana was no doubt celebrating her victory at this moment, giving no thought to all those lives she'd just taken.

Queen Levana. Cinder's aunt.

The D-COMM chip *click, click, click*ed against her fingers.

"Cinder? Are you in here?"

Her fingers stilled with the chip balanced on her pinkie knuckle. "Yeah, Iko. I'm here."

"Maybe next time we're on Earth you can pick up some sensors? I feel like I'm eavesdropping having the audio on all the time. It's becoming awkward."

"Awkward?"

The running lights brightened, reminding Cinder of a blush. She wondered if it was intentional.

"Scarlet and Wolf are saying gushy things in the galley," Iko said. "Normally I like gushy things, but it's different when it's real people. I prefer the net dramas."

Unexpectedly, Cinder found herself smiling. "I'll do my best to get some sensors next time we're on Earth." She resumed her fiddling. The chip flipped, clacked, flipped, rolled. "How are you feeling, Iko? Are you getting used to being the auto-control system? Is it getting easier?"

Something hummed on the computer panel. "The shock has worn off, but it still feels like I'm pretending to be much more powerful than I really am, and I'm going to let everyone down. It's a lot of responsibility." The yellow running lights brightened by the floor. "But I did well in Paris, didn't I?"

"You were brilliant."

The temperature of the engine room spiked. "I was kind of brilliant."

"We'd all be dead if it weren't for you."

Iko let off an unusually pitchy noise, one that Cinder thought might be a nervous giggle. "I guess it's not so bad being the ship. You know, so long as you need me."

Cinder smirked. "That's very . . . *big* of you."

One of the engine fans slowed. "That was a joke, wasn't it?"

Laughing, Cinder practiced spinning the chip like a top on the tip of her finger. It took a few tries before she got the hang of it and could watch it sparkle and dance without much effort.

"How about you?" Iko said after a moment. "How does it feel to be a real princess?"

Cinder flinched. The chip tumbled off her finger and she barely caught it. "So far it's not nearly as fun as one would imagine. What were you saying about having too much power and responsibility and feeling like you're going to let everyone down? Because that all sounded pretty familiar."

"I thought that might be the case."

"Are you mad that I didn't tell you?"

A long silence followed, tying Cinder's stomach in knots.

"No," Iko said, finally, and Cinder wished that her lie detector worked on androids—or spaceships. "But I'm worried. Before, I figured that Queen Levana would tire of searching for us, and eventually we'd be able to go home, or at least go back to Earth and live normal lives again. But that's never going to happen, is it?"

Cinder gulped and started flipping the chip over her fingers again. "I don't think so."

Click, click, click.

She exhaled a long breath and flipped the chip one last time, clutching it in her fist.

"Levana's going to murder Kai after they're married. She'll be coronated as empress, and then she'll kill him, and she'll have the entire Commonwealth under her control. After that, it will only be a matter of time before she invades the rest of the Union." She swept her hair off her forehead. "At least, that's what this girl told me. The queen's programmer."

She loosened her grip, suddenly afraid that her metal fist would crush the chip while she was distracted.

"But I like Kai."

"You and every other girl in the galaxy."

"*Every* girl? Are you finally including yourself in that count?"

Cinder bit her lip. She knew Iko was thinking back to all the times Cinder had teased Peony for her hopeless crush on the prince, pretending to be immune to such silliness herself. But that all seemed a long, long time ago. She could hardly remember the girl she was back then.

"I just know that I can't let him marry Levana," she said, her voice snagging. "I can't let him go through with it."

She held up the chip between her thumb and forefinger. Her new hand still felt *too* new. So clean, so untarnished. She squinted and let the electric current flow from her spine, warming up her wrist until the hand looked human. Skin and bone.

"I concur," said Iko. "So what are you going to do?"

Cinder gulped and let the glamour change. The flesh of her hand became metal again—not flawless titanium, but plain steel, battered with age, grime caked into the crevices, a little too small, a little too stiff. The cyborg hand she'd replaced. The one she'd always hidden—usually with heavy, work-stained cotton. Once with silk.

The girl she'd been back then. The one she'd always tried to keep hidden.

An orange light blinked at the corner of her eye. She ignored it.

"I'm going to let Wolf train me. I'm going to become stronger than she is." She flipped the chip again. It was awkward at first, making sure the fingers in the illusion moved just how they were supposed to, that the joints flexed and moved at the right time. "I'm going to find Dr. Erland, and he's going to teach me how to win against her. Then I'm going to track down the girl who programmed this chip, and she's going to tell me everything she knows about Luna and its security and all the queen's secrets."

Click. Click. Click.

"And then I'm going to stop hiding."

Acknowledgments

It's amazing how many people it takes to bring a book into the world, and this one is no exception.

First and foremost, I want to thank my four spectacular beta readers for their brilliance, patience, enthusiasm, and all-around awesomeness: Jennifer Johnson, Tamara Felsinger, Meghan Stone-Burgess, and Whitney Faulconer, you make me a better writer.

To my wonderfully supportive editor, Liz Szabla, and everyone at Feiwel and Friends, thank you for making each step of this journey so much fun. Rich Deas, Jean Feiwel, Elizabeth Fithian, Lizzie Mason, Anna Roberto, Allison Verost, Holly West, Ksenia Winnicki, Jon Yaged, and countless others who have had an impact on these books, you are rock stars and I am so proud to be a part of your publishing family.

To my agency team, Jill Grinberg, Cheryl Pientka, and Katelyn Detweiler, who have worked relentlessly to get these books into the hands of readers all over the world, thank you for continuously making me feel like the luckiest author on the planet.

I'd like to give special thanks to my editor at Pocket Jeunesse in France, Xavier D'Almeida, who agreed to look at an early draft and check for authentic setting details, helped choose the perfect location for Benoit Farms, and also saved me from poisoning the poor chickens, thank heavens.

To my 2012 debut kindred spirits, the Apocalypsies, and particularly, my local writing group: J. Anderson Coats, Megan Bostic, Marissa Burt, Daniel Marks, and Jennifer Shaw Wolf, thanks for making this year rock. I look forward to watching your writing careers flourish for many years to come.

I give all the gratitude in the world to my friends and family who have been with me every step of the way, to my brother, Jeff, for loaning me all those books on spaceships, and to my wonderful husband, Jesse—one year into our happily ever after and counting.

And last, but never least, I heartily thank all the readers, teachers, booksellers, librarians, reviewers, and bloggers who keep the love alive.

Turn the page for

bonus materials. . . .

Questions for the Author

Marissa Meyer

AS THE SECOND BOOK IN THE LUNAR CHRONICLES, HOW WAS WRITING *SCARLET* DIFFERENT THAN WRITING *CINDER*?

The most obvious difference is that *Scarlet* didn't take nearly as long to write, (about nine months, as opposed to nearly two years with *Cinder*). One of the main reasons for the difference is that, with *Cinder*, there was a lot more world-building to muddle through, along with a great deal of setup and foreshadowing for the rest of the series. But with *Scarlet*, it felt like the groundwork had been laid and I could run full-speed ahead with the story. In that way, *Scarlet* was a lot of fun to write!

But of course, every book comes with its own challenges, and *Scarlet* had the new problem of maintaining two separate plot threads—Cinder's story and Scarlet's story—and keeping them both intriguing and suspenseful, and linking the stories together in a way that felt organic. On one hand, this gave me more than one headache during the writing process. On the other hand, whenever I got tired of one storyline, I could just switch to the other, so I never got bored!

WAS IT DIFFICULT TO RETELL THE STORY OF *LITTLE RED RIDING HOOD* IN CINDER'S WORLD?

For me, using the fairy tales as a springboard is possibly

the easiest part of writing these stories. The great thing about having these archetypal stories for inspiration is that I can use the iconic moments from the tale to create a framework on which to hang all the crazy twists and world-building and character development that make it my own. I really enjoy taking those familiar elements from the fairy tale and figuring out how to give them a futuristic spin, and the rest of the story is usually built off of that. Of course, everything else that goes into writing a book—interesting characters, solid pacing, and satisfying resolutions—are going to be a challenge no matter what.

WHAT IS YOUR FAVORITE ELEMENT FROM THE ORIGINAL FAIRY TALE THAT YOU INCLUDED IN *SCARLET*?

I loved playing with Wolf's character and the concept of the Big Bad Wolf. In the fairy tale, we're told upfront that the Wolf is up to no good—that he has devious plans that involve eating Little Red and her grandmother. But I wanted to create a Wolf character who was still big and bad, but whose motivations and loyalties were more questionable. I wanted the story to have a sense of inevitability, because we all know how the fairy tale ends up, while still making the reader question everything they think they know about who this character is and what role he's playing in the tale.

WAS BOOK TWO ALWAYS GOING TO BE CENTERED ON *LITTLE RED RIDING HOOD*?

Yep, I had the four fairy tales chosen very early on, and a rudimentary idea of how they would tie together. I've known for a long time how Wolf and Scarlet's story was going to connect to Cinder's, and what role it would play in the larger scheme of the entire series.

IN *SCARLET* WE ARE INTRODUCED TO A NEW SETTING— FRANCE. WHAT TYPE OF RESEARCH DID YOU DO FOR THIS NEW ENVIRONMENT? WAS THIS VERY DIFFERENT FROM YOUR EXPERIENCE WRITING NEW BEIJING?

My process for researching the two settings was relatively similar. I spent a lot of time on Google Maps, flipping through photos of landscapes and buildings, and researching the local seasons, flora, fauna, and so on. I ate at a few French-inspired restaurants. I sifted through French real estate Web sites until I found the perfect farmhouse to base Scarlet's home on (real estate Web sites are great because they're full of interior and exterior pictures). Then, one of the greatest boons for *Scarlet*'s setting was that I was able to get my French editor to take an early look at the manuscript and offer suggestions to make it feel more authentic. That was a big help that I hadn't had with *Cinder* and New Beijing.

HOW DID YOUR APPROACH TO WRITING SCARLET AND WOLF'S RELATIONSHIP DIFFER FROM CINDER AND PRINCE KAI'S?

They're all very different characters, so it makes sense that they would have very different relationships. I spend a lot of time thinking about each character's backstory, strengths, weaknesses, what sort of things are important to them, and what traits they're attracted to and why. All those factors impact how they fall in love and how they react to someone else falling in love with them. As a writer, I feel like the "trick" to writing romances is that you find characters who really do belong together—who complement each other, who make sense, who would work well together in real life—but then you have to come up with equally compelling reasons to keep them apart, otherwise, you'll lose all of your romantic tension too soon.

WOLF, PRINCE KAI, AND THORNE ARE THREE GREAT (AND VERY DIFFERENT) MALE CHARACTERS. WHAT IS YOUR FAVORITE DEFINING CHARACTERISTIC ABOUT THESE THREE MEN?

I love each of my leading men, but for very different reasons! I adore how Wolf walks this line between being brutal and protective, but also shy and awkward. I love how Kai is fiercely loyal—he understands his responsibilities to his country and will do whatever he can to protect his people, even if that means sacrificing his own happiness. And Thorne . . . well. I've always been a fan of those quick-thinking, cocky heroes who are all too aware of their own charm. Thorne is probably my favorite of the three to write, because I never quite know what he's going to say or do next.

IS THERE ANY SPECIAL MEANING FOR YOU BEHIND WOLF'S TATTOO? DO YOU HAVE ANY TATTOOS?

Wolf's tattoo was purely story-based, but I do have one tattoo of my own. For years and years I'd planned on getting a tattoo if and when I became a published author (my childhood dream!). So to commemorate the release of *Cinder,* I got a tattoo of a stack of books on my upper back. There are five in the stack—four for the Lunar Chronicles, and a fifth for every book that's still to come.

DID YOU WRITE THE SHORT STORY, "THE QUEEN'S ARMY," AT THE SAME TIME AS YOU WROTE *SCARLET*?

No, I'd been finished with *Scarlet* for about six months before I wrote "The Queen's Army." But I felt that I knew Wolf and his backstory so well by that point that the story practically wrote itself—which was quite nice! I love being able to show readers the story behind things that are barely hinted at in the book, such as how he got a particular scar, or his deeply buried dislike for needles. So often I feel like I know my characters on these very intimate levels, and I love having the opportunity to share that with readers.

WHAT IS YOUR FAVORITE POP CULTURE OR LITERARY RENDITION OF *LITTLE RED RIDING HOOD*?

I'm not sure this counts, but I *adore* the song "Li'l Red Riding Hood" by Sam the Sham and the Pharaohs. I kind of think of it as the theme song for *Scarlet*, because I think Wolf has had many similar thoughts to the wolf in the song. Plus, it's just cheesy enough to be awesome!

WHAT IS YOUR FAVORITE RED (OR SHALL WE SAY SCARLET) ACCESSORY?

My mom is an awesome seamstress and for the *Scarlet* launch party, she made red velvet scarves for all the women in my family. Not only that, but she had a stamp especially made up that said *Scarlet* in the same font as the book cover, which she used to press the design permanently into the velvet. It's so beautiful and luxurious! I love it.

WHAT WOULD SCARLET AND WOLF BE LIKE TODAY IN OUR WORLD?

That's an excellent question! Maybe a reader can write some contemporary/alternate-reality fanfiction so we can find out. Ha!

WE KNOW YOU ARE A HUGE STAR WARS FAN. WHAT IS YOUR FAVORITE MOVIE AND WHO IS YOUR FAVORITE CHARACTER?

My older brother has informed me that Episode IV, *A New Hope*, is the best, so I already know this isn't the "cool" answer, but for my personal favorite, I have to go with *Return of the Jedi*. Because, hello, EWOKS! And Han Solo is my favorite character, no contest. He's one of my favorite characters in the history of fictional characters! You just can't go wrong with an overconfident, swashbuckling spaceship captain who happens to be best friends with a Wookiee and who falls in love with a princess. It doesn't get much better than that.

SECOND BOOKS CAN OFTEN BE MORE DIFFICULT TO WRITE THAN FIRST BOOKS. OF THE SERIES YOU'VE READ, WHAT IS YOUR FAVORITE SECOND BOOK?

Oh gosh, I could never choose just one! Second books that have completely blown me away include: *Siege and Storm* by Leigh Bardugo, *Fire* by Kristin Cashore, *Spirit and Dust* by Rosemary Clement-Moore, *Insurgent* by Veronica Roth, *Girl of Nightmares* by Kendare Blake, and *Lola and the Boy Next Door* by Stephanie Perkins.

WHAT CAN WE EXPECT FROM THE NEXT BOOK, *CRESS*? NO SPOILERS PLEASE!

You can expect *awesomeness!* At least, that's the plan. *Cress* is based on Rapunzel, in which Cress is a computer hacker being forced to spy on the leaders of Earth and report back to Queen Levana. Oh, and instead of being stuck in the traditional tower, she's stuck in a satellite that's orbiting Earth, desperately trying to find a way to escape....

Scarlet: The Lunar Chronicles
Discussion Questions

1. How is *Scarlet* similar to the story of Little Red Riding Hood? How is it different?

2. In an early chapter, Scarlet defends Cinder from the rude customers at the tavern, and we later learn that Scarlet's open-mindedness toward Lunars was largely influenced by her grand-mother's attitudes. When it comes to prejudices, do you think people are more influenced by their close friends and relatives, or by society at large? Can you think of any real-world prejudices that are similar to that between the Earthens and the Lunars?

3. Imagine you were Scarlet and your grandmother was miss-ing. Would you have followed Wolf when he offered to help you? If not, what would you have done instead?

4. What do you think was Wolf's motivation for helping Scar-let—both when he agreed to help her find her grandmother, and later when he gave her the chip to unlock her prison door? In the beginning, he tells Scarlet that he escaped from his life as a "Loyal Soldier to the Order of the Pack." Do you think he was truly on the run from his life as a Lunar soldier, or was this only a ruse to earn Scarlet's trust?

5. By escaping from prison, Cinder angered Queen Levana and inadvertently triggered the Lunar attacks. Was she right to escape after Kai had struck a bargain with Queen Levana, trading Cinder's freedom for ongoing peace? What would you have done in Cinder's situation? What would you have done in Kai's?

6. In addition to escaping from prison, Cinder aids in the escape of Carswell Thorne, a convicted thief. Do you think she made the right decision in letting him come with her, or should she have left him in the prison cell? What kind of relationship do you think Cinder and Thorne have developed by the end of the book? Do you think Thorne could become romantic competition for Kai?

7. Iko returns in *Scarlet*, not as an android, but as the spaceship's control system. Why do you think it was so important for Cinder to find a way to revive her? Do you have any hopes or predictions for what might become of Iko in the rest of the series?

8. Cinder struggles a lot with her Lunar powers and determining when it is morally right for her to use them. She learns quickly that using her powers can both help and hurt the people around her. Can you think of any situations in which it would be okay—even ethical—for someone to use brainwashing or mind control on another human being? If Lunars were to become integrated into human society, what sorts of laws might be put in place to prevent the misuse of their powers? How might those laws be enforced?

9. In Marissa Meyer's short story "The Queen's Army," we're given a look into the creation of the werewolf soldiers who are conscripted into the Lunar army as children. Children have been used as soldiers throughout history, and it is still happening today. Research one conflict in which a government employed the use of child soldiers. How did they become involved in the fighting? What happened to them when the conflict was over?

10. One of the great ethical debates of modern science is whether or not genetic engineering (altering the DNA of living organisms) should be performed on humans. On Luna, scientists modified the DNA of children in order to turn them into wolf hybrids. Do you think it is right to modify a person's DNA? Can you think of any situations in which genetic engineering would be beneficial to a person or a society? When might it be detrimental?

11. Think about the ruins of the Musée du Louvre and the Palais Garnier (the opera house) in Paris. Why do you think these national sites weren't restored after World War IV? Are there any historical buildings or landmarks in your area that have fallen into disrepair, and do you feel it's important for society to preserve these sites? Why or why not?

12. In many versions of the Little Red Riding Hood fairy tale, Little Red and her grandmother are ultimately rescued from the wolf by a woodsman or lumberjack. Are there any characters in *Scarlet* that you think parallel this role, and how so?

13. How are Cinder and Scarlet similar to each other? How are they different? Do you feel that either of them would make a good role model for young women, and why or why not?

ress has been held captive in a satellite since birth, using her skills with computers to aid Queen Levana's spy network. But her life changes when she receives a distress signal from an ailing ship, containing none other than Cinder and her band of rebels....

Turn the page for the next exciting installment of
The Lunar Chronicles

One

HER SATELLITE MADE ONE FULL ORBIT AROUND PLANET EARTH
every sixteen hours. It was a prison that came with an endlessly
breathtaking view—vast blue oceans and swirling clouds and
sunrises that set half the world on fire.

When she was first imprisoned, she had loved nothing more
than to stack her pillows on top of the desk that was built into the
walls and drape her bed linens over the screens, making a small
alcove for herself. She would pretend that she was not on a satellite at all, but in a podship en route to the blue planet. Soon she
would land and step out onto real dirt, feel real sunshine, smell
real oxygen.

She would stare at the continents for hours and hours, imagining what that must be like.

Her view of Luna, however, was always to be avoided. Some
days her satellite passed so close that the moon took up the entire view and she could make out the enormous glinting domes
on its surface and the sparkling cities where the Lunars lived.
Where she, too, had lived. Years ago. Before she'd been banished.

As a child, Cress had hidden from the moon during those
achingly long hours. Sometimes she would escape to the small
washroom and distract herself by twisting elaborate braids into

her hair. Or she would scramble beneath her desk and sing lulla-
bies until she fell asleep. Or she would dream up a mother and a
father, and imagine how they would play make-believe with her
and read her adventure stories and brush her hair lovingly off
her brow, until finally—finally—the moon would sink again
behind the protective Earth, and she was safe.

Even now, Cress used those hours to crawl beneath her bed
and nap or read or write songs in her head or work out complicated coding. She still did not like to look at the cities of Luna; she
harbored a secret paranoia that if she could see the Lunars, surely
they could look up beyond their artificial skies and see her.

For more than seven years, this had been her nightmare.

But now the silver horizon of Luna was creeping into the corner of her window, and Cress paid no attention. This time, her
wall of invisi-screens was showing her a brand-new nightmare.
Brutal words were splattered across the newsfeeds, photos and
videos blurring in her vision as she scrolled from one feed to the
next. She couldn't read fast enough.

14 CITIES ATTACKED WORLDWIDE
2-HOUR MURDER SPREE RESULTS IN 16,000
EARTHEN DEATHS
LARGEST MASSACRE IN THIRD ERA

The net was littered with horrors. Victims dead in the streets
with shredded abdomens and blood leaking into the gutters.
Feral men-creatures with gore on their chins and beneath their
fingernails and staining the fronts of their shirts. She scrolled
through them all with one hand pressed over her mouth. Breathing became increasingly difficult as the truth of it all sank in.

This was her fault.

For months she had been cloaking those Lunar ships from Earthen detection, doing Mistress Sybil's bidding without question, like the well-trained lackey she was.

Now she knew just what kind of monsters had been aboard those ships. Only now did she understand what Her Majesty had been planning all along, and it was far too late.

16,000 EARTHEN DEATHS

Earth had been taken unaware, and all because she hadn't been brave enough to say no to Mistress's demands. She had done her job and then turned a blind eye to it all.

She averted her gaze from the pictures of death and carnage, focusing on another news story that suggested more horrors to come.

Emperor Kaito of the Eastern Commonwealth had put an end to the attacks by agreeing to marry Lunar Queen Levana.

Queen Levana was to become the Commonwealth's new empress.

The shocked journalists of Earth were scrambling to determine their stance on this diplomatic yet controversial arrangement. Some were in outrage, proclaiming that the Commonwealth and the rest of the Earthen Union should be preparing for war, not a wedding. But others were hastily trying to justify the alliance. With a swirl of her fingers on the thin, transparent screen, Cress raised the audio of a man who was going on about the potential benefits. No more attacks or speculations on when an attack might come. Earth would come to understand the Lunar culture better. They would share technological advances. They would be allies.

And besides, Queen Levana only wanted to rule the Eastern Commonwealth. Surely she would leave the rest of the Earthen Union alone.

But Cress knew they would be fools to believe it. Queen Levana was going to become empress, then she would have Emperor Kaito murdered, claim the country for her own, and use it as a launching pad to assemble her army before invading the rest of the Union. She would not stop until the entire planet was under her control. This small attack, these sixteen thousand deaths... they were only the beginning.

Silencing the broadcast, Cress set her elbows on her desk and dug both hands into her hive of blonde hair. She was suddenly cold, despite the consistently maintained temperature inside the satellite. One of the screens behind her was reading aloud in a child's voice that had been programmed during four months of insanity-inducing boredom when she was ten years old. The voice was too chipper for the material it quoted: a medical blog from the American Republic announcing the results of an autopsy performed on one of the Lunar soldiers.

The bones had been reinforced with calcium-rich biotissue, while the cartilage in major joints was infused with a saline solution for added flexibility and pliability. Orthodontic implants replaced the canine and incisor teeth with those mimicking the teeth of a wolf, and we see the same bone reinforcement around the jaw to allow for the strength to crush material such as bone and other tissue. Remapping of the central nervous system and extensive psychological tampering were responsible for the subject's unyielding aggression and wolf-like tendencies. Dr. Edelstein has

theorized that an advanced manipulation technique of the
brain's bioelectric waves may also have played a role in—

"Mute feed."

The sweet ten-year-old's voice was silenced, leaving the satellite humming with the sounds that had long ago been relegated to the back of Cress's consciousness. The whirring of fans. The thrumming of the life support system. The gurgling of the water recycling tank.

Cress gathered the thick locks of hair at the nape of her neck and pulled the tail over her shoulder—it had a tendency to get caught up in the wheels of her chair when she wasn't careful. The screens before her flickered and scrolled as more and more information came in from the Earthen feeds. News was coming out from Luna too, on their "brave soldiers" and "hard-fought victory"—crown-sanctioned drivel, naturally. Cress had stopped paying attention to Lunar news when she was twelve.

She mindlessly wrapped her ponytail around her left arm, spiraling it from elbow to wrist, unaware of the tangles clumping in her lap.

"Oh, Cress," she murmured. "What are we going to do?"

Her ten-year-old self piped back, "Please clarify your instructions, Big Sister."

Cress shut her eyes against the screen's glare. "I understand that Emperor Kai is only trying to stop a war, but he must know this won't stop Her Majesty. She's going to kill him if he goes through with this, and then where will Earth be?" A headache pounded at her temples. "I thought for certain Linh Cinder had told him at the ball, but what if I'm wrong? What if he still has no idea of the danger he's in?"

Spinning in her chair, she swiped her fingers across a muted newsfeed, punched in a code, and called up the hidden window that she checked a hundred times a day. The D-COMM window opened like a black hole, abandoned and silent, on top of her desk. Linh Cinder still had not tried to contact her. Perhaps her chip had been confiscated or destroyed. Perhaps Linh Cinder didn't even have it anymore.

Huffing, Cress dismissed the link and, with a few hasty taps of her fingertips, cascaded a dozen different windows in its place. They were linked to a spider alert service that was constantly patrolling the net for any information related to the Lunar cyborg who had been taken into custody a week earlier. Linh Cinder. The girl who had escaped from New Beijing Prison. The girl who had been Cress's only chance of telling Emperor Kaito the truth about Queen Levana's intentions should he agree to the marriage alliance.

The major feed hadn't been updated in eleven hours. In the hysteria of the Lunar invasion, Earth seemed to have forgotten about their most-wanted fugitive.

"Big Sister?"

Pulse hiccupping, Cress grasped the arms of her chair. "Yes, Little Cress?"

"Mistress's ship detected. Expected arrival in twenty-two seconds."

Cress catapulted from her chair at the word *mistress*, spoken even all those years ago with a tinge of dread.

Her movements were a precisely choreographed dance, one she had mastered after years of practice. In her mind, she became a second-era ballerina, skimming across a shadowy stage as Little Cress counted down the seconds.

00:21. Cress pressed her palm onto the mattress-deploy button.

00:20. She swiveled back to the screen, sending all feeds of Linh Cinder beneath a layer of Lunar crown propaganda.

00:19. The mattress landed with a thunk on the floor, the pillows and blankets wadded up just as she'd left them.

00:18. 17. 16. Her fingers danced across the screens, hiding Earthen newsfeeds and netgroups.

00:15. A turn, a quick search for two corners of her blanket.

00:14. A flick of her wrists, casting the blanket up like a wind-caught sail.

00:13. 12. 11. She smoothed and tugged her way to the opposite side of the bed, pivoting toward the screens on the other side of her living quarters.

00:10. 9. Earthen dramas, music recordings, second-era literature, all dismissed.

00:08. A swivel back toward the bed. A graceful turning down of the blanket.

00:07. Two pillows symmetrically stacked against the headboard. A flourish of her arm to pull out the hair that had gotten caught beneath the blanket.

00:06. 5. A glissade across the floor, dipping and spinning, gathering up every discarded sock and hair tie and sending them into the renewal chute.

00:04. 3. A sweep of the desks, collecting her only bowl, her only spoon, her only glass, and a handful of stylus pens, and depositing them into the pantry cabinet.

00:02. A final pirouette to scan her work.

00:01. A pleased exhalation, culminating in a graceful bow.

"Mistress has arrived," said Little Cress. "She is requesting an extension of the docking clamp."

The stage, the shadows, the music, all fell away from Cress's thoughts, though a practiced smile remained on her lips. "Of course," she chirped, swanning toward the main boarding ramp. There were two ramps on her satellite, but only one had ever been used. She wasn't even sure if the opposite entrance functioned. Each wide metal door opened up to a docking hatch and, beyond that, space.

Except for when there was a podship anchored there. Mistress's podship.

Cress tapped in the command. A diagram on the screen showed the clamp extending, and she heard the thump as the ship attached. The walls jolted around her.

She had the next moments memorized, could have counted the heartbeats between each familiar sound. The whir of the small spacecraft's engines powering down. The clang of the hatch attaching and sealing around the podship. The vacuum as oxygen was pushed into the space. The beep confirming that travel between the two modules was safe. The opening of the spacecraft. Steps echoing on the walkway. The whoosh of the satellite entrance.

There had been a time when Cress had hoped for warmth and kindness from her mistress. That perhaps Sybil would look at her and say, "My dear, sweet Crescent, you have earned the trust and respect of Her Majesty, the Queen. You are welcome to return with me to Luna and be accepted as one of us."

That time had long since passed, but Cress's practiced smile held firm even in the face of Mistress Sybil's coldness. "Good day, Mistress."

Sybil sniffed. The embroidered sleeves of her white jacket fluttered around the large case she carried, filled with her usual provisions: food and fresh water for Cress's confinement and, of course, the medical kit. "So you've found her, have you?"

Cress winced around her frozen grin. "Found her, Mistress?"

"If it *is* a good day, then you must have finally completed the simple task I've given you. Is that it, Crescent? Have you found the cyborg?"

Cress lowered her gaze and dug her fingernails into her palms. "No, Mistress. I haven't found her."

"I see. So it isn't a good day after all, is it?"

"I only meant... Your company is always..." She trailed off. Forcing her hands to unclench, she dared to meet Mistress Sybil's glare. "I was just reading the news, Mistress. I thought perhaps we were pleased about Her Majesty's engagement."

Sybil dropped the case onto the crisply made bed. "We will be satisfied once Earth is under Lunar control. Until then, there is work to be done, and you should not be wasting your time reading news and gossip."

Sybil neared the monitor that held the secret window with the D-COMM feed and the evidence of Cress's betrayal to the Lunar crown, and Cress stiffened. But Sybil reached past it to a screen displaying a vid of Emperor Kaito speaking in front of the Eastern Commonwealth flag. With a touch, the screen cleared, revealing the metal wall and a tangle of heating tubes behind it.

Cress slowly released her breath.

"I certainly hope you've found *something*."

She stood taller. "Linh Cinder was spotted in the European Federation, in a small town in southern France, at approximately 18:00 local ti—"

"I'm well aware of all that. And then she went to Paris and

killed a thaumaturge and some useless special operatives. Any-thing else, Crescent?"

Cress swallowed and began winding her hair around both wrists in a looping figure eight. "At 17:48, in Rieux, France, the clerk of a ship-and-vehicle parts store updated the store inven-tory, removing one power cell that would be compatible with a 214 Rampion, Class 11.3, but not notating any sort of payment. I thought perhaps Linh Cinder stole... or maybe glamoured..." She hesitated. Sybil liked to keep up the pretense that the cyborg was a shell, even though they both knew it wasn't true. Unlike Cress, who was a true shell, Linh Cinder had the Lunar gift. It may have been buried or hidden somehow, but it had certainly made itself known at the Commonwealth's annual ball.

"A power cell?" Sybil said, passing over Cress's hesitation.

"It converts compressed hydrogen into energy in order to propel—"

"I know what it is," Sybil snapped. "You're telling me that the only progress you've made is finding evidence that she's making repairs to her ship? That it's going to become even more difficult to track her down, a task that you couldn't even manage when they were on Earth?"

"I'm sorry, Mistress. I'm trying. It's just—"

"I'm not interested in your excuses. All these years I've per-suaded Her Majesty to let you live, under the premise that you had something valuable to offer, something even more valuable than blood. Was I wrong to protect you, Crescent?"

She bit her lip, withholding a reminder of all she'd done for Her Majesty during her imprisonment. Designing countless spy systems for keeping watch on Earth's leaders, hacking the communication links between diplomats, and jamming satellite signals to allow the queen's soldiers to invade Earth undetected, so that now the blood of sixteen thousand Earthens was on her hands. It made no difference. Sybil cared only about Cress's failures, and not finding Linh Cinder was Cress's biggest failure to date.

"I'm sorry, Mistress. I'll try harder."

Sybil's eyes narrowed. "I'll be very displeased if you don't find me that girl, and soon."

Held by Sybil's gaze, she felt like a moth pinned to an examination board. "Yes, Mistress."

"Good." Reaching forward, Sybil petted her cheek. It felt almost like a mother's approval, but not quite. Then she turned away and released the locking mechanisms on the case. "Now then," she said, retrieving a hypodermic needle from the medical kit. "Your arm."

The Queen's Army

written by
Marissa Meyer

THEY CAME AT THE END OF THE LONG NIGHT, WHEN THE
manufacturing dome had not seen sunlight for almost two weeks. Z
had crossed his twelfth birthday some months ago, and just enough
time had passed that he'd stopped imagining glimpses of gold em-
broidery on black coats. He'd just stopped questioning every
thought that flickered through his brain. He had just begun to hope
that he would not be chosen.

But he was not surprised when he was awoken by a tap at the
front door. It was so early that his father hadn't left for the plant
where he assembled engines for podships and tractors. Z stared at
the dark ceiling and listened to his parents' whispering through the
wall, then to his father's footsteps padding past his door.

Muffled voices in the front room.

Z balled up his blanket between his fists and tried to pour all his
fears into it, and then release them all at once. He had to do it three
times to keep from hyperventilating. He didn't want his brother,
still asleep on the other side of the room, to be afraid for him.

He had known this was inevitable.

He was at the top of his class. He was stronger than some of the
men his father worked with in the plant. Still, he'd thought that
maybe his instructors would overlook him. Maybe he would be
skipped.

But those thoughts were always flitting. Since he was a little
boy, he had been raised to expect a visit from the queen's

thaumaturges during his twelfth year, and that if he was deemed worthy, he would be conscripted into the new army she was building. It was a great honor to serve her crown. It would bring pride to his family and his sector.

"You should get dressed."

He listed his head to find his brother's eyes shining in the darkness. So, he wasn't asleep after all.

"They'll ask for you soon. You don't want to make them wait."

Not wanting his brother to think he was scared, he swung his legs out of the bed.

He met his mother in the hallway. Her cropped hair was sticking up on one side and she had pulled on a cotton dress, though the static of her slip had it clinging around her left thigh. She paused from adjusting the material and, for one crushing second, he saw the despair that she'd always hidden when they talked about the soldier conscription. Then it was gone and she was licking her fingers and desperately trying to soothe down Z's unkempt hair. He flinched, but didn't fidget or complain, until his father appeared beside them.

"Ze'ev." His voice was thick with an emotion that Z didn't recognize. "Don't be afraid."

His father took his hand and guided him into the front of the house where not one, but two, thaumaturges were waiting for him. They both wore the traditional uniform of the queen's court—high-collared coats that swept down nearly to their knees and arms that tapered into bell-shaped sleeves embroidered with gold runes. However, the woman wore black, denoting a third-level thaumaturge, while the man wore red. Second-level. Z didn't think there were more than a dozen second-level thaumaturges on all of Luna, and now one was standing in his house.

He couldn't help picturing his home as it must look through the eyes of such high officials. The front room was large enough only for a worn sofa and a rocking chair, and his mom kept a vase of dusty faux flowers on the side table. If they'd bothered to look through the second doorway, they would have seen a sink piled with dishes where flies were buzzing, because his mother had been too tired to clean last night, and Ran and Z had decided to play kicks with the other sector kids rather than do their chores. He regretted that now.

"Ze'ev Kesley?" said the man, the second-level.

He nodded, clutching his father's hand and using all his will not to duck behind him.

"I am pleased to inform you that we have reviewed your aptitude tests and chosen you to receive the physical modifications and training in order to become one of the great soldiers of Her Majesty's army. Your enrollment is effective immediately. There is no need to pack any belongings, you will be provided with all that you need. As it is expected that henceforth you will have no more contact with your biological family, you may now say your good-byes."

His mother sucked in a breath behind him. Z didn't realize he was shaking until his father turned and grasped him by both shoulders.

"Don't be afraid," he said again. A faint smile flickered, then disappeared. "Do what they ask, and make us proud. This is a great honor."

His voice was strained. Z couldn't tell if his father believed what he was saying, or if it was only a show for the thaumaturges.

His chest constricted. "But . . . I don't want to go."

His father's face became stern. "Ze'ev."

Z looked at his mother. Her dress was still clinging to her slip, but she'd stopped fidgeting. The tears hadn't yet spilled over onto her cheeks. There were wrinkles around her eyes that he'd never noticed before.

"Please," he said, wrapping his arms around her waist. He knew how strong he was. If he held on tight enough, they could never force him to let go. He clamped his eyes shut as the first hot tears slipped out. "Please don't let them—"

Just as a sob tore at his throat, a shadowy new thought slipped to the forefront of his mind.

This was a small, pathetic house in an inconsequential manufacturing dome.

The people here were miserable and unimportant. His parents were weak and stupid, but *he,* he was destined for greatness. He was one of the select few to serve the queen herself. It was an honor. The thought of lingering here a moment longer made him sick.

Z gasped and pulled away from his mother. Heat was crawling up his neck—spurred by mortification and shame. How could he think such things?

Worse yet, he was still thinking them, somewhere in his head. He couldn't shake them entirely, no matter how much guilt they stirred up.

He turned to gape at the thaumaturges. The woman had a smile toying around her mouth. Though he'd first thought she was pretty, this new expression made him shudder.

"You will be given a new family soon enough," she said, in a voice that lilted like a nursery rhyme. "We have means of making you accept this and come willingly, should we be inclined to use them."

Z cringed, repulsed by the knowledge that she had seen these horrible thoughts. Not only seen them—she had created them. She had been manipulating him, and it had been so seamless, had intertwined with his own emotions so effortlessly. When his peers practiced mind control on each other or an instructor prodded him with thoughts of obedience, it felt like a new idea being etched into his brain. It was recognizable and, often, he found that with enough focus, he could defy it.

This was a different level of manipulation, one that he couldn't resist so easily. He knew it then. He would be forced to go with them, and he would become a puppet of Her Majesty, with no more will-power than a trained dog.

Behind him, he heard his bedroom door opening.

Ran had come out to watch—pulled by his curiosity.

Z tightened his jaw and tried his best to stifle his mounting despair. He would be brave so his brother would not see his fear. He would be strong for him.

Some of the terror and dread did begin to fade once the decision was reached. Empowered by the knowledge that it was his choice—that the thaumaturges had not made it for him—he faced his mother and stood on his tiptoes to kiss her cheek. She grabbed at him before he could pull back and crushed him against her, pressing a frantic kiss against his hair. When she released him, just as quickly, the tears had begun to fall and she had to turn her face away to hide them.

He embraced his father too, just as brief and just as fierce so he would know how much love was put into it.

Then he squared his shoulders and stepped toward the thaumaturges.

The woman's grin returned. "Welcome to the queen's army."

THEY SAID THE ANESTHESIA WOULD GIVE HIM SUCH A DEEP, empty sleep that there would be no dreams, but they were wrong. He dreamt of needles burrowing into his skin. He dreamt of pliers gripping his teeth. He dreamt of hot ashes and smoke in his eyes. He dreamt of a white tundra, a cold he had never known, and a hunger barely satiated by dripping meat in his jaws.

Mostly, he dreamt of howls in the distance. Forlorn cries that went on and on and on.

The waking came slowly, like being pulled up from a pit of mud. The howls began to dim as he pried open his eyes. He was in the same room that he'd been in when the nameless nurse had stuck the needle into his arm, but he knew instantly that he was changed. The walls around him were a brighter, crisper white than he'd ever known. The sound of every machine and contraption reverberated in his skull. The scent of chemicals and ammonia invaded his nostrils, making him want to gag, but he was too weak.

His limbs were heavy on the exam table, his joints aching. He wore an oversized shirt that made him feel vulnerable and cold. There was a lump beneath his neck. Forcing his fumbling arm to move, he reached behind his head to find bandages there.

As his awareness sharpened, he struggled to recall what little information the nurse had given him.

All soldiers were modified to increase their effectiveness as members of the queen's army. He would wake up *improved*.

He took in another breath and this time picked up on a new scent. No, two scents.

Two individual odors made up of pheromones and sweat and soap and chemicals. Coming closer.

The door opened and a man and woman entered. The woman wore a white lab jacket and had spiky auburn hair.

The man was a thaumaturge, but not one that had taken Z from his home. He had dark, wavy hair that he'd tucked back behind both ears, and eyes that were as black as the sky. They matched his tailored, third-level thaumaturge coat.

And Z could pick out every unique odor on them—lotions and cosmetics and hormones.

"Good," said the woman, pressing her finger against a pad on the wall. The exam table began to hum and Z was raised to a seated position. He grasped at the thin blanket around his chest. "Your monitor informed me that you were awake. I am Dr. Murphy. I presided over your surgeries. How are you feeling?"

Z squinted at her. "I'm not . . . am I—"

He hesitated as his tongue found something foreign in his mouth. He clasped his hand over his lips, then reached inside. The pad of his thumb found the sharp point of a fang and he jerked it away.

"Careful," said the woman. "Your new implants will serve as some of your most effective weapons. May I?"

He didn't resist as she pulled his jaw open and examined his teeth. "Your gums are healing nicely. We replaced all of your teeth, otherwise there wouldn't be room for the canines. We've also reinforced your jaw for additional leverage and pressure. You'll likely be sore for another ten to fourteen days, especially as we wean you off the painkillers. How are your eyes?" She pulled a contraption out of her pocket and flickered a light across his pupils. "You'll likely notice increased pigmentation. It's nothing to concern yourself with. Once your optic nerves adapt, you'll find that your eyesight has become optimized to detect and pinpoint motion. Do let your thaumaturge know if you experience any dizziness, blurred vision, or dark spots. I trust you're already experiencing heightened senses of hearing and smell?"

It took him a moment to realize it was a question, and he gave a shaky nod.

"Excellent. The rest of your modifications will evolve over the next eight to twelve months. As your body adapts to the genetic alterations, you'll notice new muscle strength, agility, flexibility, and stamina. All this will come with increased metabolism, so you'll find yourself eating more in the coming months. Even more than a normal twelve-year-old boy, that is." Her eyes twinkled.

Z's pulse began to pound against his temples.

"But we've prepared for all that," she continued when he didn't laugh. "Soldiers are provided a high-protein diet that we've created for your specific needs. Do you have any questions before I hand you off to Thaumaturge Jael?"

His breathing was becoming more and more difficult to soothe. "What's going to happen to me? In the next . . . eight to twelve months?"

She flashed a braggart's smile. "You'll become a soldier, of course." She held up the small device again. With a tap, a holograph emerged, showing two rotating images.

One, a young male, perhaps in his late teens.

The other, a white wolf.

"Based on years of research and trials, we have perfected our methods of genetic engineering, allowing us to combine select genes of Her Majesty's prized *canis lupus arctos* with those of still-developing Lunar males." She tapped another button and the two holographs merged. Z sucked in a breath. This new creature had rounded shoulders and enormous hands that were covered with a fine layer of fur and fangs that jutted from a grotesquely twisted mouth. More fur covered his face, surrounding severe yellow eyes.

Z pushed himself back into the exam table.

"Using this method," continued the doctor, "we have created the ultimate soldier. Strong and fearless, with the instincts of one of nature's greatest predators. Most important, he is a soldier who is entirely subject to the will of his thaumaturge." She shut off the holograph. "But Thaumaturge Jael will be able to explain all that to you in due time."

"Th-that's going to happen to me?"

The doctor opened her mouth to speak, but the thaumaturge cleared his throat and took a step toward the bed. "Perhaps, or perhaps not. You have undergone the modifications to give you the skills all soldiers require. But we chose to withhold the more *animalistic* changes. For now."

"Though we can complete the necessary mutations at any time," added the doctor.

"But—why not ..."

"You have been selected as one of only five hundred conscripts to receive special training. Your aptitude tests suggest you could be valuable to us as more than a member of the infantry, and Her Majesty is preparing a unit of soldiers to play a very specific role." He listed his head. "Whether or not you are admitted into that program will ultimately depend on the promise you display during your training."

The threatening look the thaumaturge pinned on him wasn't necessary. Z never wanted to be back on this exam table. He never wanted another needle beneath his skin. He never wanted to wake up with fur on his face and eyes that had no humanity behind them.

The queen was making a different kind of soldier, and he had already decided that he would be one of them.

HE WAS KEPT IN THE FACILITY FOR ANOTHER TWENTY-FOUR hours, so that the doctor could monitor how his body was reacting to the surgeries. He discovered that what had seemed like a few hours of nightmares had, in reality, been twenty-six days of being kept comatose in a suspended animation tank while his body underwent the surgeries and adapted to the mutations. Twenty-six days gone, while his DNA melded with that of a white wolf, and nameless doctors and scientists turned him into a beast to serve his queen. In that time, the sun had come and gone, plunging the great city of Artemisia into another long night.

The next day, he found a pile of clothes left beside his bed—soft brown pants, a black T-shirt, and plain boots. They fit him perfectly.

He had just finished dressing when he smelled someone coming, the thaumaturge from the day before. His nausea from his new heightened sense of smell had quelled during the night, but a new, sinking, crawling feeling settled in Z's gut as the thaumaturge entered the room.

Because another sense was missing.

The telltale vibration of energy that his people could perceive and manipulate. It was gone.

His throat clamped. "Something's wrong with me," he said, before the thaumaturge could speak. "My gift. It's . . . I think something's wrong."

The thaumaturge stared blankly for a moment, before his expression softened into kindness. The look eased Z's growing panic. "Yes, I know," he said. "That is an unfortunate result of the modifications. You see, wild animals do not have the abilities that we do, therefore we must hinder your awareness of bioelectricity so that your Lunar instincts will not interfere with your new wolfish instincts. Don't be alarmed—you are not powerless. We have simply given you a new tool with which to take advantage of your gift. It will be my job to ensure that all of your instincts and abilities are functioning properly when you're called on to use them."

Z licked his lips, finding it awkward to maneuver around his new teeth. He had to shut his eyes to force the wash of bile back down his throat.

They had taken away his Lunar gift. He was as vulnerable as an Earthen now. As useless as a shell. And yet, they wanted him to be a soldier?

"We were not properly introduced yesterday," the thaumaturge continued. "You are to call me Master Jael. You will be known as Beta Kesley until and unless your ranking changes. I am glad to see you dressed. Come then."

He left the room and it took Z a scrambling minute to realize he was meant to follow.

"The candidates for special operative status have been given their own training grounds beneath Sector 8," Master Jael said as they left the research facility. Z caught only the briefest glimpse of the glittering white buildings of Artemisia—Luna's major city—before Jael led him down into the lava tubes beneath the surface. A personal shuttle was waiting for them. "The training grounds consist of separate barracks for each pack, a community dining hall, and a series of training rooms in which you will perform formations and learn fighting techniques. This is also where you will decide your placement in the pack."

"The pack?"

"Your new family. We have found that your instincts react best when we mimic the hierarchy of wolves in their natural habitat, and so each pack consists of six to fifteen operatives, depending on the mental strength of their thaumaturge." His grin widened. "You are my fourteenth pack member."

Z turned away to watch the black regolith walls pass by the shuttle window, and tried to pretend that he understood what Master Jael was talking about.

The training grounds were in enormous caverns carved into the lava tubes. When they walked into the main room, Jael's heels clipping with each step, Z saw that thirteen soldiers were already lined up to greet them, dressed exactly as he was. He guessed their ages ranged from twelve to eighteen or older, and though they stood in perfect posture in a straight line, with their heels together and arms stiff at their sides, Z knew instantly who was their leader. The tallest and the largest and the one who's eyes flashed when they met his.

"Master Jael," he said, and in unison, all soldiers clasped a fist to their hearts.

"Alpha Brock. You have a new member joining you today. This is Beta Ze'ev Kesley."

Scrutiny seemed to pass through all the soldiers. Z forced himself to stand up straighter, though it pinched the muscles between his shoulder blades. He took the time to meet each of their gazes, thinking that, though there was a proliferation of unfamiliar aromas in this hall, he could pick out which scents belonged to each of them.

"Beta Kesley," said Master Jael, "join your pack."

Z slid his gaze to meet the thaumaturge's and his pulse skipped. There was something eager in the look. He held his gaze for a breath, not knowing what he was expected to do. Did Jael want him to bow? Or clasp his hand to his heart like the others had?

Before he could decide, Z felt a jolt through his nerves, like an electric shock. And then he was pacing toward the line of soldiers, his feet no longer under his control.

Blood rushed to his face.

Mind control.

A surge of defiance crawled up from the base of his throat. Z scrunched his face up and, with every bit of concentration he had, forced his legs to freeze. He found himself in an awkward stance, his legs caught midstep, his hands fisted at his sides. He was already panting with the effort.

He pried open his eyes and looked at Master Jael. He was surprised to find amusement, not anger, in the thaumaturge's expression. Through his teeth, he said, "Thank you, *Master*, but I can walk without your help."

Jael grinned, and with a snap, Z felt the hold on his mind release.

"But of course," Jael said. "Please, join the line."

Letting out a breath, Z turned toward his new pack.

He gasped. The leader—Alpha Brock—was now less than an arm's distance away, a snarl showing the points of his canines.

Before Z could think, a fist collided with his jaw, knocking him onto the floor and knocking the wind out of him. For a moment his lungs burned with the need for air and his head rang from the punch. The pain in his jaw was the worst, his gums still sore from the surgery. The throbbing brought tears to his eyes.

"Don't ever disrespect Master Jael again," said Alpha Brock. With a grunt, he landed a kick to Z's ribs.

Z cried out and crunched into a ball, trying to protect his stomach, but another kick didn't follow. Tasting blood, he spit onto the chalky ground. He was glad that none of his new teeth came with it.

Shaking, he risked a glance up at Master Jael, but the thaumaturge was standing calmly back, his hands in his sleeves. When he caught Z's gaze, his eyebrows rose up without mercy and he said, very slowly, "Get up and join your pack."

Standing seemed impossible. The world was spinning and he wondered if that one kick hadn't broken a rib.

But more afraid of the repercussions of ignoring an order than the pain, Z pulled himself to all fours and, with a grunt, pushed himself onto wobbly legs. The Alpha stared down at him as Z stumbled to the end of the line. The other soldiers had not moved.

"You will soon learn," said Master Jael, "that your placement in this pack is determined by strength, courage, and the ability to defend yourself. You will not see such mercy again."

Z BEGAN TO LOSE TRACK OF TIME. FIRST THE DAYS, AND THEN the weeks and months merged into constant training. Formations. Strategies and tactics. And fights—so many fights. Like wolves in the wild fight to determine their rank, these soldiers fought all the time. Constantly trying to best each other, to show off, to prove their worth, to improve their station. Almost all of them seemed to have a thirst for violence that Z couldn't claim, though he often pretended to desire the taste of blood and the crunch of bones as much as any of them. There wasn't much choice.

He didn't win all his fights, but he didn't lose them all, either. After a year and a half, or what he guessed was close to a year and a half, with neither the long days nor the long nights to judge by, he found himself solidly in the middle of his pack. An average beta. After that one punch from Alpha Brock, he had never again allowed himself to be caught by surprise, and he had developed a knack for parrying and blocking. Offensive tactics didn't come as naturally, but he could often avoid being hit for long enough to tire out his opponent.

It would never make him Alpha, but it kept him from becoming the tormented Omega.

Alpha Brock, on the other hand, remained ever on top of the pack. Undefeated, he picked more fights than any of them, like he had to constantly remind himself and everyone else how much better he was. Z tried to stay out of his way, but it was impossible to avoid him entirely, and when Brock wanted to fight, there was no denying him. Z had received more bruises and scars from those fists than he could count.

The pack was standing around watching an impromptu brawl between Betas Wynn and Troya when Z caught the scent of Master Jael approaching, along with another scent. Familiar and vague at the same time.

Z tore his eyes from the fight at the same time the others picked up on the scents. The two fighters took another moment, but in a breath, they had released each other, and together they all rushed to line up for Jael's entrance. Z recognized the cadence of Jael's footsteps, beside something awkward and shuffling. Jael had not brought anyone new to their barracks since Z himself had joined the pack.

Master Jael stepped out of the cave and into the training cavern, a new conscript at his side.

Z couldn't keep back a gasp. Beside him, Wynn flinched at the noise, and he was sure they'd all noticed his reaction. He wasn't the only one with advanced hearing.

But the new conscript was his brother. Taller now, but otherwise not much changed.

Ran took longer to notice him. Standing half a step behind Master Jael, dressed in uniform, pale and wide-eyed, he was busy scanning the faces of his new family.

Until they landed on Z and his scrutiny froze in surprise.

"Alpha Brock," said Jael, "this is the final recruit for your pack, Beta Ran Kesley."

Together with the rest of the pack, Z clasped his fist to his chest.

"Beta Kesley, you may join your pack."

Z gulped, waiting for the moment when Ran's legs would betray him and recognition would flash across his face.

And it came, and Ran's eyes did widen, but then he bowed his head and put up no resistance as his body joined the others at the end of the line and his balled fist hit his chest.

Z found that his heart was thundering. He wondered if the others could hear it.

He heard Ran's breathing, three bodies away from him, as Jael released his control.

"Welcome to your new family. Training will commence at 0600 tomorrow. You have much to be caught up on." Jael spun on his heels and left them without ceremony.

No one moved until both the sounds of his footsteps and the scent of his cologne had dissipated.

Then Alpha Brock snorted. The noise sent ice rushing through Z's veins.

The pack broke formation and within seconds had Ran surrounded.

"Well," said Alpha Brock. "You did better on your induction than your arrogant brother, at least."

Ran's gaze flickered to Z, a look of fear and uncertainty, before flying back to Alpha Brock.

"I honestly didn't think Master Jael could handle one more member," Alpha Brock continued, smirking. "You must be pretty weak-minded for him to have taken you on."

Ran took half a step away. Z could see he was still dazed from the surgeries, his pupils dilated and a sheen of sweat on his brow.

"Leave him alone, Brock," said Z, stepping into the circle. It was the only time he could recall addressing him directly.

Brock turned and peered at Z from the corner of his eye. "What's that, Kesley?"

"Give him some time. We all know you're Alpha—you don't have to bully every twelve-year-old kid who comes in here to prove it."

He thought he heard a snicker behind him, but it was stifled as Brock's expression darkened. He turned toward him fully and Z was surprised at the relief that rushed into him. At least he wasn't targeting Ran anymore.

But then Brock spun so fast, his leg spinning in a roundhouse kick, that Z wasn't sure *he* could have blocked it. Brock's foot smashed into Ran's head, hurtling him into Beta Rafe.

White spots flashed in Z's vision and he didn't realize what he was doing until a roar emerged from his throat and his fist collided with Brock's jaw.

Brock stumbled back, surprised, but it was short-lived. Snarling, he flew back at Z and used the leverage of Z's second punch to spin him around, catching Z's head in the crook of his elbow. With one arm pinned at his side, Z growled and tried to toss Brock over him, like he'd learned to throw others when they had him in such a position, but Brock was too big. Z's free hand beat uselessly, pathetically against Brock's ear.

"This is my pack," Brock said. "Don't you ever tell me how to treat them."

The second he was released, Z pushed himself away. But Brock still gripped his wrist. As Z mindlessly sought to put distance between them, he felt something sharp puncture the flesh beneath his elbow. He cried out and yanked his arm away, and the sting ripped down his skin, cutting his flesh from elbow to wrist.

Z stumbled away and clutched his arm against his chest. Brock grinned. He'd taken to sharpening his nails into knife-sharp points, a trend quickly picked up by the other pack members.

Now Z understood why.

Trying to ignore the pain and the blood dripping down between his fingers, he raised his fists for the next attack.

But Brock merely wiped Z's blood off on his pants and turned away, unconcerned about retribution as the rest of the pack watched on.

Z's stomach sank as Brock turned and spat on his brother, who was still on the ground. Brock's spit landed on his shoulder. Ran didn't back away or bother to wipe it off.

"Lesson number one," said Brock. "Never let someone else take your fights for you."

Z didn't let his fists down until Brock had led the rest of the pack away. Then he whipped off his shirt and wrapped the fabric around the wound. It didn't take long for the blood to soak through.

"Ran, are you all right? Is your jaw broken?" He stumbled toward his brother and held a hand toward him. But when Ran met his gaze, it was not with gratitude, but anger.

"Why did you do that?" he said, rubbing his cheek. "Did you have to embarrass me on my first day?"

Z drew back. "Ran . . ."

Ignoring the extended hand, Ran climbed to his feet. "You always have to show me up. I thought this was my chance to prove myself, but of all the soldiers, I have to be grouped with *you*. Stuck in your shadow, again." He shook his head and Z thought maybe there was wetness in his eyes before he spun away. "Just leave me alone, Z. Just . . . forget we were ever brothers at all."

IT HAD BEEN NEARLY FIVE YEARS SINCE Z HAD UNDERGONE the genetic modifications. Five years without seeing his parents. Five years spent underground, fighting and brawling and training. Not another word had ever been spoken about the possibility of being chosen for the queen's special soldiers, but it was never far from his mind. He frequently awoke from dreams of long syringes and fur covering his body.

There were fifty packs that had been held back from the full surgeries, and they gathered daily for an hour-long feast in the dining hall. It was during the feasts that Z felt most like the animal they wanted him to be. The stench was overwhelming—sweat and blood from all five hundred soldiers mixed with rare cuts of meat that were presented on slabs of wood and stone. They often fought over the choicest bits, resulting in yet more brawls. One more test. One more way to stake your place among your brothers.

There had been a time when Z had sat back and waited for the leftovers, living like a scavenger rather than joining the flying fists and gnashing teeth. But his hunger was as strong as any of theirs—the kind of hunger that was never satisfied—and a few years into his training, he had made the decision that he would never again be served last. After only a few victories, his pack brothers had stopped challenging him.

He still avoided Alpha Brock's wrath, despite having grown taller than him in the last year. Z did notice that even Brock hadn't seemed eager to pick any fights with him for a while, instead directing the majority of his cruelty toward mocking and manipulating Ran.

Or, Omega Kesley.

It had been clear from the start that Ran was the weakest. Z had hoped it was only because of his age and size, but soon it was obvious that his brother simply didn't have the fortitude necessary to carve out a place of respect among the pack.

Worst of all, he didn't seem to understand why he remained at the bottom of the chain. He doted on Brock, mimicking the way he talked and attempting to duplicate his fight moves, though he didn't have the upper-body strength to pull most of them off. He had even begun sharpening his nails.

It made Z sick to see it. At times, he wanted to pull his brother aside and shake him and explain that he wasn't helping himself. By cowing to everything Brock did, he was only making himself an easier target.

And yet, Ran had never given any indication that he wanted Z's help, and so Z had let him be. Had watched as his brother clung pathetically to Brock's side, hoping for recognition and receiving only table scraps.

Z was watching his brother gnaw on one of Brock's abandoned bones, the meal whittled down now to pools of blood and shreds of charred flesh, when he caught the scents.

So many aromas. Jael among them, but the others were unknown. Forty ... maybe fifty ...

He whipped his head toward the main door of the dining hall, his brow furrowed.

It took a few moments of rowdy talk and chewing before the soldiers around him hushed. A hesitation—thaumaturges never came to the dining hall—before they all pushed back from the tables and jostled around each other to form their lines, wiping the juices from their chins.

Jael entered, along with forty-nine other thaumaturges, all in black coats. They spread out so that they formed a tunnel from the entryway. Jael's gaze found his pack and narrowed. A subtle warning.

Z drew his shoulders back until the muscles began to complain.

The silence was startling after the feast's chaos. Z found a piece of meat stuck in a molar and tried to work it out without moving his jaw too much.

They waited.

And then, a new scent. Something floral and warm that reminded him of his mother.

A woman stepped out from the wide cavern, wearing a gauzy dress that billowed around her feet and a sheer veil that covered her face and drifted past her elbows. On top of the veil sat a delicate white crown, carved from shimmering regolith stone.

Z was glad that he was not the only one who gasped. He instantly peeled his gaze away from Her Majesty and stared straight ahead at the black cavern wall. His palms began to sweat, but he resisted the urge to wipe them on his pants or check his face for remnants of the meal.

The piece of meat blissfully relinquished its hold on his tooth and he swallowed.

"Gentlemen," said the queen. "I am here to congratulate you on the progress you've all made as soldiers in my brilliant new army. I have been monitoring your training sessions for many months now, and I am pleased with what I've seen."

A low rustle slipped through them—the faintest of fidgets. Z did not know how she could have watched them without their knowing. Maybe their training sessions had been recorded.

"You are all aware," the queen continued, "that you are among the soldiers being considered for a unique mission that will aid in the hostilities between Luna and Earth. This is a role of honor, reserved for those who have risen above the confines of their past, the limitations of their bodies, and the fear of the unknown. They will be my most prized soldiers, chosen not only for their strength and bravery, but also for their intelligence, cunning, and adaptability. My court and I will be making our final selections soon."

Her words were blurred in Z's thoughts and he could think of nothing past a bead of sweat making its way down his temple and how his fingers were beginning to twitch with too much energy and no outlet.

The queen, who had been as still as the soldiers until now, a faceless sheet speaking to them, lifted one arm and gestured to the thaumaturges. "I'm sure that I do not need to remind your thaumaturges that those who are in control of the selected packs will receive instant advancement in their court status."

Z dared a glance at Jael and saw that his dark eyes had gone fierce, his jaw set.

"Gentlemen."

Z snapped his gaze back to the wall.

"Your thaumaturges have asked for the opportunity to showcase some of their brightest soldiers. I look forward to the demonstration." She swirled her fingers through the air and the thaumaturges spread out into the crowd.

Jael's walk was tense as he reached them. "Alpha Brock," he snapped, "you will be fighting. No teeth, no claws—I want to show your skill. Understood?"

Brock fisted his hand against his chest. "Yes, Master Jael. Who will be my opponent?"

Jael's gaze swept to Beta Wynn. Though technically, all Betas had the same rank in the pack, everyone kept a mental record of wins and losses, of victories and failures, and everyone knew that Wynn wasn't far behind Brock in his abilities.

But then Jael let out a slow breath. "Ze'ev."

Z's eyes widened and he glanced at Master Jael, heat flooding his face. But Jael showed no humor or uncertainty, only a stern determination as he paced past the others and came to stand before him. Their gazes clashed and it was with some shock that Z realized he was now taller than Master Jael, too.

"She wants a show," he said. "This time, don't hold back."

Z's brow twitched, but he tried to remain neutral as he saluted his thaumaturge.

His thoughts were frenzied as they were marched into the largest training room. Her Majesty had been escorted onto a platform on one end and placed atop a throne so that she could watch the proceedings in comfort.

Fifty packs. Fifty fights.

Z's stomach was roiling as they began. He couldn't focus on the brawls. He was only seeing Jael's dark eyes, hearing his words over and over again. *This time, don't hold back.*

Did Jael think he faked his losses? Did Jael believe he was capable of defeating Brock, or did he only want to ensure that he lasted as long as he could?

Only once did he dare to glance over at his opponent and saw that Brock had a furious scowl. He obviously didn't think Z was a worthy opponent, not in front of the queen herself.

Ran, too, looked sullen, and although not a person in the room would have expected Ran to be chosen as one of Jael's examples, Z sensed that Ran had fantasized about such a chance to prove himself more than once.

Finally, their turn came.

Jael bowed to Her Majesty and introduced them—Alpha Brock fighting Beta Kesley.

Z could smell the blood from the previous fights, still warm and salty, mingling with the regolith dust. He and Brock trekked to the fighting circle and stared at each other.

Only when he sank into his fighting stance did he feel the panic and confusion subside.

He didn't win all his fights, but he won more than he lost. He had become strong and fast. He would not make a fool of himself in front of Her Majesty.

And if they amused her, perhaps she would choose their pack for her special mission. He would never have to go through the rest of the surgeries. He would never become a mindless beast in her army.

Brock's eyes flashed. There was a burning in his gaze that Z didn't recognize, but he was sure it carried a promise of pain.

Brock came at him first, with a right hook aimed at his jaw. Z ducked easily—too easily. Brock feinted at the last moment and drove his other fist into Z's side. Z clenched his teeth and pushed himself back, retaliating with a front kick to Brock's stomach.

They backed away from each other, bouncing on the balls of their feet, hands poised in front of their faces. A trickle of sweat dropped down Z's spine.

He squinted, watching the way Brock's body swayed, noticing how he briefly clenched his left fist.

A roundhouse kick was coming.

No sooner had he thought it than Brock whipped forward, aiming his foot for Z's head.

He caught it and pulled, throwing Brock onto his side.

Z danced out of his reach, panting. Salt was beginning to sting his eyes. Brock didn't stay down long. He flashed his sharp teeth and rushed forward—

Jab to the ribs. Elbow to the face. Sideswipe kick.

He saw them all happening an instant before they did. Block. Block. Jump. *Attack.*

Teeth snapped as he landed an uppercut to Brock's jaw. A left hook to his side.

Brock withdrew, face contorted in fury. It was difficult for Z to hide his own surprise at this newfound skill.

But it wasn't new. It was from years of sitting on the sidelines, watching and studying and inspecting every fight, every brawl, every punch thrown, every victory won. He knew how Brock fought.

And, he suspected that if he were pinned against any one of his pack members, he would have seen the same signs, recognized the same tricks and tells.

He could beat them.

He could beat all of them.

Brock stretched his neck to one side and Z heard the sound of his spine popping. Brock shook it out like a dog, then sank into his stance again.

His eyes glinted.

Bolstered, Z shot forward.

Jab. Blocked.

Cross. Blocked.

Uppercut. Blocked.

Knee—

Z gasped, pain ripping through his abdomen as five nails dug into his side, piercing the flesh above his hip bone. Brock squeezed, digging his fingers deeper into the flesh. Z nearly collapsed, catching himself on Brock's shoulder with a strangled grunt.

"I will kill you before I let you win this fight," Brock breathed against him.

He let go all at once and stepped away. Without his support, Z fell to one knee. He pressed his hand against the wounds, not daring to look at Jael or the queen, to see if anyone noticed or cared that Brock had disobeyed the rules Jael had laid out for them.

But no. They were wild animals. Predators who ran on instinct and bloodthirst.

Who would expect a fair fight from such monsters?

All she wanted was a show.

He heard a low growl and didn't at first realize that it was coming from his own throat. He dared to look up. Brock's stance had relaxed. There was blood up to the first knuckles of his fingers.

Flashes of red sparked in the corners of Z's vision. His side throbbed.

"Best just to stay down," Brock said.

Z snarled. "You'll have to kill me."

He pushed himself off the ground and lunged forward. For a moment, Brock seemed startled, but then he was blocking again, knocking away every advance. But Z was fast, and finally a punch landed against Brock's cheek.

With a roar, Brock reached toward Z's wound, but Z dodged away and grasped Brock by the wrist, pulling him so close he could smell the meat lingering on his breath. With his free hand, he grabbed Brock's throat. Hesitated.

Kill him.

The words stole into his head like the long night came upon the cities—sly, but complete. They possessed him, their command working their way into his desires and hunger and desperation and crawling down into his pulsing fingertips.

I want to see how you would do it.

He grit his teeth.

Brock's nostrils widened. His eyes glowed with disdain as he sensed Z's indecision.

Z felt the shift in his opponent's weight and he knew it was coming. Fingernails in his side, the blinding pain, the white spots in his vision.

With a roar, he let go of Brock's wrist and grabbed the back of his head.

Snap!

He dropped the body to the ground before the light went out in his eyes.

Z's heart was thumping painfully, his blood a tsunami rushing through his ears.

But outside of him, there was silence. Complete and endless silence.

Licking his salted lips, he tore his gaze away from Brock and the way his neck was bent all wrong.

His pack was watching him with disbelief and awe but, to his surprise, there did not seem to be any hatred there.

His gaze continued. They were *all* gaping at him. The other packs, the thaumaturges. All except Jael, who didn't look exactly pleased, and yet didn't seem surprised, either.

Only when the queen stood did he dare to look at her. Her head was listed to the side, and he imagined a pensive expression behind the veil.

"Clean and efficient," she said, bringing her hands together for three solid claps. She had not applauded any of the other fights. He did not know what it meant. "Well done . . . Alpha."

His stomach flipped, but the queen was already gesturing for the body to be removed, for the fights to continue, and Z had to stumble off toward his pack before she retracted her praise. Her words followed him, as kind and gentle as a bell.

Well done. *Alpha.*

He had killed Brock, and in the law of the pack, he was now to take his place as the undisputed leader.

He was the new Alpha.

He paused in front of his pack brothers. None of them seemed surprised by the queen's words. They had all known it the moment Brock hit the ground.

As he watched, they each brought their fists to their chests in mute respect. In silent acceptance of his victory. Even his brother saluted him, but there alone was bitterness. There, alone, was anger over Z's success.

Z nodded twice—once to acknowledge the show of respect, and once at his brother, so that Ran would know that he saw his disappointment.

Then he slipped past them all and headed toward the barracks. He did not care if it was disrespectful to the queen or if Jael would be furious or if rumors of his insolence would spread throughout all of Luna by the time he emerged again.

He knew that Jael's pack would be chosen for the queen's mission because of him. They would become her special, prized soldiers. Their bodies would not be tampered with again.

With that one kill, he had ensured that she would never turn him into a monster.

He knew it as sure as, somewhere on the surface, the long, long day was coming.

Paper Cuts II by Michele Boyer; Notebook Sisters;
Doing Dewey; Kaylie Austen; The-Society.NET;
Synchronized Reading; A.A. Omer's The
Fangirl Who Reads; Avery's Book
Nook; Readaraptor!; Emilie's Book
World; Effortlessly Reading;
Birth of a New
Witch

Anna Reads Jenna Does Books; YA bibliophile; Muh das Telefonbuch; In Libris Veritas;

Thank you, bloggers, for all your support!

The Literary Connoisseur; The Fuma Files; Cuddlebuggery; Love Is not a Triangle; Musing of a Blogder; RhiReading; The Biblio Philes; What Mrs. Light Is Reading; The Book Swarm; The Book Bender; Books as You Know It; On a Book Reviews 101; Wake Up at Seven; Ode to Jo and Katniss; Book Sake; The Book Rat; Teen Book Blogging; Bewitched Bookworms; A Book Blog; IB Book Blogging; Another Novel Read; Read, Breathe, Read; The Diary of a Bookworm; Peace, Love, and Fangirl; More Than Just Magic; Take Me Away...; Confessions from a Bibliophile; I Read to Relax!; Bunbury in the Stacks; Piper's Book Nook; Twilight Sleep; Mademoiselle le Sphinx; I Hope They Have Books in Hell; Little Bird Reads; Up in the Bibliosphere; The Raven Readers; A Guy, a Girl, and a Teen Book Blog; Book Dilettante; Angieville; The Hall Ways; Paper Riot; Rummaging for Answers in the Pages; Conversations of a Reading Addict; Books as You Know It; My Real Life Reviews; Attic; Tea.; Books. Love.; The Blair Book Project; Book Nook Club; City of Books; Book Nook Blog; Strange Little Bits; Carina's Books; Books and Words; Hog! Of paper and ink; Book

bookworm716; My Overstuffed Shelves; The A P Book Club; Stacked; The YA Kitten; Fic Fare; Novel Novice; Lunar Heiress;

Good Books and Good Wine; Reading the Paranormal; Cientos de miles de historias; The Midnight Garden; Xpresso Reads; Kari's Crowded Bookshelf; Alice Marvels;

Eventgate.net;
My Friends Are
Fiction; The Soul Sisters;
The Book Addict's Guide; Scott
Reads It; Alexa Loves Books; Mermaid
Vision Books; Into the Hall of Books; Supernatural
Snark; Makeshift Bookmark; Two Chicks on Books

Marissa Meyer's first two books in the Lunar Chronicles, *Cinder* and *Scarlet*, debuted on the *New York Times* bestseller list. She lives in Tacoma, Washington, with her husband and their three cats. Visit her online at marissameyer.com.